SHADOW IN THE CORN

SHADOW IN THE CORN

Jason Foss

This first world edition published in Great Britain 1993 by
SEVERN HOUSE PUBLISHERS LTD of
9–15 High Street, Sutton, Surrey SM1 1DF.
First published in the U.S.A. 1994 by
SEVERN HOUSE PUBLISHERS INC., of
475 Fifth Avenue, New York, NY 10017.

British Library Cataloguing in Publication Data
Foss, Jason
  Shadow in th Corn
  I. Title
  823 [F]

  ISBN 0-7278-4536-5

For my mother

This book is a novel. No resemblance to actual
persons living or dead is intended.

Typeset by Hewer Text Composition Services, Edinburgh.
Printed and bound in Great Britain by
Redwood Books⌐, Trowbridge, Wiltshire.

Prologue

Clouds hung still on that cold, windless night. A gibbous moon low on the horizon threw a long sharp shadow across the hillside. Other shadows moved, swayed, and circled the hallowed stone. As the moment came, one broke away. The Maiden moved forward, stripping aside the white cloak to stand naked before the moon. She shivered against the cold, trembled as she took up the knife and the onlookers took up the chant. Ethereal harmonies of another age rose into the winter air. An animal struggled away the last moments of its life, the old and wise stood back in satisfaction and The Maiden declared her need to embrace the Earth.

Soon, the Earth would embrace her.

English hills rolled green and pleasant under the weak February sun. The brick cottage lay screened by bare hedges, some way back from a sunken lane, with a long dirt drive running past its walls and into the seclusion of the hollow. The cottage was cheap to rent, from an owner who accepted cash in hand and swallowed loose alibis by those using names of discretion. Cramped and rather dirty, it served as a haven from the winter chill and from prying eyes.

A railwayman's retirement clock ticked away the seconds, and in perfect time, footfalls could be heard coming down the stair. The man had been fiddling with his black goatee and unconsciously digging his fingernails into the soft oak tabletop. He snapped out of introspection as she opened the door into the room.

"Rowan?"

She came into the room at a solemn pace, shaking her blonde hair slowly to answer his question.

"Call a doctor, call the ambulance, we should have done it an hour ago! We should have done it last night, I knew it!"

1

"There really is no point. It's much too late." Her tone was cold, forceful, her expression drained of emotion.

Every strand of his twisted life was knotted into the man's face. His muscles tensed, bringing multiple creases into high relief. He sniffed, drawing on a paper napkin to wipe at bloodshot eyes. "So we have to call the police."

"Tell me, Oak," she paused, "exactly what will you say to them?"

He bowed his head and looked into the grain of the oak table. Oak: strong, ancient, mystical Oak. She called him Oak, he called her Rowan. It was a game, a formula, a cornerstone of the life they had chosen.

"Where do you begin? How do you explain what happened? What do you plead at the trial?"

Panic raised his head at the word.

"Yes, trial. You don't think they'll understand, do you?"

"We can tell them the truth."

"And what is the truth?"

He considered it, lips faintly modelling alibis and extenuating circumstances. Rowan stood back, arms folded across her heavily knitted pullover, with its incongruously cheerful riot of black-berries rambling about her breast.

"Difficult, isn't it? Even if they believe you, do you think they will understand? Do you think they will want to understand? Do ordinary people have the capacity to understand?"

The realisation came slowly and reluctantly. "No."

Silence followed, broken only by the heavy rhythmic tone of the clock on the mantelpiece.

"I don't understand it, Rowan, I don't understand what happened."

"What on earth did you put in the brew?"

"Exactly the same as usual. This shouldn't have happened! It must be some million-to-one accident, one of those things you read about." He waved a hand to conjure up a miracle explanation. "It could be an allergic reaction, or perhaps she had a weak heart, or," he clicked his fingers, "she took something else, pills or drugs."

Rowan's face was still set in its firm, purposeful expression. Her eyes of sky blue met his of soft woodland brown. "We shall never know."

2

"Oh yes. We'll know." He had fallen back from his fit of nervous suggestions and his expression was clouding over once more. "At the post-mortem, at the inquest, at the trial."

He strangled the last word and buried his head in his hands, panting and sobbing. "What am I going to do?"

She advanced to put a hand on his trembling shoulder. "Oak, dearest Oak, don't worry, we can help you, we can protect you, all of us. No one outside the circle need ever know."

His eyes widened to acknowledge her offer. "But can . . ."

"Shh." She laid a finger on his lips. "Anything is possible, we have friends, we have the power."

"The power." A wan smile crossed his bearded lips, part in relief, part in irony. He knew where the power lay.

Rowan moved across to the window and jerked the faded pink curtain along its wire. "We can't do anything now, not in daylight. We'll come back tonight."

The shattered man watched her planning his salvation.

"We'll bring my van, and some spades."

"Rowan, no, it isn't decent."

Angry, she turned. "Decent! What is decent? I suppose we all dress in black and troop down the church and sing a few dismal psalms."

"No, but . . ."

"Oak! It is this, or face the police. It is your problem, and your choice."

Oak was fighting blasts of fear and guilt.

"Tonight?" Rowan demanded.

"We must have a ceremony," he blustered.

"No ceremony, that would be far too dangerous. I don't think the whole circle will want to know about this."

Of course, he knew she would say that. Always right, always, it seemed, capable of making the decisions.

"Yes, you're right. But it must be somewhere special, somewhere we have hallowed."

"No."

"Yes."

He surprised himself with a sudden return of spirit. "It has to be decent. If we can't have a ceremony, we have to do this at least, Rowan!"

For an hour they talked over the tragedy, with quiet logic and

3

with heated passion. Both shed tears, but Oak won his point. Rowan relented when she sensed his thoughts had turned away from despair and focused on the urgency of concealment. In retrospect, it had all been distressingly simple.

Chapter 1

A cluster of houseboats nestled within Camden Lock. Jeffrey Flint rented a small, light blue boat as an alternative to ill-furnished London flats, with their hallways cramped by bikes and black bin bags. He was in the galley, willing the kettle to boil, and the woman took full advantage of surprise.

"Pinch and a punch, first of the month!" Chrissie Collings thumped him in the kidneys, causing a yelp of alarm.

"March," said the tall redhead, "wake up, Doc, you're miles away this morning."

"Sorry, I was thinking about Easter. I'm taking the first-years to Essex. Do you want to come?"

"No, no, you're not getting me digging. Spending the whole vacation in a muddy hole is not my idea of a good time."

The kettle boiled and Flint made tea, with Chrissie sitting back on the bench-seat by the table, watching him. Poor Jeffrey, she wished she could be that soul-mate he seemed to need. Someone who was willing to tramp across rainy hillsides and spend vacations amongst dusty museum relics. Another archaeologist whom he could argue with about Post-processualism or Romano-Celtic iconography.

He was slight without being skinny, his muscles toned by years of swinging pickaxes and hauling buckets. She wondered about the long straw hair, the beard and the John Lennon glasses and whether modernising his appearance would destroy his character. Then she thought about the night before, when he had been so energetic yet so gentle. Poor Jeffrey was happy as he was.

"Now it's you who's miles away," he said as he presented her with the mug with the whale-tail handle.

"I was thinking about you," she said.

He grinned. "You were analysing me again."

"If you like."

"Do you know, Chrissie, I have a rule: I never sleep with my students . . ."

"But other people's students are fair game?" she interrupted.

"Thus far, but I think I'm going to add a second rule: never sleep with psychology postgrads."

"Aw," she took a cautious sip from the tea mug and feigned hurt, "can we still be friends?"

"Only fooling, we have a nice little relationship going on here."

Chrissie's pure-white face suddenly set into a solemn look of warning. "We do not have a *relationship*, we have a friendship. Relationships lead to rings, property and sticky children."

He nodded. "Sorry, I didn't mean to sound possessive."

"Poor Jeffrey," she said, laying a hand on his knee, "when are you going to find the woman who won't keep messing you around?"

"I'm happy," he said cheerfully. "Two slices of toast? I got some more of that wholemeal you liked last time."

Flint served the toast and apologised for the state of the hedgerow jam he had bought at a craft fair. He diverted further analysis of his sex life by talking of his plans for the Easter training excavation. Chrissie told him of a possible last-minute holiday to Paris she might make with a friend of unstated sex. Another academic morning started slowly and it was nearly ten before the pair mounted their cycles to enjoy the ride into Central College. The air was cold and the sky clear and the day promised nothing other than quiet study and the company of fellow minds.

Jeffrey Flint's office befitted his lowly rank of junior lecturer. Tunnel shaped, with a window at one end, it overlooked an internal alleyway which served as a college rat-run. Always badly lit, usually untidy, it offered room for four or five hundred books and a filing cabinet. Just enough wallspace remained for a cluttered cork board and a Che Guevara poster. He knew this was passé, but kept it as a memory of former days as a student rebel.

He collected his routine mail and ran through it quickly. Having contrived to have no lectures timetabled for Wednesdays, at least one day per week could be devoted to solid research. His mind was currently battling with the complexities of third-century Roman

Britain, or "Britain under Roman Occupation" as he liked to term it.

Professor Grant was the figurehead, but his secretary was the real power in the archaeology department. Industrious, if a little vague at times, Sally was a useful buffer between Flint's eccentricities and the ageing Head of Department's more conventional sense of order. Sally rang through on the internal phone to announce that an uninvited Dr Faber had arrived to steal precious research time. Flint grumbled assent then put down the phone in ill humour. He kept up a pretence of reading a paper in *The Antiquaries Journal* beyond the point at which the unbidden caller was asked to enter. Whatever dull academic strode in could be certain that he had interrupted precious study.

He was a she. "Doctor Flint?"

She waved away his "Doctor Faber" and said, "Call me Barbara, please."

Blonde hair, late twenties with a strong bone structure, he found her attractive in an oddly familiar way.

"Jeff," he responded, happily moving to first name terms. "How can I help?"

"I'm Lucy Gray's sister. She's in the third year."

His thoughts quickly ran through a notice-board full of bright faces. One undergraduate came to mind, with long blonde hair, sharp blue eyes and classic schoolgirl prettiness. Take Lucy, shorten the hair, add neat charcoal-grey suit, allow to mature for a few years and the result would be Barbara. She was clearly a more developed product of the same gene pool.

"Lucy, yes."

Flint made a gesture towards a soggy armchair which was squeezed in beside the filing cabinet. It was, as usual, covered with books and papers.

"Just chuck that heap on the floor." Only a hint of his Yorkshire accent remained, but slipped out in Flint's more relaxed moments.

Barbara cleared the chair, straightened her skirt then sat, tense and erect.

"I'm sorry to interrupt your work, but I wanted to know whether you had seen Lucy lately?"

The truthful answer was that he did not know and if pushed, he might have said he didn't care either. He walked past a thousand girls in college sweatshirts every day, whilst only giving half of them more than a glance.

"I don't actually teach Lucy," was his offered reply, "not this year."

Barbara appeared disappointed.

"Have you spoken to Samantha Hanley? I believe she is Lucy's personal supervisor . . ."

"She's away. I tried her." There was a barely concealed restlessness within the visitor.

"Ah, yes, maternity leave. So why me?"

"Lucy mentioned you. In fact, she is always talking about you and your ideas. I thought perhaps you were her supervisor by the impression you made."

This was flattery from an unexpected quarter. "I taught her on one course in her second year, but I think she's mainly taking prehistory units. She's not signed on to any of my classes this year."

Barbara nodded, out of ideas.

"You need to contact her urgently?"

A little pain, a little anxiety was visible. "We just haven't seen her for five weeks: our mother is getting worried. We had a wedding, you see, on the eleventh. Lucy should have been there."

"Perhaps she found it all a little dull and skipped it. Lucy never struck me as being terribly High Church." The department had seven overtly militant Christians and Lucy was not amongst them.

"But it was Janet, her old schoolfriend's wedding. They've known each other for years and Lucy was to be senior bridesmaid. We were fitting the dress the last time she was home. Janet was awfully disappointed and we all felt, well, let down."

"She's probably lying low. Have you tried her digs?"

"We've telephoned lots of times, but there's been no answer. She's in Leopold Hall. I tried to get into her room earlier this morning, but this awful man wouldn't let me."

Flint sifted through a rack of trivial information in his brain, hunting for boyfriends, society outings, major excavations, minor epidemics. Nothing came up.

"I suppose I could accompany you to the hall, it's just across the square."

8

"Would you mind? I'm sure I'm just being silly."

"Oh, no trouble."

Flint had a large and very soft spot for intelligent ladies, so the journal and its crucial article could be set aside without pain. Flint pulled on his tweed jacket with its reinforced elbows and they left immediately, taking the usual short-cuts through the bafflingly juxtaposed buildings of Central College. Barbara cast her eyes around at every turn, as if looking for traces of her absent sister. As she tried to break into casual conversation, her voice echoed along the empty corridor.

"This is all new to me. Despite the fact that Lucy has been here nearly three years, I've never actually seen this place."

"You've not missed much. It's rather tacky when you get to know it."

"Well, Lucy thinks it's the centre of the world. She's really changed since she came here."

"They all do, I did. Where did you study?"

"Edinburgh, I wanted to get as far from home as possible." Just half a smile followed the confession.

Outside, it had turned into one of those premature spring days which precedes the last shock snowfall of winter. The London air held a promise of warmth, perfumed by the smell of motorcars, whilst staccato-engined taxis punctuated what calm there was.

"So what do you do in real life?" Flint asked, hands thrust into his jacket pockets.

"I'm a doctor, a GP."

"Ah, a real doctor, as my mum always says."

"No, you're the real doctor. I always feel a bit of a fraud next to you people who have done research."

A stream of cars raced by, then the pair skipped to a traffic island.

"They give PhDs away these days," he joked, "don't mark 'em, just weigh 'em."

Four minutes' walk brought them to the nineteen fifties brick-and-concrete ediface where two hundred students were stored during term time. Flint made short work of the officious Indian porter and rooted out the deputy warden, a soft-spoken deeply Christian man with black beard of biblical proportions. The warden apologised for being of little assistance previously and accompanied them in an agonisingly slow lift to the third floor.

In the windowless hall, one of four battered wood-effect doors carried a hand-drawn disc surmounted by the words "LUCY IS". The disc offered twenty options from "asleep" to "working too hard to be disturbed". A mobile arrow pointed to the option reading "away".

A pass key turned in the lock. The small rectangular room ended in a plate glass window, offering a fine aspect of the street below, the identical hall opposite and an oblique view into the wooded square. The room was tidy and had been swept regularly by the cleaner. Barbara went over to a "Castles of Wales" wall calendar. An unvarnished nail coursed the dates. The wedding was clearly marked and other notes were scrawled reading "term starts", "go home", "fit dress", "nuptials", "diss in", "1st Exam Ugh!".

Flint scanned her posters: Roger Dean's *Another Time, Another Place*; a low-light photo of two dolphins breaking surface; a water-colour print of the Holy Grail suspended above Glastonbury Tor; a copy of Desiderata. Absolutely standard.

Her bookshelf came next and his fingers ran along a scattering of approved course reading and overdue library books. Amongst the latter was one of J. S. Flint's more recent publications. Lucy's fiction interests were clear, embracing one battered copy of *The Hobbit* plus several more sub-Tolkien fantasy epics and a Poe omnibus. Flint took down a rules booklet for the roleplaying game "Dungeons and Dragons", turning over the pages covering spells and monsters with mild amusement.

"She was into this stuff?" he asked.

A faint smile came to Barbara's lips, but she shook her head as the faintly bizarre volume of rules flicked before her eyes. It was replaced on the shelf, next to a new facsimile reprint of a Victorian tarot book. Alongside rested *The Green Manifesto*, one astrology book, Van Daniken's latest moneyspinner, plus several heavily foxed paperbacks of eccentric, semi-occult nature. Flint flicked the pages of a book of herbal remedies. Spirits and the underworld, goblins and magic. He began to appreciate the width, if not the depth, of her interests, a ripple of disquiet running through him. He suppressed it. Students enjoy being weird.

"Will there be anything more I can do?" The deputy warden spoke from the door, but was ignored.

Lucy's stereo-cassette player was on the wide mock-marble windowledge. She owned only two dozen or so cassettes, few of which were truly contemporary, consisting of offerings by Lindisfarne, Lennon, All About Eve, Mottley Crue, Blue Oyster Cult, a little folk, one Elgar compilation and a trio of whimsical New Age tapes.

A thin paperback lay on her bedside table, a small press publication of poetry by R. Temple-Brooke, whoever he was. Flint flicked to the dedication within the front cover. "To Hazel at Samahain, with love, R.T.B."

Secondhand, thought Flint, no, too new, it had to be borrowed. "Has she a friend called Hazel?"

Barbara shook her head. "I don't know."

"I'll ask around. Has she got a regular boyfriend?"

Barbara continued shaking her head. Flint allowed a little exasperation to slip through. "You don't appear to know much about your sister."

"She is rather younger than me. We don't have much in common, first I went away to college, then she came up to London almost as soon as I got back. Oh, she used to come up to Mother's once a month, but she was always full of college stories. I can't claim to know the real her."

Flint turned to the deputy warden. "You haven't seen her?"

He shook his head, mouthing an almost silent no through the prophet's beard, so Flint put the next question to Barbara. The depth of her concern had him puzzled. "Where does your family come from?"

"Durring, well, Nether Durring actually. I took up my father's practice just before he died."

"And Lucy normally stays with you in the holidays?"

"She stays with Mother, she lives about six miles from us."

Flint returned to the search, pulling open drawers looking for clues, letters, notes, hoping for a diary. Barbara found a file of documents which included Lucy's driving licence, birth certificate and passport. One possibility had been ruled out. They found no purse, no student railcard or union cards, no chequebook or banker's cards. The pocket diary she had received from an aunt last Christmas was absent. In her small wardrobe, each hanger was full, save two. Her navy blue suitcase was found stuffed into an otherwise useless ceiling-level cupboard over the sink.

"Lucy might be 'away', but wherever she's gone, it's not far and

11

she intends coming back," Flint concluded. "We've narrowed the possibilities down, at least."

At that moment, although he felt uneasy poking into someone else's life, he was beginning to gain a curious intellectual kick from gathering this negative evidence about Lucy's activities. It was almost like the thrill of discovery on site when an unlikely collection of archaeological artefacts starts to build up an answer to some ancient puzzle. Archaeologists are born nosey, they share much in common with detectives.

"We're not going to find anything here." Barbara was, if anything, even more tense. "Can we check her post?"

"It will be in the rack, downstairs," the deputy warden said.

Barbara gave Flint one glance then left the room. He followed then waited for the door to be locked. The trio returned to the ground floor by the concrete staircase, without bothering to wait for the lift. At the base of the stairs, behind the desk of the surly porter, hung a nest of wooden pigeonholes. Nine letters were waiting for Lucy, with postmarks scattered from late January to the previous weekend. Barbara made to open one.

"I can't allow you to do that." The deputy warden's hands slipped the letters from below Barbara's quivering finger.

"No, we shouldn't pry. She won't thank you." Flint tried to ease away the sense of crisis in the woman.

Angry resentment flashed across her face and tinged her voice.

"All right, do you mind if I look around and ask if anyone has seen her?"

"The common room is through that door," said the deputy warden, "and there's another television lounge on the fifth floor."

Barbara said nothing else and pushed her way through the swing door. Flint watched her go, then sat down into a coffee-stained easy chair by the porter's desk and took up an abandoned *Daily Mirror*. Twenty minutes saw the paper read and re-read and Flint was into the adverts when Barbara returned, pale-faced and tense.

"She's not been seen for weeks," she said.

"And you're sure she's not rung or written?"

"No. I mean yes. We've heard nothing." Barbara strained at the strap of her handbag, out of ideas. "Four of those letters were from us, from Mother or myself."

"I'm sure everything is okay. I'll ask around the department. If

12

you're really worried, you could always go to the police. They get paid to do this sort of thing."

"What sort of thing?" Barbara seemed dazed by the thought.

"Missing persons."

"Missing? God, no, I haven't wanted to think of her as *missing*."

Chapter 2

"We have a missing century, a century about which so little is known." Flint scrawled the first line of his paper on third-century chronology.

"We have a missing student, a student about which so little is known." Lucy Gray nagged into his brain as he tried to finish his afternoon's work. He pushed away his notepad, with its one line of text and leaned back in his chair, thinking of Lucy, student and young woman. He had never done so before, but it was a thing he would find himself doing time and again.

Lucy had arrived at Central College as a pale English rose, with collar-length blonde hair which quickly acquired red highlights as university life led her astray. After the first Christmas, she had mellowed, allowing her hair to recover its colour and to flow over her shoulders. Her face was round, almost chinless, her nose petite and her eyes were Viking blue. Her voice was quiet, but could quaver with a hint of excitement around the fringes. Flint's memory tended towards the photographic and every detail of the girl's appearance could be recalled on demand. The fashion was for dangling oversize Oxfam bargains, or chunky-knit Aran and jeans, plus the obligatory badges which proclaimed Green-tinted politics.

She had never been terribly High Church. His remark to Barbara had been a casual quip, but he quickly realised it was founded in truth. He recalled a seminar of more than a year before, when Lucy was beginning her second year. It had been late autumn when she had been competing for attention with a mixed group of second- and third-year archaeology undergraduates.

In the sunlit seminar room, nine of them had been grouped around a Formica-topped table, discussing ritual. It was an old chestnut, one that keeps both anthropologists and archaeologists in business. The slob known as "Bunny" had yawned and lowered his head on to his file, provoking his lecturer into deploying a well-tested routine for dissipating afternoon apathy. Flint put effort into his lectures, he was a born showman, an extrovert teacher and someone who loved to exercise uncomfortable thoughts.

"Okay, Bunny, if you can't relate to Neolithic ritual, let's consider the modern Catholic Church. Let us imagine an archaeologist a thousand years hence excavating the remains of, say, Westminster Cathedral. He would examine the plan of a great building and deduce from the absence of utilitarian features that it had some religious or ritual purpose."

Flint had paced slowly in front of the roller board, solidifying verbal images with hand actions. "Our archaeologist would find repeated suggestions that a cross was an important feature of the ritual. He would find artefacts, perhaps a crucifix: a man nailed to a tree. What would he deduce? What is the significance of a man suffering a slow and painful death? It is obvious: human sacrifice."

A murmur of humour escaped from a number of lips poised on the point of yawning. Even Bunny had opened one eye beneath the straggling black hair.

"Next, he would uncover statues of the saints in their niches. Obviously cult figures: this religion had a large pantheon of gods. The worshippers were polytheists."

Flint had noticed Alison, a keen Christian Union activist, fidget by his elbow. At least she had taken note.

"And what does our future archaeologist make of the repeated image of the mother and child?"

He had paused to receive heretical suggestions.

"Fertility symbol," Tyrone Drake spoke from the back corner. Assured, confident, as always.

"Mother goddess," Lucy whispered with a smile.

Flint spread his hands, satisfied they were catching his drift. "Unless a Holy Bible was recovered intact, or a book of prayer, what would our archaeologist really know of the beliefs which lay behind the ritual? What of the Immaculate Conception, the Holy Trinity, the sacrement, baptism, confession, absolution? None of that is easy to decipher from cold stone and broken statues. So what can we say about Stonehenge, whose builders' view of the world may have been both childishly simple and ridiculously complex?"

Class had awoken. Flint cringed as he recalled his own rather

15

brash and provocative lecturing style, but it was effective. Neil, the bane of the group, usually pitched for centre stage. Afflicted with a burning acne-riddled complexion, he had rambled through "evidence" relating to the properties of stone circles, ending by extolling the power of ley-lines. Flint had let him inflate his imagination so far, then ran out of patience.

"This so-called evidence doesn't hold water. If I wrote a sensible, well-reasoned textbook about Stonehenge, it would sell five hundred copies. If I wrote one claiming it had been built by space aliens after they'd finished the pyramids, I'd sell twenty thousand. Parascience is entertainment."

"But there is evidence . . ."

Square-jawed and impatient, Tyrone intervened brutally. "It's a load of crap." Alone of the students, this third-year wore a tie and a smart jacket. His blonde hair was kept in a cropped, fashionable style. Sitting beside Lucy, he could almost have been her brother, but his politics were firmly Conservative rather than conservationist. He continued to put down Neil's argument without mercy. Neil waffled back ineffectually whilst Bunny had again lapsed on to the desk top mumbling, "Bullshit, bullshit."

This was when Lucy had become agitated, trying to intervene but not finding a chance amongst the machismo.

"Lucy?" Flint had jabbed a hand at her, offering a pause.

"It isn't all rubbish, there is some sense in the New Age movement. Pagan beliefs relate to the Earth, to the world around us. Feeling and understanding."

Immediately, Flint had regretted this move, but waved down Tyrone's attempts to bully her into silence.

Lucy had continued in her wavering, gentle voice, "We don't need churches and statues and prayer books. Religion is more than just hoping for an afterlife, it is the essence of being. People are becoming estranged from the modern world and want to feel in harmony with the environment. They are returning to their spiritual roots."

Thinking back dispassionately, Flint had deserved this, as reward for putting so much effort into projecting his own alternative, anti-establishment image. Some might say that Lucy was simply following his lead.

"Okay, I think we're straying." He had tried to reimpose his authority.

16

Lucy's face had adopted an almost mystical glaze. "But Doctor Flint, no one gives megaliths their true role. Visit one, feel the power, unload the senses and harmonise . . ."

"Oh Gawd," Bunny had groaned, "let's just sacrifice a virgin."

Class had begun to slide towards anarchic cross-comments which bypassed the main argument. Flint fought back into command. "Okay, the important thing to remember is, that just because ancient people believed megaliths to be magical, and behaved as if they were magical it does not mean that they actually are magical. We are looking at belief, belief is intangible and, some would say, inexplicable."

It could have been the mantra which framed his life for the coming year, but at the time it was simply a gentle put-down to Lucy's eccentric suggestion. He had sat back and allowed the argument burn itself out before he turned back to the central theme of his seminar. More than a year had passed since that seminar, and he should have forgotten it, along with a hundred others, but fortune was not going to permit it.

Thursday afternoon saw a pair of policewomen moving around Central College questioning students and lecturers at random, disturbing the equilibrium and setting the internal rumour-machine whispering. Professor Grant had breezed into Flint's office and asked if he'd "sort things out" with the police, meaning a lost afternoon and the end of all hope of progress on the paper before Easter. The third century would have to wait, so after a day of frustration, Flint decided to indulge his love of offbeat movies. Jules Torpevitch was a tall Bostonian with an eye for animal bones who had married the delicate palaeobotanist Sasha Aziz the year before. That evening the three sat through an Alex Cox double bill of *Repo Man* and *Walker* at the ICA, then dissected the films in a late-night Camden curry house. Inevitably the conversation drifted to departmental gossip and to Lucy, Flint objecting when Sasha described her as "your student".

"She's not my student," Flint protested, ripping up a chapatti.

"The policewoman kept referring to her as your student." Sasha's Turkish eyes were almost totally black under the dim mock-candle lighting.

"She's Sam Hanley's student." Flint continued to defend himself.

"But Sam is away, someone should take an interest," Sasha purred.

"She's right, you know, kid," Jules chipped in. "You could adopt her, until Sam gets back. None of your other students are problem cases, are they?"

Flint raised his eyebrows, making his glasses twitch. "I've got Tyrone Drake."

"Oh, lucky you," Sasha said, with heavy sarcasm. "I take back my suggestion."

"Tyrone's got some good ideas on bone counts in sub-Roman deposits," Jules commented.

"But he's a fascist," Sasha protested. "Tell me, Jeff, is he as bad as he seems?"

"And worse," Flint replied, "but we don't discriminate on race, colour, sexual orientation, religion or politics, do we? We accept anyone who can think and although I hate to say it, Tyrone has a first-class brain to go with his first-class degree. He works hard, but doesn't let it make him a dull person. His problem is he needs to soften up and learn a little compassion. I was just thinking yesterday, that if we could somehow weld Tyrone and Lucy together we'd probably have the perfect student."

Tyrone Drake knew nothing of his supervisor's late-night speculations. He found Jeffrey Flint amusing and provocative and regarded the avante-garde trimmings as mere affectations. He had been in the year above Lucy, had already graduated and was studying for an MPhil, with the hope it could be converted to a PhD. Tyrone had spent the week polishing the introductory chapter of his thesis: "A critique of previous work". Flint should have read it by Monday.

As rain pattered on the window of Flint's office, Tyrone lounged in the soggy chair, fishing for compliments. "So, is it good for an upgrade?"

His supervisor sucked air, letting nothing away.

"It's got to be PhD standard," Tyrone continued. "I thought of entitling it 'De-Romanisation as analogue to Romanisation'."

"You're sticking with the fifth century?"

"It's the place to make a name. Everyone else has just messed the subject about."

Flint handed back the chapter. "Brilliant, as expected."

Tyrone let his rubber features expand into a broad grin. "So I'm on the PhD list for next year?"

"Why not?"

Flint seemed to have his mind elsewhere, he had a way of looking through people and objects when thinking.

"Is there anything wrong?" Tyrone asked.

"You know Lucy Gray, third year? Do you know if she's got a friend called Hazel?"

After a moment's thought, Tyrone delivered a definite "No."

"Does she have any regular relationships?"

"You mean a boyfriend? No, everyone says she's a lesbian."

"So much for our liberal, non-sexist elite. Is there any proof, or is this just undergraduate slander?"

Tyrone coloured, sensing he was being criticised. "She is a bit kinky, she wears a rattlesnake garter, I saw her flashing it at the freshers party last term. I've never seen her with anyone special, but all the usual jerks try to chat her up."

He listed a string of hopefuls who had hung around her neck at parties. Flint stopped him part way through and began to scribble names down the margin of his notepad. "Did you ever date her?"

"No, never, she's not my type, she's into lentils and basket weaving. Lucy's a good looker, but needs her brain retuning. She's strung a couple of guys along, but doesn't really seem to have much to do with anyone in college, or anyone on this planet as far as I can see. Why all the interest?"

"You must have heard she's missing."

"Missing missing, or just missing?"

"Officially missing. Where were you when the girls in blue came around asking questions?"

"Working."

"Okay, but if you've got any thoughts on where she is, we'd all like to know."

Tyrone deliberately creased his forehead, overdoing the impression of thinking. "I bet she's just gone off to join a wimmin's peace camp or something. I don't know why everyone is getting so excited."

"Well, everyone isn't, the police were just going through the motions and Professor Grant has asked me to liaise with them so that he won't have to bother."

"Why are you bothering?"

"Basic humanity. And, as a bonus, she's got a very pleasant big sister."

Flint kept a poker face, but not Tyrone. His square jaw twisted into a wry grin. The whole college knew Jeffrey Flint's reputation.

Tyrone had disappeared down to the computer room and the last details of the Easter field trip were occupying Flint's mind when his office door creaked open. It was going to be another interrupted day. Flint raised an eye from the sheaf of papers. Halfway down the door, a brush of short cropped black hair popped into his vision.

"Doctor Flint, I am right?"

She pushed the door further open. "Hi, I'm Vikki Corbett."

In her mid twenties, just over five feet tall, clad in an ankle-length tan raincoat and sporting huge chunky blue earrings. Was he supposed to know who she was or what she wanted?

"Can I sit?" She cleared the usual pile from the soggy chair whilst Flint allowed his mouth to hang slightly awry.

From a large leather shoulder bag she drew a notepad and clicked a pen into action. Her lipstick hovered on the edge of purple, her mouth expressed the sort of surprised pleasure reserved for meeting long-lost friends.

"Vikki Corbett," she repeated, "*Durring and Kingshaven Advertiser*."

"Oh, I thought you were a student."

"No, I'm a journalist." She over-extended her syllables as she spoke. "I hope you don't mind, but I was just passing. I'm working on a piece on Lucy Gray's disappearance, it's looking like blowing into a really big story."

She spoke rapidly with a breathless excitement which overwhelmed him.

"Did we have an appointment?"

A quick smile from the reporter served as explanation, apology or simply to override his objection. "I hear you teach Lucy Gray."

"Along with a dozen other lecturers." Flint realised he was being interviewed and allowed himself to roll out minimal responses. "I took her for one course, last year."

"So, Doctor Flint, everyone tells me you're really keen to help your students, you know, their welfare, whether they are happy, whether they're in trouble, so I thought you'd be the best person to tell me all about her."

"Well, she's not my student," he began the familiar protest, then added, "I can't say much, it wouldn't be right." What could he say? What should he not say? All he knew so far was vague slander. His stomach rumbled. "Look, I'm starving, have you had lunch?"

"Not yet. I could murder something to eat, do you know somewhere good?"

"No, but I know somewhere close."

Vikki fired off questions non-stop as they followed the complex series of stairs and corridors that led to the college refectory. Flint shrugged them off or gave non-committal answers.

"Welcome to Le Cafe Albert," he said as they joined the queue, "it's a bit crummy, like all college canteens."

She looked around at the multi-racial hubbub of students and younger staff seated amongst a litter of newspapers and duplicated sheets advertising college events. "It looks all right."

"I suppose. It's a million times better than it was. College rationalised the place last year, sacked the catering manager and staff en bloc. It caused a real stink, there were demos, boycotts, petitions, we had our own little 1968 revolution down here."

"It doesn't look like what I imagine a college canteen should look like." Vikki surveyed the mock Mediterranean decor, murals of Naples and the ice-cream-cart-style serving-hatches.

"It was put out to tender and this Italian restaurateur picked up the concession. We kept up the campaign of action, of course."

"Why? That one please . . . " Vikki pointed at the tuna lasagne.

The huge, habitually grinning Italian mamma loaded her plate.

"Social conscience . . . yeah, I'll have the veg curry please."

". . . and chips," Vikki added. "So why did your boycott end?"

"Because the food was cheap, edible and students have to eat. In the old days, even the rats refused to eat here."

They sat by a cluster of plastic palms in the non-smoking area. Flint cleared the scatter of loose leaflets into a pile at one end. Vikki slipped off her coat and shuffled her over-large cardigan until she was comfortable. She gave a guilty twitch as she sipped the Coke in her paper cup.

"This is dreadfully bad for me, I know, but I just love the stuff," she bobbed her head with the confession, "I'm just a kid at heart. I could eat here every day . . . mm, this tastes good, what's yours like?"

Flint smiled politely whilst Vikki chattered around the subject of food. He had already decided that the subject of Lucy Gray should be left to the police, his time was being gobbled up to no profit.

"I'm supposed to be asking about Lucy Gray, aren't I? Sorry. So, where do you think she is?" Vikki probed.

"Well, she's not in college."

"No, but where do you *think* she is?" Vikki's voice had a roguish tone, as though she was expecting some sort of exciting answer.

"Really, it's anyone's guess. This is your line of work, you probably have a better idea than me."

Vikki nodded. "We get these cases where people just disappear. Sometimes they turn up, you know, murdered in a motorway lay-by or down a railway embankment. We had a girl last year who went hitch-hiking and was hit by a car. She lay in a ditch for two days before she was found. And," Vikki waved a blood-red fork to emphasise the gore, "she had amnesia and couldn't even say who she was."

Flint suppressed a desire to flatten the girl's gruesome enthusiasm and posed a question. "Have you spoken to Lucy's family?"

"They contacted us. I ran a missing person story on Friday. Do you want to see it, it made the front page?"

She rummaged in the depths of her bag and drew out a folded sheet of newsprint. "LOCAL GIRL MISSING IN LONDON." Vikki cocked her head on one side to follow the text as he speed-read the story.

"You didn't read it all?" she asked as he finished it.

"I did, you learn to read quickly in my game."

She frowned with deep, sincere interest. "Working in archaeology must be really exciting."

"Only occasionally. The bureaucrats rather spoil the fun these days, they're turning us all into excavators of 'in' trays."

"Get away, it must be really interesting, I'm envious, I'd love to do something like that. Have you been to Egypt?"

"Yes, but I've never wrestled crocodiles or discovered a lost city. Life is a lot tamer than the movies."

He tried to hand the article back, but she rejected it with obvious pride. "No, keep it."

Flint folded the paper and slid it into his hip pocket, resolving to find a litter bin on the way back to his office. "So, talking of exciting careers, how long have you been a reporter?"

Her eyes flicked once at the table top. "Over a year."

He nodded, smiling at the defence mechanism. "Have you spoken to the police, down in," he thought for a moment, "Durring?"

"Mmm," she confirmed, "London police. They're not taking it very seriously though."

"And you are?"

"Not a lot happens in Kingshaven, even less in Durring. I spend most of my time doing cat shows and fires in council flats. This is something else, though, I've got a feeling I can make a really good story out of this."

Flint was concerned about what she considered a good story. It probably contained plenty of human tragedy, a thought which nauseated him and urged him to change the subject again.

"I lectured in Durring once, a couple of years back. Pleasant place, the fourteenth-century Hospitium was worth the visit. Never been to Kingshaven, though."

"Don't bother, it's a hole," Vikki said. "There's the quaint bit in the middle which is good for tourists. The rest is fine if you like docks and marshes, otherwise . . ."

She pushed her thumb downwards.

"So you have higher ambitions?"

She smiled. "Fleet Street, London."

Her roots were betrayed by the way she pronounced "Larnden".

Vikki drew out her pen and pad again and flashed her eyes. "Now tell me everything."

"A wide request." He toyed with her, not immediately sensing a change of mood.

"You know, everything about Lucy Gray."

"Her family can tell you more than I can."

"They don't know much about her. I've spent the morning asking around your college, no one knows much about her. She's Miss Mystery."

"She is a little strange."

This remark was a mistake, throwing a tiddler out to a media piranha. Vikki's eyes widened beneath the mascara, her features sharpened. "How do you mean?"

23

He tried to worm off the hook, but she had him fixed. He had taken her for a green rookie, but Vikki knew her trade and quickly prised out what little he knew. She was intrigued by Lucy's more colourful interests.

"This dungeon thing sounds really weird."

"Most of my students have weird interests. It's a way of asserting their individuality. They spend three years being as bizarre as they can, then get jobs as accountants."

The biro moved. "So all your students are weird."

"Don't quote me! And it's not just my students, it's all students." And he had fooled himself into thinking Vikki lacked the bite for Fleet Street! He continued to wriggle. "Lucy was no odder than the average student."

"So she was odd?"

He sighed, then enjoyed a thirty-second truce whilst she jotted down a note. Satisfied, she changed course.

"Well, I've covered Lucy pretty well, but I'd like to know a little more about yourself."

"Me?"

"You know, background information. You're Doctor Jeffrey Flint . . . that's a good name for an archaeologist, Flint."

"I've heard all the jokes."

"Now, you're what? Thirty?"

"Ish," was the immediate if grumpy response.

"And you're a vegetarian," she pointed to the curry.

"Not really, they just do good veggi meals here, often better than the carnivorous variety."

"I see."

What she saw was the red-rimmed spectacles, the beard, the long hair and the jacket with its patched elbows and discreet CND badge. He knew the stereotype she would create for her readers. He told her a little of himself and his past history, thinking it better she know the truth than simply find scope for creative writing. Vikki asked him about his work and he launched enthusiastically into his new theory on third-century chronology. Very quickly, her head began to nod in rhythm with his speech, she said, "Fascinating," then abruptly switched back to Lucy.

"So, Lucy was into horoscopes and dungeon games and what's this? Ley-lines? Where do they get these strange ideas from?"

She waved a laden fork in ignorance.

"Do you teach these things, is it part of the course?"

"No." His defence was just a little too snappy.

"Well, I mean." The biro end wavered towards the beard.

"It's the uniform, my image, we all carry an image, you know. Mine's the wacky off-beat college lecturer. It's what the public expect."

The sarcasm was intended, but Vikki bit back. "So whilst you're busy having demos about canteens and banning the bomb, who looks after your students?"

"They're grown-ups, officially."

Vikki had passion in her voice. "They're still people, young people. You are in charge of them. You give them all these funny intellectual ideas, you can't just forget about them when they go missing."

His left hand crushed the paper cup, anger and guilt flashing through him in waves. As he scrambled to find a witty put-down, Vikki continued her offensive.

"Lucy Gray could be anywhere, anything could have happened to her. It's your responsibility, you should know where she is."

"I'm not a nursemaid, I'm not even her supervisor. Students disappear all the time, wild parties, spur-of-the-moment holidays."

"Murdered by the roadside."

He glared at her, irritating girl.

"How many lectures has she missed?"

"I don't know. Three per week, plus a seminar."

"She wouldn't miss all that work."

"My students do it all the time."

"Her mother says she was a sensible girl."

His tolerance was gone. "She would, wouldn't she?"

"Yes, but this is her final year, do you think she would just run off?"

He shrugged, "She could be researching her dissertation."

"I'm going to find her," Vikki declared, "and I think you should help."

Flint sighed and dropped the mutilated cup on to his tray. She was right, he knew she was right, he agreed with her but was too angry to say so. All he could do was take a few deep breaths then mutter, "Okay, perhaps you have a point."

*   *   *

One hour with a manic reporter posing questions he could not possibly answer and provoking thoughts he had no time to address was a tiring experience. A lecture at two offered the excuse to run. Once the first-years' interest in Basic Dating Techniques had been satisfied, Flint checked through the class lists. In her three years, Lucy had booked solidly on the British archaeology courses, mainly prehistory with an excursion into Old English. He speed-read through the five essays she had produced for his "Approaches to the Past" seminar course. The handwriting in the first was neat, but by the fifth betrayed an unrulyness less common amongst girls. She showed good recall, some detailed background knowledge but her work contained several unsubstantiated throwaway lines that would lose her marks. "This is contentious: where is the evidence?" he had scrawled in red biro beside the point where she had glibly asserted that in her opinion, Saxons settled in the south-east of England during the third century AD. This was hardly an accepted archaeological fact; quotes were needed to back up such statements.

He was still toying with the content of Lucy's essays as he went over into the Classics lounge for afternoon tea. On the way, he passed one of innumerable cluttered student notice-boards. Buried amongst posters urging "Fight the Cuts!" or "Say no to Racism" was a photostat handwritten page reading "Dice with Dragons each Wednesday Night". That poster would have appealed to Lucy.

Chapter 3

"What are you doing?"

"Opening the door."

"Roll a dice."

"Six-sided?"

A dice clunked on to the table top. Five.

"You hear something behind you."

The girl shrieked, "Oh God, it's going to be something horrible, we're all going to die!"

Flint sat bemused in the corner of the dimly lit Upper Lounge. A few yards away, six students were clustered around a knee-high table. Five were players, one the umpire who controlled their destiny, setting fiendish traps and awarding fabulous rewards for cunning. Rulebooks were piled on the floor, the map of an imaginary dungeon full of perils was spread across the table. Adventures in a fantasy realm totally absorbed the six. Flint went down into the bar.

The reporter's barb had bitten deep, triggering his own innate nosiness. The whereabouts of the missing student, *his* missing student, had been gnawing at his conscience. Only absent six weeks. Absent for six whole weeks, over a month. A sense of balance was needed. A pint of Sam Smith's Old Brewery Brown helped.

The Lower Lounge bar was a gloomy, unpopular drinking hole with the charm of an airport departure lounge. Uncomfortable low-level mock leather chairs were grouped in eights around tables which seemed designed to remove kneecaps. Five intrepid dungeoneers soon ventured down the stairs, their careers as mythical heroes prematurely terminated. A slice of the nation's top one per cent chose one bay of chairs and bemoaned the immolation of their paper characters by a red dragon. The dungeon master soon joined them, chuckling for effect and fending off the abuse of those he had recently annihilated. Setting cynicism aside, Flint walked up to the group and creaked into one of the fading red chairs. He introduced himself and asked about Lucy.

"Lucy Gray?" A short youth in a denim jacket with unfashionably long brown hair chirped up from his stool. "She's got a gnome illusionist called Cyril."

Without blinking, Flint pressed on. "Have you seen her recently?"

"She's dropped out, it said in the college paper," a lean, gawky student informed him.

"But when did you last see her?"

"I don't think we've seen her for months, not since the autumn term." The student looked for reinforcement from his colleagues.

"The last game she played was Rod's 'Death in Skarthion' adventure," the dungeon master offered.

The others variously agreed with this point.

"But she did come here and play this game?" At last, Flint had a sliver of information. "How keen was she? Did she take it all seriously, or just come for a while?"

The one girl in the group, a dumpy individual with a QMC sweatshirt offered the reply, "She came all last year. She was really good, knew the rules backwards. It was nice having another woman along. She had a real feeling for the game, and got us out of a couple of scrapes."

"Any idea why she stopped playing?"

Shoulders were shrugged.

"Does she have a boyfriend?"

All paused, waiting for a confession. It was not offered, so the QMC girl provoked one. "Timmy." The denim-jacketed youth was given a kick under the table.

"You?" asked Flint.

"Not seriously. Not any longer."

"But you were?"

"I wouldn't like to brag about it."

"Please do." Flint stood and gesticulated towards the bar. "I'll stand you a pint."

Timmy stood reluctantly and was drawn beyond earshot. "It was nothing serious. I went out with her a bit at the start of the year, the academic year."

"And?"

The student dug his hands into his pockets and studied the mock-marble floor. "Nothing happened, you know? She's a nice girl but, you know, not really interested."

Flint nodded and ordered the drinks. "Do you know anyone else she's been involved with?"

"I know a couple of blokes she's been with, they all say the same."

He related a string of locker-room anecdotes. Lucy the lesbian. Lucy the permanent virgin. Lucy the tease. Many frustrated seducers, many long-distance admirers, many suspects for Vikki's wilder scenarios of abduction or elopement. Flint memorised the names, and would jot them down later. The girl was becoming as much an enigma as her disappearance.

"So did you fall out?" Flint asked, enjoying his second beer.

"No, it just didn't work."

The heavy-metal badges sewn to the student's jacket simply screamed scientist to Flint's eye. "I'd guess you were a scientist."

"I'm doing chemistry," said Timmy. "I've got my finals after Easter."

The last words were spoken with a sense of deep foreboding.

"And what do you think of Lucy after you broke up?"

Timmy still seemed reluctant to give straight answers. "Not much, she was just too weird."

"Was, you said was, that's a past tense," Flint said sharply.

"Well, I haven't seen her for ages."

Subtleties of detective work were hard to learn and Flint made a note to make his enquiries more oblique from that moment. "This dungeon game, it's pretty addictive, isn't it?"

"Yes, you build up points week by week. The longer you survive, the better your character becomes."

"So why did Lucy stop playing?"

"She said she was too busy, she was always going away, seeing people and getting wound up in her own crazy ideas. That's what I hated about going out with her. She lied to me, she kept things secret. We all come here on Wednesdays and play characters, good, evil, neutral and sometimes we work together and sometimes we have to double-cross each other. But afterwards, in the bar, we all become real people again. Except Lucy." Timmy seemed angry and bitter at his failure. "She carries on playing as if all this is an effin' magical kingdom and she's the fairy queen. If

29

you really want to know, I think she's mad, she needs her head looking at."

Another headline penned by Vikki Corbett ran across the front page of the *Advertiser*.

"POLICE HUNT MISSING LOCAL GIRL."

Rowan read the text for the twentieth time, then folded the newspaper. Around her, the estuary was waking up to spring. Geese were returning to the mudflats, whilst lambing was in progress on the coarse grass of the inned marshes. She sat on the sea wall, watching the birds to seaward, glancing right to confirm that a figure was growing closer. Her pulse quickened, alarmed by the headline, excited by the sight of the man striding towards her.

The Poet wore a green wax jacket and his usual tweed cap. He walked with confident purpose, his two Red Setters dodging around his heels and following his calls. Rowan watched him approach. By all the gods of earth and sky he was handsome. Rugged good looks of Mills & Boon quality set The Poet apart from the mass of middle-aged men, whilst his active brain and wide imagination left Rowan in awe.

She stood and checked that they were alone in the flat landscape.

"Rowan!" he called whilst twenty yards away. "What a glorious day, it sets my heart aflame!"

She kissed him on the cheek, then touched the head of one dog, Keats, as it sniffed at her russet woollen coat. The Poet's welcoming smile fell as she took out the newspaper. He took it from her.

"More wanton ill-informed rubbish. It's no wonder English morality has slipped so low, when the press is in the power of illiterates."

"Surely you can do something?" Rowan's tone was submissive, yet persuasive. "You must know the editor . . ."

"So I do, but I can't see any reason to create a stir. It is not as if there's a grain of sense in these articles. Why should we over-react? This will blow over and we have nothing to fear. Have the police interviewed anyone we know?"

"No." She never felt confident in his presence, all her self-will evaporated before him. "I may be wrong, but I don't think the police are very concerned."

30

"No, not in the slightest. Nor will they be," he stated with authority. The Poet folded the paper, and handed it back, sighing, "Lucy, Lucy . . ."

"No Christian names!" Rowan snapped.

His expression made clear he found her manner offensive, and she avoided his glare, turning her face to the geese once more.

"It's as you said, we must not use Christian names, it is all part of the process of denial."

"Quite," he mellowed, "and indeed, a facet of security. Not that we should be afraid, but the media can be cruel," he flicked a finger on to the paper, "our friends could be hurt. I hope everyone is being discreet?"

She nodded.

"There are ways and ways, Rowan. One does not need to be crude. This puff of publicity will blow over, and if not, I'm sure we can out-think a mere girl reporter."

"You are right, I know you're right."

He reached out an embracing arm. The Poet always excited a warm glow deep within Rowan's breast. Rebuking her, now protecting her, he played his role too.

By the end of the spring term, Lucy Gray had taken up permanent residence as one of Jeffrey Flint's projects-in-being. A box file had been rededicated in her honour and began to bulge with scribbled notes. A clean photograph of Lucy was displayed prominently on his cork board, with a series of Vikki Corbett newspaper articles dangling underneath.

The caring staff of Leopold Hall evicted Lucy in her absence. Barbara drove up to London to clear the room. Leaving her husband waiting in their Volvo estate, Barbara went into the archaeology department to seek out Flint and found him in his office. It took only a few minutes to exchange what little they had discovered.

"I can't stay long, Derek's waiting," she said.

"Derek?"

"My husband."

"Ah." Only a hint of deflation was in his voice. Ulterior motives had been dashed, but his growing interest in Lucy's welfare replaced it. Barbara had taken less care with her appearance than on the previous occasion they had met. She had dressed down into jeans and large mohair sweater, neither of which suited her. Even her hair, which had been well kept, seemed to deserve a wash and blow-dry. Barbara handed over a pile of Lucy's mail, which had been finally released into her hands.

"I've read them all, there's nothing which tells us very much." Barbara was showing the strain of waiting. After a moment's hesitation she thrust a bank statement before him.

"See this."

She watched whilst the lecturer looked at the statement, dated March 6th. There were no entries for February.

"Have you got last month's statement in there too?" Flint was frowning, students could rarely survive a month without a trip to the bank.

"In here somewhere." She ferreted out a NatWest envelope, which was unopened. Barbara sliced open the envelope with a fingernail, then withdrew the statement dated February 6th. The last item was a cheque for £9.60, clearing on the 3rd.

"Three working days to clear, end of January some time," Flint observed, drumming a finger against the paper edge. "It's not a record, not a piece of clothing, everything ends ninety-nine pence these days."

"She was careful, she wouldn't just squander money. It must have been something she had to have."

"Or do. It's about the right amount for a train or bus ticket." It was a guess, but a logical one for a girl who had suddenly vanished.

"Yes, she could have got home on that," Barbara said with pathos. "When she first started up here, I used to give her ten pounds to cover her fares, to encourage her to come home." She paused. "I wonder where she went?"

"Student railcard, day return, single, off-peak saver, coach, bus? There are a bundle of options, but a finite number of possibilities. I imagine the police could find where the cheque was presented."

"The police are not taking this seriously, they say she's just flunking her exams."

"It's the likeliest possibility."

Barbara was insistent. "But she loves it here, she wants to work in a museum after she graduates. She won't allow herself to fail."

"Students have done it before, even brilliant ones decide they can't cope at the end."

32

Barbara relaxed slightly. "When she comes back, could she retake her exams?"

"She's still got plenty of time. She'll show up after Easter, you just see. Her marks are okay, she should get through even if she misses a few lectures."

More than a few, and he knew it, but Barbara seemed partly reassured. Flint thought back to what the student Timmy Wright had said about Lucy.

"Could I ask you something, Barbara? It's probably a little personal, but you are a doctor. Did you ever examine Lucy, was she ever your patient?"

"No," she said sharply.

"Are you pally with her GP, or is she registered at our health centre?"

"Here, she's registered here."

He sensed that Barbara was uncomfortable, but put it down to some aspect of medical ethics. "In your professional opinion, would you say Lucy was okay?"

"How do you mean?"

"Fit and well, in body and mind?"

"Yes, look, I'd better go, I'm on surgery at four." Barbara stood to leave.

"Where is the rest of Lucy's stuff?"

"In the car, Derek's downstairs."

"Mind if I have a sift through her papers? It might help."

Barbara pursed her lips. "I suppose it wouldn't hurt."

"Just her paperwork, you know, letters, notebooks, things like that."

"What if the police want them?"

Pigs will fly, he thought. "I live a lot closer to their station than you do."

An archaeologist is a natural investigator. When Barbara had finally gone, leaving a pathetic pile of Lucy's books and papers obstructing his doorway, Flint tried to forget about the coming field course and concentrate his mind on Lucy. He worked late in his office that evening, reading through everything Barbara had left, but finding no diary and no letters of consequence. He then re-read all the other notes, lists of names and dates which had arisen from his haphazard enquiries.

Lucy had drawn no money since the beginning of February and

33

not even opened her mail. Easter was approaching, she should be completing her dissertation, then swotting for the finals. She shouldn't fail, no one failed BA Archaeology unless they were determined to do so. He looked at the coy smiling face pinned to his cork board. For the first time, he was genuinely worried.

If he was to find Lucy, he still needed to know so much more about her friends, her background and her past. With all the publicity of press, police and internal enquiries, the silence was astounding. Lucy had tripped lightly across the college scene, leaving few footprints. No one can become invisible, he thought, no matter how hard they might try. Something about Lucy's lifestyle held the clue to her movements and her whereabouts.

An A4 pad was on his desk, as usual, and he had doodled the word "Lucy" in the centre of the page. He sucked on the gold biro he had recieved as his graduation present, then ringed the name.

"Home town: Durring," he wrote, then drew a box around it.

"Family" was written in another box, connecting to the other two by a line.

"Tolkien etc." went into its own box.

He drew a line then wrote "Dragon games".

He drew another and wrote "Astrology etc.".

So far, everything tallied, archaeologists are naturally interested in the mysterious, the mystical and the arcane. He added a box labelled "Hazel" as an offshoot of "astrology" and "Timmy" as an offshoot of "Dragon games".

It was late, he was hungry. The switchboard was off, but he could ring Chrissie from the lobby payphone and arrange a rendezvous at the unassuming Chinese restaurant off Goodge Street. Flint wrote "Still in UK" over to one side of his chart. Something nagged at him, he had the key within his reach. He listed dates of letters, of times and places she had been seen. She was missing by the eleventh of February, the date of the wedding. She was not missing two weeks before. He sat back, sucked the gold biro a little more, then wrote "February 1st". A logic trigger went off in his brain and he reached for a colourful coffee-table book on the Celts, which sat in the pile of Lucy's books. Within a minute, he had found the page listing the four key Celtic festivals: Samahain, Imbolc, Beltane, Lugsanadh. Below "February 1st" he wrote "Imbolc", then crossed out the word "astrology" and replaced it by "occult". A cold shiver ran down his spine as he remembered Timmy's remarks, and Lucy's own dreamy speech about harmonising with the Earth. She was impressionable, but had she finally lost touch with reality?

It had been a very late night indeed, which had turned into a late morning. Flint was still reading his mail when Tyrone appeared in his office to demand attention. He had asked for comments on his paper on "London Ware" that he wanted to submit to *London Archaeologist*. It would be his first academic publication and Tyrone was keen to see it approved.

Flint suppressed a yawn as he turned his thoughts away from Lucy and on to archaeology. "Tyrone, how many 'l's are there in 'Gaulish'?"

"Two?"

"One."

Tyrone slicked a hand through his hair and sighed. "Have I botched it up?"

"Doesn't the computer have a spell checker?" Flint asked.

"Yes, but it's only got 10,000 words in its vocabulary."

"Gaulish isn't one of them, I assume. Well, spelling apart, it's fine." Flint smoothed the pages together. "What have you found out about Lucy?"

"I think she's been kidnapped by some of Neil's Space Aliens."

"Seriously?"

Tyrone produced a ring-pad with ten pages of scribbled names, dates, places. "I checked most of this stuff, it's all trivial. There are about six or seven guys who reckon they are ex-boyfriends, but they're all still around. She hasn't eloped to Gretna Green."

"Not with any of them, anyway."

"Everything else is just gossip, there's nothing reliable or substantial, so what next, Doc?"

"I'd like you to expand on the 'find Lucy' project over Easter."

"Is there any money in it?"

"Not a penny."

Tyrone's post-Thatcherite ethics were offended, he grimaced as Flint continued. "If you're aiming to be an archaeologist you should learn rule one: we all work for nothing."

The student stuck out his chin and nodded.

"I'm going to be nursemaiding first-years and trying to keep them alive in Essex next week, but can you dig around some more?"

"Sure thing."

The eighties had been a barbarous, selfish decade and Tyrone was its sharp, almost cruel product. His plans for the future were purely mercenary: an independent archaeological consultant to wealthy developers. For the moment, Flint needed to utilise his energy and his cynical realism. At some time, he would also need to utilise his car.

The pair sat talking about Lucy Gray for another ten minutes, when the phone rang.

"Flint."

"Doctor Flint?" The female voice spoke. "It's Lucy, Lucy Gray."

"Lucy, where are you?"

"Please don't look for me."

"Lucy, listen, I need to talk to you . . ."

She did not reply, all he could hear was background traffic.

"Lucy, you're wasting a lot of people's time . . ."

The phone went dead, Flint snapping brief, futile words into it before he realised he was talking to air.

"Lucy?" Tyrone asked.

"Apparently," Flint said, temporarily confused by the ten-second phone call.

"Now what?"

Flint drummed his fingers, then rang Barbara's surgery. He was insistent with the receptionist and was soon speaking to a harassed GP.

"Barbara?"

"Jeffrey Flint! I was going to ring you, we've had a postcard, from Lucy."

"When?"

"Today, this morning, at the surgery."

Tyrone was listening in. "Is it in her handwriting?" he whispered.

Flint repeated the question to Barbara.

"I think so."

"What does it say?"

"It's from Glasgow, with an Indian statuette on the front . . ."

"Burrel collection?"

". . . Yes, you're right. It says, 'Dear Ba . . .'"

"She called you Ba?"

"Yes. 'Dear Ba, don't worry about me, I'm okay. Love, L.' Then she says 'P.S. I hate the picture they used in the paper.' "

Flint and Barbara were both silent for a few moments.

"It's good news," Barbara said with optimism.

"Yes, yes. She telephoned me just now. She only said a few words, but I got the idea she wants us to leave her alone," Flint related.

"Well, at least she's safe, somewhere, whatever she's doing."

"Yes."

Silence fell again before Barbara said, "Look, thanks for ringing me, I'm terribly rushed here. You'll tell me if you hear anything else?"

"Sure, bye." The receiver went down.

Flint could not hide his growing anger.

Tyrone winced. "What do we do now?"

"We stop pissing around and get back to doing some archaeology."

Chapter 4

Summer term saw exams looming and college stood almost deserted. All the careful tutors had finished their lecture programmes by Easter, so only the occasional tutorial would interrupt research until the time came to scurry through exam scripts with the red biro. Easter had been its usual happy turmoil, with the first-years being taken on the annual ten-day crash course in fieldwork techniques. Southern Essex had taken the brunt of the offensive and the one casualty was a Greek student down with hepatitis. Otherwise the party had returned from two weeks of serious drinking and fumbling sex unscathed.

At Central College, the J. B. Stoat Library radiates from beneath a domed rotunda. In the archaeology section, Tyrone sat upright at the workdesk filling in index cards amidst a pile of journals. Bunny was seated next to him, apparently asleep with his head on the heavily worn table top. He deserved to fail, Tyrone thought, then heard footsteps from behind.

"Hi, how's it going?" Jeffrey Flint whispered, leaning his head close to Tyrone's ear.

"Fine." Tyrone sat back and shuffled his cards into a neat stack.

Bunny raised his head, recognised the lecturer then drew himself upright.

"Got a moment?" Flint asked Tyrone, then turned to Bunny. "Don't let me wake you."

Tyrone followed the lecturer and together they leaned over the iron guard rails and looked down on the circular chamber below. He had noticed a bulging blue wallet file clutched under Flint's arm.

"Do you know what day it is today?" his supervisor asked.

"Hooray hooray, first of May."

"Which is also Beltane, the holiest day in the Pagan calendar."

"Lucy?" Tyrone guessed.

"Yeah, I saw the date and it made me think about her again. Then I bumped into the Registrar this morning. He remembered I'd been interested in Lucy and told me a big fat grant cheque is sitting in his office getting lonely."

Pagan or not, Lucy could not be immune to the single greatest need of a student: money.

"Have you rung the big sister and told her?"

"Yes, she's had another postcard, Isle of Skye."

"Without a grant Lucy must be living on air."

"Or she's with someone."

"I thought you'd lost interest in her."

Flint nodded. Tyrone waited to see what erratic thought his supervisor was about to come up with.

"Sam Hanley rang in last week . . ." Flint began.

"What did she have?"

"A boy, Easter Sunday, called him Tristram. Anyway, she's Lucy's supervisor, she'd heard all the hoo-hah and wanted to check whether Lucy had handed in her dissertation at the end of the spring term. Apparently, she claimed to have just about finished it over Christmas."

"That's keen."

"Yeah, but Lucy was keen, that's why her running off really doesn't make sense. I talked to Sam and we agreed that if Lucy finally comes to her senses, she could resit her exams in October, and the department will stretch a point on the deadline for handing in her diss, but it's a month overdue now. If she doesn't hand it in during the next couple of days . . ."

". . . she fails?"

". . . she gets a third-class degree at best."

Tyrone snorted, "Same thing."

Flint pulled the blue wallet from under his arm. "I've asked just about everyone and hunted around in her stuff. I found the diagrams, all we need now is the text. There's a load of handwritten notes in here, but we know she's typed at least one draft of the final text, because Sam saw it back in January."

Tyrone thought for a few seconds. "I know which machine she uses."

"Wordprocessor?"

He nodded. "It's one of the PCs in the department. If I

can get her password, I could hack into her files and run off a copy."

Flint seemed pleased. "Go and see Brad in Computing, tell him I sent you for Lucy's password. I'll write him a memo if he gets stroppy. If we work fast, we might just save Lucy's degree."

Tyrone was happy to move off immediately. "I'll go now. What's her diss on?"

Flint adopted an ironic tone. " 'The Iconography of Earth Mother Figurines.' "

"I might have guessed."

Beltane was not the happy, joyous celebration of spring that all had expected. Disquiet spread rumours of investigation, of scandal, of social approbation. Some feared for their jobs, others their families and their friends in the real world. A real world which had suddenly edged closer to the intimate circles.

Devil's Ring was what ignorant Christians called the ancient site. Five beech trees clawed their roots into the remains of a stone circle. Nine chunks of sarsens had survived the enthusiasm of a nineteenth-century nobleman who had blown the monument apart with black powder. On a clouded evening, the Pagan circles convened at the lonely spot, placing their look-outs and taking their precautions against observation.

The Poet remained outwardly unmoved, but it was a sad and mechanical Oak who performed the ceremony in the cover of the trees. This time, there was no Maiden, no one to stand in for the Goddess. Rowan was fully conscious of the depression settling upon her circle. Time would fill the void, but for the moment, protection was what they needed. Sand would be flung in the faces of their persecutors, reporters and others. The name of Vikki Corbett was whispered and curses were raised against her, but not one pair of lips mouthed the name Lucy Gray.

A light rain fell as the group returned to their cars to dress and merge back into twentieth-century normality.

"Something is wrong with Oak," The Poet remarked to Rowan, still clad in her white ankle-length robe.

She put aside a dripping blonde lock and watched the pathetic figure struggling to pack his altar and sacred implements on the slippery grass.

"He isn't well and he misses Hazel."

40

"So do we all, myself more than most, but in Oak I sense hostility, does he still resent me?"

"More and more," she said.

"He worries me, his feelings run too deep. He thinks too much, he asks too much about The Book. There are things ordinary men are not meant to know."

Yes, she thought, how true.

The Pagans had made their sacrifices, but others, too, used May 1st to plan to save the Earth. Local elections loomed and Flint spent the evening seated on a stool in the kitchen shared by Chrissie and her flatmate. They talked as he helped her fold Green Party leaflets into recycled envelopes. He was no party member, considering their utopia as impractical as all other utopias on offer, but they won his vote on sheer imagination and novelty. Chrissie was the secretary of the college GreenSoc and the spur behind his renewed interest in politics.

"What I don't understand is why you don't join the party," she was saying. Chrissie had an elegant, earnest manner to accompany her elegant, earnest face.

"I'm an anarchist, Chrissie, you know that. I have a deep suspicion about political parties and pressure groups. No one is one hundred per cent right."

"No, but the other parties are one hundred per cent wrong."

"Well, if you don't mind, I won't sign the pledge, I reserve the right to choose."

"Apathy won't get us anywhere."

"I was in Greenpeace when you were still a Girl Guide," he said, admiring the deep red of her freshly washed hair.

"But you're not any more, you're selling out, Jeffrey."

"I got tired of protesting, I was becoming a walking cliché. CND, Ecology Party, Anti-Nazi League."

"It's nothing to be ashamed of."

"No. I've run out, gimme another pile."

Her slender hands pushed a box of leaflets across the wobbling nineteen-sixties-style table.

"I managed to get a lead on Lucy Gray's dissertation today, we may be able to save her yet."

"Did you know she was in the University GreenSoc?" Chrissie said. "Someone mentioned her when I was at the biodiversity rally. He knew that I knew you and made the connection. I asked about her."

"Didn't you know her?"

"Only vaguely, she only went to the meetings at Senate House, and only when we had a major speaker. She never came to the meetings at college, I think we were too reactionary for her."

"She always struck me as being committed to Green issues."

"Perhaps, saving whales and recycling bottles. But most of these kids have no real commitment, no concern about social issues, or nuclear weapons, or capitalist multinationals. To me, Lucy sounds as if she was rather right wing."

Flint had to smile; to be called right wing in a university was the ultimate insult. As Chrissie continued to narrate, Flint realised how deep a gulf existed between them. One day he would tire of superficial relationships and risk something deeper again.

"A lot of people who call themselves Green are just middle-class reactionaries looking for a cute hobby," Chrissie continued. "They live in expensive villages in Surrey and all they care about is keeping the rabble away. They form a protest group if a bypass is built in their back yard, but the rest of the week speed around in Range Rovers. If they use lead-free petrol they think it's okay."

"And Lucy?"

". . . Is a green-welly Green, into thatched cottages and Merrie England, which is nothing to do with the real world at all."

"This person you were talking to, he hasn't seen her?"

"Not for months, that's why he was asking me."

"Can you remember those meetings she attended? I mean she was fairly striking to look at, you couldn't have missed her."

Chrissie narrowed her eyes to indicate she had spotted a sexist observation. "She just hovered at the back, looking pretty. When we had Poritt along to speak, she asked a really immature question, but otherwise, she kept herself to herself. This chap I met said the same – he'd ask her out on weekend demos but she usually had to meet someone."

"Who?" Flint pounced.

Chrissie shrugged. "I'd guess he's not a student, we're a bit too scruffy for her."

Folding and packing continued until their paper resource was exhausted. Flint thought about Chrissie's increasing coolness and whether he was expected to seduce her that night, and if he truthfully could with a clear conscience. When he thought about sex, or women in general, Lucy trespassed in his mind and only forced wider the emotional gulf between himself and Chrissie.

What Chrissie had told him about Lucy confused him even more. Up to then he had assumed Lucy had been sincere about her Green beliefs, but she had been playing games again, obviously. She had joined GreenSoc and the CC Dungeoneers, but he strained to think of other college societies which might have attracted her. An idea came to him after only a few moments.

"Chrissie, do you remember anything about PaganSoc?"

The idea was ingenious, but short lived. Throughout the week, Flint tried to contact an elusive physics postgraduate called Gavin who had moved to Imperial to work on semiconductors. An article in an old issue of the college paper had concerned the formation of PaganSoc. The union had been ambivalent about the proposed society, but as Gavin had found the obligatory twenty members, PaganSoc was awarded its grant, despite objections.

Tracing Gavin to his lair was a minor triumph, but visiting him in the functional junior common room of Imperial College was an anti-climax. Sure, Gavin had formed PaganSoc. The prospectus included witchcraft, moonlight masses, satanic rites, all a good pagan could wish for. It had been a joke perpetrated by a group of reactionary students, partly to irk the do-gooders of the college "God Squad", partly in protest at the size of grant given to the Gay Society. They had won the minimum society handout, blown it all on one bestial party, then quietly dissolved the society. There had been no serious intent. He had never heard of Lucy Gray.

Flint cycled back across town in his shirt sleeves, enjoying the May sunshine, but cursing the traffic every yard of the way. Perhaps he should rejoin Greenpeace before it was truly too late. Chaining up his bike in the central rat-run, he was hailed from a third-floor window by Tyrone yelling.

"Doc! I've found it!"

Flint walked into the Department and passed a few words with Professor Grant in the lobby before Tyrone came down. He led his supervisor into the computer room where two PC terminals displayed a mass of turgid archaeological text.

Tyrone sat before the right-hand terminal. "I've found Lucy's dissertation. There are three drafts, cunningly numbered one, two and three."

Flint toyed with the keyboard of his terminal. "This is?"

"Version three, it seems to be the most complete version."

"Is it any good?"

"Good for a lower second if you felt charitable. It's not really finished, there's no key to the diagrams, no bibliography and no concluding chapter or appendix of data."

"So we're still going to have to find her, or finish it ourselves." Flint scrolled through the introduction.

After a few moments, Tyrone asked, "Have you spotted it yet?"

"What?"

Tyrone had a rogue's grin. On his terminal, he scrolled Version Two to the introduction. "Spot the mismatch."

"Tyrone, I haven't time, I've just seen Grant and there's a meeting in ten minutes."

"Look at Version Two: it says 'Grateful thanks to Piers Plant M.A., Curator, Darkewater Valley Museum'. In Version Three, he rates no mention. But it gets better, in Version Two she quotes him four times. In Version Three, she uses the same information without acknowledgement. That is not very ethical."

Flint insisted on being shown the facts, but of course, Tyrone was right. For a moment he thought that Tyrone had the versions in the wrong order, but soon spotted the word "Figrues" in Version Two had been corrected to "Figures" in Version Three. The acknowledgement of Piers Plant had not simply been omitted, it had been deleted.

Half to himself, Flint murmured, "I wonder why she did that."

"I think they fell out," Tyrone stated. "They must have had some sort of tiff, you know how awkward curators can get. They're trained to defend their material."

Flint hardly heard, he was rereading the text before him. "You print out hard copies of both versions and we can pick the best to hand in. I'll go and see what Grant wants, then I'll give this Plant character a ring, just for my own peace of mind."

Whilst Flint was in his meeting, Sally found the telephone number of the museum in Kingshaven. Still looking at the planned schedule of exam invigilators, Flint rang the number he had been given.

"Piers Plant here."

"Hello, my name is Doctor Jeffrey Flint, from Central College London. I was ringing to ask you about Lucy Gray."

For a moment, the curator was silent. "Lucy Gray? Are you sure you have the right number?" The voice seemed hesitant.

"I understand you gave her some information for her undergraduate project. Possibly just before Christmas."

"I get a lot of enquiries."

"Mother Goddess figurines?"

The man hummed, a thinking hum. "No, I'm sorry."

"You know she's missing? You read the papers?"

Silence.

"Have you seen her recently?"

"I really couldn't say."

It occurred to Flint that this mode of enquiry was futile.

"Could I arrange to come down and see you?"

The other made a few discouraging noises. "I'm very busy at the moment."

Museum curators are always busy, thought Flint. Doing what is undetermined.

"Look, it won't take long."

"I don't have an assistant at the moment, you see. The post has been frozen for two years. I keep asking for a new one, but . . ."

"It won't take long."

Excuse piled on excuse, meetings, school parties, a sick mother. Finally, an exasperated Jeffrey Flint put the telephone down, with an insincere "Thank you."

He had a feeling of foreboding, a feeling that he had been simply coasting, skimming the surface of something more complex than a student flunking her exams. Immediately, he opened the Lucy box file and began to reread every note that he and Tyrone had made, all her essays, her letters, her notes and the confessions of her frustrated boyfriends. When Tyrone brought them up, he read both versions of her dissertaion too.

Lucy was someone he was growing to know so well, even intimately, and the more he thought over her picture pinned to the memo board, the more empathy he felt for her. Romantic, gentle, caring, naïve, aware and confident in her own belief system. Wherever she had gone, it was down a path he could very easily have followed.

*   *   *

45

After a long evening and restless night, Flint cycled into college early. His first item of post was Lucy's April bank statement, forwarded to him by Barbara. It confirmed that nothing had cleared through the account. The February cheque was the last. Reaching his office, stepping around Winnie the cleaner, he filed the blank statement with the others. Taking a moment to flick back through the folder, he studied the statement for January, when her society subscriptions were due. The only standing order entry was for "Darkewater Val 10.00". It was enough to see him first through the library doors when they opened.

Every region of Britain has its local society and the Darkewater Valley fitted the pattern. Flint had lectured to them once, and recalled the group of mainly middle-aged and middle-class amateur scholars who referred to themselves as the "Dark Ants". The library held complete runs of most regional journals, including *The Transactions of the Darkewater Valley Antiquarian Society*, with volumes dating back to 1879. Over a hundred of the bottle-green hardbacked volumes were packed on to the shelves, the older journals becoming progressively more faded until the gold lettering could hardly be distinguished from the yellowed spines.

Flint pulled out the latest *Transactions* and turned to the list of officers. The Hon. Curator of the Society was Piers Plant M.A., Darkewater Valley Museum, Kingshaven. The following ten pages listed the members in close type, including Lucy Gray registered at her home address. The Dark Ants had no more than five hundred listed members, many of whom would be inactive and few of whom would be bright twenty-one-year-old blondes. How could any officer of the society fail to notice Lucy Gray? Flint smelt a whole colony of rats. Kingshaven, where Plant curated the museum, and where Vikki Corbett wrote her lurid articles, lay only a dozen or so miles to the east of Lucy's home town of Durring. Flint remembered Barbara's remark about £9.60 taking her home. It could also have taken her to Kingshaven.

The day was young and fifteen years based in London had given Jeffrey Flint a bulging address book. Steve Waleweski was already within the bar of The Rising Sun at Euston by the time Flint arrived that lunchtime. The pair had been thrown together as second-year undergraduates, sharing a chaotic terraced house in Fulham with three life scientists. Steve had sat Business Studies and shown an unhealthy interest in trains. Around the time they jointly graduated, Steve became entranced by one of Flint's former girlfriends and married her within the year. Two common experiences bonded the men together, but otherwise, they inhabited different worlds.

Flint thought of Steve as the sort of solid, dependable type his own mother had always wanted him to be. Steve was time-serving his way to the top in British Rail and always outwardly envious of the freewheeling, if penniless archaeologist. Forty-five minutes over chicken curry and chips was too little to relive the old times, so Flint got straight to the point. A keen thriller reader, Steve was all too willing to help in the fact-grubbing exercise when Flint passed over the information on Lucy's movements. In return, he had explained the subtle intricacies of the latest mutation of BR's pricing policy. When they separated they agreed to meet again, and soon.

By late afternoon, the facts were unearthed and Steve telephoned them through. Lucy had bought a train ticket on January 31st. Her cheque had been presented at the correct station and was the correct amount to buy a student return to Durring. She had indeed gone home, or somewhere very close to home.

Chapter 5

The Darkewater Valley Museum was a tall, red-brick building constructed through the munificence of a local Victorian entrepreneur. Its witch's-hat spires and crumbling gargoyles gave it a forbidding aspect. On another May morning, Flint made his way through the rose garden towards the Gothic monstrosity, enjoying the scent of summer in the air and certain he was close to solving the mystery. The curator had continued to be evasive when telephoned a second time. Flint had considered giving his name to Vikki Corbett and allowing the reporter to savage Piers Plant with her Jack Russell enthusiasm, but he had rejected the idea. Academia is a closed world, he and this Piers Plant probably spoke the same language.

Within the lobby, the peak-capped attendant was watching television from behind the array of postcards, key-rings and plastic dinosaurs on the sales desk. He stood to attention sharply when Flint leaned his knuckles on the counter.

"My name is Professor Birch from the Classical Institute, Cambridge. I have an appointment with the curator at ten."

Subterfuge was a necessary part of the approach. Flint was a trifle young for a professor, but knew at least one academic who had attained the rank by his mid twenties.

"I'll see, sir, but I think someone's still in with him." The attendant's accent, age and the purple-and-green General Service medal ribbon said ex-army. His upright pose and correct telephone manner confirmed it. He glanced at the clock, only quarter to ten.

"Would you mind waiting twenty minutes, sir?" he asked.

"No, I'll wander round."

A broad staircase ran up from the entrance hall, divided at a mezzanine, then came back on itself. At the mezzanine, a large brass Buddha sat cross-legged, welcoming the approach. Beneath the stair was a stuffed lion in a glass case. It was one of *those* museums, thought Flint, the type they don't build any more.

The original building had been roughly rectangular, with a nineteen-twenties annexe at the north end lending it an L-shaped plan. The archaeologist wandered past Victoriana, suits of armour, dusty fossil collections, a case of militia uniforms and much else of less interest. Even when he found the archaeology gallery, he was disappointed. Curling cards beside grey burial urns had not been amended for years. Several captions had dated, that beside the Roman coin hoard was downright wrong. A model of one of the valley's famous megaliths had been allowed to gather dust, whilst one of its plaster stones lay fallen.

Within the new annexe, the museum changed into a place where care and attention had been lavished on the displays. It housed the folklore section, bright with spotlights, shiny glass and vivid text. Twenty minutes passed easily as Flint admired rural handicrafts and read of witch-burnings and bizarre local myths. A video promised a folk-tale recital, but a sheet of paper Sellotaped across the screen proclaimed it to be out of order. It was time for confrontation and Flint moved briskly back to the lobby.

Buddha sat motionless as before, eyes closed, weighing past and future. As Flint waited, Piers Plant came soundlessly around the turn of the stair and halted before the god, one hand supporting himself on the balustrade.

"Professor Birch?"

The imposter made his way up towards the curator, taking in every detail he could. Plant was a slight, trembling man in his mid forties, dark haired, with a feeble moustache and goatee. His eyes were reddened, almost bloodshot, and his forehead was creased by successive nights of long study. Flint knew the look, but did not immediately understand his manner.

"Come this way." Plant's voice was soft, almost effeminate.

At the top of the second flight of stairs, along a passageway, the curator's office had been shoved into a corner turret. Small windows opened over the rose garden, with the remaining wall space being devoted to shelves of books and box files. Flint took in the scope of Plant's library at a glance. Most of the books were of local interest, comprising works by minor scholars, the memoirs of the nearly-famous and a set of familiar green-backed journals. It could have been the bookcase of a hundred antiquarians he had known.

"Have we met?" Plant edged around his cluttered desk, narrowing his eyes to place the face.

Flint inclined his head, thinking of the one previous occasion he had visited Durring to deliver a lecture to the Darkewater Antiquarians.

"Possibly. Look, let's not mess around. My name isn't Birch, it's Jeffrey Flint, of Central College London. We spoke on the phone a couple of times."

Plant's face showed a flicker of doubt, then almost amusement at the way he had been tricked. "Ah yes, Doctor Flint. You lectured the Dark Ants in Durring a couple of years ago. 'Celtic mutations of Roman art forms.' I found it very interesting."

"Glad to see you remembered it." Flint kept up the polite charade, but the air had become tense. He eased himself on to a creaking leather-and-hardwood chair and made Plant the centre of his attention. The man was twitching and had already started to play with a pen with his left hand whilst his right soon began to be rubbed back and forward on the table. Museum work is not noted for its high stress content, yet the curator seemed a tangle of nerves.

"How well do you know Lucy Gray?" Flint asked, seeing no profit in oblique pleasantries.

Plant's tongue appeared from those wispy whiskers and licked a drying spot on his lips. His voice set into a neutral, calm tone.

"Only vaguely, she's in the Dark Ants, one of our younger members."

"It's just that you couldn't remember her at all the other day."

"No, I was very busy. I need an assistant, they froze the post, you know. The County Council won't listen."

Flint interrupted. "You know Lucy has been reported missing?"

"Ah yes, I think I heard." The casualness was plainly forced.

"I found these notes in her room." Flint took a wad of photocopied sheets from his briefcase. It was the second draft of Lucy's dissertation. The quotations from Piers Plant were highlighted in yellow.

"Familiar?"

Plant moved his head with rhythm as he read successive lines. "Ah yes, Mother Goddesses, yes, very interesting." He scanned over the words again and again. Flint watched intently, unsure himself how the interview would end. He could see Plant's mind working over his next feeble excuse.

"Yes, I remember, she came to see me some time in the autumn."

The man was such a poor actor, making up his lines as he went along, that Flint grew angry with the deceit. "Why wouldn't you talk about Lucy on the phone?"

"I've been busy, I can't waste my time . . ."

"Have the police been to interview you?"

"Police? No. Why should they?"

"Lucy has been missing since February, well over three months. You must have seen the papers or the television reports?"

"Yes, yes I think so. If I knew something, I'd tell the police straight away."

"Really? Well tell me."

"Tell you what?"

"Why you denied knowing her. You must know her, for God's sake. If I remember that meeting of the Dark Ants in Durring, there were fifty-odd people in the room and not one under forty. You're hardly chock-a-block with college girls, are you?"

Plant said nothing, but his chin twitched and he began to colour. His head moved one way, then switched to the other as if his brain were being overcome with indecision. His interrogator continued to attack.

"When was the last time you saw her?" Flint repeated again.

"I don't know, I'm very busy here, I can't remember everyone who comes through."

"Have you seen her in the last three months?"

"No."

"Certain?"

"I don't know. And I resent this intrusion. I don't like your tone!"

Flint ignored the protest, his own adrenalin was running rich. "This year? Have you seen her this year?"

"Perhaps."

"Check your diary, it's there." Flint nodded his head towards a council-issue desk diary. "I'm sure she had to make appointments too. You are, after all, very busy."

Plant moved a hand towards the diary, breathing heavily, his trembling increasing. Flint felt the man was shrinking before him,

51

he was on the offensive, he was winning, Plant was about to crack. He stood up and leaned on the curator's desk, menacing the man with a pointed finger.

"I can ask around. I can ask other Dark Ants. I can ask Lucy's family. I can ask your staff. I can check, the press can check, the police can check."

"Who do you think you are!" Plant stood up to face him, his face bursting with fury. "You can't just act like the Gestapo, insulting people and making threats!"

Flint ceased leaning and tried switching to the fatherly tone he reserved for distressed students. "Hey look, I'm not trying to say . . ."

Plant was beyond pacification and began to rant, red faced and blustering. "I don't care what you're trying to say, just get out!"

"Okay, I'll just pop down the police station and suggest they come and see you. Maybe they'd like to read your diary."

Piers Plant's hands clenched on the table top. His pallor had been replaced by a deep red. A letter knife lay only an inch from his knuckles and his fingers were crawling towards it.

"Get out, you liar, you imposter!"

"Not until you give me a straight answer." Flint noticed the fingers had reached the blade of the knife, and his attack faltered.

"This is none of your business, what has Lucy got to do with you?"

Plant had used her Christian name and the intonantion was personal. Flint noted it and instantly switched tack.

"Do you know anyone in Glasgow?"

For a moment, genuine confusion punctured the curator's pink anger, then he returned to bluster. "Get out."

"Do you know anything of Lucy's beliefs?"

The curator started to move around the desk. "Get out!" His hand closed around the handle of the paper knife.

Flint fell back a couple of paces. "Oh well, just thought I'd ask."

He continued his slow retreat towards the oak panel door, keeping his eye on the knife, not wishing to find it thudding between his shoulder blades. When his back was to the door, he opened it and stepped outside, letting fly one final barb. "Ah, the black cooking pot in the Roman display. AD 225 or later, it isn't second century. Read my paper in last year's *JRPS*."

Flint closed the door quickly and trotted down the stairs. Once by the desk, he drew the attendant's eyes away from the television and proffered a photograph of Lucy.

"You wouldn't have seen this girl around here lately?"

"Ah, Miss Gray, what a charming girl."

Flint was in a panic to leave the building. "But have you seen her lately?"

"No sir, I can't say I have, there was something in the paper about her being up in London."

"Did she used to come here often?"

The attendant puffed out his chest. "I dare say she just about lived here some weeks."

"And she's a good friend of Mr Plant?"

"Thick as thieves." The man grinned broadly and gave a wink. Flint had no chance to respond. A figure stood beside the brass Buddha, rigid as the statue, but with a powerful anger bubbling within him. Flint said no more, nodded politely to the attendant and left.

The Mason's Arms had a half-timbered façade, plus an excellent view of the museum across the rose garden. Once through its artificially aged oak door, Flint asked for the telephone and made three phone calls. One to Barbara, one to her mother and one to Vikki Corbett. He then went to the leaded bays at the front of the bar and gazed across at the museum, contemplating his next move.

His next move turned out to be a pint of Youngs ESB and a plate of cheese and pickle. When Vikki Corbett burst into the pub, panting heavily, she found the archaeologist crunching French bread and gazing out of the window. She dropped on to the seat beside him, pulling off her sunglasses.

"Jeff, sorry, Doctor Flint, what's all this about?"

"Jeff will do." He dabbed away a crumb and grinned through his beard.

"What about this story?" she demanded.

"I have a lead on Lucy Gray."

"I thought you didn't care about her."

"I never said that. I just didn't take it very seriously at first."

"So what changed your mind?"

"Nothing. Lots of nothing, everywhere I look, nothing. An enigma, a set of questions that need answering . . ."

She screwed up her nose. "You do go on, don't you?"

"That's what they pay me for. Speaking of which, your paper seems to have gone quiet on the story."

Her aggression modified to a defensive "There hasn't been anything else to say, has there? The police have found out nothing. No one has seen her, no one knows anything about her."

"Except me." Flint had a smug expression of triumph on his face. The last crumb of French stick disappeared between the bearded lips.

Just for a moment, she detected a little charm working its way through his intellectual front. There was more to Doctor Flint than clever theories and fringe politics.

"Drink?" he asked.

"G and T."

He stood to move to the bar, digging a hand into the pocket of his jeans.

"No, let me." The reporter opened her personal slush fund and passed him a twenty-pound note. Vikki sat impatiently clicking her pen whilst Flint leaned on the bar trying to attract attention. He was soon back, sucking a finger where the beer had slopped from the glass.

"I've been to the museum, do you know the curator?"

Yes, she thought, a queer geezer with a name to match.

"Not very well," she replied, assuming he was one of Flint's weird associates.

Flint could talk very rapidly when excited, and he rattled through his reasons for visiting the museum. Vikki felt her enthusiasm pall. "Look, I'm sorry, but I need a story. This is not very exciting. It wouldn't even push Twinbridge village fête off page seven. I can't write a piece all about Lucy missing bits out of her essays and someone saying he doesn't know her."

"Vikki!" Flint interrupted her sharply, his eyes had narrowed, for once he seemed to be deadly serious, no longer laid back, no longer apathetic. "If you don't mind me saying, Lucy was a pretty, vivacious girl who would turn most men's heads. Add the fact that she has a peculiar manner of behaviour . . ."

"Peculiar? More peculiar than you originally said she was?"

"She does lots of bizarre things, but doesn't take them seriously.

54

She plays around with men, she dips her toes into all sorts of fringe activities without getting wet. She seems to hold life at arm's length."

"So?"

"As I was saying, she isn't the sort of girl I would forget. Across there in the museum is a man who is trying to make out he hardly knows her."

"And you've proof he does?"

"I phoned her mother. She told me that last summer, Lucy was up here all the time. In the autumn, she would be at the musuem almost every weekend, working on her dissertation. I know he helped her with her work, I have the proof. Then, all of a sudden, he's pretending this never happened and she writes him out of her acknowledgements."

Flint reached into his briefcase and took out the dissertation. "Read this."

Vikki started the first page, then said, "I'll take your word for it, I mean, it's clear what went on."

"It is?"

"They had an affair." She said, "She's embarrassed, because he's so much older than she is, as well as being a nerd. He's embarrassed . . ."

"Why? Most dirty old men would brag about it."

Reporter looked at archaeologist and their thoughts married.

"See why I'm worried?" Flint asked

She sucked in her well-blushed cheeks and nodded.

"He's a spooky guy and evasive as hell. He's got guilty tattooed on his forehead."

"Oh God," Vikki said slowly, "I was right, don't you know, I was right. He's done her in. She's ended the affair and he's done her in."

"Wait!" Flint objected, a look of intense pain meeting the suggestion. "Remember the phone call, the cards?"

"He could have faked them."

"No. She used a pet name for her sister, called her 'Ba'. It's nothing that sinister, but I think he knows where Lucy is, and he's covering it up. Otherwise why the act?"

Vikki was unconvinced, all her gory scenarios were coming true. Sex, jealousy and murder, with a little eccentric colour at the edges meant she could skip cat shows for the rest of that month. She slowly folded her notepad and slipped her pen into its spine. "Is he still there?"

"He hasn't come out."

Vikki downed her drink, with a "Come on."

She was on her feet before him and waiting by the kerbside before he caught up with her. Once a bus had passed, they jogged across to the rose garden, the scent of new-mown grass hitting them as soon as the diesel fumes had subsided. From her leather handbag, Vikki withdrew her Dictaphone and gave Jeffrey Flint a smile.

"Promise me you're not mucking me about."

"Vikki, would I muck you about?"

"People do."

Flint led the way into the museum, and the attendant looked up. "Hello again."

"Is the curator in?" Flint asked.

"He's left for the day, sir."

"Shit." A plastic stegosaurus bounced on to the floor as Flint's fist thumped on to the table.

"He can't have gone," Vikki felt cheated, "what do the rate-payers get for their money?"

"He said he was ill, miss. Just before noon. It seems there's something going round."

"Have you got a back door?" Vikki asked.

"Yes," the attendant pointed under the stairs, "but I'm afraid it leads to the staff car park, you can't leave that way."

"I don't want to leave!" she snapped. "I suppose he sneaked out that way just now. Does he have a car? What make is it?"

The attendant straightened his back, looking down at her with an air of mistrust. "It's one of those Russian things."

"What, a Lada, Skoda?"

"A Skoda, miss, a green one."

"I suppose he drove off just after I left?" Flint asked quietly.

The attendant looked wary and reluctant to answer.

"Look, is there anyone else we can see?" Vikki asked. "Does he have an assistant?"

"Is there a deputy curator?" Flint added.

"No, not for a number of years." The attendant was clearly on his guard, looking from one to the other.

"Don't worry," said Vikki, "I'm from the *Advertiser*. We're

56

writing a piece about the museum." She turned on her Dictaphone and gave the old man a lingering smile. "So, your name is?"

"George Carlyle."

Soon after joining her first newspaper, Vikki had learned that few can resist being interviewed. Whether politician or man-in-the-street, their ego jumps when a microphone or a notepad is pointed their way.

"So, George, there's just you and Mister Plant in this great big museum?"

"No, there's Carol, the cleaner, young Tom the technician and my relief, Jack. We get people in from the County when there's anything big on."

"Does the curator live near here?" Vikki suddenly asked.

"On the edge of town."

"Could I have his address?" Vikki spread her puce lips wide as the man accepted her pen and began to write. "Thank you, you're so sweet."

Vikki owned a scarlet Mini Metro and Flint accompanied her to Plant's address. She drove sedately, but had an alarming habit of waving both hands and looking him in the eye whilst talking and driving. Her own eyes were shielded by those deep black shades and he was convinced she could see nothing through them.

Red-brick suburbs of Kingshaven gave way to a satellite straggle of bungalows and gentrified cottages. Just as the houses began to thin, an unadopted lane ran off towards the river from the main road. Piers Plant lived with his mother, in the fourth of a line of six square nineteen-twenties bungalows. When the Metro drew to a halt, there was no green Skoda on the gravel drive.

Mrs Plant came to the window as they knocked, then came to the side door only with reluctance. Old and grey, her manner was suspicious and diffident.

"Is Piers at home?" Flint asked.

"Now, I not seen 'im." Mrs Plant displayed her slow regional drawl as she blocked entrance to her home.

"George at the museum said he'd come home," Vikki said in sympathy with the familiar tone adopted by Flint.

"Not seen 'im, my dear."

Was it deceit, or simply defiance Flint saw in her eyes? "Would you mind if we waited for him?"

"I be going out," she said as a reply, which was as good as a refusal.

"Mrs Plant, I'm from the *Advertiser*," Vikki began.

The old woman frowned.

"I'm working on an article on Piers and the museum."

Vikki was still speaking as the door closed and a chain rattled into place. Two bolts followed.

"Wrong move," Flint observed.

"Mrs Plant!" Vikki tapped on the door.

Flint was walking back towards the Metro. "Come on, we're wasting our time." As usual, he thought.

Vikki's face was clouded and angry as she strode back down the ill-sorted gravel. "She's lying, don't you think? She's covering up as well."

The archaeologist raised a tired smile. "Could you run me to the train?"

Vikki assented, urging him to get in the car. "I'll drive you to your train, but then I'm coming back. He's got to come home some time."

Chapter 6

Rowan paced across the room, her arms folded, her thin lips set into an almost invisible line. In the wing-backed armchair, Piers Plant gripped the armrests for support as he waited to be told what to do.

"Whatever came into you?" Her anger was plain, and all he wanted was understanding. Rowan reached the window and looked down into the passageway below, verifying again that no one had followed the curator.

Piers Plant strained his neck so he might check too, feeling as if he was pursued by demons. In some respects, he was.

"He came."

"Who?"

He related the intrusion by Jeffrey Flint in detail.

"He knows everything."

"Oak, you're being ridiculous. He knows nothing, Hazel has been careless, that's all. He knows nothing, understand?"

Why was she never sympathetic? Where had his lovely Rowan found this hard and cruel edge? Plant thought back to February, his muddled mind fighting the idea that the change had been his fault.

"Flint came back, with a girl. Then they went to my house. I think it was that reporter."

"Vikki Corbett?"

"I've seen her before." Plant fidgeted his feet on her hand-woven rug. Rowan simply glared at him. "I know what she's going to do, she's going to write something hideous, lying, dirty." He stopped speaking and cupped his hands.

"Go back to work," Rowan said. "Just go back and try to behave normally. Can you manage that? Can you behave like a rational person?"

"I can't go back," he stated, breathing in and out heavily. "I

59

can't, I just can't." He felt he was being overcome, a red tide of confusion was swamping his brain, blotting out all his ability to act, to speak, to think. Then she slapped him.

"Toad!"

She slapped him again. "Weasel!"

Plant held his cheek, suddenly shocked into clear thought.

"You have no option."

His lips felt so dry, he needed a drink for his burning throat. Rowan was his closest friend, she must be trying to help, anything else was impossible. Once his breathing was under control he stated, "I could face Flint if he came back. I could face that reporter girl, but if they go to the police . . . I can't face the police."

"Of course you can." Rowan's voice softened and she knelt before him, her touch on his lower arm was motherly and compulsive. She dug in her fingers as she urged him again. "Just go back and tell them the truth about last summer and the autumn. You committed no crime. You helped a student with her work, that was all."

"No." A plan was already forming in his mind. "I've got to get away."

"Go on holiday."

"I can't . . ."

"Well, ring in sick, go stay with your aunt or something."

He nodded, thinking. A slow gleam came to his face, the plan solidifying amongst the chaos of his thoughts. He said, "Yes," but not in response to her suggestion.

"Good. Where are you going?"

Plant looked at her, having hardly heard what she had said. "I can't tell you."

"What?"

"I can't tell anyone." He shook free from her arm and stood up. "You have to understand."

"Oak?" Rowan rose to her feet.

"I've got to go." He dodged towards the door.

Rowan moved to block his exit. "Where?"

He put a finger to his lips. "Secret. Trust me, Rowan, I have a plan, everything will be all right. I only have to break the spell."

"Spell?" She allowed him to pass her.

Plant took hold of the door handle. "Ring the museum for me, tell them I'm sick."

"You're sick," she repeated, without question.

Piers Plant left the room, and put whatever plan he had devised into immediate operation. To those seeking him, his disappearance was as sudden and as total as that of Lucy Gray.

"No one has seen him," Vikki's voice moaned from the telephone. "He hasn't been home, he hasn't been to work and I can't even get the police to look for him."

"I'm out of ideas, Vikki," Flint said.

"You must be able to find out something else."

"You're the thrusting investigative reporter, I'm simply a boring old academic."

"Well, use that great big brain of yours to give me an idea."

Flint squeezed his eyes tightly shut, he was too busy to delve deeper into Lucy's history. He had submitted a paste-up of her dissertation, with a hopeful covering note. That was all he felt he could do.

"Okay, try this. Lucy vanishes completely. Piers Plant vanishes completely. Let's draw up a hypothesis which says they are both in the same place."

Vikki was quiet for some time, a novelty, felt Flint.

"That doesn't get us anywhere, does it?" she said quietly.

"No, I don't suppose it does."

She rang off with only the briefest farewell and Flint put his attention back towards a large-scale map of Hertfordshire which covered his desk. Examinations had thrown a suffocating blanket of silence over Central College. Angst-ridden students had to be placated and last minute crises over question papers had to be addressed. As a distraction from exams, and from Lucy, he had Burkes Warren to occupy his attention.

For the past three summers, Flint had directed a small research excavation on a fourth-century villa in Hertfordshire. At least, it had always been assumed to be fourth century, evidence was still rather patchy. Digging took place partly under the excuse that the site was threatened by deep-ploughing, partly to enhance Flint's credibility as a hands-on archaeologist. What he really wanted to know was the kind of settlement which had preceded the villa during his pet period, the third century?

61

Twenty-four applicants sought the ten places on the digging team, all willing to work for free, keen beggars. One application had been posted in south London. Flint slit open the long manilla envelope and unfolded the message.

"My name is Death. Dig for me and I will welcome you."

His mouth dried. He read the letter again, then spent some minutes re-reading it, examining the envelope and fighting back a mix of anger and fear. Only one person was mad enough to send such a bizarre death threat. Flint peered into the envelope, half expecting to find something else, thinking about the quivering curator in Kingshaven. Vikki's theory that Lucy had met an unpleasant end suddenly became credible. Piers Plant was capable of anything.

In a fit of angry energy, Flint cleared his desk of archaeological work and brought out the Lucy file. Assembling all the facts linking Plant and Lucy, Flint dictated a long memo to the Darkewater Valley constabulary for Sally to type and post. Perhaps, there was an off-chance they might take some action.

After she had finished speaking to Jeffrey Flint, Vikki laid down the telephone and slumped into her chair. All around, the noisome, noisy newsroom clattered with life. On the screen of her wordprocessor was half a story, which hung off four alternative headlines.

MUSEUM CURATOR VANISHES

CURATOR SOUGHT IN MISSING GIRL CASE

LUCY GRAY WITNESS SOUGHT

HAVE YOU SEEN THIS MAN?

Of course, she couldn't use any of them, Arnold the editor had said so. Facts, not libel, he had demanded. Her half story of the vanishing curator was incomplete without someone showing alarm. The Museums Service were satisfied he was ringing in sick. His mother stood unruffled by his absence and no one else seemed to care. Vikki looked at the lists of relatives, friends and social contacts of Piers Plant she had visited. Each added a little to what she knew. Plant was insular and had few, if any, real friends. He had been divorced seven years previously and from then had been increasingly withdrawn into his work. The museum was his home, and apparently, his only remaining love. He was odd, no one confessed to knowing where he was and no one admitted to wanting to, either.

"Vikki, five minutes?" Vince, who was both photographer and self-appointed office stud, called across the room.

Bloody stupid Lord Mayor, who cared if he was going to pull a ribbon and say something boring at the golf club? Vikki drained her cup of cold coffee in a mood of high irritation. If Vince tried to ask her out again, she would scream sexual harassment. She saved her file, then pushed her heap of notes marked "Gray Case" into a drawer. Unhooking her handbag from the chair back, she went to meet the Mayor.

The ceremony at the golf club was only the beginning of a slow week. A Durring Tech student took an overdose (but recovered). A gang of youths set fire to three plastic litter bins in the centre of Kingshaven and evaded six policemen. The New Bridge at Twinbridge was closed for repairs to its parapet. Life was tough at the sharp end of local journalism. She fantasised that if she was forced to get very drunk that Friday night, she might just give Vince a chance to live up to his boasts. Life was getting bad if she had to stoop to that quality of excitement.

At the end of the week, the morning post brought an impersonal rejection of her application to become a staff reporter at the *Daily Mirror*. On reaching the office, the editor mumbled about wild geese and seemed to be planning to move her to the ghetto of the women's page. Vikki reached her grey laminated workstation and placed her hand on the telephone, glancing at the wall clock, wondering what time archaeologists woke up and what time they turned up for work. Just after ten, she caught him.

"How is my favourite archaeologist?" she crooned.

"Busy. I'm up to my ears in exam scripts and death threats."

"You're joking about the death threats?"

"I wish I was." Flint explained about his letter, Vikki immediately insisting she see it.

"I'll send you a photocopy, the police have the original. What are they doing on the Lucy front?"

"Nothing, apart from chasing teenage arsonists and letting them get away." Vikki paused, wondering where Flint's weak point lay.

"That letter really fazed me for a while," he admitted.

Enough of his background had emerged during her enquiries for Vikki to make shrewd judgements about his character. Flint was a committed bachelor, who fitted well into the free-and-easy college scene. He liked old films, sixties music and open relationships with women. Like all academics he had a large and very vulnerable ego.

Flint was still talking over the macabre letter when she interrupted him . . .

"I need you," she appealed.

"Need me?"

"I need you to do me an interview. I need something to hang a story on."

"A coatpeg?"

"You, tomorrow, please? I can get you the train fare and I'll buy you lunch. How's that for a proposition?"

"Sounds okay," he said after a few seconds.

"I thought we might try and see that doorman from the museum too."

When the surprise arrangement had been made, Flint made his way to the J.B. Stoat Library, thinking partly of Lucy, partly of Vikki. He liked the reporter's spirit, even if she possessed an irritating over-abundance. Whether she was soft-soaping him, or whether she was sincere, the call had made him feel good, and it would be nice not to have another train fare to pay. He was still musing whether the *Advertiser* paid appearance fees when his arm was touched by another man.

"Doctor Flint?" the hunched man in the ill-fitting suit said. "I'm Christianson, from the chemistry department."

"You looked at my resins for me, three or four years back."

Christianson seemed to have forgotten. "You are the one concerned with that missing girl, Lucy Gray."

Flint nodded, didn't he know it? Christianson shook his head. "Students! Why do we bother? I have the same problem as you, I wanted to talk to you about it. Three years of nurturing him and one of my personal students has deserted his examinations. Dropping out, they call it, well, he's simply dropped out of existence, it is as if a black hole had opened up and swallowed him."

An awful feeling of *déjà vu* crept over Jeffrey Flint. "What was his name?"

"Timothy Wright, did you know him?"

"Timmy? I know Timmy." Whatever he was going to in the library was no longer important. "Look, come up to the tea room and we'll talk about it."

Christianson gave a quaint bow of his head and they walked to the Classics lounge, comparing notes on missing students. Timmy Wright had packed his belongings into a tea-chest, which he had then abandoned in his flat with a note saying his father would collect it. He had not been seen for three weeks.

Jeffrey Flint had returned to Kingshaven once more. A chance glimpse along the High Street confirmed that he had not heeded the letter, nor paid attention to the telephone calls. The observer watched as Vikki introduced Flint to Vince and the pair shook hands. Vince offered Flint one of his cigarettes and took offence when the archaeologist was too obvious in his disgust at the suggestion. A fellow lover of clean air, if not clean living. Jeffrey Flint's soul stood some chance of redemption.

The archaeologist who pretended to be an investigator posed in front of the museum, which had fallen into the care of a locum curator from the County Museums Service. The photographer danced around, winding film, checking the light, calling out instructions, until the process became tiresome to watch. It was interesting to see the thinly veiled irritation shown by the photographer as the girl took Flint's arm and led him away towards the pub. The Bridge, a bald sandstone structure along the waterfront, was George Carlyle's habitual watering-hole. George could present a problem.

Flint led the way into the pub. "We've lost another one," he said with an air of gloom. "Timmy Wright, a chemist. He was one of Lucy's boyfriends and another dragon freak. The Central College Triangle claims another victim."

"Or suspect," Vikki said, "he could be a suspect."

Flint refused to allow Vikki to buy him another drink and glanced along the beer pumps. "Grief, it's a Stones pub, tonight calls for sacrifices beyond the call of duty."

He settled for a pint of hand-drawn Bass, which was better than he had at first dreaded. Vikki ordered white wine and soda to go with scampi in a basket.

"So you're a CAMRA man, are you?" Vikki asked. "A real Real Ale drinker."

"Yes, terribly macho, isn't it?" Flint derided his own stereotype. "I just know what I like. If pubs served decent wines, I might be tempted, otherwise, I'm a bearded hand-drawn real-ale junkie."

Vikki was shaking her head in amusement as George Carlyle walked in. Ex-Signals Regiment, now a museum attendant edging towards retirement, he was smartly dressed in his regimental blazer. Flint intercepted him at the bar and bought a pint of Stones bitter. George thanked him and they small-talked into a corner of the quiet bar. Amongst the heavy red Victorian-style decor, conversation soon shifted towards the missing curator. George must have realised he was in for close questioning.

"Name rank and number only, remember," he joked.

Flint began gently. "George, you understand what we're trying to do? To find Lucy Gray, we need to know more about her and her relationship with Piers Plant."

George looked into the froth of his beer, searching for his conscience perhaps.

"We respect your loyalty, George," Flint added.

"I'll keep it confidential," Vikki said, with too much sincerity to be convincing.

The attendant took a short breath and began to tesify without looking either in the eye. "Miss Gray used to come to the museum quite a lot. She's been coming for years, since she was a girl. More regularly in the last year or two. Sometimes they would be in his office, sometimes in one of the stores, sometimes they would go behind the woggery."

"Woggery?" Flint's hackles rose.

"It's what Mister Plant calls the north wing annexe. It's full of Zulu spears, Maori clubs, that sort of thing."

A racist too. Flint liked Plant less and less. "Do you think there was anything funny going on?"

"Sexual?" Vikki pushed the thought before him. "Were they having an affair?"

"It's not for me to say, miss. That would be insubordinate." He gave a wry grin. "We used to get packdrill for insubordination."

George seemed to be waiting for the opportunity to let the

most savoury titbit of gossip drop from his lips. He became conspiratorial, leaning close over the table and lowering his voice. "My mate Jack, he reckoned they were having it off in the store room, if you pardon me, miss. It's shameful really, she's little more than a girl. I can't see what she sees in him."

The Friday night crowd began to fill the room as George mellowed under as second pint. The air grew thick, the background whisper became a continuous rattle. George was telling them about how Piers Plant had become gradually more sickness-prone over the past year and how the museum was disintegrating under his lack of interest.

"Plant's folklore display was first rate," Flint objected, "it was easily the best part of the museum."

"I'm afraid it's the only part of the museum he's concerned with."

"How seriously is he into the occult?"

"Occult?"

"You know, witchcraft, black magic, that sort of thing."

"I couldn't say, he's got a few books on the subject."

Flint mentally scanned the curator's office, not recalling anything even mildly supernatural in content. Perhaps Plant kept them at home. Vikki frowned at the line of enquiry and was keen to change tack.

"Has he ever just vanished before?" she asked.

"No, he's malingering, if you ask me. Perhaps you upset him, Doctor Flint, he's very easily upset, is Mister Plant. Lack of moral fibre, LMF as we said in the army."

"So when did Lucy Gray last come to the museum?" Vikki asked.

The attendant fidgeted whilst he thought. Vikki was about to feed him a date, but a nudge stopped her.

"New Year, perhaps. Yes, it was when the scaffolding went up, that was just into the New Year. We're having the back wall completely redone."

George stood up. "Now, if you'll excuse me a minute, miss." George made his way to the gents'.

Flint held up a finger to impress an idea on Vikki. "Lucy's mum said she'd stopped coming last autumn. Lucy used to scrounge the train fare, stay with her mum or her sister. Let's say that some time before Christmas, she started to come here direct and stopped telling anyone. That's why there's nothing on her calendar and even explains why Piers Plant was scrubbed from her acknowledgements."

"She's ashamed to be seen with him?"

"She's trying to conceal something. Their relationship had changed and, perhaps, it wrecked the pair of them."

"What was all that about witchcraft? You said Lucy was strange, but I just thought you meant playing hobbit games."

"Sometimes I think it was more than a game with Lucy," he replied, "or maybe just one big game, who knows?"

"George Carlyle?" shouted the barman. "Come on, George! Telephone!"

"He's taking his time. Why do men spend so much time in the loo?" Vikki observed.

Flint signalled to the barman and went to see what he wanted.

"You're with George, are you?" the barman asked. "Will you take his telephone call?"

At the corner of the bar, he picked up the receiver.

"George Carlyle," growled the voice, "leave it, leave now, say nothing to Flint and the reporter."

"Is that Piers Plant?" Flint spoke. "This is Doctor Flint."

"Lucy is happy," the deep, gravelly voice said, "leave her alone."

George emerged from the gents', looking pleased. Flint put down the dead receiver with a trembling hand. It could have been Plant, or Timmy Wright, or even Lucy herself faking that Hammer Horror voice. Someone knew exactly where George Carlyle was and exactly what he was doing. That someone did not want Lucy found. Flint wiped his lips, feeling a thirst but not wanting alcohol.

Vikki came across and he told her about the call. Her mouth dangled open and her eyes widened as he spoke. "This is terrific."

"Wrong, terrifying," Flint corrected. "Don't become like Lucy, don't think this is a game."

Vikki tightened her lips at the rebuke. "So what are you going to do next?"

"Go back to Leeds for my mum's birthday. Then invigilate for the Roman Architecture and Art finals. Then I'm going to find Plant and get some answers."

Chapter 7

A weekend away was what Jeffrey Flint had needed, so the trip north had been a return to sanity. At his mother's sixtieth birthday party he mingled with relatives and familiar faces from the old neighbourhood. No one had excavated any site more ancient than his grandfather's allotment and the hired room above his father's local was an academic-free zone, with not a neurotic student nor exam paper in sight.

By Monday, he was back in London, attempting to justify his wages and regretting his brash vow to find Piers Plant. He did not have a clue where he could be, and nor did the eager Vikki Corbett. When he arrived at Central College he found she had sent him a first-class letter containing her latest masterpiece of creative fiction, WITCHCRAFT LINK TO VANISHED GIRL? She had found her story, forcing it on to the front page by the late edition.

Below the headline was a photograph of a familiar Gothic building, with an even more familiar bearded figure standing before it. Flint grimaced as he read the text, shaking his head and wondering if he was the same Jeffrey Flint being quoted in the text. A Chief Inspector Douglas was also quoted as making no comment. Stung by a throwaway line in the early edition, the Darkewater Valley Constabulary had finally strolled into action, announcing they wished to interview Piers Plant in connection with the Lucy Gray case. Flint sat back in his chair, feeling relieved from the burden of his vow. Obviously, if the whole of the regional crime squad couldn't find the three missing persons, what chance did he have.

The time of the red biro had come. "Introduction to Archaeological Processes" yielded five essays per first-year student; a mountain of gauche tedium awaited. He tossed Vikki's article on to a chair and pulled the first script across his desk and read the name Alexis da Sancha. Flint groaned as he flicked to the first question, he needed to be in a calm, charitable mood to mark Alexis' script. Coffee should help.

Once within the gloomy depths of the tea room, he encountered Tyrone reading the *Financial Times* and eating a Mars Bar.

"Hullo Doc, how's the sleuthing?"

Flint sat down beside his student, thankfully sipping the coffee. "Confusing. Dead people are much easier to investigate than live ones."

"What makes you think Lucy's still alive?"

"On Friday, I had a phone call from a guy who tells me she is happy."

"He could have been lying. He could have been speaking metaphysically."

Flint gave Tyrone a quizzical look; the shock of seeing that mound of answer papers must have addled his brain. Tyrone lapsed into philosophy. "She is in paradise, beyond the cares of the world. She is happy."

Once he had sufficient caffeine in his system, Flint grabbed an extra cup, then went back to his office, studiously plodding through the scripts one by one. Each day that week seemed to be the same: question, answers, ticks and scores out of twenty.

"Explain the principle of Seriation. On what classes of material might it be employed?" Flint scrawled a large tick at the bottom of the answer and awarded Neil Unger seventeen marks. Up flicked his eyes to where Lucy hung, pinned like a lepidopterist's exhibit to his cork board. She was coming to dominate his life, yet where was she? Alive and laughing, or dead and cold? Where was Piers Plant? Where indeed was Timmy Wright? Was the answer to all three questions the same? These were questions with no answers, zero marks. Weeks were passing in which blanks became only blanker and a cold trail became overgrown with weeds and unusable.

To complete the confused web of non-evidence, Barbara Faber had rung, full of false good spirits. She had received another postcard from Salisbury. Same script, similar brief message.

Salisbury? What remained of Jeffrey Flint's motivation led him to see possibilities. A wild goose chase to Scotland would have been ludicrously expensive, but Salisbury was closer to home. Lucy was edging into range, perhaps she was actually willing him to find her. Perhaps her postcards and calls were just part of her complex game.

Lucy's behaviour did not make sense. Piers Plant's behaviour did not make sense. Julia Stapleton-Clarke's answer to Question Three did not make sense, but at least the exam papers were dribbling to a miserable end. In the distance, a loudspeaker van proclaimed the virtues of some party or other. Of course, the elections, he wondered how Chrissie's party would perform. Badly, he imagined. Just one more script and he'd go out and give them his vote.

Chrissie Collings had first been attracted to Jeffrey Flint by his offbeat sense of humour. He was a philandering egotist, but this left her safe from an overdose of clammy sentiment which could easily stifle a young career. Sitting in the Friday night folk club, she sensed things had run full course. His humour had gone, his sex drive had been diluted, his conversation had become fixed around a missing girl, exam scripts and convoluted Marxist interpretations of the third century. It could be time to let him have the news.

In her calf-length gypsy skirt and bolero jacket, her deep-red hair swept up behind a scarf, Chrissie was conscious of how much she had fallen into his scene. Flint wore just a baggy T-shirt he had bought at an All About Eve concert and one of his smarter pairs of jeans. Yes he really looked the part of the old hippy, as, she supposed, did she. All that was lacking were the sandals.

The performer was not the best guitar player ever seen in the back corner of an Islington pub and far from the best singer. Between songs, the pair conducted a gentle post-mortem on Thursday's election results. The Greens had suffered the accustomed glorious defeat. Many votes, much credit, but no power.

"They are spoiling my world and nobody cares," Chrissie sighed over her empty wine glass. "I think we should get really drunk tonight."

The pub was dark, heavy with smoke and hardly environmentally friendly.

"We should be at Glastonbury," Flint said in response, "that's what we should be doing. Camping under the stars, singing our own songs instead of listening to these impoverished efforts. I need a festival, I really do."

"You'll still be going to pop festivals when you're fifty."

"And why not? Same again?"

Flint went to the bar and after some time, came back sipping a pop-and-orange.

"Feeling all right?" Chrissie asked as she accepted her red wine.

He responded with a bug-eyed stare. "Question Three: discuss the principles underlying the term '*terminus post quem*.'"

"You're insane." She could not resist smiling. "Is this the great Jeffrey Flint we have all heard about? Hard drinking, womanising . . ."

"Rumours, all false. I'm taking it easy tonight. I've visited every grotty bar between London and Kingshaven in the past month, sampling more grotty beer than I can take."

"Your work is getting to you."

"Bloody exams. We ought to abolish them. I can tell brilliance from mediocrity without having to read four hundred tediously repetitive confirmations. I'm going to be like Jules Torpevitch and get a rubber stamp made up embossed with the word 'Rubbish'. Save a lot of time."

"Still, the exams will soon be over."

"It's not just exams, Chrissie. It's this Lucy Gray thing. It's just the problem has lodged here," he thumped his temple, "and isn't going away."

"You're still chasing sweet Lucy Gray."

"Chasing my tail too. She sent her sister a postcard from Salisbury. I've half a hunch they've met up there: her, Piers Plant and flipping Timmy White. Another half a hunch says I should go and look for them."

"White and Gray? It sounds like someone is teasing you, getting you running around to opposite ends of the country and costing a fortune on the train. Going off to Salisbury on your half hunch doesn't make sense, so forget about it, you're not a detective. I'm sure she'll turn up."

In the background, the singer was murdering "Big Yellow Taxi" in front of forty witnesses. Chrissie realised she couldn't tell Jeff her news, not yet. He still seemed to need her.

"I can't forget about it. It's too interesting. I hate unsolved problems and I love cracking them, the harder the better. I'm a problem addict, that's why I do what I do. Can you sign me up to Archaeologists Anonymous?"

She had been wrong about the humour, it was simply blacker than usual.

"What's so interesting about a girl skipping her exams?"

"Interesting was the wrong word. Intriguing possibly. It's just so crazy, the more I find out about Lucy, the crazier it gets."

"It's as I told you, she's mixed up."

"Well, that's what I thought, but she always seemed so confident, so sincere. But you told me, and everyone else tells me, she never properly joined in, sat to one side, kept herself secret. As soon as she gets involved in something, she covers it up, pretends she's not really interested. But she was no introvert, it was a deliberate act of policy on her behalf. Most students are weird as a front, they exaggerate it as a way of showing off, but Lucy seems to have played it down if anything. The more I find out about her, the less I understand. My brain hurts."

"Then stop it. Leave it to the police, don't go getting all depressed. You can't do anything that they can't do."

"I can."

"What?"

"I can care."

Bad renditions of Joni Mitchell songs still hummed in his ears as Flint lay awake in the pre-dawn light. The houseboat offered a cosy, secure refuge from twentieth-century London. Chrissie's shoulder touched against his own. Mission accomplished, yet again, but Flint felt hollow. It was not only post-sexual guilt, or even Chrissie's whispered words about freedom and changing scenes. He looked into the shadows of the main cabin. Shadows and half-light, a girl's life clouded by incomplete truths. The towers of Salisbury Cathedral came to mind. A postcard, a clue, but why Salisbury?

Stonehenge, the summer solstice! Suddenly he knew how Lucy could live on air for five months, how she could drop out of sight completely, how she could drift around the countryside unobserved yet protected. Of course she didn't want her mother to see her, amongst punks and gypsies, hippies and travellers. A headband and beads would suit her so well as she dreamed away her summer days. The Glastonbury Festival was that weekend, with the summer solstice just a few days later. If Lucy and her friends were anywhere, they would be there.

By eight, he had shot a hasty goodbye to a confused and annoyed bedmate, found his hiking tent and cycled to Earls Court. Tyrone's flat was located in a side street just off the North End Road. Son of a "developer", he was following in the family tradition and investing in property. Given the money to buy the flat, Tyrone sub-let its second bedroom to a pair of fellow students and used the income to run his own car. Any other student would have opted for a 2CV and plastered it with stickers, but not Tyrone. Parked in the litter outside the decaying Edwardian terrace stood an old green Triumph Spitfire oversprayed with brown camouflage patterns. A huge RAF roundel graced each door whilst the owner had stencilled the letters TYR-1 down the rear wings. It was not a car in which to remain inconspicuous.

Abuse became muted when the flat-owner discovered who was ringing his doorbell. Within a few minutes, Flint was up in the front room, sharing coffee with Tyrone and a pneumatic brunette named Patsy. Both appeared sleepy and slightly hung-over. Patsy yawned over toast then said she was going to "sort herself out". Flint kept hearing that students are not what they were and that AIDS was destroying the fun, but for his students and for himself, the game of roulette went on as before.

"So what's the plan?" Tyrone began to liven up after the second coffee and the fifth piece of toast.

"It's midsummer and love and peace are in the air. Fancy going to a rock festival?"

Persuasion was hardly necessary and only fifteen minutes later, another woman was abandoned in a state of high pique.

"Chocks away!" Tyrone effused as Flint climbed into the Spitfire, stuffing his kitbag behind the seat.

Streaking away from London, Flint's mood lightened. The jaunt had a purpose, but a jaunt is a jaunt and he was going to enjoy every minute. Every minute once he arrived; Tyrone took pleasure in regarding all speed limit signs as minimums and all rules of the road to be inapplicable to drivers of gaudy Spitfires.

"Can you drive, Doc?" Tyrone shouted over the slipstream.

"I learned at seventeen. My uncle runs a driving school."

"You've no car though?"

"I have a fundamental objection to the whole concept of motor cars."

"You mean pollution and global warming?"

"Mainly what it does to society. It fragments the local economic

74

base, wrecks the national economy. Do you know that half our balance of payments deficit is due to imported cars?"

"Nope."

"Ever thought how much urban crime could be prevented if people walked home at night instead of driving? Or how much easier it is for bank robbers or rapists or terrorists to move around than before the car came to blight our lives?"

"Nope, but you've got to admit it, Doc, they're useful things to have. You can't live without one these days."

"That's the shame of it."

"Anyway, if people stopped building motorways and car parks on historic sites, half the archaeologists in the country would be unemployed."

"Your ethics leave much to be desired. Following that logic, I suppose you'd say that road accidents keep doctors off the dole?"

"Yep."

Tyrone hit eighty and zipped into a traffic gap on the M3. Flint's ecological notions were fine in theory, but even he could employ a little hypocrisy in a crisis.

Midsummer sees a curious ritual at Stonehenge: the deployment of vast resources by the Wiltshire police force to keep "hippies" and "travellers" away from the stones.

"It will be the same this year, as every year," Flint shouted into the wind, "half a million quid on overtime just to spoil a few kids' weekend out."

"The important thing is they stop long-haired weirdos damaging the stones."

"But how can you reconcile the protection of the monument with the denial of access? If the ordinary man or woman cannot experience archaeology, what is it for?"

"Ordinary man fine, but we're talking drug-crazed drop-outs."

"They still have rights."

"No right to destroy my heritage."

"Rights to experience *their* heritage."

"They can pay at the gate like everyone else."

"No one should have to pay, that's the point."

Tyrone shook his head, whilst keeping his eyes fixed on the road. "The heritage industry can't complain about funding if we let everyone in for free, then let them smash the place up. I mean, what are we bothering for?"

Impasse was reached, so Flint let the subject drop and Tyrone fiddled a Wagner tape into his cassette deck. Flint feared the Ride of The Valkyries would raise Tyrone's adrenalin, and he was right. The back end of a Telecom van rushed at them and the student gripped the wheel with fighter pilot zeal.

"Hang on, I'm going to take this truck. I've just got space . . ."

The word "just" proved accurate, but they survived to reach Wiltshire and gain a glimpse of the Monument. To their left, the Heel Stone threw its shadow across the car for a moment as they zipped by. Five days still had to pass before the solstice and the forces of reaction would not let them so close the following Friday. Over to the right lay barrows of Flint's distant ancestors and he sensed the lure of the earth, even tearing past at world-destroying speed.

Glastonbury welcomed them, as pilgrims to the global capital of the New Age, scene of the pre-solstice warm-up, official festival, fringe festival, unofficial fringe-of-fringe events. The weather was baking but here the police played things cool. Magic and earthy indulgence were all around. If Lucy had assumed that no one would spot the significance of Salisbury, her confidence was about to betray her.

"Got a tenner for some more petrol, Doc?"

Tyrone pulled up to to a small petrol station and allowed the owner to fill his tank. The bill bit into two "tenners" and whilst paying with Flint's money, Tyrone allowed the man to keep the change and smooth-talked him into keeping his car safe around the back. With bundles stuffed under their arms and Flint sensing a large hole in his wallet, they made for the Peace Convoy.

Spread across three fields was a straggle of tents and caravans, interspersed by a gaudy collection of old buses, ambulances and beat-up motor cars. Behind them loomed the timeless hill of Glastonbury Tor, supposed seat of Arthur and the focus of much mythical nonsense. Flint remembered the poster in Lucy's room, with the Holy Grail suspended above it.

"I come seeking the Holy Grail," he muttered quietly.

"But why the hell did I come here?" Tyrone said. "We're going to catch something, Doc."

A brood of unkempt children ran past, yelling obscenities. Flint kept walking across the grass, sniffing at the woodsmoke and squinting against the brilliant sun.

"Doc, we're going to get our throats cut. See those kids?"

Flint turned about and walked backwards, his face set in a mellow smile of satisfaction.

"I mean, they were so filthy . . ."

"Probably training to be archaeologists."

Tyrone continued to grumble unChristian thoughts, until Flint quieted him.

"Oi, do me a favour, Tyrone. Try to blend in. Relax, smile at people and for God's sake don't tell anyone that your dad is a Tory councillor. Then someone will slit your throat."

Flint's mind drifted leftwards as he began to visually befriend the travellers. With the smile and the welcome came a photograph of Lucy and word of the five-hundred-pound reward offered by Barbara. They worked through the converted coaches, the tents and makeshift bivouacs meeting both suspicion and helpful co-operation. Also in Flint's pocket was a photograph of Piers Plant which had appeared in Vikki's paper under the headline "POLICE HUNT VANISHING CURATOR". He had snipped off the headline, wary that Tyrone's short hair and uneasy manner would cause suspicion.

Flint did most of the work, his assistant temporarily fazed by the culture shock as they squatted with the "hippies".

"You must teach me this street-talk," Tyrone commented, as they walked away from another camp fire, "you almost seem at home."

Almost at home, but not quite. The tent was snug and its holes went untested as the week passed in a heat haze. Half naked (and fully naked) young people strolled about the fields or lolled in the sun. Groups of over-stimulated youths bunched together shrieking "Aceed!" In the background, a laid-back Somerset Constabulary turned their backs on everything bar violence. Music flowed through Flint's brain, he relaxed and regressed, almost forgetting his quest. By putting himself firmly into a role, he began to merge with the background, but was never at risk of vanishing into it. Chrissie had been right, he had grown out of festivals. The squalour distressed him almost as much as it did Tyrone and the dislocation from normality was just a little too great. The travellers had dropped out further than Jeffrey Flint ever wanted to go.

Tyrone finally caught the mood, acquired some cut-down jeans and slipped into a new mould. His survival instinct conferred an ability to conform to any norm and after two days he was able to fake a neo-hippie nineteen-sixties outlook and blend with the mellow throng. His conversion was aided by a wistful young lady who dreamed of moonbeams and loved sports cars. Flint tried not to give too much attention to the warm smiling eyes of the girls, he came there for the sake of one girl only.

As Tyrone was missing, presumed still chasing moonbeams, Flint spent the next afternoon walking alone through the tented village of the main festival. A name outside the marquee caught his eye. R. Temple-Brooke would be reciting from his own poems at three, so Flint bought a bottle of Coke and chose one of the folding seats within the tent. An hour passed gently, and he watched dispassionately as two dozen earthy folk, mainly women, wafted in to join him.

"Do you have all his books?" An immense youth in an equally immense grey T-shirt leaned over to ask the uninitiated Flint.

"I've a copy of *Eyes on a Clear Day* on my desk," Flint responded without blinking. It had been in Lucy's room, he had read none of it other than the dedication to the mysterious Hazel.

"He's really brilliant," the youth continued from behind his pebble spectacles, "he's captured the whole spirit of the age, y'know? He's the guru of the next millenium."

"Really?"

The guru of the next millenium finally appeared when his audience peaked at forty and threatened to become thinner. Like most great men, Temple-Brooke was short, but charismatic and carried a sense of his own importance. An earnest, platinum-haired woman in her late thirties announced the poet with both hands clenched to her breast and an overdose of platitudes. Flint joined in the applause then sank back to doze through the doggerel.

Poetry was never his scene and literary friends had ridiculed his own choice of Auden as his favourite poet. Temple-Brooke could have been brilliant, or awful, but to Flint, he simply seemed dull and self-opinionated. The man should be a politician, he thought. He should be making speeches about balances of payment and wage indexes. Flint watched the flies zig-zag around the tent and admired the mass of beads around the neck of the girl in the apache jacket, then applause indicated that the reading was at an end.

Temple-Brooke signed six books, then looked up into Jeffrey Flint's eyes.

"You wouldn't have seen this girl, ever?" Flint asked, with a grimace, expecting the answer to be no.

The poet gazed into the picture. "One of the Earth's fair children."

Whilst he cradled the photograph, the platinum-haired woman came around his back and looked over his shoulder.

"Do you know her?" Flint asked hopefully, but a shrug and an apology were the best he received.

It was the best he received all week. Lucy was not at Glastonbury. Flint met up with some GreenSoc people from college, sang with a folk group and danced with self-proclaimed Somerset witches. A word with a co-operative police inspector resulted in a heap of leaflets to distribute, but still the result was nil. Tyrone reappeared and half in hope, half out of apathy, they spent one midnight with UFO freaks at Warminster. Piers Plant's picture wafted around Devizes museum where someone vaguely knew of him, but no one had seen him recently.

Friday came. Anti-climax and sensory exhaustion fought against exhilaration, but one more part of the cycle remained to be experienced before the experiment was over. Tyrone powered towards Salisbury, however, some distance before Stonehenge they were stopped by the inevitable roadblock.

"Gestapo," hissed Tyrone, slowing to a halt.

"Whoever says England is a free country is wrong," Flint grunted, to be received by a shrug of the driver's shoulders.

Making ironic use of the word "Sir", the men in black turned the car around. Disruptive camouflage appears very much like psychodelia from behind visors. Backtracking, with Flint muttering "Bloody fascists" they found the Peace Convoy again. Through the evening they spoke to another two or three hundred people, the hard core, those fully committed to rejection of late-twentieth-century mores. Lucy had to be near, Flint kept repeating to himself, and to Tyrone. If she was still alive, she would be amongst people like this, out of touch with normality, but close to the Earth. Not needing her chequebook, her wardrobe, or her BA Honours degree.

Tea was shared with an extended family group of twelve, all waiting for sunset. Finding a fire and a guitarist, Flint joined in with the songs whilst his student looked on bemused. Tyrone bedded down beneath a caravan, whilst Flint resolved to talk until dawn. He failed, and was surprised when he was prodded in his sleep.

Awoken at the appointed time, stiff and cold, lecturer and student followed the procession doomed to failure. Avoiding the mêlée with authority, they struck on to the plain and stood to watch the sun rise with others who lacked the determination to fight their way through to the stones. The distant druids' horn blared as the sky brightened. Sky magic, Earth magic, this was what it was all about. A squashed red balloon was borne into the sky, its disc smeared by distant cloud. For a moment, the sun resembled Jupiter, streaked blue with a single eye winking mystery. Then it struggled free from the horizon, with burners switching to full heat. Even the police paused and watched. There is a little Pagan in us all.

Chapter 8

Ancient British rituals gave way to modern English rituals. Mrs Gray served tea from a china pot and sliced her brown bread with surgical precision. Her modern cottage-style house had replaced an earlier cottage-style cottage and the new interior had been crafted to hide its age. The dining room was small, its fake roof beams too slender to ever have performed a structural function. Between the plate-racks of Victorian blue transfer-print china, the doorway into the lounge had been left open to add an illusion of space.

After his return from Stonehenge, Jeffrey Flint had been invited to tea.

"Have you found the other boy who is missing?" Mrs Gray was an older, plumper, less intense version of her daughters, ever busy, handing round her thin but thickly buttered brown bread.

"No, his family had a postcard from the south of France," Flint replied. Cleaned and almost rested, with newly trimmed beard, he had deliberatley attempted to dress smartly, to take the week of free life out of his mind.

"A postcard? That sounds familiar," commented Derek Faber, a smooth-faced accountant slightly older than Jeffrey Flint.

"Perhaps Lucy is back in Scotland now. We might get another postcard soon," Mrs Gray said.

"It's always possible."

"I must say, you're very kind making all this effort to find her."

Flint smiled politely. Lucy had become an obsession. Some people collect telephone insulators, he chased wild geese. Mrs Gray continued to seek comfort.

"You must excuse me, Doctor Flint, you must think I'm very stupid, but I don't really understand some of the things I have been told. First I read all this rubbish in the newspaper about her

81

and that awful man at the museum." Mrs Gray's hand trembled as she made to pour more tea. "Then there is this pop festival at Stonehenge. Lucy was never interested in pop music and she hated camping when we used to go to Cornwall."

Flint was wary of any accusations that it was he who had led Lucy astray. Outside, someone started up a powerful petrol lawnmower.

"It's this New Age, Mum, I told you," Barbara said, "Lucy has found a new way of life."

Mrs Gray sat down again, momentarily. "Well, I don't understand it, do you understand it, Doctor Flint?"

"To an extent, yes. Have you ever felt the modern world was closing in on you? Too much noise, too many people, too many rules, wars, strikes, crime?"

"Well yes, everyone thinks that. I don't like his lawnmower." She indicated the direction of her neighbour's garden.

"Some people feel we're like rats in a cage, more and more of us squabbling over less and less. They think we've lost something, spirituality, the meaning of life, call it what you like. Then they start looking for something and some find it in a new religion or a new political viewpoint."

"You make it sound like the nineteen sixties," said Derek.

"It is. Another generation is going through an analogous experience to what kids went through in the sixties."

Mrs Gray was on her feet again, offering sausage rolls. "Well, I hope she keeps away from drugs, do these people take drugs?"

"Some do, some don't, Mother," Barbara said with a hint of irritation, "but Lucy took care of her body. She had more sense."

"Have the police managed to uncover anything?" Flint asked.

Barbara paused, a sausage roll perched on the edge of her lips. "No. Your reporter friend was round last week, asking about you. Mother wouldn't speak to her."

"Well!" Mrs Gray said. "The things she wrote! Witchcraft, I ask you, how silly. And this man, he's twice her age."

Flint avoided being drawn. "Anything about Scotland from the police?"

"They asked at the museum, where she sent the first postcard," Barbara replied.

"The Burrel Collection?"

"Yes, that's right, but they discovered nothing."

"I had a good look at that card, compared it with her latest essays," he said. "They look the same, but the writing appears more forced on the card. Lucy was a bit of a scribbler."

"I thought Lucy had very nice handwriting," her mother said. "Do you remember, Barbara? We sent her to that special class."

"Yes."

"That reporter had some horrid ideas about Lucy," Mrs Gray said. "She tried to say she thought Lucy had been murdered, but you know she's still alive, don't you, Doctor Flint?"

"Yes, of course," he lied badly.

She smiled an unconvincing smile. "So do the police, so do we all."

Barbara gave a cracked, stiff smile of agreement, but her eyes said no. Fruit cake followed, accompanied by polite diversionary conversation. Derek wanted to know what Flint planned to excavate that summer, so he was able to chatter inconsequentially about Burkes Warren and his Roman villa. Mrs Gray fidgeted to her feet and began clearing the table as they talked. After her second foray, Barbara nudged her husband and suggested he help wash up. Taking only a few moments to guess her game, he stood and called an offer of help to his mother-in-law.

Barbara poured two last cups of tea and suggested that she and Flint take them into the lounge. Her heel gently closed the door once he was seated on the sofa.

"Can I see that card, Barbara? The Salisbury one?" Flint asked.

"They're both here." Barbara reached for her handbag. "Mother received one too."

He took the cards, looked over them, then pulled out a wad of Lucy's essays from his briefcase.

"Could you give me a few minutes?"

Barbara sat in the wooden-framed easy chair beside the fireplace and sipped at her tea. Flint left his to cool whilst he compared word with word, letter with letter. After five minutes, he gave a little laugh.

"A rabid hyphenator!"

"Pardon?"

He waved the cards. "Rabid hyphenator! Here, she uses week-end, there, look-out."

83

"So?"

"I get them all the time. Roof-tile, hand-axe, post-hole, beam-slot. But Lucy wasn't one of them. Look at this essay: 'potsherd . . . posthole . . . rooftile'. This card wasn't written by Lucy."

Barbara had the look of an eight-year-old whose disbelief in Father Christmas had finally been confirmed. "I never liked the 'g's. They look too neat."

"This is Christmas card writing. Lucy's last two essays are a mess, look. No dots on 'i', incomplete 'a' and as you say, her 'g' loops straight into the next letter."

Barbara had lost all colour. "Now what?"

"I'll take them to the police, try to get them to move out of first gear. It's obvious that someone is sending these just to confuse us. I bet I was meant to go all the way down to Salisbury, wasting time and petrol . . ."

"Yes, I'm sorry this is taking so much of your time."

"Oh don't worry about that, we lecturers just sit around most of the day."

"No, seriously, you must have a lot of research to do. And this must be costing you a lot of money, all these train fares, then driving down to Wiltshire . . ."

She was right, of course. His bank balance had already felt the pain.

"I don't want you to be out-of-pocket on this . . ."

"No, I can't . . ."

"Yes you can, I know how little archaeologists earn these days."

"Well, I can't take money from you, Barbara . . ."

"I took out an insurance policy on Lucy's behalf when I got my practice. It's not much, but I wanted to present it to her when she finally decided to settle down. I thought, perhaps, if she got married, or when she wanted a house of her own. It's only worth three thousand pounds or so, not much. Unless she is found, she'll never get to spend it."

She paused, hating her next words. "If she is dead, someone gets twelve thousand pounds, me probably. I couldn't spend it, I'd give it to the dogs' home or something."

He picked up his cold tea and stirred it thoughtfully.

"All I want to say is there will be money available, whatever happens. Don't let lack of money stop you finding Lucy. I want you to send me a bill, every month, everything it costs you, until you find her. You can tell me now how much you have already spent."

He pursed his lips.

"It will make me happy."

"If it makes you happy."

Barbara's offer came as a relief, it opened doors, it made his retention of Tyrone easier, it made him more mobile, but it didn't solve the problem.

Barbara looked him in the eye. "You think Lucy is dead, don't you?"

He exhaled heavily, it was time for some truth. "I don't know. A few weeks back, when you said you didn't know Lucy very well, I didn't realise how little you knew about her or how little anyone knows about her. Over the past year or two, she seems to have been getting – how can I put it – increasingly eccentric. I thought she was just going through the usual fight to be different, but the more I find out about her, the less I'm sure. Starting some time last autumn she has deliberately set out to become a non-person. Unless I can find a reason, we have to assume the worst."

Barbara was hiding something. There was a polite "I hate to mention this but" straining to get out.

"My mind keeps changing, Barbara. At first I thought it was nothing, just another student being cranky. The postcards seemed fine, I had made up my mind that she had deliberately dropped out. When I found out there was something odd going on with Piers Plant, I began to worry. Nothing can explain his behaviour, nothing. No scenario short of lunacy makes a single man disappear on suspicion of having been involved with a younger girl. Then there is this . . ." He waved the postcard. "Something complex and sinister is going on and it's not just two people eloping."

"Monster," muttered Barbara.

He followed her eyes. Above the Adams-style fireplace was a photo frame. A younger Barbara standing in her school uniform and by her side a pretty nine-year-old in bunches and bows. Flint felt sick, not part of the tragedy, but sensing it all the same.

"We knew something was going on," she said. "We thought it was someone at college, a student. She never talked about him, so I assumed there was something she felt guilty about." Barbara looked embarrassed. "I thought he might be, well, foreign . . ."

Flint eased over the confession. "I understand."

". . . or married, perhaps, or even one of her lecturers."

He couldn't help raising an eyebrow.

Barbara's embarrassment deepened. "Yes, I even thought it might be the great Doctor Flint we were always hearing about. I wish it had been." The last was spoken with quiet whimsy.

"When was all this?"

"Last autumn, you know yourself that's when Lucy started changing. She became stranger, more obsessive about certain ideas . . ." Her words trailed away in a shake of her head.

Yes, Barbara was holding something back, again she was staring at the pretty little girl. "She never could, not with him." Barbara clearly wanted to deny the idea.

"Tell me, please tell me everything you know." He had to unblock that hidden piece of information.

She sniffed. "Why didn't she just get married? She could have lived with him. They could have . . ." she stopped.

He waited. A light rain began to patter on the leaded window pane.

"In this day and age, Jeff, it's not impossible. I'm a doctor, I know, I don't approve, but I know."

Riddles and trauma, but the truth was in reach.

She drew breath. "I could have told you earlier, but there seemed no point. You must promise not to tell anyone, no one, not my mother and especially not that reporter."

"Fine."

Anguished and guilty, Barbara checked the door was still closed. "I've been asking my own questions. I broke a few rules, I even told a white lie, but discovered something, and it will kill Mother if she finds out." Her confession almost choked her. "Lucy was pregnant."

Flint was as shocked as Barbara was pained. "Sure?"

She gave a reluctant nod, then quietly began relating her first suspicions and ran on to the final proof. A subtle tapping was heard at the door and after a discreet interval, Derek poked his head around it. He came into the room bearing coffees, quickly followed by Mrs Gray who was fussing over sugar lumps and who took cream. Flint saw the despair in Barbara's eyes, then turned back to playing the guest.

As the polite tea party dwindled to an embarrassed end,

thunderclouds closed over the Darkewater Valley. The electric show was limited to distant flashes and rumours of thunderclaps, but the rain intensified to ease the drought and wash the sides of the dusty British Rail carriage that rocked Jeffrey Flint back to London.

He mulled over that image of Lucy as a schoolgirl and thought back on extra titbits of information Barbara had leaked out. It had been during the autumn months that Lucy had changed. Concepts which came to mind were fertility, spring rites and Mother Goddesses. Barbara had recalled oblique conversations with Lucy concerning motherhood, when Lucy had rebuked her sister for prescribing the Pill to pollute women's bodies. When Lucy had been missing for a month, Barbara had used the old-girl network and a subtle twist of medical ethics to make contact with the College Health Centre. Only a little subterfuge had been required and the truth was known.

"Lucy the earth-mother", Flint jotted on his notepad. Even he was beginning to use hyphens. The idea of Piers Plant as the father revolted him and fought against logic, but Lucy and Plant had obviously been close and the world had seen odder matches. Perhaps they could have married and raised a brood of quirky children.

Then he came back to the enigma. Plant was divorced, neither of them had a social station to maintain, or any great wealth at risk so why would a pregnancy provoke a crisis? Perhaps Lucy could be lodged in some cottage hospital somewhere, having her sins erased by modern convenience medicine, but abortion was the work of a few days at most. Lucy had almost enough time to come to full term, unless this was another one of her games.

Dark nights, trains and inextricable plots were the stuff of murky black-and-white movies. Flint ran through all the old movies he'd seen, with Bogart or Orson Welles wallowing in tangled intrigue. In the nineteen twenties, pregnancy might have been the cause of a hurried back-street abortion, with all its risks and consequences. In the forties, it might be an exceptional cause of blackmail and murder. In the nineteen nineties, it was little more problem than a hernia, with a shorter hospital waiting list. Single mothers were commonplace, unmarried couples were de rigeur in some circles. To murder Lucy because of a child would require a psychopath.

*　　*　　*

87

The night was full of sound and movement. As Flint finally reached the warmth of his houseboat, Vikki Corbett wiped the steam from the inside of her windscreen. The past weeks had been hard graft and no reward. Piers Plant had been as secretive as he was now elusive. Few of his supposed friends could shed light on his recent past. Few would even admit to more than a nodding acquaintance at local functions. Plant had steadily grown into a social leper, with a reputation for cranky behaviour. He hardly held the credentials to charm a young woman's heart.

Mrs Plant's house was just visible from where Vikki's car was parked at the top of the narrow lane. Scandal within the quiet row of bungalows had created a network of whispered gossip, which Vikki had used persistent enquiry to tap. Mrs Plant was respected, but her senility was spoken of with gentle patronising sympathy and just one hint of a recent fetish for late-night strolls by the river was sufficient to launch Vikki on her vigil.

Radio Darke played almost below the threshold of hearing, just enough to keep the reporter awake, not enough to arouse attention. Four nights alone had been boring, but Vikki cursed herself for missing Friday. Wrong, she cursed Vince and his crazy flatmate and that snobbish girl from the florist's. Friday might have been the night.

Two streetlamps illuminated the lane, the second standing between Mrs Plant's cottage and where Vikki was parked. The thunderstorm had passed, leaving only a parting drizzle in the air and a distant crackle on the car radio. Vikki jabbed a finger towards the off button when a silver shimmer grew visible for just a moment through the drizzle. She watched the furtive shape glance around then vanish into the wet night. Immediately, she pulled up her own rain hood, then slipped out of the door, closing it quietly.

Mrs Plant had at least a hundred yards' start, so Vikki broke into a splashing jog. She left the loom of the last streetlamp at the bottom of the lane, where a slimy footpath led for fifty yards towards the river. Clinging, dripping bushes wiped at both her arms as Vikki tried to keep her distance, yet not lose contact. Ahead, the sky brightened as she slipped down on to the towpath by the canalised section of the river.

Town lights reflected from the river enabled her to differentiate buildings from trees, sky from water. Trees which lined each bank still whispered with the impact of raindrops, passing these on to

the river in heavy drips. Vikki watched for motion, but Mrs Plant
could not be seen . . .

She could run left into town or right away from town. To the left
lay a number of old warehouses connected with the defunct canal
trade. To the right, an endless possibility of riverside boathouses,
huts and an abandoned paper mill, so it made sense to choose
right. Vikki walked cautiously for a hundred yards and lost the
light. Then she paused and listened for sound that was not rain,
or trees, or river, or distant traffic. Had she chosen badly? Vikki
turned about, ran back to the end of the lane then indecision
stopped her again.

She would go towards town, cautiously and miserably, for the
rain had begun once more. For half a mile her tights absorbed
the brown water splashing up from the towpath, until with
mascara smeared down her cheeks she came to Castlereigh Bridge.
Cursing in the sodium glare, she looked back into the rainstorm.
Somewhere back there, she had so nearly found an answer.

Mrs Plant had indeed turned left, she walked steadily along the
waterfront, where only one vehicle and its owner sat waiting
patiently. Rowan opened the door and spoke to the old woman
in her assured, commanding voice. Once relieved of her carrier
bag, Mrs Plant was turned around and told to go home.

Rowan had thought she had seen movement by the old lock-
keeper's hut, so she moved towards it with renewed confidence.
Piers Plant pressed his back against the wall of the hut, saying
nothing. Raindrops dripping from a tree beat time on the tin roof,
which leaked water into the corner with a steady drip-drip. Rowan
shook her coat and lay down the carrier bag.

"Hello Oak."

"Rowan?" His voice held a hint of panic.

"I brought you some food," she said. "You were very easy
to find."

He seemed to be breathing heavily, although she couldn't
see him.

"You're running out of time, you know. The longer you hide,
the more people suspect."

"I can't go back," he stated.

"You must."

"You can't hide for ever."

89

"I can."

"Someone is going to find you, even if only by accident."

"No," he said, "impossible. Nobody knows, nobody can know."

A madman is convinced of his own sanity, she thought. Oak was so dangerous now. "That reporter is asking everyone: your friends, your relations, even the places you do your shopping." This last remark was pointed directly at him.

Suddenly, Plant slipped from a voice of absolute conviction to one of the hunted animal. "What is happening? What are people saying? What is that snooping lecturer doing?"

"I wish you would forget about damned Doctor Flint! He's far too clever for himself, you can just forget him. If he finds a clue which says Lucy Gray is on the moon, he will go to the moon. The police are being dealt with and the reporter is both young and stupid. All our enemies are running around in the dark. They know nothing, they know less than they think they do."

For a while no words passed. Only the laboured sound of Piers Plant's breath mingled with the renewed drumming above.

"You will tell me where you are hiding, you don't stay here in the daytime, do you?" Rowan had to break what resolve remained in the man's breast. "You have to let me help you find a better place, one where someone is not going to blunder into you."

"I don't hide here," Plant stated sullenly.

"You can't outwit Rowan, dear Oak. So tell me." She advanced to ruffle his wet hair, but he shrank away. "Don't force me to guess."

"No, it isn't safe."

"You don't even trust me? Me?"

"I don't trust Him."

"But he's helping you, Oak. Don't you understand? We're all helping you."

"I know what happened at Imbolc," he stated, "I know what he did to Hazel."

Rowan was glad he was unable to see her look of utter confusion. "What?"

"It was a spell of his."

"What?" she repeated, even more incredulous.

"A spell. A curse. He has the power, everyone knows he has the power."

"Oak, what has happened to you?"

"He could have tampered with the brew." Oak was excited, moving around the hut, brushing by her, knocking his hands on the walls as he gesticulated. "Don't you see how simple it would have been for him to add a poison to the brew?"

"Have some sense, please!"

"But he's evil, Rowan, evil. He's turning your mind, if you can't see it. That's why he hates me so much. He knows that I know and he knows that I can break the spell and break his power!"

Rowan stood back, alarmed, trying to think, appalled by what had happened to Oak. Hiding her true feelings, she tried to calm the hysteria. "Look, we'll play it your way, Oak. Stay in hiding, I'll try to find somewhere else for you to go, somewhere you'll be safe."

"I've been working on my plan," he said brightly, "all I need is time to complete my research then I'll be ready for them all."

"Honestly, Oak, you must be careful. Don't do anything silly."

Silly, what a grossly understated word to use. Recklessly idiotic would best describe her fear of Oak in his animated state.

"Devastating, it will be devastating when I hold the power."

"I can't talk to you like this, I'll come again when you're talking sense."

She shook away his grasping arm.

"Rowan!"

"Goodnight, Oak." She opened the hut door.

"I won't come back here!" he warned. "So don't look for me."

Rowan moderated her tone. "Goodnight, Oak, and for the sake of everything we hold sacred, don't do anything stupid. Please!"

She left the hut, quivering with anger, but strangely pleased that Oak was edging back into her power. Just the one word "research" had betrayed him.

Chapter 9

Sally looked at Flint as if he had walked into the department through the wall, instead of via the door.

"Ah, hello, Jeff. We've all been wondering about you . . ."

"Went away, then got ill."

"You were missed." She put heavy, oppressive emphasis on this last word.

"Last week of term, exams over . . ."

"People still expect . . ."

By people she meant Professor Grant.

"Messages," Sally unpinned a fan of white notes off the board, "post." She pushed a pile in his direction.

Clutching his heap and smiling apologetically, he moved out of range of the rays of disapproval. He had been listed AWOL, trouble was coming, more hassle. The corridor to his office was dark compared to the bright summer's day outside. It matched his mood.

No one had opened the office window during his absence and the spider plant gasped for air and water. He pushed the window as wide as it would go, then turned to his messages. He'd had a call from from Vikki on Wednesday: "Where the hell are you? Ring me ASAP. Very urgent, Vikki." Then every day since, the same message. He sighed, then took out the smallest envelope in the heap. It opened to reveal a greetings card on recycled paper. Flint paused to admire the naïve art parrots, then turned to the message.

Dear Jeffrey,
We've had such a good year, but I'm going home to write up my thesis, then on to Norfolk for the summer. Please understand, always be friends,
Chrissie xxx

He sucked in his cheeks and would once have muttered "easy come easy go", but living alone was never easy. The parrots slid back into their envelope. He should keep a special file of his "Dear Jeffrey" letters. He flicked through the rest of the pile, then found the enthusiasm to telephone Kingshaven.

Vikki almost bounced down the telephone. "Where the hell have you been?"

"Stonehenge."

"Look, I'm not in a mood for jokes. Piers Plant has not come back, no one can find him. He's not keeping his appointments, he's not on holiday, he's even stopped ringing in sick. I've interviewed everyone from his next-door neighbour to the woman who sells him his herbal teas. He's just vanished, or that's what we're to think . . ."

"And?"

"I know where he is. He's here, in Kingshaven."

"Eh?"

Vikki related her attempt to tail Mrs Plant the dark.

"I followed her last night, but lost her by the canal. I thought she'd go right, but she must have gone left, into town. She was carrying a shopping basket."

"Grandma visits little Red Riding Hood," Flint said dryly.

"Are you all right?" Vikki asked.

"Yes, I've just had a bad year, it will pass."

"Well, if she's taking him things, he's not hiding with friends. There are lots of places in town he can hide, abandoned churches, old warehouses, old factories, air raid shelters. He could have the key to any of those old places."

"Have you told the cops?"

"Of course not, they treat me like a child. I'm cracking this one. Can you come down today?"

"It's more than my job's worth, ma'am."

"Have you been smoking something?"

"No, it's against my religion."

"Jeff, can you be serious for a moment, just for a moment?"

Go on, said a portion of his brain, why not? "Okay, look, I expect a bit of heavy hassle, but I'll try to fix something up. I'll get Tyrone to drive me down, I think you two should meet."

"Now?"

He checked his watch. "I'll ring you back."

A quick search of the department located Tyrone in the computer room, working on his thesis. Professor Grant was walking in the direction of the staff bar as they emerged.

"Ah, Jeffrey. I was trying to track you down all last week." The professor hovered, looking up at Flint, waiting for some sort of explanation.

"Oh, tied up with research."

"Well, is everything fine for two thirty?" This line was just polite banter, there was no real question in his voice.

Flint thought "Shit", but said, "I'm sorry, Ian, I have an urgent appointment."

He topped his superior by a good four inches, his beard being roughly on the professor's eye line. The professor looked away in disgust, then burst back in a bluster, "But it's the Academic Board. The meeting has been timetabled for six weeks!"

"Sorry, present my apologies, would you?"

"This simply will not do! You have to come, what can be more pressing?"

"I'm up to here with research." Flint raised a hand to his chin, emphasising the height difference.

"Missing students? You're still hunting missing students. You're not the College Welfare Officer, when will you learn?" The bluster mellowed. "Well, you can relax, young whatsisname has turned up."

"Timmy Wright?"

"The Chemist," Professor Grant said with derision. "He was selling Coca-Cola on the beach in San Tropez. A fine waste of three years' education, but then what can you expect of northern scientists?"

He touched a finger on Flint's lapel. "Two o'clock, don't be late."

The junior lecturer was left motionless as Professor Grant shambled away. He was beyond emotional reaction, which was probably fortunate. Returning slowly to his office, he took down the file he had labelled "Timmy", poured the contents into the recycling basket, then ripped off the sticky label. If this enigma was not solved very quickly, Piers Plant would not be the only one requiring psychiatric help.

It was the following lunchtime when Flint and Tyrone met Vikki inside Auntie Joyce's Tea Shoppe. This was one of a dozen half-timbered buildings in the centre of Kingshaven that had escaped extensive remodelling by the Luftwaffe or by post-war planners. The gentrified café served a good range of teas, excellent home-made scones, and captured Jeffrey Flint's devotion with its chocolate cake. Only the sharp prices dinted the archaeologist's enthusiasm.

When Vikki and Tyrone were introduced, the student made heavy work of laying on charm, slapping his monogrammed briefcase on to the table and fiddling with the combination. Flint noticed this was 924 and winced at the poseur. Tyrone's data on Lucy's disappearance made an impressive pile, but still lacked the crucial item that Barbara had confided. Vikki, too, had to remain ignorant.

Tyrone produced a wad of ideas. "I checked his family tree at St Catherine's House – apart from his mum, his closest relative is an aunt in Oulwich."

"The police went there last week. I talked them into it," Vikki said. "She knows nothing and she's going to be in France for most of the summer."

Tyrone scribbled a note in the margin of his list. "Right, I've checked through the list of senior people involved in local archaeology, folklore and the like. I've telephoned ten to find out roughly who Plant usually associated with. There are three or four who might be classed as his friends who live in Kingshaven. Only one is in the right area suggested by the direction his mother took."

Vikki peeked at the list, unimpressed. "I've seen all these people, and, if he's with a friend, why is his mother taking him things?"

Flint interrupted. "Vikki, we agree with you that he's probably hiding out in familiar territory. He probably makes a rendezvous with his mother to pick up food, then returns to wherever he's hiding. If the police question the old dear, she only knows she met him once or twice. Even if they beat her up, she can't disclose his hiding place."

"So all we have to do is find the hiding place," Vikki said. "I've a few ideas."

A heap of photocopies skimmed across the table top. "English Heritage had Sebastian Leigh draw up an inventory of buildings for

95

potential scheduling last year," Tyrone said. "There are eighty-six, but you can cross half of them out immediately."

Vikki looked at the list for a moment, then said, "So, the sooner we start . . ."

She made a move to pay, but Flint stopped her. "We have a sponsor."

A walk along the towpath was the beginning of a long day of alternative tourism. Kingshaven's port had moved to seaward, the old wharves which had depended on the canal trade now had little use when containers arriving from Holland would be unloaded at the new cargo terminal. Warehouses, slipways, and lock-keepers' huts were as redundant as the men who had once worked there. In a maze of old brick, the trio hoped for chance sightings and searched for evidence of recent use. Hard cobbles soon produced aching shins and by eight in the evening, dining on fish and chips on the parapet of Castlereigh Bridge, even Vikki was demoralised.

George Carlyle's council house was only a mile away, and on Flint's suggestion, they tried him as a last hope for the day. Through the open curtains, they could see George and his wife sitting on their Paisley sofa, watching a TV situation comedy and drinking tea. They went to the top of the side passage and knocked at the kitchen door.

Mrs Carlyle smiled at them, shouting in to her husband after she had opened the door. George came through into the kitchen, but the face of the old soldier fell as he saw them. "I can't help you." He turned around and went back to the television.

"George, we need your help," Flint called, smiling towards the frail face of Mrs Carlyle as he squeezed into her kitchen.

He repeated his line again as he rushed into the lounge. "We need your help. Can you think of anywhere Plant might be hiding?"

George was back on the settee once more, looking deeply unhappy. "No, it's like I told the police."

"Did he have any special friends, apart from Lucy?" Vikki had also forced her way into the room.

"He doesn't want you finding him. He sent me a message."

"Yes, we were there," Flint said.

"Another one. It was waiting on our back steps last Tuesday."

96

"Oh George, don't." His wife suddenly left the room, and did not reappear.

"She loved that cat," George said, still not looking up, "but we had to give it to the police, what was left of it."

"What did they do to it?" Vikki asked.

"You don't want to know, missy."

Flint bet she did.

"That cat has all but finished me," George said.

"George," Vikki knelt beside the armchair and spoke seductively, "we have to find him before he kills a person. Who did he go to see, who came to see him?"

The attendant looked at the three faces. "You're here now, so they will have seen you, the damage is done. I might as well be shot as a hero as shot for a coward."

He breathed deeply and linked his hands across his belly as he thought. "Tim Hapgood, the librarian . . ." George began to list names. "Sir Ralph, you know, the Chairman of the Society. Miss Clewes from the teashop, though not recently . . . That Miss Woodfine from County Museums . . . That bloke with the earring from the archaeology unit, what's his name?"

"Sebastian Leigh?" suggested Tyrone. "I've got all these people."

George continued in his reluctant monotone. "Lydia Rufus-Yawl, she's the big woman who likes family history. Lady Darkeholme . . ."

The list would have gone on, but Flint stopped him. "No friends? Real friends, no one he went to the pub with?"

"He always went alone. To the Mason's usually."

"Been there," Vikki said tiredly, "no one knows anything."

"Have you got any other premises, let's say a store, or an old church under renovation, somewhere he might have had keys to?"

"No."

Vikki almost burst with frustration. "Where did he go apart from that friggin' museum?"

Adverts replaced tepid television and George looked at her. "Well, that was Mister Plant all over, he lived in the museum. He'd stay late every night after I locked up and treated it like his own personal castle. It even feels like he's there now he's gone."

George wasn't the type to be mystical, so Flint was puzzled. "Is this just a feeling, or is there any evidence? Does he smoke or anything? He doesn't leave a vapour trail wherever he goes?"

"No." George muttered a few obvious thinking noises before declaring, "But on Monday, I asked Carol the cleaner where he was, thinking he was somewhere around. There wasn't much post, you see, he usually gets ten letters a day. There was only two waiting on Monday."

"You opened them?"

"I gave them to his replacement, the lady from the County, Doctor Woodfine."

"Not Suzanne Woodfine?" Flint asked, as a disgusted aside. Archaeology was a small world, and he knew the name well.

It was as if a heavenly revelation had suddenly burst to illuminate Vikki's face. "He goes to the museum to pick up his post," she breathed in a hushed voice.

All three men looked at her, agreeing with the inspiration.

"It makes one wonder what's so important about a few letters," Tyrone said.

"It's Lucy," squeaked Vikki, "it has to be Lucy."

"Could Lucy be writing to him?" Flint asked George.

George shook his head. "I dunno, now anything is possible. I could say the Martians were writing to him and someone would write it in the paper."

"When does the postman come?" Vikki asked.

"Very early, the post is usually there by the time I get in at half eight."

"Or rather it isn't," Tyrone threw in. "He'd have to go there every morning, in daylight. Could he get in and out without being seen?"

"Is there a secret passage or anything?" Vikki probed.

The suggestion was met by canned laughter from the television.

George frowned. "I think that's just being silly, dear."

"We'll have to get in first thing tomorrow and check," Vikki declared.

Flint groaned. "If we're going to mess with the mail, we'll have to be out before Suzanne Woodfine arrives. I used to work with her sister, they're both bloody impossible."

"He would have to get in after dark, then wait till the post came, then leave again," Vikki said slowly, at the focus of everyone's attention. "It would make more sense if he just stayed there overnight. No one would know, he'll have all the keys, he'll know how to switch off your burglar alarms. I bet if we go to his office now we'd find him sleeping under the table."

"Now?" George looked concerned.

"In the dark?" Flint had seen too many horror films set in unlit museums.

"What's wrong? Scared? We can't go stomping around in opening hours, can we?" Vikki added a taunt to her tone.

"We should call in the police," Tyrone said.

Vikki quashed the idea before it could grow. "No, no, they won't be interested. And if I'm wrong, we would look bloody stupid."

Flint was still objecting. "But if we go in alone, and you're right?"

She smiled. "Then I get a bloody good story."

Chapter 10

The observer heard car doors slam closed, then saw the four people emerge from the back street, heading towards the museum with purpose. Vikki Corbett was in front, with her hands dug into the pockets of her long purple cardigan. Jeffrey Flint came next, seeming to be cajoling George Carlyle. Poor George, he should have done as he was told. At the rear was a younger man, not recognised, who could be some associate of that vile reporter.

George was directed to unlock the gate to the staff car park, which meant they would enter through the rearmost turret. The structure was under repair, scaffolding covered the whole back of the building and the group was lost to sight. Within the watcher, emotions ran cold; there was a time to act and a time to wait.

George Carlyle unlocked the staff door, then moved sharply to disable the alarm, muttering imprecations as he did so. The museum was dark and silent. It was still light outside, though an overcast sky would bring night early. George found the light switch.

Quickly, the three bounded up the stairs, past the shadowed Buddha, into the corner turret where the curator's office lay. The door was locked and anxious moments passed as they waited for George to come forward with the keys.

No curator lay slumbering below the desk. To Flint, the office looked as it had before. The desk was, perhaps, tidier, cleared now of a pile of papers which had lain on the left hand side. Flint scanned the bookcase. Perhaps there had been an extra box-file before. A gap in a row of journals caught his eye. The familiar green-jacketed tomes were entitled *The Transactions of the Darkewater Valley Antiquarian Society*.

It was a full set, running from 1879 to the previous year, with hiccups during the world wars. Two issues were missing: 1932 and 1964.

Archaeologists love rubbish so Tyrone moved straight for the waste paper bin and emptied it on to the desk, unravelling balls of paper and screwed-up envelopes, but finding no reward. Vikki searched the desk, drawer by drawer, sifting through every pile of documents.

"Does he have a file for his letters?" She stopped mid-action to ask George.

The attendant stood in the doorway, hands clasped behind his back, resolution fading. "I couldn't say, miss."

"Thanks, you're a great help." She continued to search.

Flint tapped the green volumes on the shelves, bringing attention to the dust-free voids where the two missing books had stood. "Do we know what was in the 1932 and 1964 editions of the *Transactions*?" he asked idly.

"Something worth coming back for?" Tyrone replied with another question, "We can check at college tomorrow."

"Yeah."

"Does the new woman use this office?" Vikki asked George.

"No, miss, she's taken over the assistant curator's room, that's the usual procedure."

"And how often is this bin emptied?" Vikki pointed to the mess created by Tyrone.

"Every day, I think. Carol does it."

"Pretty careless, isn't he?" Tyrone commented.

Flint swept his thoughts around the office. Careless, yes. Plant had ceased to care, perhaps all he truly cared about was Lucy. Now he was risking discovery to collect his mail.

"So he comes in at night, looks at the mail and uses his library." Flint thought aloud. "From the way the the dust is disturbed, I'd estimate he's been here during the past twenty-four hours."

"Hey, he could still be here," Tyrone stated.

On reflex, all three glanced towards the open doorway, as if expecting to see the twitching face of the curator staring back. Tyrone's hypothesis possessed enough crazy sense to be true.

"George, when we were at your place, you said that Plant virtually lived here. Could he do just that? Forget sneaking in and out or kipping here at night, could he actually live here?"

"We're not far from the river," Vikki said, "his mother could have been coming here. We'll have to look in every room, just to make sure."

Flint and Tyrone both looked at her with disquiet, whilst George seemed fascinated by his own feet.

"Come on!" she urged. "Now we're here, it won't hurt."

"Negative evidence," said Flint to Tyrone, "lateral thinking: rule out the stupidest possibilities first."

"You're so bloody smart, Doctor Jeffrey Flint," Vikki snapped, "why don't you go across the road to the pub and I'll look round on my own?"

Lecturer and student exchanged looks. The reporter had left them no choice.

Outside, the sky had clouded over and night had fallen early. Inside, the museum could have been the work of a Hammer set designer, with enough blind corners and doorways to hide a legion of undead. In the silence, it was hard not to whisper, not to tiptoe across the creaking floors, not to open doors with care. A melodramatic tension fell upon the four moving through alcoves and galleries in semi-darkness. A stuffed pole-cat's eyes glinted from the shadows. A mummy losing its shroud to moths bared its remaining teeth. Each room searched decreased the number in which the curator could hide. Each minute, Vikki talked up the chance of making a discovery.

Two floors were searched, as were the turrets, the attic over the main building, the north wing annexe. Galleries, offices, half-forgotten junk rooms, broom cupboards and dummy walls between display cases all had to be unlocked and checked by tapping and prying. On the ground floor of the north wing, two suits of armour stood guard at a doorway. One was armed with a mace.

The student went over to the armour and poked his finger through an open grasp. "What does that other suit of armour normally carry?" Tyrone asked George.

At first George seemed not to understand, then said, "A sword, a big one." He mimicked a fisherman boasting of a three-foot catch.

Tyrone slipped the mace from the grip of the dead hand.

"Treasure hunting?" Flint challenged

Tyrone waved the mace at Vikki's ever-present biro. "The sword is mightier than the pen. This Piers Plant sounds like a total loony, Doc, you won't be able to stop him just with sarcastic remarks."

George unlocked the door of the cellar. Plant would not be

found reclining in a mock Regency chaise-longue, or strolling round the archaeology gallery, but the chance of finding him huddled in a corner of the cellar was very real. If he could do to Lucy half the things Vikki had suggested, if he was indeed armed with a medieval broadsword, they were crossing a threshold into danger. Never courageous, Flint's thoughts turned to fear. George turned a switch at the top of a narrow stairway. Tyrone went first, Flint last.

The smell of dust and concrete pervaded the cellar. Old wooden racking held splitting seed-boxes, overflowing with forgotten relics. A dust-laden model galleon, a militia drum with its skin torn, a pile of architectural fragments salvaged from a local priory. In the ceiling above this pile was a smoke hatch. Tyrone climbed on to the stones and could easily reach upwards and push the hatch open.

"It shouldn't do that," George commented. He stepped forward and pointed. "It should be bolted from the inside."

Indeed, there was a bolt, rusty due to long closure. Now it was drawn back, scraped with silver lines betraying recent use. The hatch opened at the edge of an ornamental shrubbery.

"So we know how he gets in." Tyrone brushed dust from the knees of his cords.

"He really is mad if he thinks he can burgle his own museum nightly without getting caught," Vikki said.

"But it means he isn't here." Tyrone sounded disappointed, relaxing his grip on the mace.

"But he's close." Vikki wanted the options for a scoop left open. "We could mount a watch and catch him coming in."

They looked at each other for a minute or so, experiencing the anti-climax. Dissatisfied, they made for the exit, George turning off lights and locking doors as they went. By the plastic dinosaurs, Flint noticed a postcard of the museum and picked it up, frowning immediately. The postcard showed an oblique view of the building from the south-east. High on the roof of the annexe was a skylight. Flint's memory flashed an image of the first-floor room in the north wing: tall and airy, with a random collection of ethnic artefacts displayed along one side and tall picture windows down the other, facing south. A war-canoe was the central focus of attention. The room was high walled, with just a suggestion of the ceiling closing in to form the roof. There had been no skylight.

He turned the card so George could see it. "George, where is this skylight?"

George shrugged. "You can't get up there."

"I bet my life that someone can. You said that Plant and Lucy spent a lot of time upstairs, in that room with all the ethnic junk."

"The woggery, yes."

"Where exactly did they used to go?"

"Into the little room beyond. You looked in there, it's full of rubbish. I once offered to clear it out, but Mr Plant said not to."

Flint recalled the room, high but not deep, piled high with mouldering paintings and furniture under dust sheets. "He's still here, phone the police." He jabbed a finger at George. "We've got him."

"Police, sir?"

"People in pointy blue hats."

"But why, what has Mr Plant done?"

All three looked at the attendant. Flint realised he had caught the enthusiasm of the other two and allowed it to carry him away.

"Look, the station is just round the corner, five minutes' walk. Go and find someone, get them to come here."

George was going to object again, but free will had been drilled out of him many years before.

"They want to take a statement from him, okay? Go find a bored copper. Please."

"Fine, sir, but you take care with the exhibits, won't you? I don't want to come back and find you've burnt the place down."

Bemused, George unlocked the front door, then passed the keys to Flint.

Flint turned to Vikki. "This will make your scoop exclusive."

Vikki would not have heard his last words, she was already running up the staircase. Flint bounded after her, catching up just beyond the top of the stairs. She stopped. The museum was dark, only the main corridors were lit and from below came the sound of Tyrone, slow off the mark, coming up the stairs.

"Shh!" Vikki held up a hand for silence.

Flint felt his senses prickle, searching for something that lay below the sound of footsteps. Tyrone broke the spell.

"There you are!"

104

They waved him to hush, Flint tried to attune his ears to that extra, undefined sound, but no floorboards echoed above, no door creaked from behind. No raging eyes stared from the blackness.

"What is it?" Tyrone hissed.

"Nothing," said Flint.

"I heard something," Vikki insisted.

The gothic atmosphere was getting to her, Flint thought. It was getting to him, too, as he followed Vikki into the Victoriana gallery, then unlocked two very solid doors. Finally, they were within the north wing, in the ethnographic collection. Vikki stood beside the Balinese war-canoe, looking around at the haphazard assemblage of native head-dresses, war clubs and shields plundered from around the world by eccentric Victorian travellers. Myriad images of fear, hate, love and devotion dangled from the walls, bringing the reporter to an open-mouthed silence.

Flint was less impressed, thinking it all passé. Checking upwards, he examined the symmetry of the room in the abstract. The idosyncratic architecture held the clue.

"There has to be another attic. Thirty feet long, fifteen wide, perhaps eight or ten feet of head room at the centre."

Tyrone was craning his neck upwards and he nodded at the logic. Vikki moved along the near wall, checking whether the display cases would move easily. At the far end of the gallery, towards the rear of the museum, was a short corridor which led to the store room. Years of looking round churches and planning ruins had trained Flint's eye to spot an architectural flaw.

"This corridor shouldn't be here, it doesn't make sense!"

It was some twelve feet long, leading from the corner of the room. He pulled out the postcard. The store room was above a minor post-war extension added at the rear of the building to hold the washrooms. He began to bang the inside wall of the passageway.

"Looking for a secret door?" Tyrone asked, standing with his hands on his hips.

"Why not? Let's be really silly."

The wall was hollow, echoes bounced back from the cavity beyond, but there was no longer a door. "There was a door here, once," Flint was certain, "it led to a staircase which ran through the thickness of the rear wall."

"Which explains why it's so thick." Tyrone finished the logic, also banging the wall. "Or could this wall be a false one, built over an open staircase?"

"Maybe."

Vikki had come to their side now. Flint fumbled for the key to the store, found it, and went cautiously inside. Room barely existed for the threesome to stand without kicking each others' ankles. The rest of the floorspace was taken up by a pile of furniture covered with grey dust sheets. Cheap plywood panels formed the front of a set of sliding storage cabinets along the interior wall. All were locked and the bundle of keys proved useless.

"Getting warmer," Flint said.

Tyrone went back into the gallery and returned with a Zulu assegai. Flint winced as the spear point was pushed between panel and frame, but the door was easily forced open. Revealed within was a cupboard two feet deep. Vikki squeezed in and within moments had found the locked panel which led to the goal. This offered no convenient leverage point for the assegai, had no keyhole and no bolts to shift.

"What now?" Vikki asked.

"We get sued by the County Council," Flint quipped, thinking of Doctor Woodfine and her total lack of a sense of humour.

Tyrone raised his mace to strike the panel. "Okay if I test this mace?" he asked.

"Do it!"

No option remained but to destroy the panel with mace and feet. It may have taken as long as five minutes to crash their way through and by that time, they had long abandoned any idea of stealth.

Flint helped Vikki clear the debris, then stopped Tyrone from entering the void. "He'll have heard us by now."

Tyrone brandished the mace and handed the assegai to Flint. "Well, he's not going anywhere, is he?"

"Let's not do anything stupid, folks. George should have reached the cop shop by now, they'll be here in a minute."

The wall shook as the door to the gallery slammed closed.

"What!" Flint's exclamation matched a yelp by Vikki.

Echoes reverberated around the tiny room. All three were too stunned to act for a few moments, then made for the door in a rush, only to hear the lock turn and a bolt slide into place. The door was mock original, heavy, solid oak. Six fists, then a mace battered upon it.

106

"Bugger," Vikki cursed, "bugger bugger bugger."

"Double bugger." Flint stepped back, stumbling on an ankle-level obstruction.

Vikki began to clamber up the furniture pile towards a tiny square window high in the end wall.

"I can shout for help," she said, setting an old painting sliding towards them.

The others could do nothing but duck the pieces she dislodged on her way up. Balancing precariously she peeked through.

"Is there any chance of getting out?" Tyrone asked.

"No, forget it, we're right at the back, and much too high, I can't even see the street."

Flint put an ear to the door. He heard a further door slam, the one to the ethno room, then another, more muffled still. To escape, they would have to hack through at least three doors before making the main staircase. By that time, pursuit would be futile.

"That's him away," Tyrone said, helping Vikki down. "So we just sit here and wait for the Feds to let us out."

"Never put your faith in authority," Flint muttered, squeezing past him towards the concealed door. "Leave it to the police and we'll be here all night. Well, folks, as we can't get out, we might as well find out what's up here."

A staircase lay within the wall void, possibly blocked and forgotten in one of the museum's many remodellings, possibly deliberately obscured by a curator whose mind had long been bending towards the bizarre. A system existed for unlocking and lifting out the panel, but this was only obvious from behind.

A Bakelite light switch still functioned, and Vikki snapped it on. She ventured up the staircase first, snatching up the assegai and advancing in a cautious crouch. Tyrone followed with the mace. Flint went last, feeling naked.

The room at the top was still lit, although a black curtain prevented light escaping from the tell-tale skylight. The roof void had been converted into a second study, ripe to pillage for information whilst waiting for the police. Along all the available wall space was Piers Plant's impressive library. Two to three hundred books covered every aspect of the paranormal. It was immediately obvious that the curator had an unhealthy keenness for the macabre and arcane: voodoo, astrology, witchcraft, herblore, parapsychology, cryptozoology, out-of-body experience, demonology and worse.

107

Here was the source of those red eyes, Flint now knew. Secretive studies in the depth of night had turned Plant into that ghostly wreck. All the rumour and innuendo about his state of mind were finally confirmed.

An improvised bed and a pile of food packets lay on the floor.

"So he was here all the time," Vikki triumphed, "I was right."

Plant had managed to squeeze a small desk up that narrow staircase and handwritten notes were scattered on its surface. Another pile covered a stack of obscure books with damp-rotted covers. Latin verse, probably chants, Flint noted.

Vikki fereted amongst the papers, pulling out a fistful of letters with a whoop. "It's all here," she declared, "we can wrap this up in half an hour."

On the wall above the desk was an array of pictures, which drew Flint's attention. In his imagination, Flint had expected a shrine to Satan, but instead, Plant maintained a shrine to Lucy. Two dozen pictures included strips of photo-booth origin, a photograph of Lucy as some kind of May Queen, an old school photo and a poor watercolour painting of her standing in a white gown, arms outstretched. Dried flowers decked the scene as if in macabre tribute.

"What the hell has he done with her?" Flint's exhilaration at the discovery fell back to sober reality.

"Pervert," Vikki said, although without feeling.

"Look what I found," Tyrone pointed to two volumes of the *Transactions* propped up against the Lucy-shrine. He opened the 1932 volume at the contents page and spread it on the table. Of twelve papers, number four was entitled: Harken, D. P. S. "The Darkewater Megaliths".

"And 1964?" Flint asked.

Tyrone repeated the action. "The first paper is by Dowling, H. H. – 'Harriet's Stone: a re-interpretation'."

"Who is Harriet Stone?" Vikki read the title upside-down.

"A question of what, rather than who," Tyrone corrected, turning to the relevant article. "Logically, it turns out to be one of the megaliths."

He began to read the list of names on Dowling's distribution map. "Harriet's Stone, Devil's Ring, South Barn A, B and C, White Ring, Twinbridge Stones, Yarley's, Bramton East, Bramton West."

Vikki looked out of her depth. "Does this mean anything, Professor?"

"Lucy was into megaliths," Flint said, wondering about a small iron-bound box that had been carved with crude and vicious-looking runes. He took the assegai which had been discarded by Vikki and prised off the padlock.

"Oh, look at this."

Within the box lay three wax dummies. Flint took out the first, a tall figure with beard and glasses painted on to it and a cushionful of pins stuck through it.

"This explains my backache," he said dryly.

"And this is me," Vikki breathed, taking out a smaller doll that clutched a sheet of rolled-up paper in its hands and was also riddled with pins.

"Which leaves me." Tyrone took out the third doll.

"No," Flint took the doll from Tyrone, "I think not. Plant's never met you, he probably doesn't even know you exist, so this must be someone else."

The wax image was of a man, dark haired, shorter than the Flint doll but taller than the Vikki. It had a tie painted around its neck and a small square of black card under its arm. Sprouting from the sides of its head was a pair of horns.

"Candle wax," Flint said, thinking of candles, imagining he could still smell candles.

"Let's look at these letters before the police grab them," Vikki said.

Primitive senses submitted their veto. Flint was sniffing, imagining candles, but that was ludircous. The attic had electric bulbs, Plant had not needed candles, not even for the Lucy-shrine. In the corner was a paraffin heater, unlit.

"Can you smell candles?" Flint asked. "I can, I'm sure of it."

All three stopped and within moments, were certain. Filtering in from the galleries below was the acrid odour of smoke.

"Shit, he's set the place on fire!"

Vikki lost all her colour in an instant. "We'll never get out in time. He's trying to burn us alive!"

"Ideas, ideas!" Flint was close to panic.

"He must have another way out," Tyrone stated, snapping his fingers.

"Uh?"

"He can't afford to let himself be boxed in like we are, he must have another way out. He heard us come in and was able to outflank us." Tyrone swept his arm around. "Down there!"

The far corner of the void was the obvious place to try. Here the wing joined the main building, and they had already explored an attic at the same level. In a rush they fell on their knees by a bare section of plywood, thumping it furiously, probing every seam or crack with fingernails or assegai point.

"Doc, you're a film buff, ever seen *Zulu*?" Tyrone asked. "This is how James Booth escapes from the burning hospital."

"Didn't half of them die?"

Vikki thrust the spear point into a crack and jerked it sideways. Two inches broke off the end of the assegai, but the plywood panel came open. She dug in her fingers and pulled it away, then led the way towards salvation. A five-yard section of sloping roof void connected new annexe with old attic. Vikki crawled along the board across the roof-beams and declared there was another panel at the far end. The smell of smoke grew stronger as Vikki squirmed around and kicked open the far panel. Smoke flooded in.

"Keep going!" she was urged.

The main attic was unlit, only vague street-light came in through the row of dormer windows. Racking closed in on both sides, invisible detritus on the floor grabbed at shuffling feet, drifting smoke began to irritate the lungs and fear gripped the trio.

Vikki had groped her way through the discarded skulls and boxes of pottery to bang on the far door. "It's locked."

Flint came to her side, cursing a bruised shin, snapping on the light. Smoke poured under the door which led to the main staircase. This was functioning as a chimney, bringing up the fumes from below. It was no escape route. Plant's warped mind had out-guessed them again. The curator could still be loose downstairs, performing his First Mrs Rochester act with a can of petrol. He had planned this.

"We can't go that way," Flint said, then fell back in a fit of coughs.

The light died. Someone had killed the master switch, the same someone who had disabled the fire alarms. For a moment, Flint suspected George, where was he? What was he doing? Had he even gone for the police? His throat thickened at the idea, or was it smoke? They were in a trap, baited, now sprung.

110

Behind them, Tyrone forced open a paint-sealed gable window overlooking the staff car park. All three stuck their heads out into fresh air.

"Oh God no," Vikki groaned as she saw the steep pitch of slates.

"We've got to get out, this place has got wooden floors," Flint coughed.

"I'm game." Tyrone ran a hand along the slates. The threatened rain had not yet come, otherwise crossing the roof would be suicide.

Outside, the low clouds were illuminated dull orange by the lights of Kingshaven. Something could be seen silhouetted against them, tall, thin and vertical. Flint called himself an atheist, but thanked God for idle builders. They had all forgotten the scaffolding.

With smoke pouring from the ground-floor windows below, Tyrone clambered out into the night. Flint gripped his arm, whilst the student called out progress reports. The first four feet were the worst, the slates greasy with moss. Squirming on to his stomach, Tyrone found a footing on the scaffolding, then shouted he was safe. Vikki went next, cursing and blaspheming all the way. Flint was last; for a moment he felt confident, then slipped.

Two seconds were lost from his life in sheer terror, then his leg contacted a scaffolding pole and his hand grabbed at the gutter. He came to rest, panting, wishing he had stuck to theoretical archaeology.

All the ladders had been removed, but Flint had seen enough Batman serials as a child to know how to swing and slide down metal poles. Two minutes of terrified, arm-wrenching exhilaration followed before his feet kissed tarmac. Brushing rust off his palms, trembling legs at last on Mother Earth, he staggered back out of the smoke.

"You okay, Vikki?"

Vikki was in the centre of the car park, bent double and coughing away the smoke.

"Tyrone?"

"All right! Let's get the bastard!" Tyrone betrayed a killer instinct, grabbing at a short length of discarded scaffolding pole and making for the open back door.

Only the north wing was fully ablaze. Smoke wafted along the ground floor and swirled around the porter's desk. A figure moved around in the smoke, wafting it away, knocking over a heap of erasers and plastic dinosaurs. It staggered towards Tyrone, the student retreating into the yard, pole raised as a baseball bat.

Flint grabbed at the raised arm. "Hang on, that's George!"

George was helped out, then, in a state of shock, the four sat on a bench in the rose garden, amidst a growing chaos of police and firemen. George had met little response at the police station and had lacked the conviction to push himself. Too late, with the museum ablaze, the police had taken notice, dispatching squad cars in all directions to hunt for Plant. Hurried statements were taken, a paramedic fussed around, then George went home to see his wife. The other three escaped to the sanctuary of the Mason's Arms. Nerves needed steadying.

"Two pints ESB, two double whiskys, and Vikki?"

"G and T, biggish," she said with a touch of exhaustion in her voice.

Vikki paid. She stood picking ash from her hair as the barman loaded up the tray. A seat was easy to find, everyone else being out on the pavement watching the fire. Sitting down, Vikki took her G and T and stared into the distance. For a moment Flint thought he knew what she was thinking. Like him, she would feel the terror of an escape from death. Like him, she would be shocked by the destruction of the museum, even its second-rate collection deserved a better fate. Like him, she would be thinking of Lucy, doomed by a relationship with a madman.

Vikki still looked pensive. She turned to him, her expression suddenly brightening. "Bloody good story, eh?"

He had misjudged her. Vikki downed her drink in one, drew out a notepad, clicked her biro into action and began to compose.

Chapter 11

He had been a hunted animal since Imbolc, since the terrible night on the hillside, but the status of fugitive had made little difference to Piers Plant's behaviour. In the small hours of the morning, Rowan stopped her white van by the little cottage they used to rent, the one which had been the first scene in the tragedy. It was still fully dark and no lights showed through the cottage windows. Perhaps it had not been let that week.

"I wish you could have seen my little room," Oak said to Rowan.

"I wish you had shown it to me, but that was reserved for your special one, wasn't it?"

"It was. Now everything is gone."

"The radio made it sound very bad. None of this need have happened if you had told me where you were hiding."

"But you guessed."

"I worked it out, just like our enemies worked it out."

"Everything is gone," he repeated. "If only my spell had worked, if they had been trapped just by chance, we would be free."

Spells again, she noted with displeasure. The fire had almost driven him beyond the edge, but she hoped she had pulled him back again. Rowan tried to lighten his air of terminal gloom, by patting him on the knee. He gripped her hand with both his and she could sense he was looking straight at her.

"Was it necessary?" he asked.

"Yes," she replied. Oh yes, it had been necessary, only the timing had been awry.

He suddenly snapped out of his whimpering state and into that alarming voice he reserved for dangerous decisions. "I'm going now."

Oak had already taken the torch and begun to open the door.

"You're going to do it again!" she hissed, hanging on to the sleeve of his cardigan. "Oak, they will find you, you're not invisible!"

He pulled himself free and flashed his torch down the track to where he had left his car concealed. "He said we should tell everyone as little as possible."

"But this is me."

"Yes," he became wistful, "you once said you were my sister, my wife and my mother."

"And so I am, so tell me."

"You might tell Him. The fire was his fault, you know, because of Him, I've lost everything."

"Don't be silly, Oak, and listen to me. You're not well, behave like this and they will find you. Let me hide you."

"No."

She could not be defeated by one of his random peaks of confidence.

"Lugsanadh, I'll be ready by Lugsanadh. I'll bring the sacrifice too," he said.

"Good," Rowan managed a false smile into his torchlight, "I'll collect you. I know where you're going."

"You do?"

She told him and he seemed injured by his lack of cunning.

"Rowan, you read my mind."

"I can bring you things."

A light showed between the cottage curtains.

"Hurry, go now! Be careful."

He ran away down the track, his torch waving to and fro. A face came to the window of the cottage, so she pulled the door closed and started the engine. Brother, husband, prodigal son, dear Oak gave her no confidence whatsoever. The wolves were closing in and only she could keep them from hurting the one she most loved.

Tyrone slept solidly on Vikki's sofa, but in the half-decorated back bedroom, Flint rolled through a restless night. The adventure in the museum could have had so many different endings, most of them tragic. When he slipped into a dream, he was thrust into one of Lucy's infernal fantasy realms, with a dragon about to reduce his companions to smouldering crisps. He awoke to sensations of fear and guilt, knowing how stupid it had been to bungle around the museum as if on a rag stunt. The game had turned nasty, very, and any hope he held of finding Lucy alive was gone.

Saturday was spent in the smoked-glass-fronted low-rise police station which served the valley. Junior officers went through the routine paperwork, after which Flint was treated to the privilege of a one-to-one interview with Chief Inspector Douglas. Douglas was a slightly heavy man who would have only just made the height limit when he joined the force. His round face had a look of worried affability. Flint was reminded of one of his own uncles.

The office, with its one plate-glass window and view of distant council flats, was depressing in its functionalism. Flint retold the story, completely failing to amuse the policeman.

"I'm sorry, Doctor Flint, but we have no room for amateur detectives in this valley."

Douglas' balding crown showed a recent case of sunburn. Goblin-like, he stretched his long arms across his desk. It was clear he distrusted the lecturer. Flint tried to be breezy, which was a mistake. "We were just following a logical hunch."

"If you had any information, the police should have been the first to know."

"You wouldn't have done anything, you haven't done anything to find Lucy so far."

A bony finger jabbed across the desk blotter. "Look, I don't need to be told my job by some intellectual snooper." Douglas paused. "Hey, look, do they call you Jeff?"

"Er, yes."

"Jeff, look. We have missing persons reported every day. Lucy Gray didn't even go missing in this locality."

"Yes she did!"

Douglas continued to speak calmly. "So you say. If you had given us the facts, we could have done something and last night would not have happened."

Flint shook his head; protesting against this injustice would make no impression. Black was white, all of a sudden. "You can have all the facts you want."

"I'm all ears." Douglas leaned back again

Flint sighed. "You have read the newspaper stories about the links between Plant and Lucy."

"Yes, I thought them far-fetched."

"Melodramatic, yes, but the basic facts are okay. I could send you photocopies of what I have. I did that before, but you probably chucked them away."

"Let's try to be constructive, shall we?"

"Well, I'm telling you there is some pretty odd occult activity taking place and you're not believing me."

Douglas nodded. "Fine, look, I'll believe there was some sort of jiggery pokery going on, but we have to be very careful about screaming 'Satanism', Jeff, it upsets people. If we say that Piers Plant and this girl had a kinky sex life, people will be a whole lot happier."

The idea was distasteful to Flint. "Look, the man has burned down his own museum, trying to cook us in the process. It's cast-iron proof that he's a psychopath."

"So, you think Piers Plant has killed Lucy Gray?"

"Me and everyone else with an IQ of 50 or greater." Flint allowed irritation to slip through again.

"Being hostile won't help us." Douglas' unflappability showed signs that he'd recently been on some training course.

"Okay. Will you try to find him?"

"Of course."

"No more cock-ups?"

"Cock ups?"

"Plant got away from a burning building in the middle of a built-up area when hundreds of witnesses were watching. When your people finally sauntered up, they still couldn't find a madman on foot, who only had five minutes' lead."

"You can get a long way in five minutes in the dark."

"Someone must have helped him get away, then. Have you arrested his mother? She was supplying him with food."

"You forget that Mr Plant wasn't a suspect at that time. She committed no crime."

Flint nodded sullenly. "Anything else you know that I don't?"

Douglas shook his head. "Do me a favour, Jeff, no more Agatha Christie. No more snooping, no more midnight dramas, or someone is going to get hurt."

"Someone already has."

A black cloud of depression followed Flint back to London. The museum fire was not his first narrow brush with death, but without doubt, it was the nastiest. His hands trembled as he tried to read

Vikki's Saturday evening paper, due to delayed shock or the onset of post-traumatic stress disorder. He found Vikki's line about Plant "disappearing by magic" in poor taste.

Back on his quiet, peaceful, restful houseboat he awarded himself two days off sick. He lay on his bed and ran through his Dylan LP collection, humming along, trying to forget everything that had happened. What he needed was a conference, preferably abroad, somewhere with good restaurants and fine wines. What he needed was a woman by his side to unpick the knots in his soul and to care for in the quiet hours. What he might have to settle for was a month excavating in the Hertfordshire hills.

Cycling to college again, he was aware of the irrelevance of archaeology. It bore no relation to the vicious, nasty modern world, and little relation to the vicious, nasty ancient world either. Who truly cared what (if anything) happened in the third century?

Sally Parfitt had been secretary to the department for twenty years. Well spoken, correct, elegant and demure, it was her boast that she steered Classical Archaeology between Scylla and Charybdis. She claimed to remember each student who had passed between her doors over two decades and it was only she who truly knew the state of departmental politics.

"Have you been sick again, Jeff?" she asked as he extended an arm towards the message board.

"Yes, you got my message?"

Her tight lips were a confirmation. Sally pulled out a parcel and a trio of letters for his attention whilst Flint took down one telephone message from the board.

"It was your chemist, Timmy Wright, he rang to apologise."

"Cretinous erk. I should send him the bill for my wasted time."

"And Ian would like to see you. The moment you came in, he said." Her face carried a strong hint of warning.

"Bad?" he asked.

She winced as a coded signal. "Be polite and don't try any jokes. The tabloid press have been grubbing their little snouts around the department. Ian is not best pleased."

"Ten minutes?" Flint pleaded, retreating with his pile of post.

He reached his office, mentally preparing his defence against a dressing-down. Flopping into his chair, he ripped open the first envelope in the pile of mail. Inside was a dull enquiry from some West Country school teacher. It was tossed aside, the parcel at the base of the heap looked far more interesting. Book-sized, perhaps something for review. A freebie, something to shred through the intellectual mincer, something to distract the mind from Lucy, Vikki, Sally, Barbara and Chrissie Collings' slender white neck. Off came the brown paper, off came the lid, out came the newspaper, out fell the severed chicken's head.

His heart kicked, he shot backwards on his toppling chair. Regaining balance, he checked again. Staring through a half-closed eye was the bloody head of a chicken, still partly wrapped in newspaper. The stench of offal flooded out and assaulted his nostrils.

Flint spun the chair around and jerked open the window, leaned out and breathed deeply. In, out, in, out, no more shocks this week please! His pulse began to return to normal and he chanced a sideways look at the blood-soaked mess. He'd followed the red herrings, he'd had the narrow escape, this was his first public warning.

Mouth drying, he began to think logically once more. Stained dark red and stinking of death, the newspaper had a familiar look. He slipped the chicken on to the teacher's letter and uncreased the old copy of the *Durring and Kingshaven Advertiser*. It was one of Vikki Corbett's masterpieces of subtlety, the one where he had volunteered to stand in crumpled jacket before an ugly Victorian building. He examined the wrapping and the first-class stamps. The parcel had been posted in south London.

Deliberately, he relaxed back into the chair, contemplating the head, weighing up the situation. This was proof he was drawing closer and confirmation that something sinister lurked behind Lucy's disappearance. Postcards from far corners of the country, now a threat from south London? An inner feeling told him that Piers Plant had not been the one licking the stamps.

The internal phone jolted him back to reality. It was Sally, gently suggesting that the moment was ripe for him to see the Head of Department. Flint opened the window to maximum, then left the chicken where it was.

Professor Ian Grant had an office somewhat larger than that of his junior lecturer, with a view out on to the central quadrangle of college. When Flint was called inside, he was standing by his window, completely sober, gazing outwards.

"Ah, Jeffrey, I trust you are fully recovered."

"Fine," Flint lied, his mind switching between a burning museum and a decapitated hen.

"I've been meaning to talk to you about your research, but you have been," he paused, "so seldom in the department. How is your paper progressing?"

The Professor moved back to his seat and Flint sat opposite him, in the awkward chair reserved for students. Joys of the third century were briefly resurrected. The new evidence met with appreciative nods, the Marxist reinterpretation caused further furrows in an already richly landscaped brow.

"And what of your excavation, it's going to be Burkes Warren again?"

"Everything's arranged, my team is picked and ready to go. All we have to do is wait for the farmer to cut his field."

"And when do you expect to begin?"

"Second week in August."

The Professor repeated the date quietly, it was clear that academic matters were not his reason for summoning the junior lecturer to his office.

"Next year, perhaps, we might organise something abroad. There may be a villa excavation in Tuscany."

"Terrific."

"Which I shall probably be directing myself, but I daresay I will need assistance." The Professor was clearly manoeuvring around to a point of conflict. Handling confrontations and decision-making were not his happier talents.

"Since we spoke a few days ago, I hear you have been playing the detective."

"Not exactly playing."

Professor Grant pulled a copy of the *Sun* from his desk, and turned to the page four headline. The story of the fire had been lifted directly from Vikki's humbler paper, with added spice and reduced fibre.

"Have you read your contract lately? There is, I believe, a clause where staff agree to make no statements to the press."

"But she was there, she saw it all."

A finger flicked hard at the photograph of the blazing museum.

119

"How do you think this looks to the Dean of Arts, to the archaeological profession as a whole? Do you consider that burgling museums is a suitable mode of conduct for a member of the academic staff? Would you consider it a valid use of meagre university funds?"

"Yes."

The Professor gave an ingratiating smile. "We pay exorbitant rates here in London. Much of that goes to pay the police force."

"The police are getting nowhere."

"Nevertheless, we have to ask, are missing persons our business?"

"Missing student, one of our students. We can't simply lose young people, it looks careless. Makes bad reading for the alternative prospectus."

"Don't be sarcastic with me, Flint. You're not with your students now. This girl, ah . . ."

"Lucy."

"The police think she's run off somewhere."

"She was into witchcraft, satanism, something of that nature. I think she's been killed and I have a good idea who did it."

"Killed?" He looked unhappy at dismissing the weight of argument. "By this curator fellow?"

Flint inclined his head. The Professor could read a newspaper.

"Still, I must ask . . ." He began to bluster, betraying that his prepared lines of rebuke had been exhausted. "I must say that, you must feel that chasing lunatics and burning down museums . . ." That was it, the coherent sentence construction was gone. "We have our reputation to maintain."

"Reputation?"

". . . We cannot afford to have our research efforts . . . ah . . . frittered."

"Frittered?" Flint would have said more, but regard for his tenure kept a bottle of crude ripostes firmly corked. Being a rebel is one thing, but even Che Guevara kept his eye on the odds against him.

"You are paid to lecture, to conduct research and to take legitimate interests in the welfare of the students. All this is too much." Grant looked back at the paper, searching for inspiration. "You have gone too far. You have even come to the attention of

120

the Dean of Arts. I would have preferred it to have been for the production of your long-awaited paper, rather than for this . . ."

He waved the rag again. They looked at each other in silence. How old was he? Flint wondered. Fifty-five? Sixty? Time to retire the old duffer? The pause offered a chance to escape.

"I had better get back to my research," Flint said, with only a hint of irony.

"Quite." Professor Grant was unused to berating his staff. Thirty seconds after Flint left the room, he would lunge for the bottom left-hand drawer of his desk.

Enraged rather than chastened, Flint stomped back to his office, to find Tyrone loitering outside the door, about to write a note. He was invited inside, and shown the head.

"Did they read the entrails first?" Tyrone asked, kneeling on the floor and staring the chicken in the eye. "The jungle telegraph said that Prof was giving you a ticking-off."

"Said I was frittering our research effort." A pencil cracked down on to the table as Flint exploded. "Frittered! Most research effort is frittered! Frittered on bonking undergraduates, going off on foreign jollies and pissed away down the ceramic pipe in the senior common room!"

"You told him that?"

"No."

"Good job. So you're still my supervisor, then?"

Unconstructive anger had been vented on the empty room. "The shit came from above, the Dean of Arts." His hands simulated pigeons dumping on his head. "I wonder when they dug him up. If I was paranoid, I'd sense a conspiracy."

"Why not? It would explain other facts." Tyrone was so relaxed, almost unflustered by the museum drama.

"Such as?"

He blinked heavily. "Why the police are being so pathetic."

"You're fantasising." Flint dismissed the comment verbally, but his mind continued to play on the word. "It's not a conspiracy, it's just more complex than we first thought. It's like digging a test pit through a site of unknown depth and function. It just keeps going down, deeper and deeper, making less and less sense."

Tyrone remembered one of his supervisor's favourite quotes. "Mark Twain: 'We have already thrown much darkness on the subject, and if we continue we shall soon know nothing at all.'"

"Not quite, but almost."

"It will make sense sooner or later, when the pieces fall together. Just you see."

Flint gave a heavy sigh. Despite the chaos at the museum, despite the warnings, he wanted to keep digging. The hole yawned wide, and tantalisingly deep. He pointed at the chicken's head.

"You happy to continue with this game, Tyrone? Back out if you want to. It could get very nasty if Plant isn't found."

"I'll give it a couple of weeks. I've nothing planned until August."

"You could come to Burkes Warren, if you're feeling bored by then."

"No, I'll give that a miss. Me and the lads are hitting Italy. Red wine, white marble and brown-skinned girls for one whole month."

"You'd give up four wet weeks in Hertfordshire for that?"

"Easily."

"Right, Tyrone, you've a month to crack this one."

Tyrone stood up and indicated the severed head. "Is this evidence? Do the police want to see it?"

"They'd probably toss it in a casserole."

"If you throw it away, remember to keep the stamps and wrappers. Do we know anyone who lives in south London?"

"What does your computer say?"

"Do you want to come and see?"

Flint supposed it was research of a sort, so allowed Tyrone to lead him to the computer suite to see his relational data base. Prepared to accept data for his thesis, he was testing it on the Lucy case. Every fact, supposition, statement and piece of research had been reduced to computer-friendly form.

"Excellent." Flint thumbed the mouse and watched the data flood by. "Do you have a working hypothesis too?"

Tyrone switched to a text file, then began to summarise his theory. "Lucy left hall on 30th January, it was a Monday. She went to the station, bought a student return ticket for £9.60 and travelled to Durring – Kingshaven is fifty pence more. At Durring she met someone . . ."

"Piers Plant?"

"There's no other candidate. She arranges to stay somewhere overnight, perhaps. Late on the night of the 30th, they drive to one of your megaliths, meet the other weirdos and do whatever weirdos do on February 1st. That's Imbolc, the feast of the lactating of ewes, it says in my book."

The air-conditioned hygiene of the new computer suite was an incongruous place to be discussing Pagan ritual. Flint cast his eyes around the rows of empty terminals, themselves reminding him of an avenue of standing stones.

"Then what?"

"Before your Piers Plant tried to sauté us in the museum, I thought we were dealing with a group of harmless cranks. People don't go crazy, hide in attics, torch museums and burn people alive just to cover up an elopement. I think something pretty nasty happened to Lucy. I bet they sacrificed her."

"Uh?" Flint sat back in shock; the idea appalled, yet seemed curiously possible. "That's horrible, and it's hardly likely."

"The tabloids are full of that sort of stuff."

"Yes, but is it true? Don't tell Vikki, whatever you do, she would love that. Can't you see the headline? 'SEXY SEDUCTRESS IN SATANIC SACRIFICE SHOCK SENSATION.' Anyway, Plant was obsessed by Lucy, every fact we gather points to that."

"Most murders are crimes of passion. He's a loony and his friends are probably all loonies too."

"Friends." Flint hung on the word. "Everyone says he has no friends, but he must have had help, and I don't just mean his mother. There's too much going on for one crank to organise. Fake postcards, phone calls, two disappearances, fingerlickin' chicken in a bag . . ."

"And the museum fire," Tyrone said.

Flint nodded. "Four a.m. this morning, I had some very uneasy thoughts about the whole museum caper."

"Timing," Tyrone said bluntly.

"We go upstairs. Plant hears us hack down his door and escapes through his rabbit hole. While we're making idiots of ourselves in the store room and quietly reading his library, he gets no more than five minutes to set light to the whole museum. Then, he manages to skip out of the building without bumping into George and disappears before the police turn up three minutes later."

"Magic."

123

"Let's say we don't believe in magic. There is something missing."

Tyrone looked back at his theory on the computer screen. "You're saying there are more people involved?"

"That's my hypothesis. So before we try any more heroics, we do more research, get a full grasp of the subject, find the other people. We really ought to do the rounds of those blessed megaliths too. Can you drag up the relevant data, get me some map references too?"

"Okay, but this is taking stacks of my time."

Flint stood, slapping him on the shoulder. "This is for the good of your fellow students."

"It's applied research, so can I submit it as my thesis?"

"Don't be daft."

The third century could whistle. Once the chicken's head was in the dustbin, Flint set about reading all Lucy's books on the occult. After only an hour he found the reference to the rattlesnake garter, the one Lucy was supposed to wear; it was the mark of the witch. He suppressed irritation at the idiocy of the parascience books, but read on. The J. B. Stoat library had another fourteen which touched on the subject, Senate House library a few more. It took three days to plough through them all, finding notes to feed to Tyrone. It was a poor research base, but Lucy would have read all the books on the subject she could easily get hold of. He already felt he knew her so well. To follow her shadow, Jeffrey Flint needed to enter her mind.

Chapter 12

The books and papers which had once filled Piers Plant's attic room had been turned into black ash and mixed with the rubble of what had been the north wing of the Darkewater Valley Museum. Half an hour's access to that information would have been sufficient to solve the case, Vikki had observed. Plant knew this too, and had been willing to sacrifice his lifetime's work to save himself. Vikki sat at her desk, ignoring a trio of less pressing stories, looking at the four letters she had managed to grab in the panic to escape the museum. In the post that morning she had received something different, something odious and crude. What was worse, it had been delivered to her home.

Her hands still trembled at the thought, whilst her fingers hovered over the telephone buttons. Jeffrey Flint – no, sorry – Doctor Flint thought she was stupid, didn't he? It had been her idea to raid the museum and by inference, her fault the place now lacked a north wing. It had been a grotty dump, after all. She tapped in the telephone number, wondering if all that junk had been insured?

After three minutes, someone found Doctor Flint in the library.

"Jeff," she said sweetly, "did you like my story?" she asked.

"'*Demon curator in arson drama*'?" he recited with unrestrained irony. "I have it pinned to my wall."

"I bet you'd prefer something a little more pretentious?"

"No, it was fine. Write to the market."

"Do you know what some bastard did to me today?" she asked.

"Present in the post?"

"Dog shit. A parcel of dog shit, wrapped in one of my articles, posted to my house. Somebody out there is really sick."

"Oh, but I got the top prize: *poulet cru au papier*."

Was she supposed to understand him? "Stop mucking me about."

125

"Honest, a chicken's head neatly gift-wrapped in one of your pieces. It was like *The Godfather* on a low budget. Gave me a real turn."

A smile came to her lips. Where did he get it all from? "I guess someone didn't like the way I write." Vikki was more offended by this than anything else.

"Maybe they didn't like my photo."

"No, it's because I upset someone, by revealing that witchcraft is involved. Well, if they think this is going to frighten me, they're wrong. What about you?"

He sounded very relaxed. "I'm not going to chicken out now things are getting interesting."

"Very funny," she groaned. "Now Jeff, I've been looking at those four letters. Three of them are just routine junk, but the other is an odd one. It's a card from a book dealer in Holborn. I don't understand it, but you will. Do you have a fax?"

"You kidding? We're an archaeology department, only just getting used to having our own photocopier. Still, I imagine the Business Centre does. If you hang on, I'll try to hunt out the number."

He shuffled paper whilst she waited. "How are you feeling?" he asked.

"Fine, why?"

"I'm glad to hear it."

When Vikki had rung off, Flint walked across to the Business Centre, marvelling at the reporter's ability to shrug off all life threw at her – including dog excrement. When the magic message scrolled from the machine, it revealed a standard card from a Holborn antiquarian book dealer which read simply: "Dear . . . *Mr Plant* . . . Thank you for your enquiry regarding . . . *De Nigris* . . . We regret this book is not in stock."

The usual offer to order the book was crossed out. Underneath was handwritten, "Sorry, but we've no record of this book at all."

Curious, he thought. He was still thinking about the card the following day when a meeting at UCL gave the opportunity to visit the bookshop which had returned Plant's request. In the gloomy but rich depths of the shop, Flint found himself quickly distracted by the archaeology section, touching his finger against the spine of a good few familiar volumes in faded hard jackets. Alongside was

126

the section labelled "paranormal". Why did bookshops always do that? It made no sense.

When asked if he needed assistance, Flint unrolled the fax. The tired shopkeeper looked at the facsimile of his card and shook his greying head.

"I must say, I've never heard of it," he said with confidence, "it's not in any of the catalogues."

"It could be something to do with folklore, or witchcraft."

"We do specialise in books of that type, but I've never heard of it."

"Did you know Mr Plant? Did he ever come here?"

"I think so, he's a young man, about your age."

The shopkeeper proved to have a patchy memory for names, faces and facts unrelated to books, so still without an answer, Flint thanked the man and left the shop. It was only a short, sunny walk to the British Museum, where Flint dangled over the porter's desk, quoting names of people who might help.

Mandy O'Hearne was an old favourite. She was a year older than Flint and he had spent a few futile parties flirting with her as a young undergraduate. Married, then divorced, she had become heavily involved in the movement of stock to the new British Library at St Pancras.

"Hello Jeff." Her tone was attuned to the priestly quiet of the Reading Room. Mandy had not aged well, her smile wrinkled both cheeks up to and beyond her big hazel eyes, her face now framed by hair turning a premature grey.

They walked towards the Library, with Flint explaining about Plant, the book and the mystery. "Can you hunt it out on the BL's catalogues?"

If the British Library didn't hold a copy, no one would.

"*De Nigris*," she frowned, "that's familiar, but I can't think why."

"A fellow named Plant hasn't written to you by any chance?"

"A museum curator?"

"That's the one."

They were in through the high brown library doors. He'd miss the old place, Flint thought, no new building would be the same.

"Plant, yes, two or three months ago. He came in. He'd written a pile of letters to us and said he'd had no reply."

"Can I see them?"

She stopped, "Jeff, you might have all the time in the world, but I'm busy . . ."

"It's life or death, Mandy. Worth a pizza and a glass of cheap plonk . . ."

She looked around herself and smiled wryly. "Still chasing the ladies?"

"Old habits die hard. I'm meeting Jules Torpevitch and Sasha, you remember them?"

"Sasha was my flatmate for a while," Mandy said. "Okay, come on."

It took nearly an hour to locate the letters. There were four, mostly repeating the same information. *De Nigris* was a grimoire, a magic book, written by a man named John Eastney in 1698. Plant claimed to be a student of folklore and his earliest letter dated to the previous autumn, well before Lucy had disappeared. This was Plant's project-in-being.

Mandy found the young librarian who had worked her way through the catalogues and verified what she thought. Flint shrugged and Mandy ran her fingers through her hair as she apologised for being no more help.

"I'm afraid that's it. So far as we can tell, *De Nigris* does not exist. We've checked the manuscripts, the unpublished works, even our lists of lost books, it isn't anywhere. There's no record of John Eastney either, so this poor man is in for a big disappointment if he keeps on trying to buy a copy."

Mandy had earned her Pizza Veneziana and Chianti at the Holborn Pizza Hut. Jules and Sasha had been there some time, their first bottle of wine already looked a little sorry by the time Mandy and Flint waved hello through the window. Over the second bottle, they chatted about Plant.

"Do you know, he was really nervous?" Mandy said. "It was as though he was ashamed to be asking for this book."

"Or frightened?" Flint asked.

"He could have been."

"Has he told you about the rooster's head yet?" Jules asked, with a nod towards Flint.

"No corpses at lunch, we have a rule," Sasha intervened.

"He told me," Mandy said, "but I don't want to think about it, not when I'm eating. I'm glad I never knew how crazy this museum curator really was."

128

"But is he crazy enough to hunt for a book which does not officially exist?" Flint asked.

"It happens constantly. People get the author wrong, or the name wrong, or they confuse a reference then become convinced they are right. We're always getting people looking for non-existent books."

"How about occult books?"

She sipped the wine then accepted a piece of garlic bread from Sasha.

"All the time, it seems that we're the last refuge of the insane. We get a few regulars, who are mostly harmless. They all seem to be seeking the Holy Grail or Excalibur or the Arc of the Covenant. Mostly they end up with Frazer's *Golden Bough* or reading up Doctor John Dee."

"Names?"

"Oh, I couldn't say, there are so many."

"What of your harmless regulars, are there any who still have at least ten per cent of their marbles?"

Mandy refused the last slice of pizza, so Jules took it. In the background, an Asian waiter dropped a tray to a cacophony of laughs and curses. The whole group craned their necks to watch, Flint being first to want the conversation back on track.

"Mandy, you were saying?"

"Oh, cranks. There's one sweet old fellow, with half-moon glasses, you can imagine the type. He calls himself a professor, although I'm not sure what of." She narrowed her eyes. "Leopold Gratz."

"Go see him, Jeff boy," Jules joked, "get that man, solve that crime."

"Make yourself useful, pay the bill, Jules," Flint responded, hooking out a note from his pocket, but not taking his eyes off Mandy.

The librarian talked more of Gratz, and of others who often came to finger manuscripts of dubious potency. Most were men, most greying and bookish. Flint walked towards UCL with Jules, thinking of what he would do once the meeting was over. There were not many Gratzes in the London phone books, and only one "Gratz, Professor L. K., Occultist".

Leopold Gratz was a self-parody, who had set his mind on an image and moulded his character around it. He lived in a basement flat

129

near Barons Court tube station underneath what he called his office. A blinking, bespectacled man in his mid fifties, he still had thick black hair and beard, but was wishing it to grey. His parlour offered a view of ankles and bicycle wheels and was decorated in antique-shop style. Its mean date was Edwardian, with trinkets tailing back into the nineteenth century and tip-toeing as far as art deco.

Gratz greeted him with gust. "It's always good to meet a fellow student of the occult arts," he said, indicating that Flint was to sit in one of the reconditioned Chesterfields.

"I'm not really an occultist, my main interest is ritual, the occult is very much a new field for me. I thought you could give me some basic pointers."

"And the British Library recommended me?" Gratz seemed a little surprised, if obviously pleased to be finally recognised as a scholar.

Flint could not play his full hand of cards immediately, so began to probe Gratz, offering tiny bits of information. From the corner of his eye, he could just catch a glimpse of a woman in an ankle-length Paisley gown who drifted into the room and out behind him, her hair tied up in a jade turban.

"*De Nigris . . . Black Book . . .* John Eastney . . . no." Gratz shook his head. "I have read all the major occult works, that one I do not know." He had a hint of Brogue about his voice. It was possible that the East European name was just another part of the veneer.

"But why should a man search for a non-existent book?"

"Perhaps he is deceived. There are many non-existent books about the occult."

To Flint, this seemed a contradiction. "Such as?"

"The *Necronomicon* is a good example. A writer of science fiction invents a book of arcane lore as a plot device. His fans take it seriously and ask where they can buy it. Now, it is published in paperback. Several versions, all different, none genuine."

Flint mulled over the thought and bought thinking-time by asking, "What precisely is your own field of interest?"

"Sceptic," he stated with a smile. "The paranormal has always fascinated me, but always disappointed me. I was once, after a fashion, a mind-reader who thought he could foretell the future."

One glance at the basement flat qualified the extent of his power.

"As you see. Now I study and write about the occult. Ghosts, witches, demons. It is a fabulous field of study but sadly lacks substance. And you, you too are a sceptic."

He did read minds, thought Flint, or rather had trained himself to judge characters. "I am investigating a cult."

"What sort of cult?" Gratz asked, his deepening interest betrayed by a twitch of his eyebrow.

"I was hoping you'd be able to tell me. I've done some regular reading, plunged through *Golden Bough* this week, but I still need some up-to-date data. How much is horror-book nonsense and how much is real?"

Gratz linked his hands across his paunch and began to twiddle his thumbs as he thought over the request.

"Where can I begin? This is a vast field. There are many forms of occult practice in the modern world. People call this the New Age, new religions, old religions, a guru for every taste."

"I'm an archaeologist. I've dabbled with traditional religions and analysed ritual in an academic sense, but I'm not familiar with the substance of pseudoscientific beliefs. I've always regarded them as dangerous nonsense, illogical, defying common sense."

"Common sense, no, it is a question of belief. Millions of ordinary people, mainly women I might add, dabble in such things as astrology or tarot cards. It is a form of belief, although most are simply finding ways of justifying their own actions. Now, that sort of person won't interest you. You want to know about people such as myself in younger days, who feel they have some hidden power or need a new mysticism in their lives. So we have ESP, mind-readers, palmists, diagnosticians," he sighed, "faith healers, dealers in herbs and homoeopathic remedies, I could give you a list a yard long."

"What about magic?"

He smiled. "Magick, with or without the 'k'. Even in this day, even in the Western world you will encounter witches, warlocks and covens."

Gratz began to go into deep detail, Flint nodding all the time and taking the occasional note to show he was paying attention.

"The purest follow Wicca, the ancient religion, what you might call white magic. Others follow a more corrupt line, black magic.

More obscure still are the true Pagans, followers of Celtic or druidic lore. Not so ancient as Wicca, but tuned to the powers of the natural world and enjoying a revival, I feel. Your cult may even be Satanists, followers of the Devil. Satanism is, of course, just an inversion, nay a perversion of the Catholic belief. Black masses are like holy masses, with words spoken backwards, inverted crucifixes . . ."

"I've seen the films." Flint weighed up the alternatives.

"Of course there are many more beliefs associated with other cultures: voodoo . . ."

"These cultists are British. Very British, folklore and maypoles, a little herblore. Potions and latin spells, moonlight masses. I can't be more precise." He thought over the strands of evidence remembered from Plant's office.

"Some modern witches' covens do mix their sources: a little true Wicca, a little druidism, a little astrology, even a dash of black magic to spice things up. They are confused, of course, but most settle down to their own rules, their own ceremonies."

"What about sex?"

Gratz raised both eyebrows. "Sex is important to some. Crowley's Golden Dawn was centred around ritual sex-magic back in the 1920s, but that sect was dominated by men. The true ancient British cults are female-dominated and female-orientated. They may involve fertility rites, but these are more than simply an excuse for perverse behaviour."

Flint now had a clear picture, he had read so much, it was time to throw in the key question. "Okay, so what part does human sacrifice play?"

Gratz frowned.

"I'm searching for a missing girl."

"Aha! *That* missing girl, Lucy Gray, stray student."

"You read the papers."

"I have followed the case, Doctor Flint. The burning museum, the disappearing curator. Fascinating, you must tell me all about it."

"But human sacrifice?" Flint pushed the point, disappointing his host.

Gratz gave a worldly sweep of an arm. "It would be highly unlikely in this day and age. Most witches are harmless, whilst serious students of the black arts are too intelligent to risk such outrageous behaviour."

"Even Satanists?"

"Especially Satanists." He flashed his eyes. "They can be cruel, obsessive people, but they live in the normal world. Eating babies and sacrificing virgins is too perverse even for the blackest cult."

"You're sure?" Was the man genuine or covering up for friends? "There's a lot of Satanist accusations in the papers . . ."

"Even if a cult were evil enough to want to sacrifice humans, it would simply be impractical. Ninety per cent of murders are solved. People cannot simply disappear these days like they could in the Middle Ages. There are many true followers of the old religion who will not even sacrifice a goat . . ."

". . . or a chicken?"

"Indeed a chicken, but as I said, there are no hard rules. Many follow the occult way simply because of the freedom it permits."

"My student vanished without trace. Let's just suppose the practitioners have totally lost touch with reality. Suppose they have become so locked up in their fantasy world they have driven themselves insane?"

"Many are in the technical sense. If to believe in magic, demons and the spirit world is to defy conventional logic, then most of what you call practitioners are, by definition, insane."

"I've met the occasional witch in my time," Flint recalled the summer solstice, "but they are all on the social fringe. Are there many people involved who might be considered sane and respectable?"

"Undoubtably. If sane and respectable people can openly worship Mohammed, Buddha or Christ, I see no reason why they cannot worship the Mother Goddess, or Odin without being ridiculed."

"But can these sane respectable people practise magic?"

"Oh yes. The foundation of magic is belief. If you believe a Hail Mary will bring absolution, it will. If you believe a curse will do you harm, it will."

Flint had recited similar lessons to his students, Lucy included. His thoughts turned directly to Lucy, Lucy plus unborn infant. He found himself tugging at his beard in thought. "If I wanted to penetrate a coven, would it be easy?"

"Almost impossible if they knew they were under investigation. They are closed and secretive. Even if they have committed no criminal offence, members face ridicule and suspicion from people of more conventional outlook."

"But I could catch them in the act?"

He nodded. "If you knew enough about them, could find their meeting places, or identify one of their members."

"I think we have some sort of sub-Celtic cult operating in the Darkewater Valley," Flint stated, "perhaps witches, less likely Satanists. Have you come into contact with anyone from that area?"

Gratz thought. "One or two, but no one who confesses to being a true practitioner of magic. I could give you a few names, if that would help."

Flint passed over a pad and for five minutes watched Gratz scribble names, cross them out and rewrite them, all the while qualifying his decisions by muttering. The list came back, with two dozen lines filled. More work for Tyrone.

"I thought I'd add everyone in that region. Sometimes coven members have to travel a fair distance."

"How many are there likely to be?"

"Well, they like to pair, but revere the number three. Three pairs of pairs is twelve. Thirteen to a coven, twelve plus one. Larger gatherings might be, say, of forty, three thirteens and one, but that would be exceptional."

"Who is the one?"

"In pure Paganism, the priestess."

"Not a high priest?"

"Possibly, but the power is vested in the woman. A priestess will normally officiate, but a priest may also be present. Perhaps a young girl will play the role of The Maiden, standing in for The Goddess. One day, she may become the priestess herself."

An eerie creeping sensation made Flint shudder on impulse. He knew the perfect girl for the role of The Maiden.

"There are other titles, other roles depending on the strand the coven follows." Once Gratz was in full narrational flow, he was unstoppable. As he talked on, a cup of herbal tea was served by the woman in the green turban, who never spoke and was never introduced.

"So how do I catch them?" Flint asked when the tea cups had been emptied.

"Identify their members, or identify their meeting place. If they are a large coven and feel secure they may chance to meet at an ancient site."

"A megalith?"

"Yes, it always strikes me as being terribly melodramatic, but I suppose that fact helps the magic. Now, the next major Celtic festival is Lugsanadh, which is August Eve. As it is the festival of gathering, one might expect them to assemble in an agricultural region."

"It's a sort of harvest festival," Flint stated.

"Precisely. It's *the* harvest festival. The C of E have simply added a few hymns."

On the far wall, a dark oak bookshelf carried a range of hardbacks which would have cheered Piers Plant's heart. Gratz picked off one book and passed it to Flint with a degree of pride. Published by an obscure press, *Occult and the Wise* by Professor L. K. Gratz retailed at six pounds ninety-five pence. Plenty of copies, at least a dozen, peeked from a Victorian dresser and Jeffrey Flint thought it politic to buy one before he left.

"Six ninety-five?" He handed over seven pounds.

Gratz kept the five pence and came to the door to see Flint out, "If you find out anything, I'm always keen to know."

"I imagine you'll read it in the papers."

"But what do the papers know?" He had a twinkle in his eye.

Flint halted and turned to him. "You do believe, don't you?"

"Believe?"

"All this talk of being a sceptic; you believe there is something behind all this nonsense."

"I think we all need to believe there is something else, something beyond our comprehension."

"But I'm a scientist. I believe everything can be deduced given the evidence."

"Yes, I thought you were very calm," Gratz's voice had acquired a strange tinge, "you show no fear."

What was Gratz getting at? "I don't understand," said Flint.

"Are you familiar with the concept of a guardian angel? Well, the opposite can exist too. Beware the Horned Man, Doctor Flint."

"Now you're being mystical."

"No, practical. I am a sceptic, I investigate, I expose, but I know when to keep my head clear of danger. These people you are investigating could not do the things you describe and expect to get away with them. They may be more than just a handful of harmless Earth-worshippers. They may be dangerous and you may not know how dangerous until it is too late. Just be careful, Doctor Flint."

Chapter 13

Kingshaven Council and the County Museums Service held a joint enquiry into the museum fire, and both Flint and Tyrone were asked to attend. Chief Inspector Douglas was satisfied that arson was the cause and Piers Plant MA, "Acting under motives not ascertained", was the suspect.

The four almost trapped in the museum were questioned closely and suspiciously. If their motives for the museum raid sounded perverse, the antics in the ethno gallery were almost farcical. Dumb awe greeted Flint's description of how they had been locked in.

Jeffrey Flint was acquainted with one of the panel, the earring-decked, crop-haired Sebastian Leigh, who had risen to a senior position in the County Museums Service. Once the panel had wound up its business, Leigh was persuaded to take a quiet cup of tea in Auntie Joyce's Tea Shoppe, and over a buttered scone was induced to talk. Poor George Carlyle was being disciplined for infringing various rules on the night of the fire and Flint wanted to plead his case. Vikki had left to cover a dispute at the container port, but conversation inevitably turned to Lucy.

"I assume you know that she applied for a job with us," Leigh said, his public-school manner always grating against Flint's leveller instincts. "Piers wanted an assistant, to replace the one who resigned when he couldn't take it."

"When would that be?"

"A good two years ago. As I was saying, when this guy resigned, the post was frozen because of the cuts. Piers whinged about needing a replacement, but the answer was always no way. When Lucy wrote and asked for a job, I knew they were involved, so it stank too much of nepotism to me. When the post is unfrozen and we can appoint an assistant curator for that fleabag museum, we will do it properly and advertise. Even then, they need a botanist or a zoologist not another folklore freak. We made the same mistake before, when old Mr Ellsworthy demanded to have Piers as his assistant. Ellsworthy was raving mad too."

Of course, Flint realised, that secret room of Plant's had been there for decades, he had inherited it rather than built it himself. This saga obviously tailed back deep into the past.

Leigh went on to cover old ground, with tales of Plant's macabre obsessions and Lucy's eccentric behaviour. "I wondered what was going on between the two of them, and now we know."

"We do?"

"It's obvious," he sneered. "She was always a bit of a tart," Leigh said, hands itching over his tobacco pouch.

"You used to say you liked buxom blondes," Flint said, hiding his anger at the denegration of his student.

Leigh twitched at the subtle riposte. "I met Lucy at a few Dark Ants meetings. She was always the most beautiful person in the room, so full of herself and the way the old men would drool after her. She was an arrogant snob." He glanced at his wristwatch. "Look, I've another appointment, can I leave this with you?"

"Sure, we're off to do some megalith-bashing."

"Great." Leigh rose to leave. "Good to see you, Jeff."

Tyrone watched the receding back, then rolled up his nose. "What a turd, Lucy was never that bad."

Flint examined the bill. "I suppose it depends how much you fancied her and how many times she told you to get knotted. She was a funny girl, our Lucy."

"Everyone I've met says your chum Sebastian is gay."

"Sometimes he is, but that doesn't make him a bad person."

Flint ignored the latest demonstration of Tyrone's intolerance. He paid the bill with Barbara's money, then student and lecturer walked back through the old centre of Kingshaven, intent on looking into a couple of antiquarian bookshops on the way to the car. Down a narrow passageway opposite the Tea Shoppe lay a green-fronted health food shop. Flint went inside, Tyrone made some joke about rabbit food and stayed outside.

Odours pierced his nostrils as the door was pushed open. Joss-sticks burned in a wire frame, whilst pot-pourri baskets lay open to catch the tourists. At floor level were ranged tubs of wholefood and sacks of pulses. Above where the owner sat knitting a winter-weight Arran, a row of sweetie jars had been recycled to hold herbal teas. The music was ethereal and the atmosphere mellow. The platinum-haired woman turned a creased smile his way.

"Can I help?"

Flint bounced on his ankles, surveying the wares. "An ounce of Breakfast Apple, please."

As he watched her take down the jar and measure out the tea, he remembered something that Vikki had said about teas. She had come here asking questions.

"Would you know the museum curator?" Flint asked on impulse.

Something in his suspicious nature expected a flat denial; instead, he was presented with a packet of tea.

"Mr Plant, yes, he used to come in here all the time."

"Seen him lately?" Just a hint of apology was behind his enquiry.

"Not since his disappearance." She gave half a laugh. "Are you looking for him too?"

"In a way."

"I'm sure he'll turn up."

"Excuse me, I've been watching too many black and white thrillers lately, I'm expecting to find clues everywhere."

"You're the man in the paper, the sociologist." Her pale green eyes met his.

"Archaeologist."

"It must be fascinating."

"Sometimes."

"Eighty pence."

The pound slid across the counter. Flint fought against *déjà vu*, but he was sure he recognised the woman. "Excuse me, but were you at Glastonbury?"

"Yes I was," she raised a finger, "and so were you, at the poetry reading."

"R. Temple-Brooke."

"Did you enjoy it?" she asked.

Flint found he liked something in her wholesome warmth. Perhaps it was the alluring odours of the shop or the lilting tones of the New Age pipes playing from a quiet cassette. "It was different. I was there chasing curators, it's become an obsession of mine."

She frowned. "Obsessions burn the heart, you are clearly not a born policeman."

139

"No, I certainly am not."

"So where are you digging?" Her face was still stocked with polite shopkeeper interest, she folded her arms and tilted her head to listen.

"Nowhere. No, that's not true, Hertfordshire, next month."

"St Albans?"

"No, Burkes Warren. It's a Roman villa."

"I've got friends up there, I might just pop by. I always wanted to see a real dig, it must be totally absorbing."

"Please come, everyone and his grandmother normally drops in to see us, stops us getting lonely up there. Bring some tea."

"I will."

"Better go, I'm off to stomp around a few megaliths. More clue-hunting, I'm afraid. Thanks for the tea."

"Come again."

He left the perfumed air and went back on to the cobbled street. Flint felt better for the interlude. Red herrings and wild hunches were turning him into an enquiry nut.

Covering the docks dispute put Vikki in a bad mood. Why were union leaders so thick? Why were trained lizards always employed as management spokesmen? She pondered what she could make of the fire inquest, and decided it held no scope beyond bland repetition of the facts. A little grin came to her face, thinking her colleagues would welcome something bland. Her barrage of shock headlines had brought overnight prominence not welcomed by the time-serving veterans. She had even been accused of manufacturing news.

In ill temper, she worked into the evening preparing a background piece on that dispute. Self-catering demanded too much organisation, so she ate supper in the reporters' local, fending off Virile Vince whilst working through gammon and chips. Heading home, happy at last to be alone, she parked her Metro, cursing the owner of the blue van who always parked in front of her nineteen-thirties semi. Each house was much like the next, built before cars for the masses were thought of, so built without space for drives.

Her back door lay beyond a brick archway. Vikki opened the black iron gate and a fingerful of rust again reminded her it needed repainting. A fingertip ran around the key ring looking for the Yale as she went under the brick arch. It was dark, she should really get a porch light.

She was falling, she threw out her hands, then for a moment, the world blinked out of existance. Her head, something had struck her head!

And again, Vikki felt her elbow strike concrete, the impact overwhelmed by the pain bursting into the back of her head. Dizzy blood clouded her sight. Hot and heavy hands clasped her ears and hair and drove her face down into the concrete. For a moment, Vikki lost contact with reality, all she could hear was a coarse voice snapping out threats and warnings.

The voice thumped around her head as she rolled on to her back and focused on a slit of dark blue sky. Feet echoed away down the street. Dazed and sobbing she sat up slowly, feeling for parts to rub and to mop. Her handbag had gone, at least it had been robbery, not rape. Keys dug into her hand.

Vikki opened her door and slammed it behind her. Safe, for a few moments. Her pulse stayed high, blood trickled down her cheek and mixed with the tears. She spat out two dozen choice obscenities and snapped on the light. Her mind searched for culprits, the voice had been gruff, common, she remembered the smell of tobacco, sweat and drink. Had she offended a docker? It could not have been the effete Piers Plant.

She shivered with shock, trying to remember where her telephone was. She'd call an ambulance and get herself checked over. Then, whilst waiting, she would go to the bathroom and would wash away the pain. When she felt safe, clean and warm again, when her thoughts were her own again, then she would phone Chief Inspector Douglas and give him a hard time.

Harriet's Stone, Devil's Ring, South Barn A, White Ring, Yarleys, Bramton West. Jeffrey Flint was dreaming of megaliths, a dozen of them, cold and proud in hissing summer lawns. Feet clumped above his head, feet on the deck of the houseboat? Flint yawned and rolled over. He was alone and momentarily thought of Chrissie Collings. It had never really worked, not from the start. He'd have that inscribed on his tombstone. No alternative remained but for him to regress back to the bad old days of chat-up lines and one-night stands. Bachelor-land could be a gross place.

He turned his watch the right side up. Seven thirty, no lectures, much too early to stir. The boat moved almost imperceptibly, as if it were suddenly lighter. His pulse rate advanced just a notch and he looked out of a porthole to riverside. Tourist boats sometimes chose him as a mooring point, but not that morning. Irritated, he put on his glasses, then slipped out of bed and covered his naked body with an old blue towelling robe. Barefoot, he padded through the galley to the door.

Outside, early morning at the Lock was brilliant, blue and quiet. There was the ever-present London traffic hum, but for a few moments, Flint stood on the deck, enjoying for once seeing the world at that side of nine a.m.

His mail box lid was part closed, its mouth choked by a packet too large to fit. It was too early for the postman, Flint realised as he cradled the brown paper parcel. He examined it in detail, the wrapping reminding him of a certain chicken's head. Yes, the parcel had been posted in south London.

He checked the quayside and the other boats. One girl was cycling past, but no one else was about. He went back into the cabin, and set the parcel down on the bed. Leaving it whilst he pondered the subject, he lit the gas stove and put a kettle on.

"Right, what nasties have we here?" he murmured, then thought of the police. Would they be interested? Douglas might, just possibly, if he hit him over the head a few times with it.

The parcel was the size of a shoe-box, wrapped in brown paper and weighed about a kilo. It had a generous allowance of stamps, surely first class, but was post-marked five days before. Footsteps on the deck came to mind. Could it have been an early, enthusiastic postman making up for the delayed parcel, or someone more sinister? If the latter, why waste money on stamps?

His address had been typed on to an adhesive label much too large for its purpose. He began to pick it off and within moments, had an answer. Just beneath the label, an area of the brown paper had been cut away. The package had been posted, delivered, reopened, the address removed and his address added. The bizarre act only made sense if the parcel now contained something that wouldn't travel through the post, but had to appear to have done just that, so he would open it. He sniffed, expecting offal or excrement, but a tart smell came to his nose. Mothballs, napthalene, firelighters came to mind.

"Not on your life, mate!" Flint backed away from the parcel,

142

unsure what to do. He could take it on to the quayside, throw it in the water, or he could leave it on the bed and phone the police.

Perhaps ten minutes had passed since he first awoke. The kettle emitted a high whistle and he stepped into the galley to silence it. He had decided to take the package on to the quayside, then call the police. Moving back into the cabin, he reached for the parcel, then stopped as the outer paper began to turn a deeper shade of brown. Mesmerised, he watched as brown turned to black, then to blue. The package burst into flame.

An infernal curse, a hex on his meddling! Romantic terror struck him as an incendiary bomb, the anarchists' plaything, burned into the sheets. After a few seconds' confusion, he grabbed at them, dragging them to the door, but scattering the contents of the spitting package over the houseboat floor. He jerked the burning bedclothes out of the door and yelled a pathetic "Fire!" as he turned them overboard.

Back inside, a curtain was ablaze and naptha cubes were fizzing all over the cabin. He grabbed the kettle and threw boiling water at the nearest threats, then remembered the extinguisher.

As he scrabbled beneath the sink, smoke reached his nostrils. Out came the extinguisher, off came the cap, then he paused to cough away the smoke. Out came the pin, up went the nozzle. Plywood was beginning to peel around the burning curtain as he took aim at the seat of the fire. A cloud of snowflakes burst into the room with a roar, then Flint backed out of the galley door.

A vest-clad neighbour was staring at him with mouth agape.

"Fire!" Flint repeated, then chanced to put his head back into the cabin. Taking a few lungfuls of air, he made a sortie into the galley, exhausting the extinguisher towards what would have been the root of the fire. Smoke continued to pour past him as he retreated for air. Then he remembered the propane cylinders beneath the gas stove and retreated to the shore. For the second time in a month, a group of onlookers gathered to watch Jeffrey Flint rub smoke from his eyes.

His reflex action had saved the houseboat. Flint sat on a bollard in his bath wrap and a pair of borrowed trousers watching firemen finish off the work he had begun. After two hours, he was admitted back on board to see what remained of his possessions. His bedding was gone, his clothes in the under-bed locker, a couple of posters

143

and a clock were lost. Most of his books were in his office, his CD player was safe, but his Dylan LPs had been splashed with sooty water. The taped casettes of the Bogart season seemed to be okay, the television and video had been flooded, but both had needed fixing. His thoughts turned to hassle with insurance companies and the landlord.

At the local police station, a keen constable took delight in explaining how easy it was to make a fire bomb with a drop of acid, some firelighters and a condom. No magic was involved. Pity, thought Flint, he almost wanted to believe in spells, so he could weave a circle of protection or buy a talisman to ward off the evil eye. No, these devils operated in the real world with tangible weapons. He was mortal and in danger.

That afternoon, Flint moved in with Jules and Sasha whilst his life emerged from the ashes. Jules came back from college with the message to ring Vikki immediately. He gave a heavy sigh, then did just that.

"Jeff, where have you been all day?" She sounded very annoyed.

"Sweeping up. Our pyromaniac had a second go at me." He went on to relate the drama of the dawn in his terse, documentary style. "It's another warning, Vikki, close this time."

"Well, I spent the day at the hospital," she said, as if firebombs were trivial devices.

"You okay?"

"No, I had my skull X-rayed and they wrapped so many bandages round me I look like one of your mummies." It was Vikki's turn to spin a yarn, one full of violence and terror.

Flint felt sickened as he listened. Already he knew he would have to abandon his houseboat and find somewhere anonymous to live, but the assault on Vikki was something else. Something innate and macho urged him to protect her.

"Vikki, you've got to take care."

"Why just me? It sounds like we both had a brush with death last night."

"Not death, Vikki. If someone really wanted to kill me, he would have come along at 3 a.m., doused the whole boat in petrol and given me a Viking funeral. My arsonist wanted me to escape with a warning."

"He didn't seem to be bothered in the museum."

144

"Not Plant, we're talking someone else. Lots of someones, probably, we've stirred up a whole bunch of lunatics. One has bombed my boat, another beat you up – or paid some thug to do it."

Vikki sighed heavily. "I'd better send Vince up to get photographs of your boat."

"No no. Not this time. Every time you do a story, someone likes it so much they try to kill me."

"Only once, you're exaggerating!"

"Once is enough, Vikki, I'm not a cat. And neither are you. I want to find Lucy, not join her."

"Right! Right, so we'd better find these lunatics of yours before they get us again."

"Vikki, this was a warning . . ." he began.

"Look, stop playing the pacifist liberal, we've got to nail these bastards. Now you've done all the research, you've read the books and met the people, you're the one with the computer full of information, where do we look to find them?"

"We have to leave this to the police now."

"Douglas is a useless twat," Vikki snapped. "I'm seeing him tomorrow, what do I tell him he's got to do?"

After a pause to reconsider, Flint reluctantly said, "I do have a plan."

To be truthful, Tyrone had a plan, one which his supervisor regarded with scepticism. The next morning, Flint cycled into college via the insurance office and picked up a claim form. It was late by the time he strode into the postgraduate room, which reeked of stale coffee and was empty of all but one researcher. A large chart hung from the wall, presenting a two-dimensional maze of facts. It was a worked-up version of the first diagram Flint had sketched in his notepad. Now the chart was a metre wide by two long, composed of recycled computer print-outs Sellotaped together. With Tyrone watching, he added the latest details with a felt pen, Tippexing out mistaken hunches.

One word lay in the centre of the diagram: LUCY. From this, lines radiated to dozens of inter-connected boxes, mapping out the problem. Somewhere, deeply buried under an overburden of trivia, lay the solution.

Tyrone drew attention to the new line connecting LUCY and

PLANT, which converged on a box reading BABY. Barbara's confidence could only be carried so far.

"You're sure he's the father?"

"No," the pen squeaked to a pause, "but I'm fresh out of other candidates. He seems the logical choice. He may have been hopeless in normal life, but then Lucy wasn't interested in normal life."

"So, she gets pregnant during some orgy and he bumps her off," Tyrone stated, "or am I being simplistic?"

"Guesses, all we're doing is guessing." Flint gazed at the chart. "Too much white paper up there. Needs filling in. Our problem is, we're trying to out-think a madman, put rational explanations behind irrational acts." Flint sucked his pen. "The past holds the keys to the present."

"That's a good old archaeological cliché, but with respect, Doc, I'm only here another week."

"Traitor!"

"Sorry, but it's all booked."

"Tell me of this crazy plan of yours."

"No self-respecting witch would miss Lugsanadh, so we've got two options. Plan A is to find where they meet and stake it out. Plan B is that we take that list of people Gratz gave you, and try to follow them to where the coven meets."

"Okay, I'm game for plan A, I feel daft enough to try anything."

Tyrone's plan went ahead immediately. He scoured the Ordnance Survey maps in tandem with archaeological journals to identify prominent Celtic or pre-Celtic sites. Vikki was officially on sick leave but spent it in Kingshaven library running through back numbers of her own newspaper to check reports of unusual behaviour on past Pagan festivals. Adding both data sets together produced a distribution map, which was also pinned on the wall of the postgraduate room. A dozen sites of definite occult interest were identified immediately, plus another two dozen likely candidates. It was only a case of taking a gamble and guessing: in no way could they cover them all.

As time began to run short, Vikki went to tackle Chief Inspector Douglas once more. Her eyes puffy behind the sunshades, she trailed along in his smokestream as he paced down the corridor of the Kingshaven station.

"You didn't see him, you've no idea who it was, so what can we do?" Douglas gave most of his attention to a heap of typed papers.

Vikki's mood was determined. "You could start taking this case seriously."

Douglas stopped outside his office, knowing that if he let the reporter inside, all hope of catching up on the paperwork was gone for the morning.

"I am taking it seriously! We found a man who saw Piers Plant's car out near a cottage on the night of the fire. That same cottage was rented in January by a man calling himself Johnson, but who answers the description of Plant. Satisfied? We are not flat-footed idiots!"

"Where's the cottage?"

He gave the location, which was oddly close to Jeffrey Flint's favourite cluster of megaliths.

"So when do you arrest Piers Plant?"

"Tell me how and I will," he said earnestly. "Give me half a clue what is going on and perhaps we can even find dear Lucy Gray."

"Lugsanadh," Vikki said by way of response.

"What?"

"The prof, you know, Doctor Flint. He told me that the last evening in July is some big Pagan festival."

"So he's still chasing witches?"

"He's worked out where they meet."

The bland cynicism of the policeman's face was replaced by wary interest.

"Where?"

Vikki showed him a list scribbled on her notepad. "These are all stone circles; that's where these people get together. Some of them are near this cottage."

Douglas looked deeply troubled. "The Witchcraft Act was repealed in the nineteen fifties."

"But don't you see, Piers Plant will come out of hiding to go to the ceremony."

"What makes you so sure?"

"It would be like the Pope skipping Easter."

147

Douglas shook his head and looked at the list. Vikki continued to bob in front of him, demanding attention.

"Even if he isn't there, his friends will be. They might know where he is, or what happened to Lucy Gray."

"Lucy Gray." Douglas muttered as if the name haunted him. "See, there are twenty places on this list, are you proposing I put all these sites under surveillance?"

"Yes."

"Forget it."

Vikki dodged into the doorway as the policeman tried to enter his office.

"One car. It can drive around and record number plates. All we need is one number plate, one name and address, then we have them."

Douglas looked upon her with the look a weary uncle bestows on an unruly niece. "One car?"

Rowan regretted the loss of the cottage. It was in the columns of the infernal local newspaper that she read of the one sighting of the fugitive Piers Plant. The cottage had been handy for so many sites, a refuge for cold winter nights, somewhere to rendezvous and change from the camouflage of twentieth-century dress. She thought back to when the girl had lain in the bedroom, shivering and unaided. Alternative lifetimes passed through her mind, what should have been said, what should have been done.

She laid aside her knitting to slip on a cassette of medieval rounds, then sat back in her chair and began to hum to soothe her nerves. No doubts, no regrets, everything was as it was meant to be. But the archaeologist was becoming a nuisance. Unhappy accidents seemed not to daunt him, he should be left to defeat himself. It could be arranged, but it would be an unpleasant, final solution to all her cares.

Her thoughts were drawn towards Oak, dearest Oak as she called him. A pathetic, trembling fugitive who threatened everything. He was coming to Lugsanadh, he said. She knew the risk that entailed, she knew the threat his dwindling sanity posed. How would he behave at the ceremony? Would he cause a scene? She would have to tell him of the change of plan – the official change of plan. There would be more sadness and more deceit; the plot grew deeper and thicker.

Chapter 14

As August eve approached, Plan A took on more credible form. Jeffrey Flint seemed in a buoyant mood when Tyrone and he met Vikki at Durring railway station with their maps and camera cases. She walked up to them with a black cardigan tied around her neck and a smile breaking through the fading bruises. Her tight boutique jeans were tucked into short yellow wellies, making her as country as she would ever be.

Flint wore a digger's ensemble of shapeless jeans and lifeless sweater. Tyrone came prepared for action in army surplus pullover and camouflage trousers. The student shared his supervisor's bouncy optimism, Plan A was flawless, everything had been worked out in the finest detail and the logic was impeccable. Piers Plant had been researching the Darkewater megaliths, of which three had dramatic settings: Harriet's Stone, South Barn and Devil's Ring. All were in the farming belt of the valley, all sat in or overlooking cornfields. All were within five miles of the cottage Plant had once rented.

Tyrone sat in the back of the Metro, thinking a little about Italy, mostly about the twisting trail of Lucy Gray. In the front, Vikki was small-talking her way to the sites with her London accent and her hand-waving. If she watched the road, she could drive faster, he thought. Flint seemed happy too, chattering away without making any obvious chat-up lines. It was a pity if Chrissie had dumped him, but Tyrone had never liked her left-wing affectations. You wouldn't get Chrissie out in the fields on midnight witch-hunts. Tyrone felt for the big multi-bladed Swiss Army knife in his thigh pocket, then thought of Pagans, weird and violent. Bunny and his tribe of drunks should have been asked along, they were always game for a brawl.

Just before sunset, Vikki parked her car in the yard of a derelict farm, leaving a walk of just over a mile to Harriet's Stone. Passing no one, they trudged the footpath at the edge of the cornfields. It was just a little far from civilisation to attract dog-walkers and teenage lovers, just far enough to attract others, perhaps. As they came to a crest, the sun set gloriously over the hills on the far side of the valley, warming Tyrone's heart at the sight. Then it was chilled by the stone. Tall, alone, dominating, the single finger of granite poked from the wheat in the centre of a field. The finger of a mythical witch, Harriet, doomed to spend eternity holding up the fabric of the Earth. If there was any magical site in the valley, it was here.

Low sunlight cast shadows across the field. Long grass stood about the base of the stone, and around this, another circle within the corn fell into dusk first, giving the illusion of a depression. This was the place, he was certain.

Flint suddenly pointed. "My God, look!"

Vikki was startled by the outburst.

"Look at the shadow in the corn around the stone, the way the light hits it! The corn is shorter there."

"So?" Vikki asked.

"It's like a cropmark." Tyrone realised what was being suggested.

"Imagine a whole troupe of people trampling around the stone in the spring, bruising the corn shoots, compacting the earth so they grow less well."

"Really?" Vikki screwed up her nose.

"This is the place, look, we've got to hide."

Tyrone had never seen such animated excitement in the lecturer, not even in the wildest debate about racism or imperialism or any other -ism. A beech hanger lay some four hundred yards to the south and offered cover. Jogging to its edge, the trio went to ground amongst the bracken. Over the fields they would be able to hear songs and chants, or, at least, motor cars delivering the modern witches to their sabbat. A cautious advance at midnight might reveal fires and dancing figures under the stars. Flint lay down, panting with the exertion. Tyrone flopped on to his back and pulled a Mars Bar from another pocket.

Time has an immensity only obvious when nothing exists to fill it. Flint sat, poised on the edge of excitement for three hours. Vikki kept whispering things of no consequence. Tyrone looked up at the trees, thinking of all the Tolkien he had read in the past fortnight.

A breeze rustled the branches and bats skitted about against the darkening sky. Yes, he could see how someone impressionable could start to see fact and fantasy merge.

"Do you know anything about trees, Doc?"

"No."

"Nor me. Vikki?"

"No."

"We wouldn't make very good Pagans, they're into trees in a big way. Do you know they have to apologise when they cut timber?"

"Really?" asked Vikki, hardly sounding fascinated.

"And they ask permission before picking an apple."

"You're making this up."

"It's all in the books," Tyrone said, then lost enthusiasm to talk.

Bright yellow-white, Jupiter made its debut, then Vega, high and winking, was the first true star to grace the night. His throat dried, senses tensed for action. Nameless things scuttled about in the undergrowth. Flint shuffled his legs. Vikki would whisper "What's that?" whenever an owl hooted, something scurried through the undergrowth, or a distant dog barked. Flint gave way to asking him the time at increasingly short intervals.

"What time is it?" he asked.

The luminous dial of Tyrone's watch glowed in the night. "Ten to twelve."

"It's bloody damp lying down here," Vikki whispered.

A motorbike grumbled along the nearest lane.

"You'd better be right about this, Jeffrey Flint," she warned. "Oh God, I'm all wet, my leg's all wet."

"Shh!" Flint urged. "What time is it?"

"Oh, sod this." Vikki stood up and began to probe her way forward. Tyrone rose and followed. Flint came last, hissing warnings. They advanced cautiously to the edge of the field and beheld the stone, still silent, still alone in the moonlight. Magic was there, reaching out, calling, but no one came to answer it.

The moon blinked out as cloud rolled in above. Unable to see, they squatted to await the passage of the cloud.

"Car!" Tyrone warned.

At an instant, the three were swishing back through the corn. Corn stalks tugged at Tyrone's ankles, he began to bound to avoid

151

tripping, but Flint gave a yelp then fell noisily. Vikki used the F-word, then she too went sprawling into the dark. Tyrone stopped and waded back to help her up. Flint crawled towards them, then all three dropped to the ground.

A light could be seen dodging around in the dark. Tyrone could hear the others breathing close, he groped again for that knife and teased open a blade with one hand. The torch came nearer, two figures could just be seen silhouetted against the night sky.

"Nothin' here, Phil."

The policespeak tones were clear as the voices muttered together. Flint stood up and made himself known.

"Doctor Flint, is it?" one said. "We've been round your list and there's nothing, nothing at all."

"Which ones?" Flint asked, clearly in doubt.

"All of them, all your list. No witches or Satanic masses, not even any boy scout camps."

The two groups came together.

"But are you sure you've been to them all?"

"Read him the list, Phil," the voice without a face was irritated.

"No, it's all right." Flint sounded suddenly subdued.

"So we're off back into town now, sir. To make our report," the last words were barbed.

"Fine."

"Mind how you go," the policeman said.

"Don't meet any bogeymen," the other added under his breath.

The police left them in silence. The moon did not reappear and as they stumbled through the corn towards the Metro, a fine rain began to fall.

"Twat," muttered Vikki under her breath.

"What?" asked Flint after a few moments.

"Twat," she repeated, "you, dragging me all the way out here to catch pneumonia."

"I didn't force you!" He sounded hurt.

"Don't say anything, just don't say a word," Vikki snapped.

Tyrone coughed as Flint dropped back to his side. "So tell me, Tyrone, who was the genius who composed Plan A?"

Lugsanadh was a night to be forgotten. Tyrone and Flint stayed the night at Vikki's house, then left in the morning, with Vikki's temper still as black and brittle as her toast. After the farce at the stone, Flint would not see Tyrone again for six weeks, and envied him the carefree jaunt to Italy. More, he envied his ability to shut off any emotional or moral involvement without notice. Flint made a resolve to make the summer vacation pay, to stop brooding over his ill-fated love life, to achieve things on his excavation and to make progress with the third-century paper.

Once back in his office, he took down Lucy's photograph and removed all the wall-mounted evidence into box files. The desk had its annual clearance, then with satisfaction, he unrolled a plan of the Burkes Warren villa upon its clutter-free surface. It was time to think about archaeology again. Whole days of bliss followed, in which no students demanded his attention, no meetings disrupted research, librarians were smiling and co-operative and even the third century began to make sense at last. Sasha had flown back to do some fieldwork in Turkey, allowing Flint to take over the cooking for the bachelor flat whilst Jules paid attention to the wine list. Stuart Shapstone, the site supervisor for Flint's excavation, stayed for a few days and they ran through the logistics of spades, buckets, finds trays and tea urns. Life was looking good. Then the call came through from Vikki.

"Hello Doc, it's me, sorry I called you a twat the other night."

He gave her a moment's distant contemplation. "That's okay, people call me a twat all the time."

"So you'll forgive me? Just this once? Well, you had the right idea, but chose the wrong spot."

Was his mind going dim or what? Wheels clicked, then he issued an exclamation of delight. "What?"

"My editor wasn't happy when he found out I'd spent my sick leave chasing your daft ideas. He said we would have been better off covering the illegal rave at Caesars Camp."

Caesars Camp. Flint knew the name vaguely, it had sat at the bottom end of Tyrone's list of Pagan sites. Grey cells started to work on the possibilities.

"There's this couple, right? They retired from London, he was something in the City, but they bought a converted farm close to this Caesars Camp. It happens all the time these days. Anyway, they complained to the police that a pretty rowdy party was going on."

153

"August eve?"

"While we were freezing our bottoms off, there was a party on the opposite side of the valley. Anyway, the police did nothing, so this snooty couple complains in all directions. So I rang them next day to get a story. They didn't want to talk about it, said I was to forget it. They said they heard just a few cars, but raves have thousands of people, hundreds of cars and loud music, so I thinks, midnight mass."

Flint weighed up the evidence.

"Am I smart or am I smart?" Vikki demanded.

"Brilliant."

"After these old fogies kicked up a stink, someone must have leaned on them, put them in their place and told them what living in the country really meant. This is one for you, Prof."

"Look, Vikki, can you hold on a second?"

His arm swept the desk clear of archaeology and the O.S. map of the Darkewater Valley took its place. Caesars Camp was a hill fort, Iron Age, probably nothing to do with Caesar. It was a wooded hill, guarding a spine of high ground along the valley's northern wall a good fifteen miles from Harriet's Stone and about as far away from the Darkewater megaliths as one could get without leaving the county.

A muffled voice complained from the telephone. He picked it up, pacified the excitable reporter, then arranged to meet her at four that afternoon.

Before he left Central College, Flint had found all the published references to the fort, which had been excavated twice in the first half of the century. Photocopied plans, sections and grainy photographs were stuffed into his briefcase by the time British Rail made more money at Barbara's expense, shaking him down to Durring.

Vikki bounded up to him and pecked him on the cheek, taking his arm whilst he was still startled. "This is my daft idea now, if I'm wrong, we're quits, okay?"

"Okay."

Once again he was captive to Vikki's driving habits as she dodged out of Durring just before the evening rush. The summer continued to be glorious, it was the sort of summer Flint's grandmother always could remember, it was the summer we didn't have any more.

They crossed the Darkewater at Twinbridge. Flint had picked

up an obscure treatise of very peculiar folktales about the valley. One thing it had taught him was that odd moonlight activities had a long tradition in the farming community.

"I spoke to them newcomers again," Vikki said as she drove along the lanes. "But they said all they wanted was peace and quiet."

Peace and quiet. This part of the valley carried an ancient charm: cornfields being harvested, green spinneys bursting from their midst to throw a colour contrast across the golden landscape. Deep in rural England, with poppies in the hedgerows and kestrels hovering overhead, the window was down and Flint's arm trailed out into the slipstream. Warm, wheat-rich air blew in, reminding him of one of whatsit-Temple-whatsit's poems. The thought was anarchic, but deliciously seductive.

Caesars Camp was invisible from a distance and invisible from close-to, a fortress created by only slight modifications of the topography. One ditch encircled the hill, and within it, the upcast earth formed a rampart. All this lay screened by birch, beech, oak and bracken and was reached from a sunken lane that cut through its lower slopes. The Metro bumped upwards over stones and potholes, then the slope began to lessen. A layman could pass within the ancient stronghold almost without noticing. Flint glimpsed just a trace of the ditch-and-bank system as they passed through the gateway. Then the trees ended abruptly.

The centre of the fort was a flat, oval field of ten acres, with a coppice growing in one corner. Over to the left lay a low mound, according to the records possibly pre-dating the fort itself.

"Is this it?" Vikki asked. "Where do I go? It's huge, and my gearbox is about to fall out."

Flint told her to stop anywhere she liked. The car was abandoned, heeled to one side on the rutted track's end and Flint took a few things from his satchel before they walked towards the mound.

"It's not much of a fort." Vikki turned and walked backwards, shielding her eyes to see whether she was missing anything.

"It's too big to see," the archaeologist commented, "you only get the true effect of these places from the air."

"Where are the walls?"

"It never had any, it's not really a fortress, it's more a refuge. The local tribesmen would have brought their families and

155

cattle here in times of trouble. Iron Age warfare didn't include sieges."

An evening breeze ruffled two T-shirts as their owners moved into the open. His, tight and white, bore the Radio Caroline logo, hers hung baggy around her slender frame. Over the suggestion of a left breast was emblazoned a designer label. He found something alluring in her fragile, schoolgirl figure. His eyes came away, back to archaeology, a good passion-killer.

"Of course, the Romans spoiled all the fun, brought up the siege engines, hopped over the bank and killed anyone they took a dislike to. Methodical people, the Romans."

Vikki looked around, turning up her nose at the idea of mass slaughter. Flint had meanwhile spotted something.

"Look at this," he went down on his knees, "see the flattened grass, all about this mound?"

Two days of heat had punished the bruised stems, the worn grass browned under the sun.

"Just like the other place?" she asked. "They dance around this little hill, what is it anyway?"

"A tumulus, burial mound, late Bronze Age. All the goodies were robbed centuries ago."

She took out her notepad. "Right, you're going to have to tell me about this hill again, I need all the facts so I get it right."

"Later . . ." he was walking around, looking for clues, "it's a long and boring story."

A circular burnt patch had been neatly scraped of debris.

"This is new." He bent down and put a hand to it. "Anyone circling this mound would have scuffed this ash into the grass."

The grass contained wind-blown wood ash and charcoal, not crushed by prancing feet. Over towards the trees was a suggestion of a track betrayed by lightly crushed grass and the odd dash of ash. It happened on site, people never carried buckets without a little dribble of soil betraying them.

Like a Mohican he was on the trail of spillage, across a chicken-wire fence and into trees. Here, the bracken was crisp and gave away the slightest disturbance. Vikki followed slowly, asking him questions which he hardly heard. He told her what to look for and in ten minutes she had found a patch of newly broken earth. From the rear pocket of his jeans, Flint plucked a trowel.

"Be prepared!"

156

Her surprise was met with a flourish of his trusted digging tool.

"Pointing trowel, four inch, cast blade and tang, work-hardened steel. Never leave home without one."

He began to scrape away at the soil. Once four inches, his trowel had been reduced to three, with a useful curve worn into each edge.

"Standard issue posing equipment for veteran site-wise archaeologists and the best all-purpose implement known to man." Flint chattered as he dug, totally within his element, swapping the tool from hand to hand, flicking away the soil with forensic care.

"You can dig with it, build walls, screw screws, peg section lines, knock in nails, cut cake and stir tea."

He glanced up at Vikki. The reporter seemed in a trance, standing with arms across her waist, face set in amused wonder. Five minutes saw the topsoil removed, revealing a patch of dispersed ash and charred wood. It still held an imagined whiff of warmth. The trowel point flicked upward to pick out a bone.

"Is that human?" Vikki knelt down close, breathing a shared fear.

"Animal. Ribcage, sheep or goat, immature. Could you nip back to the car and get my satchel. There's a dozen polygrip bags, bring the whole lot."

He continued to dig and by the time Vikki returned with his satchel, six ribs, a few vertebra, the top of a skull and a horn lay on the grass beside the excavation. All were heavily charred and partly calcined.

"The smart money is on goat." The excavator continued to disperse the ash, picking out more fragments. "I'll take these back to Jules for an expert opinion, he's our bones man."

Flint pointed out the key features and she eagerly began to scribble notes. He stayed her writing hand. "No shock horror headlines on this one."

"What?"

"Let's see what it tells us first. We can't keep on giving the game away. Next time you publish a feature, you might just get us killed."

"It's my job! It's my living!"

"Well, if you want to keep living, no article, not yet. Promise?"

She pursed both her lips into a kissing pose and thought about it, then promised. The bones went into zip-lock bags which were bundled together in Vikki's carrier bag. Both took a film of photographs of the site, then walked back along the path to identify other areas of evidence: a place cars might have parked, a torn shred of white cloth on a branch. Vikki wanted to drive straight for London to meet Jules, then stay the night with her mother.

The kitchen table in the north London flat became an impromptu laboratory.

"Goat," Jules Torpevitch announced after twenty minutes' post-mortem. "Mature male. Is this a ritual sacrifice by your Satanists?"

"My guess. Can you tell anything else about it?"

"The breed is unusual, it looks like one of the ancient breeds. See how the horn is flat and twists outwards part way up."

"An ancient breed would be about what we expected. These people like to get the detail right."

Jules laid on his mock Frankenstein voice. "Come to my laboratory, in ze morning." He began to pack away the evidence. "Tomorrow I'll have a root through the textbooks, see what I can find."

Vikki stayed for burgers and Budweisers, then left for her mother's.

"Nice brawd," Jules said, sinking back on to the sofa.

"Sexist remark, ten pence in the box."

"Sasha's not here, sexism box is closed," Jules responded, tugging off a Budweiser cap.

"Vikki and I don't quite see eye to eye," Flint confessed.

"You're eight inches taller than she is."

"Ha ha. You'll be analysing her bone structure next."

Jules pointed the can at Flint. "She has excellent bone structure."

"Boorman's *Emerald Forest* is on tonight. When does it start?" Flint suddenly switched tack. He was not going to be drawn on the subject of Vikki, Chrissie, Lucy Gray or any other member of the female sex. It was time to relax.

By the next afternoon, Jules came up to Flint's office bearing a heap of textbooks. On top of the plan of Burkes Warren he

158

displayed an open page bearing a photograph of an ugly-looking short-haired animal. Flint had expected something hairier, more dignified.

"Your goat has to be an Old English, a popular medieval breed, but almost extinct earlier this century."

"Jules, this is perfect, what do I owe you?"

"Just stack up those beers," the expert said with a grin.

"How common are goat breeders these days?"

"In England? I couldn't tell you."

"Where do you get your samples for reference collections?"

"I know this butcher in Covent Garden, but he just does the usual stuff. You could try the Rare Breeds Society."

Getting hold of the Society magazine took a few hours, then finding a local member in the phone book took until the evening. Flint asked about Old English goats and whether there were any breeders resident in the Durring–Kingshaven area. The call was returned next morning. Amelia Winter, Forest Farm, Oulwich, some nine miles from Durring in the Forest of Axley. Flint thanked the caller, with a voice inside his head saying "Winter".

He put down his phone and walked to the empty computer room. Flint keyed into Tyrone's data base and searched on "Winter".

"Plant, Shirley Elisabeth, nee: Winter."

Plant's mother had once been a Winter. Amelia Winter was the aunt the police had interviewed several weeks previously and who had denied all involvement. She bred goats, those goats were used in the sacrifices, she was involved after all. This was a gift.

Chapter 15

Jeffrey Flint commuted along the increasingly familiar line from London to Durring that Sunday in early August, watching England slip by. It was the season of gathering, the wheat was coming in and the farmer at Burkes Warren had telephoned to confirm he had harvested the crop over the villa. Stuart Shapstone had been sent on ahead to set up camp, clear the ground and organise the diggers, but for Flint, there was one more distraction. A bluebottle buzzed around the dusty carriage window. An expressionless youth sold his mind to the incessant tsst-tsst of a Walkman headset. Mandatory engineering works on the line saw the train arrive twenty minutes late. He was coming to loathe this journey.

At the station, Vikki hooted him from the short-stay parking bay and he walked across to her car.

"I brought a map," he said as he climbed inside.

"Oh, I know where we're going," Vikki chirped, "I went there last night."

"Forest Farm?"

"Just to have a quick look."

"Alone?" He pulled the door closed a little too firmly. "Wasn't that a little stupid, suppose you had been seen?"

Vikki turned and faced the road. She may have coloured beneath the deep tan and the ubiquitous sunglasses. She started the car and moved off with a jerk. He let her sulk for a minute then curiosity overcame anger. "Okay, what did you see?"

"Just some goats and a dog barking its head off, nothing else. Nobody mugged me, am I forgiven?" Her last note was heavily ironic. He let it pass.

"The old aunt is away, I asked in the village."

"Who feeds the goats?"

"One of the yokels usually looks after the goats and lets the dog out."

"Usually?"

Her smile split her suntan ear to ear. "But not this year. So who is at the farm?"

Beyond Durring, the forest of Axley runs in a broad sweep into the valley, broken by fields into clumps of open woodland. Oulwich lies away from the main roads and consists of five houses plus satellite farms. Forest Farm was one, lying half-a-mile from the hamlet down a single track lane.

Vikki turned into the lane, then squashed her car into a passing place to allow a tractor past. Abundant vegetation scraped against the paintwork, her radio aerial catching in the foliage, then whipping back into position as she moved off again. A mixed deciduous wood lay on the right, a thinner screen of trees on the left. Beyond were more cornfields, ripe for harvesting, and in the hedgerow, green berries prepared for the date they would turn black.

Just before the farm came a denser area of woodland, mainly of silver birch. Vikki pulled into a gateway she had used the night before and they climbed out, closing the car doors quietly.

"It's not far now," Vikki said, "I keep thinking we should have told the police, but then, I don't think I'm flavour of the month with them."

A dog could be heard barking before the farm came into view and a padlocked gate barred a short rutted track beside the signpost reading "Forest Farm". They skipped over the gate and dodged right, into the woodland. Moving as quietly as possible through tangled brambles and a carpet of fallen twigs, they arrived at a vantage point behind a young birch. An off-white, single-storey building could be seen through the edge of the trees.

"The witch's cottage," Vikki breathed.

"Except no gingerbread and pretzels," Flint quipped.

Amelia Winter's cottage stared at them square-on, with a couple of rundown outbuildings to either side. The manner in which the tree tops opened out suggested that fields lay beyond.

"The goats are round the other side," Vikki said.

"Ugly short-haired things?"

"They're horrible, all brown and black, not proper goat colour, if you follow me."

"Sounds right."

A dog barked again from within the cottage, but no human

seemed to respond to the warning. An old water tank provided cover.

"Ready?" Vikki asked.

"What for?"

"We could sneak round the side," she gesticulated right, "then we can have a good look first."

Flint wondered about Amelia Winter, what sort of person she could be, who she had hired to look after her farm for the summer and how the unknown person would react to people skulking around the yard.

Vikki mistook his hesitation for fear. "Come on then, chicken!"

She was off, scuttling around towards the nearest outbuilding. After a few moments, Flint sprinted after her, making quickly for a blind spot around the corner of a long wooden shed. Vikki halted with her back to the rotting timber, panting. He scowled at her. "Stop pissing about, this is not a game!"

Vikki glared back at him, then stuck out her tongue by way of reply. His heartbeat pulsing with anticipation, Flint put a hand into the door of the shed and opened it a few inches. Inside was a car, the green Skoda which belonged to the curator. Its front nearside tyre was flat and whilst he dwelled on the significance, Vikki came to his side.

"He's here," she whispered. "It's time for that interview. And don't try to stop me, Grandad."

"Vikki."

Without waiting, she darted around the corner and across to the cottage, with Flint in her wake trying to grab her elbow. He caught her just as she reached a small square window in the side of the building. She came to a reluctant halt.

"Bully."

He chanced a glance through the window. The contrast between dazzling sunlit whitewash and shadowed interior was blinding, but his eyes made out a small dingy kitchen, a clock and a leg. He released Vikki's arm.

"Ow." She shook the offended arm.

He hushed her and she looked puzzled, before she too allowed herself a long look through the window. "There's someone lying on the floor," she whispered.

A fly thumped against the inner window, then another. Moving on the balls of his feet, Flint cautiously advanced around the back of the building. It was L-shaped, with a scullery or dairy tacked on to the rear. Lime wash cracked in the sun, grass grew in the gutters and the whole place seemed very rundown.

A dog began to bark wildly in the rear of the house. At any moment an irate Rottweiler, or an unstable museum curator was going to burst from hiding and punish their daring. Flint reached the corner of the extension, realising that Vikki was gripping his hand, or vice versa.

They edged around the third corner, to view the back of the house. Only the dog still challenged them. Vikki released her hand from the archaeologist's and tried the scullery door. It opened to reveal clothes soaking in a basin of cold water. A stale slaughterhouse smell pervaded the room, becoming stronger as Flint followed Vikki inward. The dog had fallen silent.

Slowly, Vikki opened the door from the scullery into the main body of the house. Squadrons of flies flooded out, and a putrid stench assaulted the senses. Batting away the vile, buzzing creatures, Flint was hardly aware of the rattle of claws on a tile floor. Frothing and barking, the Labrador threw itself at Vikki. She fell back against the wall, hitting out wildly with feeble slaps. Flint grabbed for the collar, yanked the dog away and was immediately bitten on his right hand. Forming fists, he hit out at the dog, punching, left, right, left, right. Its jaws snapped around the fist but couldn't close. Flint retreated into the scullery, with the dog now gripped to his sleeve.

"Find a weapon," his primitive instincts urged.

Flint's uninjured hand grabbed at a tin washtub, pulling it down ineffectively against the dog's flank. Swinging the tub with violence, he caught the dog on the head, causing it to yelp and step back. Grasping both tub handles, he charged the dog, using the tub as the Roman legionnaires used their heavy *scutum* to shunt the enemy backwards. The dog began to lose its grip on the floor, its legs scrabbled for a hold, it leaped up and was caught in mid-bound, falling back and out of the door into the yard. Flint slammed the door closed, leaving the dog outside, barking, and the intruders inside, panting and swearing.

Man had defeated beast, but Flint felt the pain well up in his arm and his hands. Vikki needed his help before he saw to his wounds. She was standing rigid in the door to the kitchen amidst the reek of rotten flesh. Beyond, human remains lay on the tiles, half covered in swarming bluebottles. Most of the clothing had been torn from the body, leaving the visible skin blackened and putrid. The dog had been shut in the house for days, with the torso as the only source of food. Much of it was spread around the room.

The expression on Vikki's face said "I'm going to be sick". Flint echoed the sensation. The room was unlit, dark, chaotic and appalling. The grandfather clock by the corpse was silent, time had stopped. For a moment, only the buzzing of gorged flies could be heard. Piers Plant, demon curator, lay in pieces. One of his arms was in the corner of the room where the dog's basket lay. Other parts of his anatomy were strewn around the charnel house, mixed with dog excrement. Flint recognised the goatee on the semi-detached head. He looked away, and tried to find a focus for his stunned mind.

The kitchen table was set for one. A stewpot sat in its centre, a bowl had been mostly finished. A teapot stood cold and a cup drained. Plant had eaten his last meal alone.

No words were said as the two drifted around the room, taking in facts at random. A row of herb jars stood along Amelia Winter's top shelf, a few books of quaint rural recipes lay on a dark oak sideboard. Over the blackened and cold kitchen range hung a shotgun and in the sideboard drawer lay a box of shells. Flint took down the gun and worked out how to load it, knocking away gluttonous flies as he broke the weapon. The abbatoir lacked a telephone and at least one starved and manic dog stood between them and the sanity of Vikki's car.

"Find a few bags, can you?" he asked.

Vikki nodded through the handkerchief she held to her mouth.

"The police will take this place to pieces, so we have to be smart. Just take a pinch of each of those herbs and we'll need samples of the stew and the tea. Watch for fingerprints."

He found three zip-lock bags still stuffed into his jeans pockets and scooped up some of the stew, then dregs from the teapot. Fighting back nausea, Flint gathered up the samples he needed, but could endure no more than three or four minutes in the kitchen. Forcing himself to act, Flint left the cottage by the front door and walked into the centre of the yard. Animal lover, pacifist, sometime vegetarian, he stood awaiting the Labrador. When it appeared, snarling and rushing to do battle, he raised the shotgun and fired.

The body of the dog was left in front of the cottage and Flint walked to the far side of the farmyard and sat down on a heap of firewood, shotgun on his knee. Vikki broke into a run, making for her car. Whilst he sat guard, she drove to the village and telephoned the police and a staff photographer.

She returned within ten minutes, bringing a pair of local farmers and a first aid kit. Vikki and Flint dabbed and bandaged each other's wounds. They were sitting in close contact when the first police car arrived after another ten minutes had elapsed. More cars followed, with officers of increasing rank wanting repeat statements. Douglas arrived within the hour, saying little before he had been treated to the chamber of horrors.

The Chief Inspector came out of the house shaking his head, which seemed balder and greyer than usual. Flint wondered if he ever wore a hat. The senior policeman looked at the archaeologist who was sitting on the logs, tugging at grass stalks with his good hand.

Douglas leaned on the bonnet of his squad car, fumbling in his pocket. "When we last met, I asked you to keep out of my investigation."

"At least we found him." Flint had been deep-breathing to calm his nerves and clear away the nauseous odour.

The policeman gave a harrumph and lit another cigarette. "This is a . . ." He paused and tried his lighter again. "This is a horrible business you're mixed up in, how long did you know Piers Plant was there?"

"I didn't, it was a lucky guess."

The policeman closed an eye. "Guess? People like you don't guess."

Flint was in no mood for debate, fiddling with a bandage around the mauled hand.

"Okay, it was the result of deductive thinking. Hypothesis plus evidence equals conclusion, New Archaeology applied to a modern problem."

He stopped bullshitting when Douglas began to discolour. "I'm not your enemy, Doctor Flint. Honest. We want to find your Lucy as much as you do."

"But you're not doing anything."

"Wrong, Sherlock. We came here three weeks ago. Miss Winter said she knew nothing, we had a look round, found nothing."

165

"And you know where she is now?"

"The Dordogne. She has an old penfriend, who invites her over for a month each year. She usually gets a lad from the village to look after her goats." Douglas appeared pleased with himself. "See, we're not imbeciles. You don't need five degrees to unravel a few basic facts."

"Amelia Winter is involved in the coven, we have proof now."

Douglas took a long drag then nodded. "We have her for aiding a suspect in the arson case. We'll be charging her when she returns."

Vikki strolled up, folding out her notepad. "Can I have a comment, Chief Inspector?"

He straightened up, stamping out his stub in the grass.

"No comment as yet. Enquiries are continuing?"

Weary of the whole affair, Flint returned home to Jules' flat. Jules was about to fly out to Turkey to join his wife and passed on an invitation for Flint to join him in September. The thought was very refreshing, but first came Burkes Warren, and before that, college. First thing on Monday morning, Flint took the pocketful of bags he had filled at the cottage and spread them out on to the work surface of the environmental lab.

All white coat and black hair, Sandra "Doc" Savage fingered each in turn.

"What are these?" she asked, fiddling her huge glasses. "Let me guess, more vital evidence in your man-hunt?"

"Food samples." Flint took out a fax sheet that had awaited him that morning. Vikki's banner headline "WITCH'S COTTAGE DEATH RIDDLE" explained it all.

"Read this, but not over lunch."

Sandra scanned down the page. "Yuk yuk yuk. This must have been awful."

Understatement. Flint had suffered appalling nightmares overnight and hardly had any sleep.

"I know he wasn't shot, the place was a mess, but that was the dog, I'm sure. My money is on poison, a natural poison."

"So you want me to test these?"

"Scoop of soup, dregs from teapot. Pinch from half a dozen jars in her spice rack."

166

"Well, this isn't a forensic lab, you know. I'm pretty busy, I've got to get up to Hexham by the weekend."

"Come on, Sandra, you're the only one left manning the boat."

"Really, Jeff, my work schedule is behind. I keep getting . . ."

"Please?" He gave his most appealing little-dog-begging expression.

She looked at him, expressions masked, then multiplied by the huge, thick lenses. "Okay, you win." She opened one packet, professional interest clearly rising. "Chromatography is your best bet, I'll give it a go. Sasha is off digging, so I'll have to do it myself."

"You're a heroine. Try a look under the microscope first. See if you can spot anything herbal – death cap mushroom, belladonna, anything of that sort."

"Real Agatha Christie stuff." She nodded with a wry smile.

"More than real, too real."

"Well, I've spent the last four months identifying cereal grains from Scotland. I suppose it's a change."

"Give me a pad and I'll scribble a number for you. I'll be at Burkes Warren for the next four weeks. It gives me a chance to do some real archaeology again, get me away from all this."

He needed a break, by all the ancient gods, he needed a break.

Chapter 16

Piers Plant lay cold on the Kingshaven mortuary slab and the trail of Lucy Gray lay equally cold. Forest Farm had been a dead end, the final burial place of Flint's line of investigation. Piers Plant was the link to Lucy, now Piers was dead, with Douglas finding no evidence to implicate anyone else. Amelia Winter was returning to face questioning and there was no further role for the archaeologist. Vikki Corbett managed one last gruesome feature, then was left facing a summer of agricultural shows and church fêtes.

Burkes Warren beckoned, the harvest was over and time was ripe for a raid into the past. Leaving the city, if not his cares, behind, Flint made for Hertfordshire and a month in the country. The dig had been left in care of Stuart Shapstone, a reliable if dull graduate of the previous year who had not yet found fulltime work. Life on the digging circuit was uncertain, but Burkes Warren offered him four weeks' food, accommodation and pocket money.

Stuart had begun the excavation as Flint remained embroiled in the affair of Forest Farm for a fair chunk of the first week's digging. The site lay on the southern slope of a gently rolling hill, with the villa itself lying concealed towards one side of a large cornfield. The plan for the season was to work on the west wing of the villa, slowly peeling back the soil, grubbing up finds, teasing out the evidence. Finds of pottery, stone or iron would be placed in trays, then brought to the top of the field where a grey plywood caravan stood across the slope.

Nightmares followed Flint to Hertfordshire. Plant was dead and the verdict of the newspapers was suicide. His motive was obviously Lucy, so Lucy too had to be lying dead, somewhere. The failure of the investigation to produce any tangible or positive result left Flint

168

feeling cheated. He had outguessed Plant in the end, but Plant had broken the rules.

Flint walked through the gate into the field, giving the nearest diggers a cheerful wave that was little more than a veneer. He experienced dizziness from delayed shock following the trauma of the bloated body at the farm. Sickening thoughts welled up each time his mind wandered on to the affair. Had he and Vikki not pressed the investigation so hard, perhaps the curator would still have been alive. Perhaps a different strategy might have resulted in Plant confessing what had happened to Lucy. Perhaps, if he had taken notice of Lucy's drift towards the lunatic fringe, he could have saved her too.

Stuart was shouting hello, several more diggers were stopping work to greet him. It was like wishing Schrodinger's cat to be alive; events could not be reversed. He had to think positively, urge himself back into his chosen life and adopt a professional attitude to the task in hand.

The weather had become more subdued as August progressed, the sun tending to play hide-and-seek with the clouds. Pacing around the stubble of the cleared cornfield, Flint slowly relaxed and slowly reverted to type. Breezes blew across the hill, the sun burst on the scene for a few blazing minutes and he knew he was out in the field once more. The challenge of discovery occupied his thoughts, whilst the studied quiet of the digging team gradually calmed him. Few sounds penetrated the peace of the dig; a distant tractor, the occasional farm animal and the ever-present clink-clink of trowels. At intervals a volunteer would cry out a crude curse or yell a joke. Another would burst into song. After three days, even Jeffrey Flint found himself singing again.

A sudden, unexpected peak in his spirits came with the arrival of Vikki, unplanned and unannounced. In thigh-length puce T-shirt, black sunglasses and a heavy dose of suntan, she strode down from her car to the crest of the hill to where the command centre was situated in the lee of the caravan.

"Vikki, I never expected to see you."

"I thought I'd just pop up and see how you were."

His heart started to increase its pumping. Here she was, vibrant, happy, bobbing up and down on the toes of her sandals, showing concern for his welfare. Masked as usual by an array of equipment, Vikki offered solace for physical and mental pain.

169

"How are you?" she asked. "How's your arm?"

He displayed the battle scars, flexing his fingers. "Fine really, and you?"

She poked a trio of clawmarks on her right arm. "Healing up."

With the anxiety of one seeking to impress, Flint took her downslope to where a pair of trenches meeting at right-angles occupied most attention.

"The villa faces south, this is its west wing."

"There's not much, is there?" She stopped at the edge of the excavated area and peered into the shallow trench. "You know, I expected more, with it being a Roman villa, I expected something grand."

"Marble columns and statues sticking up out of the dirt?"

"Something like that."

"The villa was just an upmarket farm. It would have looked pretty grand in its day, but local peasants robbed out all the stone from the walls back in the Middle Ages." He pointed into the empty hole. "This is just the trench the Romans dug for the foundations."

Vikki picked up a triangle of chunky red roof tile. "Is this valuable?"

"Not in a financial sense."

At noon, she sat with the diggers in the dirt, drinking tea from cracked mugs and gazing out across the bright fields. Vikki had brought a box of sandwiches, with extra supplies of Swiss roll. She was an instant hit.

"This is lovely," Vikki romanticised, "what a way to spend your life!"

Stuart pulled long brown hair away from his face. "You should have come on Wednesday."

"Why, what happened on Wednesday?"

"It rained," Flint said, "then it looked like the Somme down there."

For twenty minutes Flint was happy, watching the neat jawline chatter inconsequentially, the brown eyes squint when the glasses were removed, the nose wrinkle when Vikki was expressing opinion. A door had been opened in his life, a new interest, a new objective. She had cared to drive all that way to see him. He started to construct expectations, not noticing her drift away from intimacy.

Vikki had been toying with a daisy plucked from between her feet. "You know what you suggested? About hiding?"

"Yes, have you been all right?"

"Fine, it's been dead quiet, I've been at my cousin Pat's, anyway, but nothing has happened. How about you?"

"Anyone who can read the college notice-board knows where I am. But so far, zilch."

"I thought there might be some of those nutters still around, you know, friends of Piers Plant."

"If they are, they're keeping quiet."

"So it was him all along," said Vikki, "sending those postcards, paying someone to burn your boat and rough me up."

"You're probably right." Flint was fresh out of explanations. "We can all go back to living normal lives." He managed his widest, most seductive grin.

"Is this your holiday?" she asked.

"No, after this, I'm going to Turkey. I'm staying with Jules and his wife, they have the right idea, they dig where it's sunny all the time. I'm going to try to get to see Ephesus and Aphrodisias."

"That sounds wonderful, have you room to squeeze me into your luggage?"

"Yes," he said, a little too sharply.

Vikki gave a little laugh before she let him have it on the chin. "I bet it will be a bit more exciting than Corfu. Me and Vince are going there next week."

"Vince?"

"Yeah, you know, my photographer."

"Oh yes, Vince." All leather jacket, fake Rolex watch and roll-your-own fags. This was the limit, Flint reeled in confused disgust; where was her taste?

"We're off on Tuesday." She seemed immune to the fact that she was hurting. "I'll send you a postcard, does this place have an address?"

She chattered for another ten minutes or so, but his enthusiasm had gone. The red Metro kicked up dirt, then was just memory, where no room remained for self-pity. Flint grabbed a wheelbarrow and set to work to sweat out the devil in him.

Leading from the front, getting his hands dirty, it all served to keep mind and body occupied, and it impressed the volunteers by example. Ten of them assisted the work, with a fifty-fifty mix of sexes. Four were Flint's undergraduates, two hailed from other colleges, the remaining four were an ad hoc assemblage of keen amateurs. Mr Death's application to come on the excavation had been turned down.

A steady stream of visitors flowed through the excavation; people from the local archaeological society, colleagues from London, friends from the Hertfordshire field unit. Tea breaks, lunchtimes and evenings were enlivened by old acquaintances stopping by to drink, gossip and trade tales of digs gone by.

After a fortnight, the uncovering of third-century rubbish pits beyond the villa started to excite Jeffrey Flint's interest. All he had to do was to find the house which went with them. He had just finished explaining this to the farmer when a white Vauxhall van drove into the field and parked beside the college Land-Rover. As Flint walked uphill, his eyes made out the name Naturella Wholehealth Market stencilled in blue along the side of the van. A tall woman clambered out, her silver-blonde hair glittering in the sun.

"Hello," she called.

He greeted her, recognising the woman from the Kingshaven shop.

"You said I should drop by, so here I am." She grinned brightly, bringing out a few wrinkles, but Jeffrey Flint liked the colour of her eyes, first green, then blue as they reflected earth and sky.

"I brought some tea, I couldn't remember what type you bought, so I chose three varieties for you to try."

Flint took the paper bags and thanked her, then offered to show her around the excavation. "I'm very sorry, I don't even know your name."

"Monica Clewes."

"I'm Jeff," he said.

"Oi Doc!" called Jeremy, the big bluff amateur digger.

"They also call you Doc," Monica said. She had a soothing way of speaking, always backing up her statements with a smile. Instantly, Flint was happy she had come. He led her over to Jeremy's trench and inspected his find: a trio of small cubes of fired clay.

"Ho ho ho!" Flint exclaimed. "So we had a mosaic, did we?"

172

"The ploughing's fair buggered it up though," Jeremy said, "that's all that's left."

When Monica was allowed to touch the artefact, she trilled with delight.

"Isn't this wonderful? We're touching the past," she said.

Her enthusiasm demanded to be rewarded, so Flint gave her a detailed, deluxe tour of the site and their finds. She was captivated, bending down by each trench, soaking up each morsel of information thrown out by the diggers. Running her fingers through the shards of pottery spread out in the sun to dry, she sighed.

"I always wanted to go on an excavation," she said, "a dig." She added the word with embellished excitement. "You must need all sorts of qualifications."

"The ability to make tea and a fondness for sitting in the dirt."

She laughed. "Is that all? You're teasing me."

"Last year a pair of American tourists just walked up to me and asked if they could help. They stayed a fortnight in the end, the wife was really handy with a trowel, she was a natural digger."

Monica's eyes were in their green mode, a little smile sneaking up one cheek. "How about me? I need a week off from the shop."

Within a few moments, the team had been expanded to twelve. Monica drove off to her friend's house to change whilst Flint informed Stuart about the new recruit. As he walked away from the trench, Flint knew what the diggers were thinking. That reputation of his was dragging him down again, would people never let him escape it?

Two days after Monica had joined the team and found a penchant for washing and marking pottery, Jeffrey Flint sat brooding whilst filling in the site notebook.

"Cheer up, Jeff."

The pen stopped doodling in the margin and he threw attention Monica's way. Her anxious beam cut through his depression.

"Sorry, things on my mind."

She waved a heavily abused toothbrush. "But it's a lovely day."

"Again, again, good thing too. You can't dig this soil in rain, it goes all plasticky."

She picked up another small potsherd, dipped it into the plastic washing-up bowl between her knees and began to scrub. "Do you know, if I could do this for a living, I'd never be unhappy again. You are so lucky, you know."

"Doing this?" He pointed to the pile of record sheets at his feet.

"No, this." Monica pointed the toothbrush out towards the horizon. "You don't even have to dig in England, you could go anywhere in the world. You're so free and so lucky."

"Yes," he said, "I suppose I am. I ought to cheer up and be thankful."

"You should."

Slowly, as they talked, Flint became aware he was moving into into chat-up mode. It was subconscious, aimed at erasing both Vikki and Lucy from memory. Jeffrey Flint's golden rule came to mind: never seduce your students. It had a corollary: never seduce your diggers. Monica was another blonde, an older English Rose with a love of life. He gazed out over the fields again, making silent vows against slipping into low life as an antidote to depression. Monica was not a sex object. Mentally, he wrote this out a hundred times and was pleased with the result. Chasing women had been his way of life and he knew some academics who were still at it at fifty. To avoid turning into a campus lecher, he had taken serious steps to stop chatting up women on reflex. Monks must find some pride in celibacy, he thought.

"Penny for your thoughts," Monica said, "or is it a denarius?"

"Sorry, I'm brooding."

"It must be those horrible things that you were tied up with. I read all about them in our local paper, it all sounded shocking."

Shocking, yes, Flint had again begun to dwell on Lucy. She might be dead, but she did not die in his mind. Ever, she returned to haunt him, sometimes he imagined her still alive and playing a complex game of hide-and-seek, beyond his understanding.

"But it's all over now," she said, "you should try very hard to forget it."

"But is it over?" Flint asked with a wistful note to his voice. "You knew Piers Plant, didn't you?"

"Yes, I think everyone who moved in local society knew him a little."

Flint shook his head. Random thoughts zig-zagged through his brain as he sat in the cane chair, filing cards, making notes, gazing across the stubble of the cornfield. He thought of other cornfields he had visited that summer. Harriet's Stone and Devil's Finger: the names had mystery about them.

"I thought I'd found him," Flint began to confess, relating his self-doubt and confusion over Piers Plant's motives. Why had Plant taken those volumes to his attic and marked those pages? Why had the coven rented a cottage near by? What importance did the megaliths hold?

"Poor Jeff," Monica said, in her sincere, sympathetic tone, "all that midnight stalking simply isn't you, is it? And as for all this business with the megaliths . . ."

"But you were at Glastonbury," he cut in, "you must know people who are into fringe New Age practices."

"I sell wholefood, I sell New Age books, I have a friend who writes Green poetry and I like folk music. I can see what they see, but," she paused and sighed – Monica had very dramatic mannerisms, "one meets an awful lot of fools."

Flint tossed aside his index cards and allowed himself a stretch. "You're so right. I mean, I'd like to believe in most of this stuff. I vote Green, I hate modern materialism, but most of the stuff I've found out in the past six months is sheer nonsense. I just wish people would realise where to draw the line."

"You blame yourself for something," Monica said.

Flint nodded. "You knew Plant, a little. You know the area. Where would a madman with intense Pagan beliefs bury the girl he had once loved?"

"Gosh! That's a question. Are you sure this girl is dead?"

"It wouldn't be just a shallow grave by a motorway embankment, but somewhere holy, romantic, even magical."

"One of these stone circles?" she guessed.

"Perhaps, but Inspector Douglas of the Darkewater CID is not going to relish digging up two dozen scheduled monuments to satisfy a wild hunch."

He recalled a shadow in the corn around a finger of granite. Had it been at Imbolc when the coven had met at Harriet's Stone?

Thoughts of shadows stayed with him until the day that Ralph and Judy Slack, the man-and-mate team from Cambridge visited Burkes Warren and pushed air photographs under his nose. "Your site, 1943, we came across it in our records."

The photograph was familiar, but Flint bubbled thanks. He had given them the usual tour, apologised for the lack of exciting discoveries and offered them Oolong tea. Monica had been the archaeologist's constant, and welcome, shadow, but she had taken a day off.

"Well team, what do you think?" They sat in the dirt as a stiff wind propelled a solid bank of clouds above their heads. "No earth-shattering discoveries, just plain old dirt archaeology."

Big, brash and bearded, Ralph made an envious grunt. "I wish I could do some. It would be so good to get out in the air, pick up my trowel and be a real archaeologist again. I spend most of my time in the dark room these days."

His gypsy-complexioned colleague protested at this. "What he means is I spend time in the dark room while he goes off to meetings."

"Oh, you've not become a meetings animal, Ralph?"

"Not deliberately, it just happened."

"Don't you feel that the bureaucrats are taking over these days? Everyone I meet does less and less archaeology, and spends more and more time sitting on committees and responding to directives. The route to the top these days is to excavate paper."

"Aw Jeff, you get more cynical all the time," Judy commented.

"Well, I'm in archaeology to discover, not to sit in meetings and expend hot air."

"You're right, you're right," Ralph said, kicking at a loose piece of spoil with his sneakers, "but you'll never make professor with that heavy dose of attitude."

"Maybe not." It was time to squeeze in an ulterior motive for inviting the couple to visit the site. "So, meetings apart, what are you into at the moment? Still the aerial survey of megaliths?"

"As ever," Ralph replied. "Things are progressing, as they say. We're a little behind, but then that's only to be expected."

"Are you including the Darkewater Valley Group?" Flint pounced.

"We did them last year," Judy intervened.

Damn. "All the sites?"

"We did six or seven," she added.

"How do you fancy doing them again?"

"No way," Ralph said firmly, "it's too late, in any event, all the fields will have been cut by now. A month ago it might have been possible."

"Pity."

"They've been cutting early this year due to the heat."

"Greenhouse effect," Flint commented gloomily. "I suppose air photography is useless on stubble?"

"Unless it snows," Judy came back, "then only if it hasn't been ploughed. Are you looking for clues? We heard you were on some kind of man-hunt."

Flint told them about the chase for Lucy Gray.

"It wouldn't be smart to bury someone in a cornfield," Ralph said, "you'd leave a hole in the crop which would be easy to find in summer, and afterwards, deep ploughing would be sure to bring up evidence."

It had been a futile hope, a stab in the dark, another wild idea discarded. The couple came for a drink in the evening then returned to their college. Monica returned next day and spent two final days with the dig before departing back to the Darkewater Valley. Flint walked to her van as she was taking off her short boots for the last time.

"Thanks for coming along."

She reached out and touched his hand, tiny crows' feet gathering behind her eyes to complement the smiles. "Jeff, I've loved it, but I'm afraid I have to return to real life. If you're ever in Kingshaven, do drop by and say hello. I may even have some bargains you can't resist."

"Now you mention it, I'm in Durring again tomorrow, the dead won't lie down."

Her concern was genuine. "I thought all that was over."

"It is, or it will be," he corrected. "It's the inquest, I've got to attend, like it or not. By tomorrow night, it will truly be over."

"Then you're free to resume this wonderfully carefree life you lead." Monica stood up in her driving shoes and took Flint by the elbows. She planted a short, social kiss on his lips. "Thanks for letting me help out."

"It wouldn't have been the same without you."

Chapter 17

Jeffrey Flint rarely drove, so taking the college Land-Rover to Durring was both a novelty and an escape from the monotony of British Rail. The inquest into the death of the curator taught him little, as his own laboratory was efficient and accurate. Digitalis, the product of common foxgloves, had been mixed with the stew in killing proportions. Amelia Winter had collected herbs, including a few foxglove leaves in a jar, but Plant had apparently picked a fresh batch for his final meal and left the remains on his chopping board. The date of death was the first to third of August.

Amelia Winter, robust and oddly jolly, testified to Plant's diminished mental state. She related his obsession with death and his dreams of horned men and demons. An expert psychiatrist presented an interpretation that Piers Plant was suffering from schizophrenia and Chief Inspector Douglas stated that no evidence had been found that anyone else was involved. The verdict was suicide. Case closed.

The old woman was on police bail and staunchly refused to be driven back to Oulwich in a squad car. Vikki Corbett, highly suntanned, highly chic, was shunned by a swish of blue knitted shawl when she tried to speak to the woman. Then Jeffrey Flint stepped forward, his red tie almost straight, his jeans almost free from Hertfordshire mud. He offered the old woman a lift in his Land-Rover. She smiled at him and took hold of the crook of his arm before allowing him to lead her from the court.

Once at Forest Farm, Flint could not suppress a shudder at the memories, but Amelia Winter seemed hardly ruffled by the prospect of re-entering the cottage of death. They walked around the rear, Flint apologising in an awkward manner for what he had done to her dog.

"I had Toby from a pup," Amelia Winter said as they walked, "he was just six. Ah well, that's the way of things."

They came to the rail fence at the edge of her fields and she turned her eyes to her goats. She pulled her shawl close and screwed up her ageing eyes against the thin autumn sun.

"I'm sixty next week, in case you want to know," she said.

"Have the police charged you?"

"Aye. Aiding a fugitive. He was flesh and blood, Doctor Flint. I had no choice. Piers was a sad boy, but he never did all those things I read in the newspaper."

"Do you know who did?"

"Now you sound like the police."

"Sorry." He was almost offended.

He was hoping for a titbit, a crumb of evidence to fill out the fragmented picture left by the verdict. Suddenly, unexpectedly, he was deluged by a whole feast.

"He loved that girl, the one they say he done away with. He brought her here once . . ."

"When?"

"Last year, to collect one of my kid goats. His eyes shone in that way men's eyes shine." She sighed.

"What did Lucy do, I mean, did her eyes shine?"

"Not in the same way. He could have been her dad, the way she seemed to look up to him."

"Not her lover?"

"Lover? That's one of those newspaper words which makes it all sound so dirty."

"I think he was the father of her baby," Flint stated baldly.

"Piers? No." She seemed very certain, even amused. "Not Piers. That was his undoing. Did you know his wife? No of course you wouldn't, well she was called Patricia and she ran off with a schoolteacher. Do you know why?" Amelia held up a finger. "I'll tell you now, because it will hurt no one. She wanted children."

"And Piers didn't."

"Couldn't." She nodded in emphasis.

The past, as ever, the clues lay in the deep past. Suddenly Flint had a motive, a reason for Plant to become increasingly desperate and finally to lose all reason. He had a motive for murder and a final excuse for suicide.

"Mrs Winter."

"I never married . . ." She almost sang the words. "That's why I go out to France. You see, my Percy was in the army and he

179

couldn't decide whether he would marry me or my best friend
Dolly. Guess who he chose?"

Flint was wrong-footed by such intimate admission by a stranger.

"Dolly, you guessed." She gave a little laugh. "Anyway, to show
there's no hard feelings, we still meet up. They keep goats too, now
isn't the world strange?"

"Miss Winter, you must know what Piers did with your goats."

"He had his little ceremonies."

"You were involved?"

"Oh no, oh no. People think that if a little old lady lives on
her own, with her dog and her goats, she's a witch. No, Doctor
Flint, I never went that way. It was all too silly for my liking. I
love the woods and fields, like Piers did, I taught him his herbs,
but I didn't go for his antics."

"Do you know any others involved with Piers', um, antics?"

"None of them. Piers asked me to breed these goats six years
ago, I had ordinary breeds then. I let him have one, he pays me
and we have a business deal."

"Did he ever mention names?"

She pulled her bottom lip inside her upper teeth, giving an odd
smile. "Now, I suppose that question could hurt someone."

"I need to find the truth."

"For the newspaper?"

"I'm nothing to do with the newspaper."

Amelia Winter looked at him, through him, even. She was
still weighing him up, judging him as friend or enemy. "He was
always cagey, was Piers. Sometimes he talked about Rowan and
sometimes about Hazel."

Hazel? Flint remembered the dedication in the poetry book
which had lain in Lucy's room. "Was that a male or female
Rowan?"

"Female?" she guessed slightly. "Piers was never happy with
men, he was always with women, all his life. I think that was why
he liked his little games."

"He enjoyed the power?"

"He must have enjoyed something."

"He was in charge, then, he was the head wizard or whatever?"

"I suppose he must have been."

"Have been?" He recognised the implied past tense.

"Oh, it's all too silly for me. I don't get involved, look what it did for poor Piers."

"Is your sister involved?"

"Dear Shirley, poor Shirley." Amelia touched her forehead. "She's no longer all there, we don't really talk any more. They say it is a sickness which runs in the family. I am free, so far."

"But Piers never talked about men? You've no idea who the father of this baby could have been?"

"He never talked about men, not real men anyways."

Flint strained to think of a new angle on the same question. "At the inquest, you said he dreamed he was being chased. Did he ever talk about it?"

"Every day, poor child."

"I suppose that was my fault. You must really hate me for that."

"No, dear. I don't hate you. Why should I? Piers wasn't frightened of you."

"Well, it was me who put the police on to him, made him go into hiding."

"He wasn't hiding from you."

Flint was puzzled. "If not me, who?"

"He was frightened of dreams. He said a horned man was after him and that you were just one of his demons. Oh every day, he kept talking about Him and how he needed the spells to defeat Him. Poor dear, there was nothing I could do."

Something in what she had just said held a clue, but Flint couldn't connect it with facts he already knew.

"Piers wanted me to go to France, as I always did. I wanted to stay and look after him, but he said he had work to do. He asked me to post letters for him, but I never did. I thought it dangerous whilst the police were looking for him."

"They were not, by any chance, to bookshops?"

Amelia Winter's eyes opened wide. "So they were, bookshops in Paris and in Germany. Have the police shown them to you?"

Of course not, thought Flint. "Did he ever mention a black book?"

She thought hard. "There was some book he fretted about all the time."

Flint knew which book. Which non-existent book of non-existent spells, presumably with which he would fight non-existent demons. How could the logic of a madman be unravelled?

At length he decided he had drawn as much from the woman as possible. He thanked her and apologised again for his part in the tragedy. She was phlegmatic, if deeply saddened.

"You go home, Doctor Flint, and don't you worry. None of this was your fault, you were only looking for that girl. I'm sure Piers would want you to find her too."

Amelia Winter's parting words sent Flint driving back to Kingshaven and down the lane in which Shirley Plant and her late son had lived. Some arrogant sense of righteousness had persuaded him that if his snooping was acceptable to Amelia Winter, her sister might be brought around to the same attitude. He was wrong. He parked the Land-Rover, got out, took one look at the green Skoda parked on the unmade drive, then rapped on the door. Mrs Plant looked around the curtains at him, then returned inside. He knocked again, then went around to the side door and tried his luck. A bolt and chain slid into place when he knocked. He went to the kitchen window and she began to pull the blue curtains closed. Finding this both futile and invasive, he retreated back to the head of the drive to think. He had to speak to her, solve the final riddles. Perhaps she knew something about Lucy.

Then Flint noticed the car. Its front nearside tyre was taut and firm. He remembered it being completely flat at Forest Farm. Of course, he realised, the police would have changed the wheel to drive the car back! He bent down to examine it, quickly spotting that the layers of dirt and rust matched those on the other three. This was no spare tyre, he would bet the spare was still under the bonnet somewhere, clean and rust-free. The police must have pumped up the tyre to move the car.

Piers Plant had driven himself to Caesars Camp and contracted a slow puncture on that awful dirt track. His tyre then had a whole week to go completely flat before the car was found, so much was logical. Flint walked back to his Land-Rover, started the engine and drove back up the lane, a discomfiting thought worming its way into his head. This same tyre had been pumped up by the police and stayed fully inflated for a month, so it could not have any sort of puncture.

*　　*　　*

The final days of the excavation were a happy riot of jokes, songs and last-night parties. Flint left his team to clear the site and flew out to Turkey for a fortnight of sun, dark coffee and glittering white ruins. It gave him a perfect excuse to miss Piers Plant's cremation.

Vikki Corbett wanted one last interview to close the file. Arnold, her editor, had yawned when she mentioned the moribund Lucy Gray story and it was only the macabre quality of Plant's suicide that made another article worthwhile.

She had mingled with a dozen people willing to be recognised as friends and relations of Piers Plant at the crematorium. The ceremony had no religious content and the curator's body was simply burnt for disposal. Afterwards, Vikki had made a discreet enquiry and arranged to be present when Mrs Plant collected the ashes.

On an overcast September day, Vikki advanced from the cover of scaffolding shrouding the front of the ruin that had been Kingshaven Museum. She had followed the bent figure of Mrs Plant from the crematorium and she knew what lay in the white plastic carrier bag the old woman hugged to her chest.

The reporter had contracted some of the archaeologist's erratic logic, hoping the curator might have asked to be buried at some sacred spot. Perhaps, the same sacred spot where Lucy also rested. It contained the germ of a story, so Vikki was prepared to let it grow.

Mrs Plant had stopped by the rose beds in front of the museum. She took a cylindrical container from her carrier bag, removed the lid, then froze. She turned a stone face to Vikki, halting any action she had intended. The reporter faced the challenge and advanced towards her.

"I'm sorry to intrude . . ." said Vikki.

"I'll not do it while you're watching."

"Mrs Plant, I'm very sorry."

"I hope they paid you a lot of money for what you wrote."

Vikki's mouth went dry, a spasm of guilt and uncertainty halting her usual resolve.

Rain began to fall, droplets exploding on the fading plants.

"He loved these roses," Mrs Plant said.

"Will you tell me everything, Mrs Plant?"

"No."

"I need to know who his friends were . . ."

"He had no friends."

"I need to know, I need to . . ."

"I'll tell you nothing. If I knew anything, I'd take it to my grave." The cold grey look remained. The urn lid stayed poised.

"Sorry." Vikki backed off, part disappointed, part ashamed. It's only a job, she told herself, I'm only doing my job.

Mrs Plant was still impassive. Vikki waited a few more moments, feeling awkward, then turned down the path to the road. She glanced over her shoulder, but Mrs Plant was still immobile, prepared to wait indefinitely for privacy. Vikki turned her head back towards the road and resolved to look back no more.

Evening closed in and rain continued to fall, as another figure walked slowly into the rose garden. Rowan had not been to the crematorium, she saw the risks and she saw no benefit. Beneath her umbrella she looked around the roses.

Oak, poor Oak, how had things gone so badly?

Standing in quiet reverence, Rowan thought of Oak, and the women who had treated him so badly. That bitch who had divorced him, his crazy aunt, his even crazier mother, the vicious reporter and of course Hazel. All this had been Hazel's fault, Rowan would never forgive her for any part she had played. Only one woman had understood poor Oak; she had been his mother, his sister and his wife.

Rowan pulled her collar closer, thinking of the fifteen years they had shared a dream, a dream that would soon be brought into being. She had read of the inquest verdict, she had seen the evening edition of the paper with its terse account of the cremation. Vikki Corbett's colourless article was proof that the reporter had lost the scent of the trail. Rowan had also learned that even Doctor Flint had run out of ideas and enthusiasm. Things would return to normal, she would put aside the unhappy year, then she had plans for the future.

Looking down at the flowerbeds she was sure she could see a trail of fine grey ash between the roses, slowly mingling with earth and water. Piers Plant had returned to the elements.

Chapter 18

Central College was the same in late September as it had been in August, except the toilets had been repainted and stank of turps. Flint found his office looked too clean, too empty, so messed it up deliberately on arrival with notebooks and permatrace plans from Burkes Warren. He would be supervising the projects of three postgraduates in the coming year, and the keenest one came to demand attention that first morning.

"It looks like I missed all the fun." Tyrone surveyed the newspaper headlines he had escaped. The dun sports jacket was new, expensive and Italian.

"It was hardly fun at Forest Farm."

"Aw, seen one stiff, you've seen 'em all."

Flint gave him the most disgusted look he could manage.

Full of high spirits, suntanned and over-relaxed, Tyrone stretched himself to almost-horizontal in the soft chair. "I hear you went to Turkey with Torpevitch, what's it like?"

Thoughts of the sun-bleached walls of Aphrodisias came back to mind and Flint felt instantly warmer. "Wonderful."

"And was Burkes Warren a barrel of laughs?"

"The social life was okay. I'm still undecided on the dig, we may have stripped the wrong wing, not much there."

"I told you Stuart was a waste of space, everyone wondered why you took him."

Was Tyrone just trying to be irritating? He was succeeding in upsetting the happy state of equilibrium which had been cultivated so carefully in Turkey.

"My fault, not his."

"I heard you found a new woman." Tyrone was trying to be chummy now, brimming with tact as ever. Gossip travelled the department at the speed of light, Flint supposed that Monica was the subject of the innuendo, but merely grunted a denial, refusing to be drawn into Man Talk.

"So what's on the menu for this term?" Tyrone continued his attempts to jerk some sort of response out of his supervisor.

"Back to archaeology. Real archaeology. I'm teaching, you're thesis-ing."

"You're forgetting all about Lucy?"

Flint looked at the keen, earnest face. "All the clues led us to Plant. All the other evidence is scrappy and contradictory."

"So the official police viewpoint is correct? Plant goes mad, kills Lucy, plays all sorts of dirty tricks on us, then kills himself."

"Well, it's plausible."

"But you're not convinced?" The suntan cracked into a one-cheek smile. "If we had something to go on, you'd carry on looking?"

Flint was reluctant to admit it, reluctant to start over again. Lucy was last year's business and he avoided a direct reply.

"Any more bombs? Head-in-a-box, hate mail?"

"No, thank God."

"But you're still in purdah?"

"Yes, but I'm in college every day. They know where to find me."

"Who is 'They'?"

"'They' are the ones we never knew about. Perhaps Plant was behind it all, or perhaps his friends are happy for us to think that."

"His suicide was very convenient," Tyrone said.

"You're not going to come out with more conspiracy theory stories?"

"No, but it stopped the police asking questions. It stopped us finding Lucy."

"Lucy, yes, poor Lucy. I've a few ideas where she might be buried, if she is dead, and we still don't know for sure. To be really sure, of course, we'll have to turf-strip about four square miles of ancient monuments. That or wait for a convenient snowfall and drag Ralph and Judy Slack out in their Cessna."

Flint could see something welling within his student. Tyrone's face was adjusting to suit his next statement.

"I've had time to think, you know, sitting in street cafés, sipping cappuccino, watching the sunrise over Florence. So when I got back yesterday, I had a scurry through the files, just to get my grey cells going again. Thanks for the photocopies by the way, I added all the new stuff. Do you want to come and look?"

"No, but I suppose I must."

A square, grey-painted room had been allocated to Tyrone and another postgraduate student. Along most of the free wall hung the Lucy wall chart, with all the key information displayed in its spatial relationship. Tyrone ran through it item by item, step by step, using a felt pen to scrawl a few new notes in the appropriate places. After a few minutes, Flint stopped him.

"Tyrone, what is the point?"

The student, who looked more like an advertising executive, pointed with the felt tip and adopted a serious, hands-on-hips pose. "If this was the data for my thesis, and I drew the same conclusion as the police have, would you be satisfied, as my internal examiner?"

Flint played the game, following all the arrows, spotting the errors, omissions and unused pieces of evidence. The cracks in the arguments yawned wide, the links were tenuous and much white space begged to be filled correctly. Last year he had marked an MA thesis with identical flaws. Many intriguing lines of enquiry had been opened, but none followed to a satisfactory solution. The mature student involved had slapped on a ludicrously inappropriate conclusion and left the oral examination in tears.

"Present it in that state and you'll fail."

"Why?"

The examiner began to point out and identify problems.

"One, who is Hazel?

"Two, who is Rowan?

"Three, who was behind that organised hate campaign: I don't believe Plant had the backbone, or the opportunity to organise it.

"Four, who helped Plant escape, other than his mother?

"Five, who was Plant scared of, or was he really in a fantasy world?

"Six, who is the father of Lucy's baby? We know it can't have been Plant.

"Seven, if Plant was depressed enough to commit suicide, why did he bother to collect fresh foxgloves, when there were plenty already prepared in the cottage?

"Eight, what was wrong with the front tyre on the Skoda?"

"Nine, why the hell is that book so important?"

"Ten, last but not least, where is Lucy?"

Tyrone nodded. "That all?"

"For the moment." Flint was downcast. Sleeping dogs refused to lie, but continued to roll and scratch in discomfort.

Tyrone sucked the end of his fat felt pen for a whole two minutes. Then he started to draw new lines, connecting many points to one word he labelled "SECT". Below this he drew a deliberately long line. At the very bottom of the wall he ended his line in a box, filled with a question mark.

He jabbed SECT with his pen. "This is Them, all these unknown people who are involved. There could be dozens of them for all we know, all as mad and fanatical as the late Piers Plant."

"Who is that?" Flint kicked a toe towards the skirting board.

"That is what is really behind all this. The thing or the person we're not supposed to find. The thing which is being protected."

Both contemplated the empty box, making wild, unreasoned guesses at what it might be. Hairs prickled on Flint's neck as something crawled from his memory. "Beware the Horned Man."

"Horned Man?"

"Something old Leopold Gratz said to me, I thought he was just being mysterious. 'Beware the Horned Man, Doctor Flint.' Old Amelia Winter also said something about Plant being chased by a man with horns, then there was that wax doll at the museum. That was a man with horns."

Tyrone came straight back. "Satan. Plant thought he had been cursed and pursued by Satan, that's obvious."

Flint was deflated. "Of course, well, we can't have Satan arrested for complicity, can we?"

"We could add him to the suspect list."

"Don't be juvenile. How many people are on it?"

"Fifty or so, I'm putting Amelia Winter and Mrs Plant right at the top, they'd both make good witches. I've got several lists, drawn from different sources: friends of Plant; relatives of Plant; members of the Dark Ants; local people with known occult interests; Lucy's old school chums; that list your Professor Gratz gave you. I'm sure that with enough data, I could use cluster analysis to produce a heirarchy of suspicion."

"Is there anything behind that wad of jargon you just used?"

"Yes, we compile a whole set of lists, based on different types of evidence, then see who occurs in most lists and get the computer to plot the relationships mathematically."

"Okay, but that's not going to stand up in court, is it?"

"No."

After a considerable, heavy, pause, a decision was taken. "Look, Tyrone. Last year was a disaster, we lost Lucy and we ended up making idiots of ourselves. If we're going to open up this bag of maggots again, let's be sure we do it right and let's decide now that we're going to see it through."

"Fine, I'm game."

"So, first objective, we need to satisfy ourselves that your sect really exists." Flint tapped the SECT box. "Then we need to get these people out in the open. The question is how."

"What about the book?" Tyrone suggested. "Plant thought *De Nigris* was really important, so suppose his friends do too? What happens if we get a copy and advertise it for sale?"

Flint congratulated himself on his choice of assistant. Two brains worked better than one, especially if the one was partially addled. He nodded slowly, then felt his pulse quicken. "If we get any reaction at all, we're on to something."

"If not, we've lost nothing."

"No, and we don't even need to find a copy." Flint's depression swung round to instant mania. "Brilliant! All that education wasn't wasted on you."

"Shall I knock up some adverts, then?"

That afternoon, a small ad was sent to several newspapers and posted in notable occult and antiquarian booksellers' windows. Flint even sent one to Monica down in Kingshaven. The card she posted in her window read: "For sale: Eastney, John, 1698, *De Nigris*. Facsimile copy. Bound. Offers . . ."

Many people must have seen the cards and the adverts and most would have ignored it entirely or have been briefly mystified, but when Rowan's eyes fell on the wording, it was as if her soul had suddenly plunged down a cleft in the earth. Someone was still prying and it took little imagination to guess who. All at once she felt vulnerable and fearful for others who were still close to her. She had to speak to Him, she needed comfort and reassurance and her spirit needed rebuilding. Something different would be required this time, a sacrifice to preserve the greater good. He would never know what she had done to save Him.

Three days passed before The Poet returned from his journey, which meant three days of angry anxiety for Rowan. When at last she spoke to him on the telephone, she had made her plans and was resigned to them.

"Ah Rowan, did you read the small ads in that rotten newspaper?" The Poet asked calmly down the telephone.

"I have." Rowan knew her voice must have lost its certain edge.

"Can it be a coincidence?"

"No," she stated, "someone is still nosing around."

"Could you find out who it is?"

"I know who it is," she muttered. "Doctor Flint of Central College London."

"So, you were wrong when you stated – with deep certainty – that he had ceased to chase our shadows."

"I was, but I have a new idea, one that will work."

"No, Rowan, no more dramatics, let us sit tight. He's clutching straws, you see. He has found this name, this book, from something Oak left behind. It will tell him nothing."

"You must know someone in London," she said, "someone who can do something."

"Yes, London, of course. I'll see what I can do. Now, my wife is expected back shortly, so I should ring off."

"You haven't told her about us." Rowan fell sullen.

"No, dear, it's complicated, especially now. Let us wait until things fall quiet again."

"Promise?"

"No promises."

The freshers burst upon Central College with the usual mix of gauche exuberance and innocent wonder. Fifty new faces for Flint to recognise, fifty new names to repeatedly forget. Classes were full, the new intake was still keen and not yet succumbing to the attrition of lie-ins, hangovers and note-swapping deals. He was on his toes, breaking them in gently, taking one shuffling group after another on forays into the British Museum. College was exhilarating and hectic, social contacts were renewed and he had little time for brooding or plotting. Like a creature trapped in a Buddhist resurrection cycle, his life renewed itself each autumn.

He vacated the spare room in Jules' house and took another in a house rented by a trio of medics. If the advert succeeded in stirring up trouble, it would be best if he made himself difficult to find. Only four nights into the new term, he was called down to the phone by a bemused medic.

"Mr Selby?" The medic held the receiver as if it were infected.

"Ya, Grant Selby," Flint faked a suburban yuppie accent as he took up the telephone.

"I came across your advertisement, advertising a book?" It was a man's voice, educated, with a slight regional accent.

"*De Nigris*, yes."

The other paused. "Is it genuine?"

"A facsimile. I collect manuscripts relating to mythology. This does not quite fill my requirements."

"May I ask how you acquired it?"

"Some time ago, almost by accident in a Brighton antiquarian bookstore. I believe it is closed now."

Another pause for thought. "And what price would you be asking?"

Impromptu lies tumbled from Flint's lips. "I have been offered two hundred pounds, but of course that's way short of the mark."

Silence greeted the price. Were it original, were it genuine, the book would be priceless.

"This is the John Eastney version?" The caller was familiar with it. Of all the casual callers who had rung that week, this one knew what he was seeking.

"Sixteen ninety-eight, yes. A nineteenth-century facsimile. Latin. Leather bound, a little eaten at the corners, I'm afraid, and there are a few rather torn pages . . ."

He embellished his story whilst the man picked at details, all the time deeply sceptical and deeply knowledgeable. This was the fifth call about *De Nigris*. The first to respond to the advert had been Leopold Gratz, who was amused to discover who the bogus Mr Selby really was, then chattered at some length about the turn of events at Forest Farm. Two further callers had been professional enquirers, obviously mystified, wondering if they were missing a bargain. The fourth had been a woman, obviously well acquainted with the nature of the book, who asked clumsy and rather naïve questions with a distinctive Irish tone. She was called Michelle and had left her number: south London, 081 code. The fifth caller was more discreet.

"I'll have to think about the price," he said. "I'll ring you back . . . don't sell it, will you . . ."

In a moment the line hung empty, with no name and no telephone number this time. Flint had sensed some indecision at the far end and it excited him. The book did not, or should not, exist, yet this was the second stranger familiar with it, and idly, he wondered how many copies he could fake and sell. Then he remembered that reverse telephone directories were on sale, enabling people to deduce addresses from telephone numbers. If his hunch was right, one, or more, of his callers would be interested in his whereabouts. It was time to move house again, or buy another fire extinguisher.

The following day, he sat at his desk, ignoring a pile of internal memoranda and concentrating on the Lucy file. His interest was growing, he could feel that a solution was within his grasp.

"Hullo." Tyrone came into the office without knocking. "Would you like to see some pictures of pots?"

"Not really." Flint hardly looked up from his papers.

"How about the name of your mystery woman?"

"Come in, there's a draught."

Tyrone had also used a reverse directory to discover that the Irish woman was named Michelle Kavanagh and lived in Dulwich. She had not rung back about the book.

"Michelle Kavanagh eh? Is she on any of your lists?"

"No."

Flint had her secretly pencilled in as "Rowan" or "Hazel". He was also aware that his unwelcome parcel post had always originated in south London.

"I'm going to have to meet her."

"I will if you like," Tyrone said.

"Tyrone, come on, she could be at the centre of all this. A coven needs a high priestess – it could be Lucy for all we know, but it might be this Michelle. If she's the one posting parcel bombs, she may not be a nice person to know socially."

"I'll risk it."

"No, I've lost enough students this year. You get on with those lists of suspects. Ring Vikki and ask her to root out some dirt, I'm hoping to see Monica again and ask her to keep an eye on her clientele. She put up our advert for free."

Later that day, Flint gave his first Roman Art and Architecture lecture to the second year, then caught a bus for Dulwich. Jammed between a cross-section of London society he began to compose a character for Grant Selby and sketch out a life history. He would need to remember all his fiction and keep his act consistent, but this was something he was used to. Whenever he stood at the lecture podium, or before a camera or a microphone, he put on the act of the confident intellectual. Whenever the common room debates became heated, he slipped into the role of laid-back liberal anarchist. He remembered a lecture tour he had once guided around Rome, and a dealer in antiquities who had been a member of the party. Grant Selby had a role model to follow.

Still in his lecturer guise, he strolled along the Dulwich back-street, with its parallel rows of parked cars and its opposing walls of terraced houses. The design was standard for the older suburbs, brick-built circa 1910, with one bay window on each floor and a slate-roofed extension at the rear housing the bathroom. A few frontages were graced by mock stone facing, and looked ridiculous. Many of the others had been divided into two flats, one on each floor and Ms Kavanagh lived downstairs in one of these. She had decorated the sad windows of 37a with a dozen fetching Celtic designs painted on to small sheets of glass, but Flint dare not go closer without a disguise. His heart pumped hard as he longed to get inside the dark brown door and meet this Michelle. Who was she and why did she know about this book?

He returned to his flat, where everything he owned was once more packed to move, then made contact through the sanitised safety of the telephone. Flint lied as he had never lied before. He had been let down, the man had failed to come up with the money, would she like the book?

"I'm not sure I could really afford it," said the soft Irish voice.

"Can I show it to you? That might make you change your mind, this really is something special."

Michelle Kavanagh made thinking noises, clicking with indecision. "Yes, it won't hurt, will it?"

"No, can I pop round? Where do you live?"

She caught her breath, obviously daunted by this strange male voice. "We could meet somewhere."

"Fine, any ideas?"

"The Sunday Market at Covent Garden. I've got a stall."

"Selling?"

"Craft jewellery, paintings, batik prints, you know."

"Yes, there are quite a few of those."

"I've got a little dragon pendant I fly from my stall. You can't miss it."

"See you Sunday."

Down went the reciever. Flint thumped the air with his fist. "Yes!"

One of the medics was squeezing past in the hallway. "When are you moving out?" he joked.

"Saturday," replied Flint.

Saturday would be the day of sacrifice. The rugged outdoor-man stereotype beard had to go. Cultivated over so many years it had afforded Flint a "real archaeologist look" in younger days, but now it was a liability. A girl from the London School of Fashion lodged upstairs in the address he was moving into. For a pound she cut his hair short and neat, then for another she dyed it a deeper shade of brown. A bottle of instant tanning lotion sufficed to hide the join between raw cheeks and paler areas revealed by shaving off the beard.

From one of the cardboard boxes which filled the floor of his new attic bedroom, he fished out an older prescription pair of spectacles: gold-rimmed and square. The world fuzzed around the edges, but with a little eye-strain, he would get by. Tyrone had loaned him a car coat, a little large, but it suited Grant Selby's image. Flint critically assessed the new man in the dressing-table mirror: neat, smart, almost trendy. The thought revolted him.

Sunday morning was kind to the market. In autumnal warmth, tourists mingled with Londoners out for a bargain and new students out sampling the big city. Flint wore the car coat and a new personality. He both looked, and felt, like a spiv seeking to unload a bundle of nylons on the unsuspecting girl below the little dragon.

He could absorb research like a sponge. Occult and New Age literature had been consumed and digested in bulk, sceptical and analytical approaches to the subject had also been fodder for his mind. The psychology of those who placed faith in the paranormal had been a vital ingredient in his research. He had learned that certain people, of certain backgrounds, of certain states of mind could be drawn towards the occult. The insecure, the inadequate, the frustrated and the dissatisfied had always been attracted by counter-culture.

Placing a mirror against what he knew, Flint felt he could almost draw a personality profile of the woman before they even met and Michelle fitted the part. Squinting just a shade, he judged her as a little too heavy for her own good. She was probably around thirty, large boned, with a broad, sunwarmed face. Her hair was black and long, mingling with the shawl around the shoulders. Flint had always been attracted by brain rather than superficial appearance, but he remembered he was Grant Selby, the man in the car coat. Michelle was not Selby's type, her neck was too fleshy, her chin almost double and every aspect of her clothing and manner screamed against established order.

Unaware she was being analysed, Michelle Kavanagh looked one way then the other at the would-be clientele. She seemed bored, even alone, but then, the text books said she would be. Flint composed his image, then strolled across and picked up a pair of dragon earrings. They had been hand-crafted from some modelling medium then baked and painted a translucent green.

"These are splendid, do you make them yourself?" Grant Selby had been given a languid, self-satisfied voice.

"Yes," she said, "I make all these, everything you see."

She had talent. He looked up at the silk scarves painted in pastel blues or vivid red-and-golds.

"I'm sorry, I should have introduced myself. I'm Grant Selby."

He began to regret the name, it had dropped from a route atlas and seemed as good as any other.

"Ah?" She tried to place both name and face.

"You rang about a book, *De Nigris*?"

"Oh, oh yes." She was either embarrassed, or excited, or both.

"Actually, I came to apologise. I sold it this morning, just before I was due to come here. The man came back to me after all, with an improved offer and cash in hand and of course, I had to take it. Sorry."

195

"Oh." She managed a little laugh. "I probably couldn't afford it anyway."

"No, it was rather expensive in the end."

"So why did you come?"

"To apologise. I thought it might mean a great deal to you . . ."

"No, not at all."

Keep up some momentum, he told himself, so found a new item on her stall to pick up and admire. While he talked, he was observing. This could not be the high priestess, she had a nervousness which would prohibit her from posting dismembered animals. Michelle bobbed her head to one side when he praised her work, with a lack of sophistication the real Grant Selby would have found repellant. She had an air of despair about her, an air which fought against the gaiety of her designs. Celtic and fantastic, dragons and wizards. Michelle was another dreamer who found reality a little too dull to bear. He talked and kept talking.

"Yes, the Celts always fascinated me." Flint had the knowledge to back up this story.

"And me, being Gaelic, like."

"Do you like Clannad?"

"Yes, of course."

"I've got everything they pressed into vinyl." Here he was beginning to let some truth slip. Truth is a wonderful camouflage for deceit.

"Me too." She smiled, and as she smiled, an idea began to hatch in Flint's mind. Less hatch, fester and breed perhaps. She had hazel eyes which widened as Flint flashed his teeth, spoke authoritatively on the Celts and claimed the same musical tastes as she. Yes, she was lonely, those eyes said it. They dilated as he talked, barely flicking on to other potential clients who picked at her wares.

"Do you take lunch?" This slick Grant Selby tried to ooze charm.

"I've got sandwiches. I get my best trade around lunchtime."

"Ah well, I was just going to find somewhere, another time perhaps, by way of apology? I'd love to talk about where you get your inspiration from. Do you market these? I mean, other than sell them yourself?"

"No."

He sucked in his cheeks, thoroughly enjoying his game of

deception. "Could alter that, I know one or two outlets which might take them."

Monica's little shop, for one, he thought. He may have to waffle a little more if she swallowed that bait.

"Well, I don't know." She glanced around at her wares.

"I know a good folk club in Islington, they have an excellent double act on this week. You must come along."

Michelle thought for a good twenty seconds, then gave a nervous grin. "Love to."

They arranged time and place, with Flint suppressing both glee and disgust at what he had achieved. It shouldn't have been that easy, but Flint had at least thirteen years of studied practice at the pick-up behind him. University had taught him more than how to date coins.

Chapter 19

Michelle enjoyed the Islington folk club. An Anglo-French couple performed a superbly professional set, but the French (and female) half stole the evening with a hilarious and talented imitation of a pig on a truffle hunt.

"So what do you do?" Michelle asked the heavily disguised Flint.

"This and that. My granny died and left me a house. I sold it and used the proceeds to finance my life of ill repute. I do a little dabbling here and there. Books mainly, a few artefacts, you know, scarabs from Egypt, pots from the Aegean. I buy and sell, it doesn't make one rich, but it's quite distracting. It allows me to travel and meet people."

"Have you been to Egypt?"

"Twice." Once would have been truthful, twice made a better story. Flint discovered he enjoyed inventing fiction, especially when he could back up every unlikely yarn with a heap of anecdotes. All the diggers' tales he had heard over the years were dredged from his memory and subtly altered to fit Grant Selby's globetrotting lifestyle.

"And what about you?" he asked, already bored of this boorish Grant Selby character.

"Oh, I don't do anything interesting really. I came over three years ago with my brother. He got married and went back to Kilkenny. I hate him anyway, he's such a sod."

"And have you many more family over here?"

She shook the black cascade of hair, then in the interval began to relate a sad life of a ruptured family, failed love affairs and failed careers.

"I'm just a mess, you see."

"Oh, you seem okay to me."

Just okay? her eyes said, pleading for someone to take notice of her. Her tattoos called out for attention. Dragons and snakes intertwined on the ample tapestry of her upper arms. Flint felt a stirring in his darker self.

"You seem to have built yourself a nice little niche."

"I survive, it pays the rent. You said you might know someone who wanted to sell my things."

He was a hostage in his own plot, he could not even risk Michelle and Monica meeting, so his one plausible contact was lost. Flint gave an inward curse and began to ferret for an excuse, but she saved him the trouble.

"I thought about that, and I decided it wouldn't be right," Michelle said. "I worked in a factory once and I don't want to again. I design my own things, I make them and I sell them. It's my world, see, I don't want to be a capitalist."

Flint smiled, thinking how odd it felt not to have those hot bristles crowding his cheeks. He wondered if she could see straight through his naked expression.

"You're a woman after my own heart. People have said, 'Grant, come into business with me,' but I just won't have it. My life suits me as it is."

He bought her a fifth pint of cider. Grant Selby would have been disgusted, but Flint passed no comment. The girls on his digs all drank pints and most of them knew when to stop. Squeezing himself in by the bar he looked back at Michelle, deeply saddened by what he had heard. Her attitude cried out a textbook of psychological tags: neuroses, anxiety, depression and lack of self-respect. She would get drunk frequently and she would sleep around. He knew it because he had once walked the same snake-strewn path. The pints came into his hands and he pushed back towards the welcoming face.

She touched his hand. "Thanks. I haven't paid for one of these yet."

"Don't worry, I've had a good week."

Her hand squeezed his and he squeezed back. Now what? He had learned nothing of value, but had absorbed enough hints that Michelle was in some way linked to Lucy. One of his anecdotes mentioned the obscure and dull market town of Durring and she had replied "Oh yes" with authority. He used a great many Celtic and occult references and again she accepted them without a murmur. Only when he switched to Classical allusions did she admit to gaps in her knowledge.

199

A bell rang out last orders.

"Another?" he asked, hoping for the answer no.

"You must think I'm a lush," she giggled. "No, no more."

"Fine."

There was a deep lonely longing in her eyes, it grabbed and held him each time he glanced her way. Seduction would be so easy, but completely wrong and not even necessary. His resistance began to crumble as another voice in his head whispered that it had been a long time since that anaemic romp with Chrissie Collings in the houseboat.

Michelle squeezed his hand again and gave a sigh he interpreted as "it's getting late". He was reminded of the lyric of the Hazel O'Connor song, "Will you?" Its saxophone drawl buzzed around in his head and refused to go away.

The barman rang his bell for the second time. Would it be cruel or kind to say yes? Would it help him get closer to the truth? Can any single man resist the come-on?

"Well," Michelle said, expecting something of him.

He had been through so many one-month, one-week and one-night relationships in the past. One more would not be out of character, he could forgive himself in the end.

"Do you live near here?" she asked.

Flint saw the question was loaded. "Out of town, Kent, Bromley way." But Grant Selby was a predator who would pounce, devour and retreat. "I could murder a coffee," he added.

"You could call in at my place, it's almost on your way."

Flint was saddened that he could smile, keep hold of her hand again and say yes.

Night passed into day in slow, sordid turmoil. At dawn, Flint slipped out of Michelle's devastated bedding and made an excuse to run. He offered another rendezvous rather than a simple promise to call her, or look her up. Sleepily and happily, she accepted.

Back at Central College, a yawning and hungover Jeffrey Flint delivered the first lecture of the day to two dozen yawning and hungover students. After an hour they were freed with his final burst of frenetic theory.

"Right, so have I turned you all into little Marxists?" Flint asked the class. "Go away and think about how you can apply Marxist theory to the Roman Empire. If you agree with me, I want to know

200

why. If you disagree, I want to know why. Essays in by December 1st, anything later I use for Christmas wrapping."

The class clattered to their feet and shunted from the main lecture theatre. Political interpretations of archaeology was a bit steep for the poor dears in the second week of term, but the prospectus had never promised things were going to be easy. Whilst his voice had purred about the Old Imperialist attitude, his mind had relived the previous night: rough, sweaty and squalid in an erotic sort of way. Partly elated, partly disgusted with himself, Flint stood down from the podium, thinking that Freud would probably be able to explain his conflicting emotions quite succinctly.

He pushed out of the doorway. Tyrone was waiting, file in one hand, plastic cup in the other.

"Suppose I said 'Horned Man' to you?" he said.

"Say it and try me."

"Horned Man."

Flint shook his head. "Nothing, I'm afraid."

"Got a minute to come to the computer room?"

"Sure, but let me grab a coffee first."

Tyrone was already within the computer suite when Flint, caffeine supply and pack of chocolate biscuits joined him. Tyrone already had a terminal active and fingered a key to conjure data on to the screen.

He accepted a biscuit and input "orned".

"It's easier than searching on 'Horned', it avoids glitches. Here we go. The Horned Man. Sometimes known as The Protector or The Overlord. Person of influence who is outside the coven, but uses his power to protect it. In the Middle Ages, he might be a rich landowner who provided a place for the witches to meet in safety. He might appear at a sabbat in the guise of a horned figure, here read the rest . . ."

"I fed you this data, remember?"

"Well, we've had three hints that Plant was afraid of a horned man."

Flint looked highly dubious. "Go on."

"Your postulate was that there was someone else involved in the Lucy business, in the cover-up if nothing else. Someone has helped tidy things up, making sure that once Plant was out of the way there were no more clues. Suppose there really is a Horned Man, someone higher than Plant, someone who doesn't want you

201

to find out the truth about Lucy, or just doesn't want you poking around in his business."

"Assuming it's a him. Let's not get sexist."

"If it was a woman, she wouldn't be called The Horned Man."

"Okay, okay. Any more daft ideas?"

"It has to be someone important, someone powerful enough to frighten Plant. Now what about this for an idea, perhaps he is powerful enough to influence the police."

Flint looked at him. "Serious?"

"They were very casual about the whole case, so I've got a who's who of the area and I'm adding all the senior policemen, judges, politicians . . ."

"Hang on, I'm supposed to be the anarchist, you're the budding pillar of society."

Tyrone looked sagely at Flint. "My dad's a councillor, a builder and a Freemason. You wouldn't believe what goes on in the real world."

"Perhaps I would."

"Right, so I'll put them on. How far did you get with the bint?"

What did he mean, precisely? Flint became instantly defensive. "She's not a bint, she's very sad and very lonely."

"But is she one of them?"

"If she isn't, she damn well should be."

Flint went back to his room, set thoughts of Michelle aside and turned his attention to preparing his night school class. He had entitled it "Aspects of Roman Archaeology", which gave him licence to talk on any subject he chose. That Wednesday he had promised to summarise architecture and town planning, so all he had to do was fish out forty of his slides of Rome, Ostia and Pompeii.

The class had grown since the beginning of term and now featured six ladies the far side of fifty, a couple in their mid-twenties and another half-dozen students of mixed sex and ages in between. Just as he was loading up his slide projector in the seminar room, a familiar tall figure walked in.

"Hello, Monica."

The tendons in her neck tensed as she whispered an embarrassed hello in return. "I'll just sit here at the back," she said.

The skeletal columns of the Temple of Castor and Pollux at

202

Rome slid on to the screen and Flint turned off the main lighting. His talk went well, he worked without notes, simply chatting about each holiday snap as it came on to the screen. Class scribbled furiously, then afterwards peppered him with questions. Monica was the last to leave when the room cleared at nine.

"That was very good," she said. "I've never been to Rome."

"You must." He poked an errant slide out of the carousel projector, then closed his slide box. "So, are you joining my class?"

"I thought I would, if you don't mind. Wednesday is my half-day closing and I always need an excuse to come to London."

"It's a long way."

"Oh Jeff, don't be so modest. You know why I'm here, I missed you. Thank you for your card, was Turkey wonderful?"

"Yes, I should have talked you into going."

"If only I could have." She pulled her dramatic sad expression.

Why is life so complicated, thought Flint. "Are you going straight back?"

She shrugged and again her face made apologies for her action. Flint found the mannerism cute and assumed she was embarrassed making advances to a younger man.

"There's a pub just round the corner which serves eight real ales and sixteen country wines, interested?" he asked.

Yes was the answer and within ten minutes he held a pint of Marsden's Pedigree whilst she sipped at the plum wine. Flint felt the awkwardness melt away as they talked, it was a relief to be talking straight once more, after the charade with Michelle.

"And what have you done with your beard?"

"New term, new image. It always looked a bit nineteen sixties, I just need to have my jeans surgically removed and I'll be a real person."

"I like you as you are."

Flint enjoyed a brief fantasy in which he cohabited with the owner of a wholefood and alternative lifestyle shop. It was the sort of hippy heaven he could warm to.

"We haven't seen you in Kingshaven since the summer, I thought you might be down."

"I'm trying to avoid the place – not you – just the place. It brings back unpleasant memories."

"I put your card up, but no one's shown any interest in it. What is this *De Niggers*? What are you up to?"

Flint touched his nose. "I have a cunning plan."

She wiggled a finger around in the air. "This is something to do with your mystery, isn't it?"

"It is, but I can't tell you what."

"Go on, brighten my life." She leaned forward to encourage him.

"No, Monica, people get hurt. I've got a hunch, but I'm keeping it to myself. I certainly don't want anyone in Kingshaven to know. Word might leak from somewhere, or Vikki Corbett might splash it all over her newspaper."

"She's a real bitch, don't you think?" Monica screwed up her eyes.

Actually, no, Flint didn't think that at all, but Monica continued to dig in her claws.

"I know someone who used to work with her, I've heard all the stories about Victoria Corbett."

"She always seemed okay to me. A little manic maybe."

"Be careful with her," Monica warned, "she's not what she seems, she has only one person's interest at heart, and that's her own. You can be sure she'll get nothing out of me."

Wow, he thought, Vikki must have sure trampled on a few toes in Kingshaven.

"Could you do me a little favour?" Flint asked once the character assassination was complete. He told her about Tyrone's list of suspects and how he was trying to glean intelligence on each one.

"Some of these people must come into your shop," he said, "could you do a little spying for me?"

She raised one eyebrow. "So you think the people you're after might come into my shop?"

"Frankly, yes. It would suit them perfectly."

"Where did you get all these names from in the first place?"

"We're archaeologists, we dig around. It started out with this ghost-hunter who calls himself Professor Leopold Gratz. He's written a couple of books, do you stock them?"

"No, are they any good?"

"No, well, they're par for the course. I find a lot of this New Age stuff is complete garbage."

Monica glanced around in case the crowded room was full of her clients. "To be really truthful, so do I."

"Can I be really truthful now, Monica?" It was time he displayed his hand. "I want to tell you something about myself."

"Please do."

"Ask anyone at college about me and they will tell you I'm an unrepentant womaniser."

"I did," she grinned. "I know what the diggers said about your reputation, but I'm an adult, I'm not frightened. Frankly, I was surprised when . . ."

"I didn't try something on at Burkes Warren? So was I, so was everyone else, I expect. I'd like to see you again, Monica, but I'd like to take things slowly."

"Is there someone else?" she asked gingerly.

"No," he said sharply, then wondered whether this was a lie. "It's just that I've grown out of one-night stands."

"That's nice," she said with deep sincerity, "I'm not a prude, but I'm not a bed-hopper either."

So Monica was apparently content with the quiet affection he had shown and she had returned to Kingshaven alone. Flint felt better for the evening with the mature woman, it prepared him mentally for the next night with Michelle. Whatever transpired, whatever the cost, he had to get back into her room and inside her mind.

On his next visit to Michelle's flat, it was as chaotic as he had remembered it. They planned to see a revival of *The Rocky Horror Show*, and Flint had called early. Michelle had met him in a saffron bath wrap, kissed him fruitily, then left him alone in her room as she went to shower. Her new lover sat on her secondhand black patent sofa and moved his attention from one to another of five paintings signed "Michelle". One was a self-portrait, in which she cast herself as a tall, thin seductress on a rain-swept down. For Flint, there was too much grey, too much heavy black rain. She must have been really depressed when she slashed it into existence.

He wondered how safe he was, sleeping with a woman whose mind seemed set on another plane. She had told him about the attempted overdose when her drunken ex-lover had walked out a year before. She had told him a group of friends had saved her, but offered no detail about who they were.

Flint padded across to the loosely nailed planks beside the chimney breast which served as bookshelves. Art books replaced archaeology texts, but otherwise, this could have been Lucy's collection. One spine caught his eye, a book of poetry, entitled *Eyes on a Clear Day* by R. Temple-Brooke. He pulled it out, smiling at the pretentious photograph of a tweed-jacketed man posing against a tree trunk. He stopped smiling, Lucy had owned this same collection of New Age doggerel. He flicked to the first page.

"To Willow, with love – R.T.B."

Hazel? Willow? Rowan? A hand seized his heart and stayed there. He had been right, Michelle was close to the centre of whatever was going on. One hunch, one lucky break as Bogart might have said, and he had broken through.

Michelle came from the shower, rubbing her hair with a towel, another inadequately draped around her breasts.

"This any good?" Flint showed her the book.

"Yes, I find poetry very relaxing, don't you?"

"Of course. I've never heard of this guy though."

"Oh he's marvellous, I've heard him recite."

"Where?" Perhaps the question shot out of him a little too sharply.

"Oh, at festivals. You know I'm really into the New Movement. I go to sell things. He swapped me this book for one of my dragon plaques at Glastonbury."

He tried to recall having seen her at the poetry reading. Perhaps she had sat next to the girl with the Apache jacket.

"Is Willow your middle name?" Flint played at playing with the dedication.

She discoloured. "It was a sort of in-joke."

Michelle went to dress, leaving Flint in a state of high excitement. Everything was coming together wonderfully and at last, he had a good idea who Hazel was.

Chapter 20

Rowan knelt within her special room. Naked, she wore only the protection of the pentagram. She gazed up at the sky she had painted herself and concentrated with all her power. She was like a householder who sees a line of damp above the skirting board, and without the skill to arrest it, watches the decay advance up the wall day by day. First the wallpaper is stained, then the plaster bursts, then the very fabric of the house comes under threat. What was Flint doing? What could he know? She knew beyond doubt that he was ferreting around again, possibly at random, possibly with something certain to work on. Samahain was drawing close; it was the date by which she had to act.

Tyrone was aware of Rowan only as a name. He had a role for her, too, but as yet he had not connected the pair. Part of the time he spent in the computer suite, he was constructing his bibliography for Late Roman Britain. At intervals, he switched to the directory of files labelled LUCY.

It was late on a Wednesday, the day which most London University students took as sacrosanct, but Tyrone would skip sports and society meetings to have the run of the computer room and a quiet library. A pile of print-outs lay across the workstation, containing all the names mentioned by each person interviewed by Vikki, or by Flint, or known to be associates or relatives of Plant. Tyrone had added Barbara (inheriting £12,000), Mrs Plant, and Amelia Winter (double bluff). He still needed a Horned Man and a father for Lucy's unborn child.

Chief Inspector Douglas went into the list together with a pile of local dignitaries, politicians, a pop star, a second rate novelist, two judges (one retired) and the head of the local masonic lodge (information via his father). He had added R. Temple-Brooke, as the name appeared in four lists; the list of Lucy's contacts; the list of Michelle's contacts; the who's who of the Darkewater Valley and the list supplied by Leopold Gratz. Other names kept swimming to his attention, names which meant nothing without proof to nail them as suspects.

Turning off the machine, he went into his study room to lock up and study the wall chart again. Flint had added a box labelled "Michelle = Willow". He had also written "Hazel = Lucy?" and both were connected by the book of poems. Tyrone knew a game was being played, with Jeffrey Flint on one side trying to outwit an unknown opponent who manoeuvred his pieces unseen. This was not like archaeology where the facts remained stationary, waiting to be found, it was more akin to postal chess.

He locked his own office. Outside, the corridors were dark, almost everyone had gone home, or back to what passed for home during term time. Light showed from under the door marked "Dr J. S. Flint", its occupant presumably waiting for his night school to arrive. Monica would be coming too, Tyrone expected. She was too old for Flint, someone should tell him. Tyrone knocked.

"Come in, Tyrone."

Tyrone pushed the door open. "How did you know it was me?"

"Your Hush Puppies squeak."

"Sorry."

"Plus, everyone who lacks your dedication went home at lunchtime. Have you read this?"

The lecturer held up Lucy's copy of R. Temple-Brooke's *Eyes on a Clear Day*.

"Should I?"

Flint opened the book at a marked page. "Read. Be enlightened."

Tyrone cleared his throat and read the passage aloud.

> . . . All earth's blackness I despise,
> For *De Nigris* shields mine eyes,
> And holds the power to thwart them still,
> I shall endure, survive I will . . .

208

He groaned, "What a heap of dross."

"And so it goes on."

"I'm surprised anyone published it." Tyrone dropped into the soggy chair, flicking idly through the remainder of the poems.

"He uses a vanity publisher. They try to solicit my business all the time."

"So, in effect, this Temple-Brooke person has to pay people to read his poems."

"Not quite. He seems to like giving copies away to young ladies."

"Lucy and your Michelle?"

"Hazel and Willow."

"Those names are pathetic, don't you think?"

"They may be designed to confuse people – they confused us for long enough."

Tyrone flicked the pages of the book again, running from back to front. He still hadn't mastered Flint's knack of reading pages at a glance. "To save me reading all this, are there any more mentions of *De Nigris*?"

"No, but you can see why I'm curious. *De Nigris* does not exist, so why is this cretin quoting it as if it were the Bible?"

Perhaps it did exist, Tyrone had argued before Flint had evicted him from his office. Perhaps it did, but the night school came first, with more pretty slides of mosaics to illustrate a talk on villas and rural settlement. Monica was there, taking notes as assiduously as the rest, and afterwards Flint took her for a drink in what looked like becoming their usual place.

Monica had been telling him of how she had become dissatisfied with teaching and found a new meaning to life through healthy nutrition and meditation. He had related a couple of inconsequential college dramas which had kept the air alive after the excitement of freshers week. Monica wore a high-necked blouse she had embroidered herself, with a small blue gem hanging at her throat. She would toy with it from time to time as she listened to what he had to say.

"Monica," he said, changing tone as he moved on to business, "did you make any progress with that list?"

"No, I'm sorry, most of my customers are faces, I rarely know their names."

"I'll try to get pictures if I can." He thought of Michelle and how touched she would be if he asked for a photograph, then winced at the hypocrisy.

"Bring it, please, anything I can do." She was all well-worn smiles as usual.

"The other thing is that book, *De Nigris*, the one I advertised. Have you ever heard of it before?"

"No."

"It's just that there's a poem which mentions it, I have it here." He reached into the pocket of his jacket and pulled out *Eyes on a Clear Day*. "It belonged to Lucy."

She took the book without a word, then turned to the dedication. "It says Hazel here."

Flint waved away the anomaly. "Lucy had it, I haven't quite worked out who Hazel is yet."

He instructed her how to find the poem, noticing how she fumbled with unfamiliarity.

"You introduced the author at Glastonbury, I thought you'd know his works well."

"Oh yes, Rupert's an old friend."

"I must meet him again, try my list on him. You could set it up."

"No," said Monica sharply, "I couldn't, he wouldn't thank me for it. He's a very private person. He enjoys his public readings, but normally he keeps to himself." She hesitated. "I only ever see him at readings."

Ah, thought Flint, Monica had been name-dropping and now regretted it. He should give her space to retreat. "Tell you what, I'll drop him a line."

"Do that."

Monica seemed less well at ease that night and wanted to leave before last orders. She had a long drive, so Flint could hardly blame her. He sauntered back towards the Tube station, feeling the cold in the air, thinking he needed something smarter to wear than a surplus RAF greatcoat. Monica might be less help than he had first hoped and he had not enjoyed the evening so much as the previous week. Perhaps he had again met someone to whom he was mismatched.

A gang of youths screamed and ran from the yellow mouth of the Tube station. Flint watched them go, checked there was no danger, then turned his eye towards the telephones, thinking of that accursed book. He drew out his diary and searched for the scrawled telephone number beside the name "Gratz, L."

Leopold Gratz proved reluctant to meet Jeffrey Flint again, certainly not at his home, certainly not at half a day's notice following a midnight phone call. Flint was insistent and they compromised. Gratz was due to visit the British Library, and agreed to a casual rendezvous in the British Museum.

The following afternoon, Flint loitered by the Elgin marbles, feeling rather nostalgic for hectic days of love and adventure in Greece. The Parthenon in Athens had been the scene of another cloak-and-dagger mystery, now many years in the past. His life seemed crowded with women now, but in those days there had been only one and his throat dried at the memory. Where was she now? Did she ever think of him?

He switched his concern to the present. Where the hell was Leopold Gratz? As he waited for the occultist he wondered if years must elapse before the knotted cords of Lucy's disappearance could be untangled. Twenty minutes passed, then a familiar figure stalked into the gallery, a pile of books and papers pushed under his arm. He was looking the wrong way.

"Professor Gratz!"

Gratz gave a start, then reached out for a hand to shake. "Leopold, dear man, call me Leopold."

"Good to see you here. I could easily have come to your place."

"No, no. It's better if you don't. I was coming here anyway. Otherwise, I'm keeping a low profile." Gratz glanced one way, then the other, then back again.

"Low profile?"

"Yes, I said low profile." The Scots Brogue was stronger than ever before. He nodded for melodramatic emphasis.

Flint found the temptation to glance around irresistible. "What's going on, Leopold?"

"I warned you about dabbling; I told you that some people can be determined." Gratz spoke in low tones, nodding his head and bringing his eyebrows down to shield his eyes.

"Leopold, everything is cool. Since I found the body, no one has threatened me, no one has tried to incinerate me, I've had no more sick parcels . . ."

211

"Perhaps you have not, but I have!" Gratz broke in. "On Saturday I received a letter dipped in blood. Ox blood I daresay, but blood all the same. It is not a message I would ignore."

"What does it say?"

"You may have it." He drew a rolled plastic bag from his pocket. "You may add it to your collection."

Strong odours of dead animal pierced Flint's nostrils as the bag was unrolled.

"It's a little reekie." Gratz passed over the bag.

Two Japanese tourists had stopped and payed close attention to the English ritual of passing the blood-stained letter. Flint glared at them and when they hurried away, he turned his attention back to the macabre object. The lower third of a stiff cartridge sheet had been dipped in blood, which had now turned a crispy brown. Above the gore had been typed a two-line couplet:

> Blood flows down The Darkewater Valley,
> Do not let your veins feed the river.

"Very theatrical. Posted in south London?"

Gratz grimaced. "So you are a mindreader too."

Plant had been a long time dead still to be issuing threats. It was odd that someone should suddenly feel threatened by Gratz, odder still that they even knew about him.

"Shall we move?" Gratz was becoming nervous, so they strolled towards the Assyrian room. "I think this is my fault, I have been making a few enquiries on your behalf."

"And somehow the message has got back?"

Gratz nodded. "So if it's all the same to you, I'll stop asking. A dead man, a burnt boat and now this . . ."

He touched the top of the bag which Flint had pushed into his own jacket pocket.

"Well, that's your choice. Pity. Did you find out anything?"

"Since we last spoke I've been to a couple of conventions. I asked about your book, *De Nigris*. Interesting."

"It exists?"

"Something of that nature seems to have appeared on the scene. There is a rumour, a persistant rumour that a powerful and unknown grimoire has been found."

212

All around the walls of the museum was evidence of the antiquity of fearful religious belief.

"It's nonsense though, Leopold. Tell me it's nonsense."

"So it's nonsense." He stopped and spread his hands skywards. "Those who wish magic to exist are always spreading rumours of a Great Book, or a Great Leader. At the moment, we have both this book and a sort of Black Messiah."

"Like your Horned Man?"

"Indeed. He will be discovered to be a charlatan, however, just like all the others."

Flint watched a group of schoolgirls pass, thinking fleetingly of Lucy Gray, the reason for all this mind-warping incursion into the occult.

"Leopold, what can you tell me about R. Temple-Brooke?"

Gratz cocked his head to one side. He was rather shorter than Flint and had to gaze upwards. "He's a minor writer who hangs around the New Age fringe. I met him some time back in the summer and mentioned your problem. He lives in your area, so I thought he might know something of what's going on, but apparently not."

"Is there any chance he's involved? I have three mystery women involved in this coven, but I'm desperately seeking male suspects."

"Temple-Brooke seemed to know of that Piers Plant character but dismissed him as a crank. He has what you might term a philosophical perspective on the New Age and he's always been very scathing about the paranormal."

"He seems to know all about *De Nigris*, to the extent of writing a poem about it."

"Has he indeed? I always found his literary criticism very astute, but his poetry is not his best work. That does not stop some of his younger adherents calling him The Poet . . ."

". . . memories of Aleister Crowley?"

Flint had read all about the founder of Golden Dawn, the inter-war cult of sex magic.

"Temple-Brooke is no Crowley," Gratz said with confidence.

"You know him that well?"

"No, but the leading occult figures are well known to me and he is not one of them. If anything, he's on our side of the fence. He's very conservative."

213

"What does he do, I mean, how does he make his living?"

"He doesn't. He inherited a little land out near the coast and he married money to keep it going. His real name is James Rupert Tempelson and R. Temple-Brooke is his pen name. I suppose calling himself Rupert Brooke would have been a little too presumptuous even for him. He has standing, of sort, in the locality, I understand he's a failed politician."

"He sounds the right sort of figure to be your Horned Man. My assistant has a devious and colourful conspiracy theory."

"Temple-Brooke has a high public profile in other fields, he's a publisher, I've even written in his magazine *New Sceptic*. He is not your Horned Man, but you might find it worthwhile speaking to him on your own account."

Flint shook his head. "I've stopped tackling people head-on. The last thing I want to do is stir things up again. Too many people got hurt last term."

Gratz pulled out a pocket watch and found an excuse to go. He slapped Flint on the arm. "Well, I won't be getting hurt either, you take care, m'boy."

It would be another one of those terms, Flint could see it coming. Archaeology was already taking a back seat to playing detective, as Professor Grant would put it. After talking to Gratz he only had three hours to kill before meeting Michelle. A conference in Bradford was expecting to hear his third-century critique and he had still not had time to work enough jokes into his paper. Flint slipped the bloodstained letter into his briefcase, then decided to go back to his flat. He would work on the paper, take a shower, then dress up in his Grant Selby costume once more.

Supper comprised chicken in black bean sauce, chop suey vegetables, special fried rice and a bottle of something execrable. The pair spent the evening seated under the stairs in one of Soho's cheaper Chinese restaurants. Feet clomped overhead as patrons hunted the loo.

"So can you read Latin?" Flint, as Grant Selby, glugged the last of the wine into Michelle's glass.

"What?"

"Medieval Latin."

"God, no, I failed all my 'O'-levels, except Art and English."

"Then the book would have been useless to you."

"What book?"

"*De Nigris*, John Eastney. Remember, it's what brought us together."

"Oh, yes, I suppose so."

"I was intrigued by the number of people who were after it, I mean, I'd never heard of it. What on earth made you want to own a book like that?"

"I dunno. Just curious."

"You know what it is?"

"I think so."

"It's a grimoire, a spell book."

"Yes," she gave a little laugh and looked into the wine glass, "I told you, I'm interested in that sort of thing."

"So am I, in a sort of way."

"I know, I can tell. I do fortunes."

"What method do you use?"

"Tarot, and I read palms."

Flint extended his right hand.

"Oh, I've had too much to drink."

"So we've got an interest in common . . ." he began.

"Another interest," she corrected, "we like the same music. We fit together well."

What did she mean by that? He studied that round face, trying hard to like her, not to look down on Michelle. She took his probing for interest and seemed inflated by it.

"You intrigue me, Michelle." Flint was telling the truth for once. "There is more to you than meets the eye."

She giggled, almost happy for her obscure interests to be drawn out.

"Your book collection is something else."

"I bet you've got ten times as many."

"So I do."

How should he attack the subject? When should he attack the subject? Flint hovered on the brink of plunging into an interrogation, but drew back. Michelle could turn and walk away and he would lose the only firm grip he had on the situation. Game playing had to continue. Lucy would have understood.

"You know you said you wanted to see *Cats*?" Flint started another oblique ploy.

"Did I? Yes, I've wanted to see it for ages."

215

"I got us a pair of tickets for next Tuesday."

"Oh . . ." Her enthusiasm was punctured as she realised the date. "I can't, not then, can you change them?"

Something within Flint cheered. Tuesday was October 31st.

"I don't know, I'll try," he replied after letting her dangle for a few moments, "I could always take my landlady."

"Is she pretty?" Michelle was downcast.

"She may have been in 1953."

Her anxiety relaxed. "Could you make Wednesday?"

"No, I have . . ." he almost said "a night school to run". "I have an appointment."

He had so nearly tripped up and betrayed himself. Flint made a note to keep on his guard, but began to worry in case he had already let tiny clues slip from his lips. When the meal was over, they took a taxi back to her flat and she went through the charade of making them coffee whilst he again looked at her books.

"You're really into the occult," was his comment as she came back in with the two mugs, each the product of an English craft potter.

"It's a sort of hobby," she said.

"A growing hobby," Flint continued to flick through an A to Z of Weird Britain. He closed it with a snap and whirled around. "Do you know, I read that neo-paganism could be the growth religion of the new millenium."

She sat down, looking worried.

"And not before time," he said, joining her and extending an arm, "we could do with some decent home-grown religions instead of importing everything from the Middle East."

She touched his thigh and dug fingernails through the leg of his slacks. "Do you really mean that, Grant?"

"Sure, I've read up on just about every religion there is. The way I see it, neo-paganism brings everything and everyone together. Man, woman, animals, planet. I met this coven of witches when I was at Glastonbury," he went on to detail his moonlight dance with the West Country girls. "It was all terribly jolly, it beats psalm-singing any day."

Michelle gripped him tighter. "Make love to me, Grant."

"Now?"

"Now."

After half an hour, Flint lay on the bed feeling as a whore must

216

feel. He felt nothing for Michelle, and had covered this by the intensity of his erotic assault. Inwardly he grimaced, these people were dragging him down, slowly, into their pit. Stonehenge had been the beginning, so many flirtations with obscure books and eccentric beliefs had followed. Now there was this degrading use of a fellow human being, one who was willing, even happy to be used.

Michelle lay half on top of him, making purring noises. "Grant, would you mind if I were a witch?"

His pulse quickened, but he allowed himself to relax. "Are you a good witch or a bad witch?"

"Good." She ran her fingers around in the hairy patch on his chest.

"Hmm, you're very good," he said in character, thinking this was the sort of comment lovers made.

"I've got these friends . . ."

"Who call you Willow?"

"You guessed!"

"I've read all the books, seen the films, I know. I'm a minor expert in this field."

"You should join us," she said softly, "we'd be ever so happy together."

First she had seduced him, now she was recruiting him, this was becoming serious. Either he was succeeding in getting through her defences, or she was breaking through his. Who was using who, he wondered.

Chapter 21

A new wine bar had opened beside South Kensington tube station. Halloween week provided the excuse to string up a few paper bats and allocate ghastly names to the cocktails.

Vikki Corbett never missed an opportunity to come up to London and was intrigued by the invitation to dinner. Jeffrey Flint was normally penniless and might not even own a tie.

She had made herself up heavily, too heavily, she decided on the Tube when it was too late to rectify the damage. How did Jeff like his women, with make-up or without? Clean, or caked in mud? On being shown to her table, she was stunned by what she saw. Jeffrey Flint had a smoothly shaved, rather weak chin and wore a well-cut navy blazer with co-ordinated tie.

"Jeff, I didn't recognise you." She gave the waiter her long purple coat and slung her handbag over the chair back. "Honestly, you look ten years younger."

"What, like a fifteen-year-old?"

She took a few moments to absorb the quip. "And where did you rip off that jacket?"

"I borrowed it, off one of my hard-up students."

"I'll bet it was that Tyrone."

"It was."

"He's a real wide boy, that one."

A ghostly waiter passed a menu over her shoulder. She ordered a Vampire Venom to clash with Flint's Blue Demon and opted for the steak.

"Stake, vampires, get it?" She pressed a pun of her own.

He got it, groaned at the joke, then opted for the tagliatelle. They small-talked around her holiday in Corfu and his in Turkey.

"Vince was a real reptile," she admitted, "I thought he'd improve on holiday, but he was worse, always boozing and leching."

Flint's expression appeared to brighten. When her drink arrived, the archaeologist began to tell her about the Bradford conference where the establishment had savaged his iconoclastic paper on the third century.

"I called it 'Crisis, what crisis?', after the old *Private Eye* scandal. The radicals loved it, the red-nosed classicists were outraged and both reactions gave me the utmost pleasure."

She thought she would draw him away from archaeology in case he decided to explain his paper in detail. "Do you bring women here all the time?"

"Oh, I'm a reincarnation of Casanova, haven't you heard? I've done nothing else this past fortnight but date women."

"Jeff! That's not funny."

"It was a joke."

"It's still not funny, now what's going on? Why are you lashing out on all this?" She indicated the vault-like interior of the wine bar.

"I'm on expenses."

"Of course. Doctor Barbara Faber, née Gray. She doesn't like me. She thinks I'm a vulture."

"And why would she think that?"

"Is she one of your women?" Vikki prickled with hostility, wondering what his game was.

"No, I'm avoiding her. I send her bills, she rings me up and becomes melodramatic. Her mother took the fun at Forest Farm very badly."

"It proved that Lucy is dead."

"Hmm. I have a growing hunch about what happened to Lucy, and where she is."

Vikki had switched her eyes towards the steaming plates being brought fresh from the microwave. Her attention snapped back at his words.

"What?"

Slowly, Flint began to narrate what he had done since the summer, the clues he had unearthed, the questions which he wanted answering. He would stop and concentrate on his food at intervals, perhaps using the time to edit his story.

"And I thought it was all over." She sawed away at the steak as Flint related the tale. "You should have been a detective."

219

"I am, after a fashion." Using his fork as a trowel and his tagliatelle as a model, he began to expound.

"I'm an archaeologist, they train us to think, stick together bits of incomplete jigsaws that don't really make sense on their own. When we excavate a site, Vikki, we first strip off the overburden, that's all the modern junk which gets in the way of what we're looking for. Then we dig the archaeological deposits layer by layer, slowly going back in time. Fifteenth century, fourteenth century and so on. Gradually the whole picture emerges, but it is only when the process is completed that you can look backwards at it and reconstruct the history of the site."

"But how do you know when to stop digging?"

He dug his fork viciously into the mutilated pasta. "When I strike natural soil, undisturbed by man. The deepest layer, where there is nothing left to excavate. Then I know I've found everything I can."

"So you're digging? How far down are you?"

"Extending the metaphor, somewhere in the Dark Ages. The superficial has been removed, the deepest secrets are still to be revealed."

"Very mysterious." She had lapsed back towards disbelief. "You've ruined your meal."

"Well, I've had better. How's the steak?"

She pushed aside a strip of fat with her knife. "So-so. I was surprised to hear from you, but I came because I had the same ideas. After the cremation of Piers Plant I met his ex-wife and we had a woman-to-woman chat. You know why she divorced him?"

"Impotence?"

"Shoots blanks." Vikki had a tongue in her cheek as she nodded. "So we know why he went into all this kinky stuff. He felt inadequate, especially in the company of other men. She said he became more and more unbearable and started to act oddly."

"What did he think of children?" Flint had still not told Vikki about Lucy's pregnancy.

"He loved them and so did she. She talked about adopting, but he just wanted to try a few crazy remedies and it all fell apart. She ran off with another teacher and they've got three sprogs now. I asked her if Plant had any close friends, and she said, 'Have you spoken to Monica?' She said that this Monica and Plant used to be like brother and sister. It was something else his wife hated."

Flint's eyes narrowed. "We're talking what, seven years ago?"

"Something like that. Anyhow, I did talk to her before Plant disappeared and I went back again after the funeral, but she says she hasn't had much to do with him in the past few years."

"Nor has anyone else. I know Monica, she came digging this summer, we get on well."

"Is *she* one of your women?" Vikki was both intrigued by the older woman and also oddly jealous of her. Monica Clewes was all beads and joss-sticks, perhaps Jeff's new image was purely cosmetic.

"We get along, she's been helping me round up the evidence. But more important, I've met a girl, who I'm sure is part of the London branch of whatever network Plant and his friends belong to."

"What's her name?" Vikki reached for her handbag. The notepad was out in an instant.

"No names."

"You don't trust me, do you?"

"As they say in the best movies, I don't trust anyone."

He bared all his teeth in a wide grin, the smug bastard. "And I thought we were friends."

"Guess what happens if you print a story advertising my latest theories. Someone killed Lucy, I'm certain, and it wasn't the Demon Curator. That same someone then tidied up the plot by arranging for poor demented Piers to commit suicide. If he can kill two, he can kill four." Flint unrolled a computer print-out. "This is Tyrone's list of suspects. I want you to find out everything you can about them."

She looked at the list. "This will take for ever."

"No it won't. Next Tuesday is Halloween, Walpurgis Night, Samahain, one of the two holiest days in the Pagan calendar. Somewhere out there, our friends will be enjoying a rather cold moonlight party."

"I'm not staking out another one of your standing stones, we've played that game," Vikki warned.

"No, Tyrone has another cunning plan, Plan B, he calls it. I think it stands a chance of working. We'll run around in the moonlight whilst you telephone everyone on this list. If they're at home, cross them off."

Vikki looked at the list again, a frisson rippling though her. She prodded Flint's glass, which was empty save puddles of ice cubes. "What did that blue stuff taste like?"

"Paraffin."

"Let's go for the green ones, then."

She called the waiter and ordered two Glowing Ghouls. "Witches meet for moonlight mass, would make such a good story for Halloween," she said with a hint of whimsy in her voice, but Flint cut her short.

"No stories!" He thumped his empty glass on the table.

Vikki sat back, suppressing a giggle. "I'm only teasing, don't hate me for it. My lips are sealed. Now tell me all about Plan B."

Tyrone had not enjoyed the Bradford conference. He hated northern towns and his bias was increased by the rough ride his paper had been given. It may have been a mistake to imitate Flint's cavalier style of delivery so closely, but more of a mistake to launch incomplete ideas on to an unreceptive audience. "The end of Roman Britain is a fallacy" had been a suitably Flint-ish title, but Tyrone realised he still had much to learn.

Plan A had been a farce at Lugsanadh, but for Samahain, Flint had suggested a resurrection of Plan B. This time there would be no mistakes, Tyrone would have the personnel and the equipment required to ensure success. The Hunt Saboteurs loaned their three walkie-talkies for a small bribe, whilst a rental company provided two mobile phones. Beers bought volunteers from members of the college AeroSoc and by Tuesday, October 31st, he knew he was going to make the breakthrough.

Tyrone had always wanted to tail someone, so Halloween saw his wish come true. He sat inside his Spitfire watching No. 37a, with one of his volunteers lounging in the seat beside him. They had seen Michelle close her curtains as it had grown dark, then waited for two toe-numbing hours.

A brown Allegro slowed to a halt and stood with its motor running amidst a cloud of steam, flushed orange by the street lights.

"Glyn! Scramble!" Tyrone hissed.

"Is that her car?"

"Tart at two o'clock."

The figure of Michelle was seen briefly darting from house to car, and as soon as she was inside, it moved slowly away. Tyrone started his own engine, barking out the registration number of the

222

Allegro for his co-pilot to jot down. Flint had safely predicted that Michelle would catch a train to one of four stations in the valley. Plan B was already going awry.

Glyn had practised with the mobile phone, communicating with Flint in the Durring station car park. He took up the phone and after a few minutes' repeated attempts, got through. Tyrone took the handset from him and talked whilst he followed the Allegro into traffic. "She's been picked up in a car."

Flint let out a clinical obscenity.

"Hey Doc, we've got one registration number and I'm hard on his tail."

"Tyrone, you'll lose him before he leaves London."

"But there's only one road he can sensibly take, wait Doc."

Tyrone told Glyn to hunt out the OS map. They then suggested that Flint and his Land-Rover full of AeroSoc students wait in the layby for the Allegro to pass. He would chase from behind.

The Allegro was lost within ten minutes. Tyrone tapped his wheel whilst his companion hopefully checked cars elsewhere in the traffic queues. It was one of those damp, clinging nights with a fine mist never quite turning into rain. Traffic thinned as the city was left behind, then Tyrone stamped down his foot and accelerated into the night. If he reached the Land-Rover without seeing the Allegro, it was somewhere behind him. Otherwise, he would catch it, unless it too was driven by a frustrated fighter pilot.

"Shit!"

Through the spray at almost ninety miles per hour, the unmistakable hunched shape of the Allegro was visible after ten or fifteen minutes. They had already checked two such cars at close quarters, but after tail-gating the third car for a mile, Tyrone was able to read the plate and drop back.

"Tell ground control."

"You're a prat, Tyrone," his passenger commented.

"Just do it, or get out and walk back."

"I could have gone to the Halloween disco."

"Just dial."

They saw the Land-Rover fleetingly as they passed the lay by at fifty-five. Behind them, headlights sprang to life as Flint made to join the chase. The Allegro took the Durring bypass, then headed inland, away from Kingshaven. The Darkewater megaliths were ignored, the car turning on to minor roads beyond Potter

Bramton. Sometimes, Tyrone could see lights in his mirror. Flint was too laid-back for this, the college Land-Rover too knackered and abused to keep pace.

Suddenly, the Allegro was gone. As they breasted a hill, Tyrone snapped on his beam and had a clear road ahead of him. He stamped on his brakes, then began to reverse. In the dark lane, and the thick night, he could see nothing. He engaged forward gear and trundled forward until he found a field gate, then performed a clumsy five-point turn. Slowly he made his way back up the hill, towards the approaching headlights.

"That will be Flint," Tyrone said.

"That way!" Glyn had spotted a minor lane on the left and Tyrone skidded to another halt, almost colliding with an oncoming Range Rover. Both cars stopped dead at the junction. The Spitfire stalled.

Tyrone had been winding down the window to speak to Flint, but Flint was not the driver of the Range Rover. The man could be heard muttering "Fool" as he made a wide turn around the back of Tyrone's car then vanished up the lane.

"Number?" Tyrone asked.

"Sorry."

It was Tyrone's turn to swear. The number plate had been out of angle and all he had seen was the circular sticker featuring a Red Setter. He restarted the car to await Flint's arrival.

Flint did not arrive. After ten minutes, they tried the mobile phone, then the walkie-talkie. Another car turned up the little-used lane, so Tyrone decided to follow it. He had no problem in following the car for mile after mile until it turned into a farm gateway and stopped. Tyrone pulled up at the side of the road in a state of complete demoralisation.

"So much for Plan B," he said.

If Tyrone had consulted his OS map, he would have noticed a long, narrow valley terminating at a spring about five miles south of where he sat. Flick through an antiquarian guide to the valley and Holywell Syke is listed under sites of minor historical interest. Over the mouth of the spring is a large erratic boulder, reputed in local myth to be connected with the ancient Celtic "cult of source".

In the seclusion of the hills, under the protection of a benign farmer, the covens gathered around the well. Anxieties of the summer could be forgotten, cares were released in worship of the Earth, before they huddled into the warmth of the barn.

Rowan had assembled three circles and, yes, The Protector had appeared in his horned guise and delivered a deep, reverential prophesy from The Book. The weather was damp and cold as Samahain often was, so the revellers soon put back their clothes and huddled within the barn, fired by the brew and animated by the prophesy. When the rites were over, they fell back into the straw, finding cosy niches to chat or simply to lie with friends.

"Willow, it's good to see you so happy." Rowan laid a gentle hand on Michelle's black shawl. Michelle sat on a bale before one of the mobile heaters, drinking blackberry tea.

"She's got a new feller," Hawthorn said, with a knowing look.

"Not one of us?" Rowan was little concerned. Her people could live double lives, there were no rules.

"He might be, one day. He's very interested in the New Age, he even owned a copy of The Book for a while."

Rowan blinked. "Pardon?"

"He advertised it, it was on a card in Walker's bookshop . . ."

"Did you mention tonight to him?" Rowan's tone switched to a stern interrogative.

"No, why should I? I just rang him about the advert." Michelle began to tremble. "I'm sorry, I didn't mean to do anything wrong."

"Come with me a moment, could you?" Rowan took Michelle by the arm and led her from the barn, out into the wet air of a new November. In the lee of the barn, Rowan released her.

"I want you to tell me everything about him."

Michelle was questioned closely and sharply. At first, she gave straight answers, confused by the interrogation. Then she became hesitant as Rowan pressed her.

"A dealer in antiquities?" Rowan said in her most cynical voice.

"Yes."

"And rare books?"

"Yes, what's wrong with that?"

"And he's rich, and handsome?"

"He's okay."

"I bet he's anything but okay."

"How do you know . . ."

"Willow. Listen to me!" Rowan bit deep with her nails into Michelle's arm. "People who hate us are out to destroy us. I want to know about this man. Who he is, where he lives, what he looks like, where he goes."

"Why?"

"Because he is lying. He cannot have a copy of The Book, believe me, he cannot. The Protector himself has told me."

"But he's really nice . . ." Michelle began to sob.

"Grant Selby, great gods, what a name! He sounds too nice, Willow, why on earth should someone like that take a fancy to you. You were a drunk, you took drugs, we took you in, we saved your soul and you go back to sleeping around like a common slut. You slept with him the first night, didn't you?" Rowan knew she had the power to command answers.

"Yes," came the sob.

"And where is the sanctity of your body?"

"I just want someone."

Just for a moment, Rowan felt a shard of sympathy. She too had a fear of being unloved and growing old.

"Do you know who your someone is? Doctor Jeffrey Flint, BSc, PhD, FSA, MIFA, thirty-one years old, born in Leeds. He's five feet ten inches tall, eleven and a half stones, has straw-coloured hair, blue eyes, he's clean shaven with red glasses."

"His glasses are gold."

"So he changes his glasses, you stupid bitch!" Rowan struck out at Michelle, swiping the slap across her cheek. Leaving the girl in a hysterical huddle, she went back inside the barn.

Elm stood talking by the far wall, jogging the keys of his Allegro in his hand.

"Take Willow home, she has betrayed us," Rowan said, quivering with rage.

He was a middle-aged, paunchy man who everyone in the Balls Pond Road thought was Jewish, like his ancestors. Elm missed the point of her thrust.

"Do you know, Rowan, I had the oddest sensation tonight. I imagined I was being followed . . ."

Rowan suddenly remembered the idiot who had nearly rammed the Range Rover. "By a sports car with an RAF sign on the door?"

226

"It was a sports car."

Rowan had reached a stage of panic. She ran into the middle of the room and yelled for attention. The circle must break up at once.

The field and the barn were deserted by the time a mud-splashed Spitfire and a Land-Rover reached the top of Holywell Syke. Flint, Tyrone and the six lads from AeroSoc had managed to make radio contact and rendezvous just after two o'clock. Using maps, guidebooks, research notes and logic, they had identified the sacred spring and driven there within half an hour.

Beside the gateway, the field had been churned into mud by a dozen or more vehicles. One at least had been a minibus with twin rear wheels. Damp and dispirited the group formed a skirmish line and advanced towards the erratic boulder, much as when field-walking on ploughsoil.

Tyrone came up to Flint and showed him his finds. Something glittered in the torchlight, the foil of a condom wrapper.

"Looks like we missed the party," Flint said.

The hunt was abandoned and they drove in convoy back to Durring. One of the college lads swore that he was insured, then drove the Land-Rover back to London. Flint went with Tyrone to Kingshaven, nodding off to sleep just as they reached the street where Vikki lived.

Vikki let them in, her eyes half-closed and her make-up incompletely removed. She invited them into the lounge and switched on the gas fire, before snuggling herself into one of her cheap armchairs and pulling the vermilion housecoat closer around her. Flint made them all coffee whilst Tyrone yawned through the story of their adventures.

"You two really are the limit."

She had spent four hours on the phone, ending after midnight, when the replies had become too brusque. Flint handed her a coffee and she cradled the mug in her hands, ignoring the four empty cups which already sat by her chair. He took her list and looked down the names. Something over half the names had been eliminated by confused responses.

"Could I have some toast, Vikki?" Tyrone asked.

A finger pointed towards the kitchen. "The bread's in the bread bin."

Tyrone went to make toast, whilst Flint read out the names of those who had been out on Halloween.

"Monica Clewes, Monica, where were you? . . . Barbara Faber . . . Leopold Gratz . . . Tim Hapgood . . . Michelle Kavanagh, obviously . . . Sebastian Leigh . . . R. Temple-Brooke . . ."

Tyrone responded to each name by shouting a qualification: "Fancied him . . . she was a favourite."

He came back into the room, handing around toast. "We do have a car number plate and someone drives a Range Rover with a doggy in the window."

"The police could find out who owns the car," Vikki said, without any of her usual buoyancy.

"No," Flint said, "we'd be showing our hand. Having an orgy in a barn isn't illegal. We just have to keep plugging away and hope for snow."

"Snow?" asked Vikki, with tired confusion in her voice.

"They say it's going to be a cold winter," said Tyrone with undue enthusiasm.

"When it snows, we can drag in the cops. Until then, team, it's softly softly."

"Well boys," Vikki stood up, "softly softly, I'm going to bed."

Chapter 22

The Poet and Rowan drove back towards the coast in the Range Rover. Windscreen wipers sliced through the thin rain and his words cut through the darkness.

"I did not like the hysterical scene, Rowan. Everyone was distressed, you know you distressed them?"

"Yes." She kept her tone submissive.

"Things should never have reached this state."

"No."

Rowan looked out at the featureless night, wanting to say nothing.

"Tell me what you fear," he said, patting her knee with his spare hand.

She thrilled to his touch, then told him what Willow had done.

"I was never truly happy about Willow," The Poet said, with nonchalant dismissal. "She has a," he paused to choose his poetic insult, "base crudeness."

"Willow could say things to hurt you. We can't have her at any more meetings. She might have been followed tonight, she might have told Flint everything."

"So, what does it matter?"

"Think of the embarrassment. He'll whip up a story and that bitch reporter will magnify it and you will be made to look ridiculous."

"Can't Willow just," he paused, "go away?"

"Like Hazel?" Rowan managed to whisper the suggestion.

Poetry was lacking from the situation, so she was not surprised when he refused to answer.

"Have you spoken with your people?" she began again.

"No, but I must."

Yes! she screamed within herself, he must and soon!

"You could perhaps have a word with Elm and the others in

London," The Poet suggested, "we can't let one stupid girl spoil things, can we?"

"No." She held the hand that was resting on her knee.

"This academic will get bored one day, you just see," The Poet said.

The Range Rover was approaching street lights, with the driver punctuating the quiet with pronouncements at intervals. "Yes, I'll speak to a few people, I'll see what can be done. Now you'd better go."

He pulled up to the side of the road in the lifeless town.

"I'd better go," Rowan echoed. "One day, can we be together and not hide our feelings or our beliefs?"

"You had better go."

Morning came late for everyone involved in the muddy fiasco at Holywell Syke. Vikki had already gone to work, late and bleary-eyed, when Flint awoke at eleven. He cleaned the mud off his clothing in her bathroom, which like every other room in the house was incompletely decorated. Tyrone was still dozing on the sofa, showing no sign of moving, so Flint dropped a note by the toaster and let himself out.

He had decided to walk the half mile into the centre of Kingshaven to find breakfast (or lunch). His chin bristled with unshaven whiskers, but he felt oddly fresh after the night's excitement. It had been a near miss and only bad luck had prevented a breakthrough.

Walking along High Street, he turned into The Passage and pushed open the rainforest-green door of Naturella Wholefood Market. Monica was serving red lentils to a hairy young customer, but she recognised Flint immediately the door tinkled and waved one spare finger. Flint waited until the customer had picked up his bundle of recycled carrier bags and left the shop.

"Hi there."

"Jeff, how are you?" Monica asked in a voice full of empathy for his dishevelled state.

"Tired and scruffy. We were out on a witch hunt last night, but it was more of a wild geese hunt in the end."

"I thought you were too old for Halloween games."

"Do you close for lunch?"

"I can, it's one of the joys of being self-employed."

She turned the "closed for lunch" sign and took off her unbleached linen apron. Flint escorted her across the road to Auntie Joyce's Tea Shoppe.

"Do you come here often?" he asked as she sat down in one of the slender dark wood chairs.

"No, it's for tourists, how often do you go to Madame Tussauds?"

"Good point."

"It's very expensive and I have three times the range of teas at home."

"But have you tried the chocolate fudge cake?" Flint purred over the menu. "I'd kill for chocolate cake."

Tea and cake arrived in good time whilst he went through an edited version of what had transpired during the night. He decided against mentioning Michelle's part in the affair. The question "who's this Michelle?" could wreck a fragile friendship.

"So have you any joy for me?" Flint asked.

"Oh we always talk about the same thing," Monica said with a hint of depression in her voice, "do you only want me for my information?"

"No, no, sorry." He spoke around an unwise mouthful of cake. "Look, Monica, I've wrecked one relationship this year blathering on about my investigation, so I'll forget it. We'll talk politics, or the weather."

She reached across a hand to touch his. "Silly! I just worry that you are becoming obsessed."

"Sorry, I'm getting close to the truth, but I'm using up friends fast. One of my contacts in London has been threatened and won't have anthing more to do with me. I tried to ring old George at the museum, but he's been scared off. I had six willing students helping me last night, now they're totally pigged off too. So, apologies, but you're one of my last hopes."

Monica looked at the table, saying nothing.

"Monica? Hello?"

She looked up. "There's something I didn't want to tell you."

Oh no, he thought, here comes the push-off line.

"Last night," she continued, "I had a strange phone call."

"That would have been Vikki, I'm sorry."

But Vikki had said Monica had been out, he realised. How reliable had Vikki's phone survey been?

231

"No, it was a man, a horrid heavy-breather," Monica continued, "he told me what would happen if I helped you any more."

"Monica." He gripped the hands she had offered him.

"He's going to come along at three in the morning and set fire to my shop, with me inside."

"Did you tell the police?"

Monica stifled a sniff. "What can they do against this madman? I just went to bed and pulled up the sheets."

Flint sat back, released her hands and drummed impatient knuckles on the table. "Can you see why I want to stop him?"

"Can't you just leave him alone? The police will get him sooner or later, they always do with madmen."

He had lost another ally, another friend and another avenue of information. "You have to do what you think is right, Monica."

"I'm sorry, but after what you've told me, I'm scared. I can't come to night school tonight."

"I'm going to ring in sick, anyway."

"I probably won't come any more, but once this is over, I'd like to see you again."

"Fine, it will be nice to see you."

"That's if you're still interested in an old maid."

"And if you're still interested in an old hippy."

Her anxious wrinkles flattened into a smile. "Do take care."

Flint returned to London with Tyrone and took time off to think and recover. He dropped by on the Friday for a lecture and a meeting, was scowled at by Professor Grant, then prepared himself for another night with Michelle. He watched the night from the window of the London bus, with Michelle occupying his thoughts. For three weeks he had followed Che Guevara's maxim: huddle as close to the enemy as possible. Too close for them to know they were being observed. Too like them to be distinguished as hostile.

For three weeks he had dated Michelle as often as possible, been intimate as often as possible. He had spent liberally from Barbara's funds, making the role of the suave Grant Selby easy to play. What a name, why had he chosen such a daft name? Flint distracted himself by drawing circles on the misting windows, guilty ideals fighting practical realism.

He had been exposed to the full depth of Michelle's dreams

232

and emotions after only a few hours of frantic passion. Some men probably never learned to understand their wives as well as Flint thought he understood Michelle. Lonely, desperate and gullible, she was not one he could ever love, but she was one he could use. Animal pleasure and subtle interrogation was the stuff of nineteen-sixties spy thrillers, but Flint had never liked James Bond.

Their relationship had remained on narrow tracks: drinks and sex. A meal and sex. Sex and sex. They had something in common, but it filled him with distaste.

That night it would be Woody Allen at the local multiplex cinema, as he had forgotten all about the promised trip to the theatre until too late. Afterwards, she would expect more of the love-substitute he provided. Sleeping with Michelle was like sleeping with Lucy, whose image was before him every day, and who he knew as well as any lover. Michelle was another friend of the Earth, someone else who read horoscopes and hummed folk music. Like Lucy, she was a harmless victim of a world which no longer had room for such fantasy.

Michelle was not ready when he knocked. As she opened the door, he immediately sensed the change.

"Oh, hello," she said, almost biting her lip.

"Let me in out of the rain."

She nodded, walking away into the hall. He closed the door and followed her into the bedroom. She was wearing a long shapeless plum jumper and jeans with ripped knees. She flopped back on to the unmade bed, one arm over her temple, the other by her side.

He felt uneasy, she had none of that vulnerable innocence about her.

Her expression hardened. "So, I suppose you want to fuck me."

Flint was stunned for a moment, then began to stammer with confusion.

"No, actually, I thought we'd go to the pictures," he tried to make a joke.

"Ah," she said, "then you'll fuck me afterwards? Which way do you want me?"

She rolled on to her stomach.

"Michelle!" He was angry at this taunting, but the taunting

233

ceased. Michelle remained prone on the bed, ceasing to fight, beginning to weep.

He sat beside her, gently and warily.

"I'm ready," she sobbed, "just tell me how you want it."

"I don't understand."

"Who are you, who are you really?" she said into the pillow.

So she knew, or someone knew. The game was over and Grant Selby could be put back in the wardrobe and forgotten.

"I'm sorry, Michelle, but I know everything about you. I know where you went on Tuesday, on Samahain, brown Allegro, off to the Darkewater Valley to meet the coven."

She gulped, then shook her head.

"Okay, come on." He shocked himself with brute force, rolling her to face him.

"What do you want?"

"One of my graduates works for the Sussex police. He told me that car belongs to Jacob Goldberg."

"You bastard."

She struck out, but he blocked it with a reflex of the right wrist.

"Don't, just don't. Don't try anything, I hate violence."

Michelle choked back a laugh. "What? You are that lecturer, the one in the papers."

"I am, this is the real me."

He had dropped all the Grant Selby mannerisms immediately.

She simply shook her head, a tear-track working its way around her cheeks. "How could you? After all we've done."

Flint sat up, guilt waves washing through him. "I had to. Do you remember Lucy Gray? You might have called her Hazel."

Her expression was a mixture of anger, depression and fear, but it gave nothing away.

"You have two choices, Michelle: tell me about it, or tell the police. I've got a shelf full of box files, overflowing with information. I could write a book! Once the CID start investigating, they will break your coven wide open."

"We've done nothing wrong. It's like going to church."

"They don't kill people in church, Michelle."

"Neither do we. You don't understand."

"Yes I do. I sympathise with your views, I understand what you believe and what you feel. Honest, I'm not a total fraud. I

234

ride a bike, I eat wholefood, I wear a beard but what I won't do is subordinate myself to priests and priestesses at moonlight rituals."

"You think I'm silly, don't you?"

"No, I think you're sincere, but that won't count when Vikki Corbett and her friends have a list of names and addresses. Even if you say you have done nothing wrong, the publicity will destroy your friends. I mean, isn't Jacob Goldberg supposed to be a nice Jewish father?"

"Don't hurt him, don't hurt any of them."

"All I want is the man who killed Lucy Gray. Once I have him, I'll leave the rest of you alone. Call it a deal if you like, but that's what I want."

She searched his eyes for truth. "That's all you wanted. You never loved me."

"I never said I did."

"You didn't even enjoy it, any of it?"

He almost wanted to weep himself. All this emotional drama was too much. "Another time, it would have been," he searched for a word, "different."

Michelle sat up, breathing deeply to control her dismay. She was an addict finally being brought into therapy. "I knew this was all too good . . ."

"Now, I don't know what kind of games you and your friends play, and I don't really want to know, but murder and intimidation is beyond a game."

"But it was a game," she said wearily, "just a little fun. You know I never had any luck with men, I'm too fat and I'm hopeless in the house and I just fall underneath anyone with trousers on. My family are all shits, but the circle is my new family, all friends, all lovers."

"Do you have a regular partner?"

She looked at him, as if wanting to say yes and hurt him. "No, it sounds dirty, doesn't it? Christians hate sex, but we're not perverts, not Satanists like the newspapers say. We just worship the Earth, sky-clad, celebrating the ancient rites. We are at peace with the Earth and the Earth is at peace with us."

"How many are you?"

"It depends. Just four sometimes."

Something came to mind about terrorists, the mafia, the

carbonairi, the IRA. All had four-man cells for security, with none knowing more than three others. The sect had been organised in the face of the eventual witch hunt. Flint knew the ancient, and modern formulae for secrecy.

"So, a pair of pairs, but that is not enough for a circle. How many groups of four meet at the ceremonies?" He guessed. "Three fours and one? Thirteen?"

She said nothing.

"More? Three thirteens and one? Forty?"

A glazed, apprehensive look met the questioning. Was he still wide of the mark?

"Thirteen thirteens and one?" He did a quick mental sum. "One hundred and seventy?"

Michelle smiled broadly. "Now you see, I have many friends, and they have many friends, each of whom has many friends too, all over the country, circles within circles, it is growing, you can't stop us."

She spoke in riddles, hinting at hundreds. Hundreds would encompass more than bank clerks, students and shopkeepers. Someone, somewhere, was important.

"Who is in charge? Who is the priest? Piers Plant?"

"You killed him," she stated sourly.

"Who is the priestess?"

She shrugged. "She is called The Priestess."

"Rowan?" Another wild guess, but Plant had been close to someone called Rowan.

Michelle almost choked, but admitted nothing.

"And they call you Willow? The purpose of the woody names presumably being to stop the coven being penetrated."

"Rejecting Christian names is part of the process of denial."

These were not her words, she was speaking by rote.

"Okay, so tell me about Hazel."

A long silence followed. A silence broken only by the heavy breathing of the oppressed woman, the sporadic noise of a passing car, the periodic patter of a tear striking the bedding. Between sighs, Michelle continued the confession.

"Hazel was The Maiden who stood in for the goddess. There will be a new Maiden chosen in the spring, it might have been me."

"What happened to Hazel? When did you see her last? February, Imbolc?"

"There's no point in telling you, is there, you know it all."

Flint led her on, turning his floating thoughts into concrete fact.

"Did anything strange happen?"

"It was cold, we all had too much of the Kat . . ."

"Kat . . . sacred potion, right?"

She gave a little laugh. Flint knew they would be high as kites, the holy draught was based on hemp.

"Did anything odd happen to Lucy, sorry, Hazel?"

"She performed the rite, she said she felt ill, they took her back to the cottage, then we all went home."

"Who took her home?"

"Oh, I don't know."

"And you never saw her again?"

"No. At Beltane we were told Hazel had gone away and we were really upset about what the newspaper was saying."

"Piers Plant was there?"

"Oak was so sad, everyone was sad. I always loved the May Games," Michelle sighed. "One May Day, I will claim a man for my own."

Narrowing his eyes, Flint's memory swept across pages of research. "Claim a man as a husband? But only if you were pregnant by him."

"But I never was."

Something in her gleeful naïvety depressed him, but he could envisage the kind of joy such a union could bring to the hopelessly lonely. Lucy would have been pregnant on May eve, so who could she have claimed by ancient right?

"Lucy was pregnant, Michelle. Conception might have been around Samahain last year, a convenient time for union of god and goddess. Piers Plant was not the father. Any ideas who her partner was?"

"No."

"Okay, let's try another tack. I know there is someone beyond this Rowan and your High Priest, someone Piers Plant – sorry, Oak – was afraid of."

She shook her head too vigorously.

"Who is he?"

"I don't know, no one knows."

"I doubt that, Michelle, seriously. He is important, powerful?"

This he could tell from her manner. Lucy's partner was no ordinary coven member.

"He knows the path to ultimate harmony, he knows the ultimate spells."

Spells, the ultimate spellbook, Flint felt almost sick with excitement.

"This is the Horned Man?"

"He wears a horned head-dress, you know it's the tradition."

"And whoever it is owns a copy of *De Nigris*?"

"You know he does."

"And that's why you wanted it."

"I was just curious."

So Gratz had been right and someone did hold a copy of the semi-mythical book. So why had Plant needed to find a second copy? Something in the twisted logic of the circle had to explain it. Flint began to fire names from Tyrone's list, fishing for clues or for any sign of recognition.

"Tell me about Lugsanadh. Was Piers Plant there at Caesar's Camp? It doesn't hurt to tell."

"Yes."

"And he drove himself there in his green car?"

"Yes, I think so, what does it matter?" Michelle's resistance seemed to be stiffening.

Flint had another crucial fact locked tight and switched tone. "Look, can I be honest?"

"It would make a change." There was anger in her voice, perhaps she had said too much and was realising it at last. "What do I call you, anyway?"

"Call me Jeff."

"Jeff? Huh. I thought it was the real thing between us."

"I am sorry, you won't believe me, but it's true. You don't deserve this, I know I've been a real bastard."

"Then don't ask me any more questions. My friends know I'm seeing you, they won't let me attend any more of the rites and it might mean I have to leave the circle."

"Can you do that?"

"Of course, I haven't made a pact or anything. You seem to think I'm in some sort of mad cult . . ."

"You are."

"Not that kind. You don't seem to understand that we wish

238

no one harm. It's not like a video nasty. Witches don't ride on broomsticks, we're thoughtful, caring people . . ."

"Who have other people killed . . ."

"Piers Plant did all that, don't you see? You'll never find Hazel now, so why not leave it alone? You should let things rest, stop upsetting people."

He wondered how deeply Michelle believed what she had just said or whether she had been primed. She had fallen into his bed so easily he had never ceased to suspect some sort of complex trap. He had been allowed to make progress in the case, without threat or attack. Paranoia started to slowly creep up on him.

"One more question, then I'll leave you alone. Where did you meet at Imbolc?" Flint asked. He turned to face her, staring into her eyes, watching for the flicker of acknowledgement as he broke through. "Was it Devil's Finger? Caesar's Camp? Harriet's Stone?"

At the last name, Michelle's expression gave away the truth again, but she extended both arms. "We could still be friends, I don't mind calling you Jeff."

She had switched emotional tack again, what was wrong with her? She put two hands behind his neck.

"Just hold me, just love me, forget all this. People are getting hurt, you can't imagine the damage you are doing. The New Age is dawning, Jeff. Everyone is turning Green, no one goes to church any more. People's consciousness is rising. You should join us, join the New Wave before it sweeps over you."

The stark buzzing of the doorbell made him throw off her hands much too roughly. She sat up, annoyed and hurt once more.

"Who is it?" he hissed.

She gave a careless shrug.

"Is this a set-up? Have you just been telling me lies?"

Michelle shook her long black locks in disdain. "I'm the wicked witch, remember."

He levelled a finger. "Just don't start cackling just yet!"

She slid off the bed and walked down towards the bell, which buzzed again. Flint beat her out of the room and went into her kitchen. The back door was closed by a single bolt which he had open in moments, wishing Tyrone the departmental thug was by his side. Thought of Tyrone made him grab at an empty wine bottle as he darted into the dark yard behind the house. He couldn't waste time playing with the back gate, so vaulted straight over the brick wall at the end of the yard.

No mob of fanatical cultists awaited him in the alley beyond, so he lay down his bottle and broke into a run. Another source had been closed, but more questions solved. If Michelle could be believed.

Michelle halted in front of the door and let the bell jangle. She put her back against the painted wood and listened to the sound of her dream love escaping to the rear.

Someone knocked on the door.

Christmas was coming and the Christians were getting fat. Her dragons would be seasonal golds, reds and greens. Her modelling clay could be worked into a tree-stump entwined with mistletoe, with just one goblin peeking out at the world.

Someone tried the handle.

She rubbed away a headache forming in her left temple. Crawling repeatedly out of the quagmire of life, she seemed fated to slide back in. Now she was once again in the slime with the reptiles. There were some things a man simply couldn't fake and perhaps if she helped him, he could drag her free.

Her doorbell spluttered its erratic jangle. Someone battered the door knocker again and she turned to give it attention. Pulling open the door, she was shocked by the three faces, two male, one female friend. Friends so close they had never dared come to her door.

"Willow." The one who spoke was the man who had first hoisted her on to this plane of higher awareness, the one who had first pulled her away from her former, squalid life. Married, and comfortably successful, he had most to hide and most to lose.

"Let us inside, Willow. We have to talk."

Chapter 23

Jeffrey Flint hated his new flat and toyed with the idea of finding another houseboat. One of Jules' friends lived in a converted Thames barge near Putney and wanted another bunkmate. It would be a possibility once the Horned Man had been laid to rest, but whilst he was stalking around issuing threats and controlling the game, Flint had to maintain a low profile.

No longer need he pretend to be Grant Selby, but the new image was hard to shrug off. Flint had bought himself a new jacket with a whiff of Italian styling and decided to keep the beard away for a few more weeks, to experiment with the feel. His office also felt the change: Che Guevara came down and a poster of the Portland Vase took its place. So long attracted by alternative lifestyles, his experiences had left him thoroughly disgusted, the affair with Michelle ranking as the final indignity. There was to be no more low life, it was time to reshape himself and his standing at college. Jeffrey Flint, scruffy rebel, began to fade.

His first tutorial as a born-again-lecturer went badly. His voice rattled away about the villa system and the imposition of land ownership, but his mind was firmly fixed on a single track: women.

Michelle had not answered a single telephone call since the melodramatic Friday night. Who had knocked at her door? Was she in danger from her former friends? He should have stayed to find out, what a rat he'd been, running away to save his own skin. What an utter chicken.

Poor Monica had been drawn into the ring too. Poor smiling Monica, always ready to hear a wild anecdote, or to dispense a chunk of cheerful philosophy, hardly deserved midnight phone calls. Having her ask questions of her clientele had thrust her into danger.

And what of Vikki? Would she start ferreting about where

she was unwelcome and would the Kingshaven thugs stop at a black eye next time? Flint had to stop that, he must not simply stand by.

"Did all the Britons live in villas?" asked one of the fresh-faced lads in the tutorial group.

No, cretin, listen to what I'm saying! Flint thought, but after only a moment to re-engage his brain gave a more polite, more professional answer. He too had once been an oik asking banal questions of Professor Grant, or the late (and great) Henrietta Honey.

What of the late Lucy Gray?

What about Barbara Faber and Mrs Gray, still waiting for an answer?

"We're talking rural settlement," Flint said aloud, squeaking the chalk across the blackboard, "not just villas, but a whole living agricultural system."

All this was rot, he knew. It was utterly irrelevant and useless to every student sitting in that seminar room, plus everyone else in the known universe. Everyone to whom the villa-system mattered had been dead for sixteen hundred years.

"Look, shall we round it off there," he said.

The room erupted into motion before he had finished the sentence. Feebly he called out the title of an essay, knowing that it meant he would have to mark a dozen scripts. Once the inevitable keen student had asked his final question, Flint was left alone and he strolled back to his room. He tried to phone Michelle again, but again had no reply.

Along in Tyrone's office, he found the postgraduate sticking pictures of pots to index cards. The Libyan student who was supposed to be sharing the room had not turned up due to visa problems, so Tyrone had colonised both desks and all the wall space. An airbrush print of a Stealth Fighter over the Arctic had been fixed to the back of the door. Flint disapproved but said nothing.

"Sub-Roman pottery," Tyrone said, "mathematical modelling of its distribution in the Roman/Post-Roman interface should enable me to draw up a chronology for the fifth century."

"Oh."

"Sounds great, doesn't it?"

"Yes."

242

Flint removed a roll of drawings from the Libyan's chair and sat astride it, elbows upon the back rest.

"This is a Lucy visit, isn't it?" Tyrone said, laying aside the cards. "I haven't done much since Thursday, I thought I ought to do some thesis."

"You're right, you're right, carry on, don't let me stop you."

Tyrone fidgeted with his cards whilst Flint sat in silence for some minutes, watching his student in the failing light of the afternoon.

"We're buggered," Flint said, at length. "They know I know about Michelle, so nasty things start creeping our way again. Gratz, George Carlyle, now Monica, they have all had their warnings."

Tyrone gave a smile which betrayed suppressed excitement, perhaps even the hint of fear. "They know they can't frighten us off, so they're picking off the easy victims."

"It might mean you're next," Flint cautioned.

"Oh I'll be okay. If they try anything, we can bust them. We've got two names, we'd soon get more if you could get back into that Michelle's place and swipe her address book."

"But what can we prove? That a group of people have an offbeat way of having fun. Okay so we name four or five or six minnows and perhaps we get sued for slander and meanwhile the real villain creeps up and incinerates us."

From the rat-run below the office window came the sound of breaking glass. Constantly paranoid, Flint sprang to his feet and checked for a threat. Eight or ten students were criss-crossing the yard, making Rugby passes with milk bottles, chanting a supposed Zulu war cry.

"Who are those rejects?"

Tyrone came to his side. "There's Bunny."

The familiar rounded shape jumped to catch a bottle as it lofted over his head. He missed and it shattered against the wall.

"What are we doing letting him come back for an MA?" Flint muttered.

"See the big hairy one? That's Ape Anderson, he's the ring-leader. They call themselves the Animals, it's a piss-artists' off-shoot of the Rugby club who give themselves animal nicknames, and spend all their time in the Union Bar having drinking races and puking. It's totally juvenile."

243

"Ali zumbah zumbah zumbah . . ." echoed from below. Another bottle shattered.

"They were the ones who were nearly arrested for invading Chelsea College last week?"

"Yup, trying to steal trophies."

Flint had been an equally puerile undergraduate. He remembered the pub crawls, the rag stunts and yes, even the mascot-hunting raids on other colleges. The bright, frivolous memory sparked briefly before his mind turned back to darker thoughts.

"My thesis is still going to fail unless I get some hard facts," he said. "I'm going to Dulwich to see Michelle and I need someone to watch my back."

"You've been watching Clint Eastwood movies again."

Flint shrugged. "Or Henry Fonda."

Tyrone grabbed his leather flying jacket and within minutes they were out in the late afternoon air, stepping over a scattering of broken glass. Flint wore his RAF greatcoat with its CND patch, so the pair leaving Central College resembled crewmen from some alternative air force.

"We could have asked Bunny and his mates along," Tyrone said as he set the pace of march. "Then you'd be safe."

"Safe in jail."

"We could get them to invade that Jew's shop and cause a distraction whilst we look for evidence."

"Then we'll certainly end up in jail."

A bus came after a forty-minute wait, then they crawled the commuter-clogged route to Dulwich. Opposite where they sat, an advertising panel urged people to "Teach English as a foreign language". After his excursions into folklore, myth and magic, Flint felt he could hold a course on "England as a foreign land". A land which became stranger and more alien by the day.

It was dark by the time they reached the row of terraced houses. Tyrone found a shadow to loiter in, whilst Flint crossed the road to No. 37a. Where the gate was missing, he stopped at the end of the short brick path. The curtains of the ground floor flat were open, but the cheerful Celtic images which had brightened the uniform façade had gone.

Flint peered into the front window, resting his hands on the glass to shade his eyes. The sitting room was lit only by diffused street lighting, and had been stripped of all possessions beyond the

244

cheap furniture provided by the landlord. Bare rectangles marked the former positions of Michelle's wild paintings.

The scene of the torrid affair was deserted, the rug had been firmly tugged from beneath Flint's feet and now even the dust had been swept away. He knew there was no point seeking out a forwarding address, there would not be one. Cold crept upwards from the path into his shoes as he realised Michelle lacked the drive, the organisation and the money to perform such an instant move. She had been helped, she had been pushed, she had been forced. She had disappeared as neatly as had Lucy.

He kicked the drab brown door in frustration. Tyrone jogged across the road to his side and looked through the window for himself. Flint simply stood there, at a loss as to what step to take next.

"What now?" Tyrone asked.

"Either we give up, let them win, or we start again."

"If we leave it a bit, something might come up," Tyrone said.

"And we might get a white Christmas. Do you fancy getting really plastered? At my expense?"

"Yeah, don't mind."

The hangover was still thick when Flint arrived at Central College the next day. He had never had a "drink problem", but could easily see how one could arise. Sally stopped him as he passed the photocopier. She was wearing her apologetic prophet-of-doom expression.

"Can you see Ian PDQ?"

"Bad?" Flint grimaced.

Sally glanced sideways. "The Dean of Arts has sent him a letter."

He shook his head. "If I had a dog, it would have died this morning."

"Pardon?"

"Is he in now?"

Professor Grant had been reading the reviews in the back of *Journal of Roman Studies*. When Flint came in, he set it aside and started to look for something else.

"Ah, Jeffrey."

He had called him Jeffrey, it was an ominous portent.

"You've been ill, again?" Grant paused and appeared to be licking his teeth behind his lips. "My, you don't look well today."

"No, it's part of the same thing, it keeps hanging on."

"Not hanging over?" The Professor tried to laugh.

He stopped forcing jokes and produced the letter. The Dean of Arts had been made aware that Dr Flint had cancelled lectures, seminars and a night school class on the pretext of being ill. He held proof that this excuse had been totally spurious.

"We have to fill in forms, Jeffrey. We can't lie to the DSS, or whoever gets them."

The letter went on. Flint had been associating with persons of dubious repute (unspecified). He had been using college resources (Land-Rover, computers, telephones). He had drawn students away from their work (Tyrone plus the AeroSoc boys).

Grant closed the letter. "I understand," he said, "I realise what you want to do, but I talked to the Dean this morning and he told me things that were not even in the letter. I cannot control your private life, but ask yourself, should someone who is teaching fresh young minds be spending his nights with an Irish witch?"

Would an English witch be okay? Flint kept his face straight and his expression submissive. He was bottom of the staff list, the first one out in any cutback.

"Who has been putting the screws on?" he asked, but the question was ignored.

"I can only put it so strongly. There must be no more phoney illnesses, no more jaunts with witches, and no more distraction of students. That boy Drake gave a terrible lecture at Bradford."

"Tyrone will learn."

"Yes, but what will he learn?"

When the ticking-off was complete, Flint apologised, then left for the coffee room, found Tyrone with his nose in the *Financial Times* and told him the news.

"No more Lucy, it's official, the Prof says so."

"All that work down the drain?"

Flint shrugged. "I shall ring Vikki, then it's back to solving the pressing questions of the Roman Empire."

Whilst Flint was still sipping coffee and talking departmental trivia with Jules Torpevitch, Tyrone slipped upstairs to his own room. In part he was depressed by his lecturer's surrender to authority,

246

but also he felt a sense of freedom. This was his project now, he could work on it whenever he chose, no one cared when he came or went, nobody cared whether he did any work or not. He could quite easily do nothing for two more years, then fail his PhD without anyone in the department being aware of it. Plenty of other students did.

Within his room, Tyrone looked at the big wallchart and drew a few more lines, looping up from the box he had labelled "Horned Man" and bursting into the boxes for Gratz, Carlyle, Flint and Monica Clewes.

He wondered what she and Flint had seen in each other. Knowing Flint's appetite for nocturnal athletics, the relationship must have progressed beyond prune wine and nut cutlets. She was forty-two, Tyrone had discovered, and she was Top of the Pops. Each of his suspect lists was composed along one line of enquiry and Monica came top in most of them. She was so obviously New Age, she had such a high and quirky profile that she entered most of his lists as favourite. She was in the Dark Ants, she had known Plant, she sold wholefood, she sold New Age books, she associated with this Temple-Brooke character, she had once written an article on folk songs for the *Transactions*. To his prejudiced eye, Monica Clewes was an obvious candidate for any fringe activity that could be imagined.

Flint had drawn a red biro line through her name. Perhaps she had been too obvious, but now the telephone threat had ruled her out of the running. Pity, it would have been a nice twist.

Tyrone deleted the name from his other lists, then looked for a male suspect. Tim Hapgood, the librarian, had suffered a stroke before Halloween. Strike him out. The red biro paused over the name of Sebastian Leigh, the County archaeologist and sometime practising bisexual. Tyrone took pleasure in leaving Leigh in the list and planned to dig around his past a little more. He was certain that the computer files breached the Data Protection Act (1984), but this only added to the fun. He should ring Vikki and inform her who was now in charge of the investigation.

Tyrone continued to work on "his case", without saying anything to Flint. His supervisor seemed to be playing the new role well, keeping his lecture schedule, giving his night school classes and speaking only of archaeology in the tea room. Lucy was taboo, so Tyrone played the game, talked sub-Romans and methodology and ever so quietly continued to dig.

Sebastian Leigh had been eliminated: he had been at a conference in Utrecht on May Day. The Bishop of Durring-and-Sembolt had been eliminated, having launched a twin-pronged public attack on the paganism of Halloween and the godless nature of a new shop in Eastport. Adding the Bishop, and the judges, to the list had always been an offbeat idea.

The shop damned by the Bishop was called "Final Frontier" and sold graphic novels, paperbacks, videos and boardgames with a science fiction/fantasy/horror flavour. Both members of staff were male, in their twenties and on Tyrone's list, but it had been Vikki who discovered that it was owned by James Templestone. The same James Templestone owned a small publishing company called Samphire Fields, whose output embraced the myth-busting *New Sceptic*, the wistful poetry quarterly *Lost Lands*, the political magazines *New England* and *Green Concern*. Whatever the fringe interest, James Templestone also made it his interest, even if it conflicted with causes he supposedly espoused. Tyrone had straight political beliefs and one basic moral position on any issue. It was confusing to think of Templestone, or Temple-Brooke, changing his chameleon image to suit his audience.

All the new information went into his computer file, and Tyrone's pulse quickened on sight of the resulting output. Flint had always wanted a man at the top of his suspect list.

Vikki had spoken to Tyrone almost every day for a fortnight. She never escaped the feeling the boy was trying to chat her up, or impress her with his wild ideas. She put down the telephone and consulted her pad. All around, the jarring bustle of the *Kingshaven Advertiser* office continued as normal. She'd have to visit that shop, Tyrone was still plucking at straws. Eric, the sub-editor, placed his cigarette hand on her shoulder.

"Uh?" She screwed up her nose.

"Sorry Vik, the gaffer wants a word."

Suspecting nothing she entered the editor's office with a cheery "Good morning, Arnold."

Fifteen minutes later, a chastened Vikki Corbett emerged from the office feeling trampled and ill-used. She went to her desk and collected her coat and handbag, then walked slowly past the racks

248

of leather bound back numbers at the top of the fawn mock-marble staircase. In her handbag was a pad full of Tyrone's latest names, addresses, deductions and insane guesses. In her ears, the sound of the editor professing deep boredom and irritation with the Lucy Gray story. Plant was dead. The story was dead. No more witchcraft, the punters were becoming angry.

"Look lass," he had said, "the tradesmen don't like this picture of the town you're putting out." Nonchalant in his shirt sleeves, the big man had put the little girl in her place.

"The tourists love it," she had fought back.

"The Chamber of Commerce don't, and I have to lunch with them. No more witches and warlocks, Halloween is over."

Vikki took the stairs one at a time. Rotten, crummy paper. Rotten, crummy town. She'd been beaten up for this story. She'd spent cold days and nights out in cornfields. It was the only story she had ever covered in depth. It was what she came into journalism to do. It was her child which the editor was trying to strangle.

No way. She thought of the list of names: crosses, ticks, hints and denials marked her progress towards a solution. That annoyingly analytical lecturer had told her to avoid face-to-face interviews and direct approaches, as if he was the one in charge. In some respects, he was right, but Flint's oblique approach fought against her nature. She wanted to confront, denounce and fight her way on to the front page, not cower and pick at evidence with a trowel and soft brush.

She burst from the swing doors into the car park and the rain. The cold grey sky suited her temper. Arnold the editor had almost confiscated her Lucy Gray file, but she had snatched it back and made excuses that it contained confidential information. She knew that one more fruitless excursion into the story would sink her career, a few G and Ts were needed to settle her nerve.

Hooray Henry's was a smart town-centre wine bar which hyped its mock-chic image so well, it had become chic in reality. Feeling like a TV-movie slut propping up the bar, Vikki dug over the facts in her mind. She could no longer rely on Jeffrey Flint, if she could ever have relied on him. First, he started hanging around with that healthfood woman. Then he had become embroiled with that girl he refused to name, and lost her. Finally, he had backed out of the scene without giving her all that juicy information he had gathered during the summer. Even the kid Tyrone was keeping things back, she knew. Vikki could not wait until the laid-back intellectuals had humped and fumbled their way around the problem.

Harry Knowles came into the bar and folded his brolly. Harry was nearing the end of his innings, but lived on in hope of a gong for the twenty-five years he had given to the Tory Party. Councillor, greengrocer, ex-RAF, ex-mayor, he cheerfully stood drinks in Henry's Ascot Bar for the charming Miss Corbett. With only the suggestion of wheezing, Harry wrapped his bony fingers around the drinks and carried them to a booth and she followed.

"You don't smoke, do you?" he asked.

"No."

"Wise girl. I had to stop, doctor's orders. He wants me to stop this too." He raised his G and T. "Here's to the after-life."

Vikki fenced around the subject, then passed over her edited-down version of Tyrone's suspect list. Harry scanned it in disbelief.

"I've been reading your paper, of course, but all these people cannot be followers of Satan."

"They're witches, not Satanists. It's a very fine line, I'm told."

"Well, whatever."

"And not all of them are involved, this is a sort of a shortlist."

Councillor Knowles returned to the list. "I see you have that Rupert Temple-Brooke character."

"I heard he was something in the Party. Didn't he apply for selection as replacement for Sir Lewis when he retires from the House?"

A deep rumbling came from within the Councillor. "I think his wife put him up to it. She's a funny old stick, she thinks he ought to make something of himself. Between you and me, he never stood a ghost."

"Why?"

"The man's a bloody fascist, that's why. Have you read any of his poems?"

"No."

Harry raised a finger, and it trembled before her eyes. "He writes bad poems, so I hear, which are full of romantic claptrap about a New England rising from the ashes. The man himself is even worse, mad as a hatter and convinced he's right. He's made your shortlist, but didn't make ours, no. He changes his name too. In the old days he was just James Templestone. We can't just give seats away to the opposition."

"What does he do, other than write bad poetry?"

"He inherited a manor farm, out towards Eastport in the marshland. It's mainly sheep and cattle I think, but someone else actually runs the place. His wife has the real money and does a lot of charity work around the county; people say it gives her an excuse to get away from that dreary old swamp. She's the keen Party man, he plays laird of the manor, but they're both on every committee you can name." He waved his hand. "He's a Rotarian and on the Golf Club committee, she's WI and a parish councillor."

"They get around?"

Harry touched Vikki on the hand and she gave him a nervously polite smile.

"They're meddlers, dear."

"What is her money in? I heard he's also a publisher."

"Is he? I know her money was from publishing. The family firm deals in magazines – cooking, knitting, that sort of thing."

Fingers in lots and lots of small pies, thought Vikki.

"Did you know he goes to pop festivals and science fiction conventions?"

"Wouldn't surprise me in the slightest."

"Is Monica Clewes a member of your Party?" Vikki asked on impulse, trying to make the connection that bound the two together.

"The chick-pea lady? Goodness no, I'd guess she was a Green or one of those damned Social whatsits."

"Oh."

The liquid lunch moved onward, Vikki jotting down notes, failing to enhance her own list of plausible suspects. As soon as Harry had cheerio'd from the door, she telephoned the Temple-Brooke residence and invented a few poetic lies of her own. The laird of the manor himself had come to the telephone, sounding pompous and self-important and demanding how she came to know his ex-directory number. He would not talk to the press at such short notice.

Yes he would, Vikki Corbett smiled as she put down the

telephone. A new branch of Waterstones had opened only a hundred yards from where she sat. One of their fortnightly literary events was a poetry reading by six local writers. Someone could not resist being one of the six.

Chapter 24

Rowan was approaching a state of ecstasy. Doctor Flint had finally been put in his place, whilst Vikki Corbett's job hung by a silken thread. Willow had ceased to be an embarrassment and the police still remained torpid. The Poet would be giving a reading, but more delicious was the thought that his wife would be travelling to Europe for ten days in December. So much could be accomplished in ten days.

She often went to the literary evenings at Waterstones, so attending on this special night would not cause complications. Sitting before her mirror she quivered with anticipation as she dabbed at her face with cruelty-free cosmetics. Only natural products would touch her skin, and then only to obscure the advance of years, not to titilate or entice.

A long wool coat would protect her from the bitter November night, whilst she walked the two hundred yards to the bookshop. The other shops were bright with plastic Santas, reindeers, fake holly and exhortations to spend, with not a Christ-child in sight. The whole English population was ready to celebrate a thoroughly Pagan festival in a thoroughly Celtic orgy of feasting, drinking, gift-exchange and lovemaking. The Poet was right; their time was coming once again. How she wished this year would pass, so that a new cycle could be begun and the new dawn be a season closer.

The Poet sat with all the other poets in the front row of forty tubular steel chairs deployed in the tubular steel surroundings of the new bookstore. He was number four on the bill, promising to read his epic "Visions of Verges", published by a small press held in his wife's name. Rowan arrived precisely on time and sat at the back as most of the chairs were taken. The attendance had possibly been swelled to forty by the prospect of a free glass of plonk at the management's expense.

Rowan ignored everything the first three nameless nobodies had to say and kicked her feet impatiently as members of the audience strove to demonstrate the extent of their own literary appreciation. When the evening was well advanced, The Poet was called to speak and rose to polite applause.

She knew his 120-line eulogy for the English hedgerow by heart and moved her lips to the rhythm of his words. For Rowan, there were only two people in the room, the presence and the opinion of the rest were irrelevant. She sat back bathing in the glory of his vision, certain that the audience was as entranced as she was. Many new followers would be born that night, it was certain.

Two more readings may have followed, but Rowan simply re-recited the poem she had heard and tried to catch his eye. Once he blinked in her direction, then actively ignored her. She had transgressed again, it seemed she could never please him.

Poets and public mingled after the readings. Rowan made a direct line for R. Temple-Brooke as the formality began to dissolve.

"Wonderful!" she exclaimed.

He did not acknowledge her with his eyes and quite simply rebuffed her.

"Go away, immediately. That reporter is here."

Rowan looked for the direction his strong blue eyes were pointing as they swept around the crowd. One woman was just too casual, too interested in their two-line conversation. The woman looked away, but her face had been seen. Somehow, the reporter Vikki Corbett had slipped into the room after the reading had started. Rowan's despair fell to alarm.

"At your car, I'll wait."

"No!"

But Rowan was moving away from him, watching the reporter watching her. She bowed her head to shade her face, then made for the exit.

Through the rush of punters making for the free wine, Vikki tried to see who the tall blonde woman was. By the time the crush cleared, the woman had left the room, so Vikki made straight for the target.

"That was a really nice poem," Vikki said, then wondered if the poet would think "nice" was an insult.

"Thank you."

He was only some five feet six inches tall, dark-haired, with deep blue eyes. The even pallor of his skin, the plasticity of his good looks and the neat controlled hair immediately reminded her of her little brother's Action Man. Even his motions seemed jerky and poised, as if always prepared to strike the right attitude or ensure light was falling correctly on his profile.

"Vikki Corbett." She thrust out her slim hand and he shook it with a compelling grip.

"Delighted to make your acquaintance." He gave a slight bow of his head, and addressed her eyes with an intensity that made her falter. This man had charisma with a capital C, plus a touch of good, old-fashioned chivalry. "Tell me, would you write for the *Advertiser*?"

"Yeah, I do, but here I'm on my own. I'm not working." Ooh you liar Vikki Corbett, she thought, but Arnold would spit blood if he knew what she was doing. Temple-Brooke was in publishing, wasn't he? Could he be the one stirring up trouble against her?

"Reginald!" Temple-Brooke turned to greet a friend with another hearty handshake.

"I wanted to ask you if I could do an interview," Vikki said across the greeting.

Temple-Brooke glanced her way just for a moment. "You're not working, remember? Give me a ring from your office."

"I did."

She had been "cut", quite effectively too. Without making a scene, she could not intervene in the hands-on-shoulders man-talk which had begun in earnest between the poet and his crony in the Rotarian tie. Vikki would not be thwarted, she would simply wait on the fringes of the meeting then accost the poet as soon as he attempted to leave.

A glass of Riesling was pressed into her hand and she leaned against black shelves of paperback fiction to wait. An art-lover who topped six feet and wore intellectual spectacles came to lean a hand on the case beside her and began to talk poetry. She smiled and for ten minutes allowed the sound to pass through her head unprocessed. All in a rush, she noticed that the object of her attention had gone.

"I say, what's your name again?" the art-lover asked as she kicked away from the bookshelf and began to hurry towards the exit. She gave the man a flicker of a wave as she rounded the top of the staircase, then left his life for ever.

She ran into the sharp winter air like a fly meeting a car windscreen. Struggling into her coat, she looked right towards the High Street, then left down the pedestrian precinct. A hundred yards away, a couple walked with arms interlinked, the woman some inches taller than the man. Vikki broke into a jog across the frosted paving until she had halved the separation, then slowed her rush and moved into the lee of the shop fronts, replacing the urge to confront with a desire to follow.

The couple crossed the precinct and disappeared up a sidestreet. Vikki followed, knowing that was where a line of parking bays stood. By the time she rounded the corner, they were already inside the Range Rover and she burst into a full sprint. The engine started as she ran around to the driver's door and banged on the glass.

An electronic hum accompanied the appearance of a narrow vision slit above the steamy window. The poet's eyes could be seen. "Yes?"

"It's me, about the interview."

"Goodnight, Miss Corbett."

The window slid closed and a forward gear was engaged. Vikki stood back, noticing the sticker in the window of the back seat. A Red Setter lolled its tongue towards her, below the legend "A dog is for life".

"What a moronic act of lunacy!" The Poet said as the Range Rover lurched away from the parking space.

"What a bitch!"

"Not her, you! Here I am, asking favours of everyone I know to close up the situation, and there you are parading yourself in public like the Queen of Sheba!"

"Don't be angry, please!"

"Oh Rowan, this whole affair with Oak and Hazel has gone too far."

"I thought you had dealt with that reporter?"

"So did I."

"Have her sacked, you can do it."

"I cannot be so crude."

"Sack her, talk to Arnold Brass, take him out to dinner, buy shares in his paper."

"Rowan, I am not a millionaire."

"Yes you are."

"Not a real millionaire, I don't have great heaps of money in offshore deposits, my money works for England." He concentrated on driving out of town. "It's tied up, I'd have to work out a very expensive arrangement."

"Is your wife at home?"

"Yes. We'll drive around for a while, then I'll bring you back to the edge of town and you can get a taxi home."

Neither said anything for several minutes.

"Rupert!" Rowan crooned. "Won't it be delightful when your wife goes abroad?"

"Perfectly," his tone changed to one of jollity, "you must come to stay at Foxstones. We'll have a whole crowd of people to stay; poets, free thinkers, artists, you'll love them all."

"I will."

"You'll have to cook us one of your banquets."

"I shall insist."

He was concentrating on watching a set of traffic lights. Once they were moving once more, she advanced a more tempting idea.

"It could be like that all the time. Couldn't you arrange it, one day?"

The Poet said nothing in reply, but he never addressed that question whenever she asked it. She could only hope for a plane crash, or Parisian muggers or an unfortunate fishbone in a West Bank restaurant. Rowan could ask the goddess to remove the inconvenient woman, and free The Poet from her thrall.

Kingshaven faded into petrol stations and ribbon development, then the black hedges of the countryside replaced the streetlights. To their right, the river glinted ancient and cold in the frosty moonlight.

The Poet had been quiet, obviously preparing to speak. "Listen to me, Rowan, I have decided that we cannot risk being seen together again in public, not until this whole Hazel affair has been forgotten. If there is any whiff of scandal, my wife . . ."

"Oh forget your wife!" Rowan lost control.

"Rowan!"

"Tell her, for God's sake tell her! Let's go straight back to your house now and get it over with."

"Sometimes, Rowan, I can't understand you."

"I love you, can't you remember that for one moment? Rupert, I love you, I would do anything for you. Tell her and get rid of her, she's no use to you, she only gets in the way."

"Life is not that simple, my wife is an asset to our cause, I cannot afford either the scandal or the financial cost of separation."

"I have money, I can sell my property."

"Pennies, Rowan, pennies. I would lose all the companies, all of them." He spoke in short bursts of objections now. "And my farm, it loses money, you know that, I couldn't even keep the farm."

"But she doesn't see you for what you are."

"Yes she does, in her own way."

More silence, road noise, the sound of the petrol-guzzling engine.

"She is useful," he said again.

"And me? Am I useful?"

"Irreplaceable," he said in a softer tone, patting her knee as he drove, "you are the right hand that wields my sword."

His right-hand woman said nothing more as they drove around the lanes then back towards Kingshaven. Fate would have to contrive too many fatal accidents before her life could be complete. Fate might need a hand.

November ended in cold, swirling sleet and the promise of worse to come. It had been a chilling year and a frustrating year, Vikki mused as she sat before her wordprocessor writing a totally neutral account of the poetry reading. She might go up to London for Christmas with the family; she could see the lights and find someone to take to a show, if she could wangle the tickets. She could look up Jeffrey Flint, he probably knew a whole range of exotic bistros tucked away in side-streets and he wasn't half bad once he stopped using jargon and descended to the level of everyday conversation.

Vince passed across her line of vision with a bundle of mistletoe for the secretary to Sellotape at strategic points. The office party would be the drunken shambles it had been last year, so she ought to contrive a headache that day and leave for London early.

Christmas cards, damn! If she didn't organise herself soon, all the best selections would be gone, leaving her to send naff ones as usual. It was almost noon and launching into the push-and-shove of Christmas shoppers appealed to her. Quickly, Vikki left the building, working out how many cards she needed to send. From the Press Office she had a brisk walk to reach High Street, passing the scaffolding-clad museum on the way. She crossed the junction at the lights, then entered the pedestrianised "Old Quarter", as the Tourist Board had dubbed it. As she reached the end of The Passage, she thought of Jeffrey Flint and of his sometime girlfriend in the wholefood shop. It would be a touch ironic to buy him a little something from Naturella Wholefoods.

The shop was double-fronted with its woodwork stripped and repainted rainforest green. Its door was adorned with narrowboat-style floral paintwork, which Vikki had never appreciated before. She had been here twice to speak to Monica Clewes, but had been too full of the hunt for truth to pay much attention to the shop itself. The door jangled as a Chinese wind-chime caught the air. Inside, the odours were enhanced by extra Christmas pot-pourri baskets lining the window. Up above the cash desk were the glass sweet-jars of herbal teas. Vikki thought of another top shelf lined with herb jars and wondered where Amelia Winter had done her shopping.

Monica Clewes sat behind the desk, half hidden behind Vikki's own newspaper. She wore a one-piece homemade dress, basically black but with a wild riot of jungle plants and toucans breaking up its shape in dazzling camouflage. Her hair was swept back into a ponytail and either prematurely grey or naturally platinum blonde, unless the wholesome Miss Clewes had found a little peroxide to fudge the issue. A hand-knitted shawl dangled around her shoulders whilst heavy brass hung from her neck. Vikki felt she ought to ask to have her fortune told.

"Can I help?" the shopkeeper asked.

Vikki could see what Flint saw in the clean face and those grey-green eyes. Monica recognised her.

"Hello again, it's Veronica, isn't it?"

"Vikki."

"Yes, sorry."

She wasn't sorry at all, thought Vikki; she could spot a catty remark any day of the week.

"I'm afraid I don't have anything to tell you."

"I was just passing," Vikki said, "window-shopping, I thought I'd pop in and see what you have."

"Please do." The shopkeeper's eyes fell back to the paper.

Vikki walked slowly into the body of the shop, which changed direction, level and lighting at the rear. This had once been another room, two steps lower, which ran at right angles to the first creating an L-shape. A green-painted staircase ran upwards and below this were four shelves of books. Vikki stopped beside them and read the titles: save this, recycle that, alternative lifestyles, alternative cosmologies, Arthurian Tarot, Green politics, herblore. Food for the body, food for the soul. For a few minutes, Vikki browsed, half-captivated, half-bemused, wondering if there was anything in this New Age nonsense. She fingered the facsimile herblore, then the definitive work on mushrooms. Organic winemaking might appeal to Flint, she could send him a book through the post. Then she saw the short row of poetry books by the little-known local author.

She heard footsteps coming down the staircase and moved her attention to a rack of eco-friendly, politically correct postcards and plucked out one card at random. Its recycled paper featured an ethnic-art dolphin leaping from the sea. As the shopkeeper approached, Vikki turned to notice how tall Monica Clewes was. Those extra eight or nine inches made Vikki feel like a schoolgirl caught shoplifting.

"This is an interesting place to work," she blustered, on reflex gesticulating towards the sacks of beans on the floor.

"Are you interested in wholefood?"

"Well, I've never given it a try really."

"You should, it enhances body and soul. You could try my cosmetics too."

Vikki was conscious that she had dressed in a rush that morning and had probably applied too much blusher, whilst she knew the purple eyeshadow had been a mistake.

"They're cruelty-free, not tested on animals and made from only natural ingredients," Monica continued, "they might save your skin."

Vikki felt herself colour beneath the blusher as her lifestyle clashed with the shop owner. She pointed to the bookshelf. "What does all this black magic do for you?"

Monica discoloured. "Are you here to buy something?"

Vikki waggled the recycled card. "You know Jeffrey Flint, don't you?"

A slow smile came to Monica's face. "Yes, we're good friends."

"I was looking for something for him."

"I have the very thing." Monica went away and Vikki followed back to the desk. She was presented with the Yule gift pack of special teas.

"Wonderful, thank you." Vikki drew out her purse to pay. The reporter was replacing the Christmas shopper as Vikki found another angle. "You've got all Temple-Brooke's books back there, do they sell?"

"Very well."

"You were at his reading, over at Waterstones?"

"Yes," came the slightly irritated reply.

"Look, you're a friend of his . . ."

"I am?"

Vikki took a wild stab in the dark. "You were in his car, when I tried to speak to him."

"Me?" If Monica was lying she was exceptionally good at it. "That must have been his wife, they're very close."

"Ah, sorry. I just want to interview him for my paper."

"Oh well, I'm sure you could try ringing him."

"He's ex-directory."

Monica glanced towards a pensioner who had just set the wind-chimes tinkling.

"Why didn't you go to Piers Plant's funeral?" Vikki asked directly.

"Look, I'm busy. I hardly knew him and I hate funerals." Monica turned to the man. "Can I help you?"

Vikki slipped the gift pack into her Harrods shopping bag, then left the shop. The slit of sky above The Passage had a greenish hue, there was snow in the air and she shivered against the icy chill which had formed as she had spoken to Monica Clewes. Jeffrey Flint deserved better, she might just give him a ring.

Chapter 25

It was Wednesday, and it was snowing. Jeffrey Flint was sketching the plan of a typical "playing-card" fort on the blackboard of seminar room 246 when he heard the sound of fingernails tapping on glass. He stopped talking and glanced towards the eye-level window in the door. Tyrone mouthed the words "it's snowing".

Flint signalled for him to come in. The first-years looked up at the postgraduate as their lecturer clapped him around the shoulders and turned Tyrone to face the class.

"Tell us all."

Tyrone paused, looking foolish. "It's snowing."

Flint banged on the table: "This! This is the power of observation that we demand of our students here at Central College."

The class tittered and Tyrone frowned. Flint waved his hand at the class. "Class closed, disperse, go away." He turned to Tyrone.

"That wasn't fair," Tyrone said.

"Life's unfair. I know what you've been up to and I stand a good chance of losing my job because of it."

Beating the students out of the room, they marched down towards Flint's office. "Okay, tell me about it."

"I've spoken to Vikki every day."

"And?"

"We've crossed most of the suspects off, and found a lot of dirt on James Templestone."

"Who?" Flint asked, then remembered, "Ah, Rupert Brooke reincarnated as Aleister Crowley, or the other way around."

"He and his wife own all sorts of weird outlets for books, videos, games and they publish a whole load of magazines, not just Green ones. They're into just about everything, right-wing politics, left-wing politics, church committees, Tory council, it's completely mad."

"He could be a liberal, wanting to express all shades of opinion."

"But it's all the same opinion, isn't it, Doc?"

Flint halted outside Sally's room. "You've noticed?"

"Yeah; right wing – keep out the immigrants, left wing – keep out the capitalist multinationals; Church of England – let's respect our betters, Pagan cults – let's live in the past. Even the video games and Lucy's dungeons and dragons form part of the same scene. His poems are all about rural landscapes, he hangs around with hippies like Monica Clewes . . ."

"Wait." Flint held up the flat of his hand and stuck his head into Sally's office.

"Jeff?" She looked up from the typewriter.

"Sally, I'm going to be sick," he said.

"Oh no," she said in alarm, then her expression quickly changed. "Would this be one of your convenient illnesses?"

"I feel it coming on already."

"Jeff, I wouldn't . . ."

"Be a hero and cancel my night school people."

She frowned.

"And everything else until next week."

Sally's voice sank to a whisper. "Ian will go mad."

"A man's gotta do what a man's gotta do," Flint drawled in his best John Wayne voice.

"Can't you wait until the end of term?" Sally's utterly readable face was awash with anguished pleading.

"Lucy Gray won't wait that long."

"You've found her?"

"Give or take a few hundred yards."

It was a hunch, but one based on growing certainty. By dawn the following morning, Flint was packed into a high-winged Cessna with Ralph and Judy Slack. It had taken an afternoon and evening of frantic telephoning, plus bribes, to persuade them to take to the air. The snow had been fitful during the afternoon and lay still on the freezing ground overnight. By mid-morning on the Thursday, it would begin to melt and no more was forecast.

The morning sky was was clear, the sun weakly sparkling across frozen marshland as the Cessna swooped over Kingshaven. Ralph turned inland, passed the smokestacks of the industrial estates and

263

flew on to the gently rolling farmland beyond, with the curving river as a guide. Judy navigated, with Flint hugging his map and spotting the landmarks one by one. A red smear in the distance had to be Durring, with curls of the Darkewater snaking towards it.

Some snow still lay on the fields, it lined hedge banks, clung to paths and hid in furrows. Changes in vegetation or surface height were sufficient to alter the pattern of white, so that even the faintest hollow showed up as a brighter concentration amongst the dusted brown or green fields. Ralph pointed out ancient features invisible from the ground: field systems, ring-ditches, enclosures, droveways, it was all text-book stuff.

Flint knew all the Darkewater megaliths intimately. He had read all the references, seen all the sketches and visited each in turn. One held his quest in its cradle and only tiny strands of evidence, plus gut feeling told him which one. Harriet's Stone passed beneath them, the finger of the old witch pointing upwards at those come to steal her secrets. Ralph throttled back and lost altitude, flattening out for his first run. Cold air blasted upwards through the open hatch in the Cessna floor, which permitted Judy to take the photographs under a barrage of instructions. Flint was reminded momentarily of "The Blue Max" and thought how Tyrone would love to be up there with them.

Ralph suggested that five of the sites were suited to air photography. Several passes were made at each until all three were satisfied and Ralph turned the plane back towards Cambridge. Flint should have been taking tutorials at that moment, instead he risked his career in the skies over southern England. The exhilaration was worth the expense, but it would be several hours before he knew whether the results justified the risk.

Tyrone had driven Flint overnight to Cambridge, then hung around with some old school mates until the expedition returned. Several more hours elapsed whilst Judy developed and printed the film, so it was evening before any progress was made.

Ralph set up a stereoscopic viewer to compare vertical photographs of each site, with those taken the previous year. Pictures with their ghostly echoes of peoples long past were scrutinised to millimetre accuracy. One was examined closer than any. Harriet's Stone cast a black stripe across the photograph, like a giant sundial in the ploughed field. Less obvious was a white blurr some twenty yards in circumference surrounding the stone itself. This was not in the previous shot, it was the result of the snow settling in the long grass and taking time to thaw. It was not the proof sought.

"If you were a murderer, Ralph, where would you dump a body?"

"In a ditch."

"But farmers recut ditches."

"In the cornfield," Tyrone said.

"You foul up the shoots and create a nice empty patch."

"But in the autumn, the farmer ploughs it . . ."

"And brings up the subsoil you've disturbed, plus bits of clothes, bones et cetera."

Judy hung over their shoulders. "It's complex, being a murderer."

"I'd choose a field of rough grass," Flint said, carefully checking the images, looking for a smudge no more than half a centimetre long.

"If you had a new grave in grassland," Ralph thought aloud, "it might just retain some snow on the surface."

The field around Harriet's Stone was surrounded by a hedge and perimeter ditch. No marks showed in the Yule-log texture of snow sprinkled on evenly ploughed soil. The adjacent field was arable, with a faint path leading from its corner towards the nearest country lane. Snow clung more stubbornly along its course.

"You keep away from the path, because that's where the predictable man-with-dog walks." Flint continued to narrate his thinking on the psychology of murder.

Lower downslope was an area of swampy marsh, bordering a broad S-bend of the river.

"Are you sure you know what you're looking for?" Judy asked.

"Piers Plant had an obsession with this place and this girl I met implied it was here that she last saw Lucy."

It would be somewhere close to the stone but not too close, not too obvious. Towards the top edge of the field adjacent to that with the stone, a white oval stood out from the mottled shade of the rest of the field.

"How long is that?"

Ralph laid a ruler along the mark and moved his whiskered lips to calculate. "Two or three metres. I'll check it's not a piece of dust on the negative."

Flint laid the ruler from the stone to the white blob, then looked at the orientation marks Judy had applied.

"South-east, roughly. That could be the direction of the mid-winter sunrise, I can see Piers Plant loving that idea. I've walked across this field, it's an old-fashioned meadow, with rough grass grown long for cattle feed. No one would plough it, people only walk dogs down the far edge and the spring growth would bury any disturbance in the winter."

Water came to his eyes. He knew what had been found.

Organisation takes time, people had to be mobilised, cajoled, and this was not easy by telephone. Central College operated on an archaeological timescale, things did not normally happen overnight, but overnight was the schedule that Tyrone and Flint worked to.

Arrangements were complete some time after midnight, when Flint bedded down on a camp-bed in Ralph and Judy's barely heated study. As he tossed fitfully and tried to keep warm, he found himself somewhere else, barefoot and exposed on the cold, windless night. A gibbous moon low on the horizon threw long shadows across the hillside. One shadow was longer, sharper than all the others, which moved, swayed, circled and touched the hallowed ground. As the moment came, one moved forward, stripping aside the grey cloak to stand naked before the moon. She shivered against the cold, trembled as she took up the knife and the onlookers took up the chant. Ethereal harmonies of another age rose into the winter air. An animal struggled away the last moments of its life, the old and wise stood back in satisfaction and The Maiden declared her need to embrace the Earth.

A tall figure in a horned headpiece blew a blast on the hunter's horn, then raised a cry to the night and the cry was answered. Something dark moved, clawed its way out of the blackness, summoned by the blackest of spells from the blackest of books.

Stupid, idiotic nightmare! That was not how it had happened! His logical brain fought back against the fear of darkness and loneliness as he forced himself awake.

It was edging towards four o'clock when his heartbeat returned to normal. He was cold down there in the study, surrounded by visions of demons and monsters, but in the morning, Jeffrey Flint would have to face the scene of that nightmare.

Before it was light, they drove back to London in Tyrone's car and called at Flint's flat to collect warm digging clothes. Next they drove on to college to change mode of transport. In the car park, Stuart Shapstone and Bunny Beresford both leaned on the Land-Rover, looking ill-kempt and unhappy. They had already packed the rear with the tools of the archaeologist's trade and were uncertain what the rest of the day held.

A wintry shower accompanied them on the drive towards the valley, but the rain had moved on by the time the Land-Rover lurched down the country lane and pulled on to the verge behind the red Metro.

Muffled to the point of disappearing, Vikki met the team in a flurry of introductions, then gave Flint half a hug in the excitement.

"So this is it!"

"Don't look so thrilled," he warned. "If I'm wrong, we could still look very foolish and if I'm right, it's not going to be nice."

"I know." Vikki's face fell to a sober equilibrium and she helped the men unload the equipment.

Grimly, they walked towards the objective, a ragged group of excavators laden with their tools like a gaggle of dwarves. Soon, Harriet's Stone could be seen through the low hedgerow, glinting wet after the lunchtime rain. They passed the stubble field and into the meadow beyond, which had been cut in the autumn to leave rough and uneven grass. No further snow had fallen.

"Explain how you know where to look," Vikki said, after the students set about their work. "I don't really understand."

The lecturer kicked at sticky earth. "Any disturbance of the soil alters its character. Perhaps it holds water better, perhaps less well than before. That will mean that snow or frost will exhibit differential settling, differential thawing. Especially down here, we're near the bottom of the hill, the drainage will be affected. Then, if you dig a pit, chuck in a body, you get a mound, so you have to disperse the spare earth. But, if you backfill it to produce a level surface, the contents will settle and compact over a period of months, creating a slight depression. This may be enough to retain a light snowfall for a few hours longer than the surrounding fields."

"And this is what the photograph shows?"

"A little white shadow. In the summer it would have been a little black shadow, but I missed my chance then."

Using a map drawn up from the photograph, Stuart identified a pair of trees and a gatepost which had shown up clearly on the picture. It was a simple matter of twenty minutes to triangulate the position of the white smudge with a pair of surveying tapes. They then laid out a square, five metres to a side, around the point the air photograph suggested the disturbance might be. Bunny took up a four-foot-long piece of iron and began to drive it into the ground, following a pattern of points spaced at half-metre intervals within the square. He systematically drove the rod downwards as far as it would go, which in most places was only one foot. The point of the spike was pulled up each time, red with the clay of the subsoil. In the centre of the grid, Bunny's rod sank two to three feet without undue effort.

"Here, Doc, a fiver says it's here."

Flint quickly dished out orders: Bunny and Tyrone take the spades and cut the turf, he would wield the turf-cutter, whilst Stuart lugged the turves and piled them well clear of the area of excavation.

"I don't mind getting dirty," Vikki said.

"You write the story, we'll dig the hole and the union will be happy."

She took out her camera and took a few working shots whilst they cleared away the turf.

"This is too easy," said Bunny, "someone's done this before."

When he looked closely, Flint could see a slight change in the vegetation which suggested turf had been crudely torn up and even more crudely replaced. This gave them an area to work and it was cleared before Vikki gave a yelp of alarm.

A figure was coming across the field from the bottom, walking purposefully in their direction.

Bunny stopped.

"Keep digging," Flint said.

A one-foot-deep excavation existed by the time the figure was close enough to shout. He wore a green wax jacket and flat cap and carried a broken shotgun under the crook of his arm. A border collie ran away from his heels, barking.

Another bloody dog, thought Flint, swapping turf-cutter for a mattock.

"Oi!" The challenge came from long distance, then was repeated as the challenger drew closer. "Oi, what the hell are you doing?"

"Hello," Vikki yelled back.

"What the bloody hell are you doing?"

"We're excavating!" The girl was so irrepressible, she could make grave-robbing sound blasé.

The dog reached the diggers and halted, growling. Flint kept the mattock at the ready.

"You, what are you doing in my field?"

"Are you the landowner?" Flint asked, one eye still on the dog.

"I farm it, same difference! And who the hell are you?" Ruddy features were further reddened by anger.

"We're looking for a buried body," Vikki said.

"Body? What body?"

The dog took interest in the hole, ceased being hostile and began to scrabble by Tyrone's spade.

"You know, a dead person," Bunny added, "a stiffie."

"You're all crazy, now just clear off."

The man stood immobile and impotent, his gun clearly reserved for rabbits. Whilst he blustered threats and abuse, Tyrone, Bunny and the dog continued to dig. Pawfuls of dirt spattered over the farmer's wellingtons. Vikki scrabbled in the soil, arising triumphant with a strip of sodden white cloth.

"I'll make an archaeologist of you yet." Flint took the strip from her.

"I'm calling the police," the farmer exploded, "this is trespass."

"Good, get Inspector Douglas," Flint said, "and tell him to bring the forensic boys along."

"I'll bring the bloody green van to lock you lot away!"

The farmer retreated, yelling threats and calling his dog to heel. The hole was two feet deep now, with Flint urging them to dig with care, not to go too deep but work across the site to keep the digging platform level.

"Doc, we know what we're doing," Stuart protested.

"Just testing." Flint stepped out of the hole to direct, rather than interfere. The two diggers expanded the hole into a rough square, tossing their soil into a bucket, which Flint would pass to Tyrone. Each bucketload was poured through a sieve and scoured with a trowel, Vikki helping pick out possible clues into a seed tray.

"Grave cut, Doc." Stuart straightened his back and stood out of the hole.

The sub-soil lay red-orange and undisturbed below where Stuart had worked. In Bunny's half of the hole, the brown topsoil continued downwards, mixed with disturbed clods of orange clay and grass. Stuart bent down and flicked away at the top of the disturbed soil with his trowel. Within moments he had exposed the clear junction of the two soil types.

"Okay team, spades down, trowels out!" Flint said, sniffing against the cold, wondering how long the farmer would be in bringing back the police.

Even Vikki fell to her knees and learned how to trowel. Once the edge of the grave cut had been identified, they began to work systematically along its edge, clearing away the topsoil to reveal an oval of brown earth within the cleaner orange. This was what the aerial photograph had revealed: the shadow of the last resting place of Lucy Gray. A blurred frosty patch had been her only marker.

"Do we go on?" Vikki asked, wiping at her clay-caked knees.

"Do you really want to go on?" Flint asked.

"She won't be very pretty," Tyrone added.

After ten months in the ground, Lucy would not be pretty at all. A distinctive smell was already issuing from the hole.

"No," Vikki said, after toying with the idea for a moment. "I suppose the police would be narked if we did."

The diggers suspended work and moved a respectful distance away from the hole. All but Vikki had known Lucy, albeit briefly, so the jokes had stopped and few words were exchanged as they sat on the gate, or on upturned buckets and waited.

First to arrive was the local bobby, walking down from his panda car in company with the farmer. Whilst the lawman listened to, and disputed the story, the farmer stood in the background muttering, "Bloody students." Vikki subdued both men with her press card and the voracity of her interview technique. Grudgingly the farmer gave his name, brightened up, then fleshed it out with a potted life history. The constable walked to the hole, refused the offer of a spade, then radioed for assistance.

A procession of policemen flowed from headquarters: a mobile patrol, the scene-of-crime officer, the murder squad and at last, Chief Inspector Douglas.

Flint sat back on the gate awaiting the inevitable interview with Douglas, coping with the mixed emotions which ran through him: pride, sadness, and a sense of anti-climax. Barbara would have to be told before Vikki's inevitable scoop hit the news-stands and it was not a prospect to be relished. He managed a grin to his comrades as the figure of the Chief Inspector could be seen working his way down the stubble field.

"Now, let him ignore this!"

Tyrone hummed an objection. "Mind you, we're going to look ridiculous if this turns out to be a neolithic warrior burial."

Vikki was not entirely responsible for the blown-up Hammer Horror fantasy which appeared in the late editions of the *Advertiser* that night. Flint had encouraged her in order to throw confusion at the hidden enemy, and make them think he was still wide of the mark. On her part, Vikki needed a story so sensational, no editor could refuse to print it. The front page headline ran: "LONELY GRAVE FOR WITCH SACRIFICE. Victim of Demon Curator Found Murdered."

Chapter 26

Vikki spent the following day hanging about the fringes of the official police excavation, with Vince taking reel after reel of photographs. The once deserted field was full of men in blue boiler suits and the lane choked with police and media vehicles. Her story had been syndicated to radio and national press, so Vikki would have felt good but her pride was tinted by the tragedy to which she almost felt witness.

She had wanted to interview Mrs Gray, or Barbara Faber as second choice, but something held her back. Flint had been unusually silent after he had made the phone call which delivered the news. To pry too quickly would be to injure his grief too.

The great grey finger of sarsen reared above her as she watched Flint coming down the field once more, his wellingtons caked with mud and stormclouds running across his face.

"Hi, what's wrong?"

"Effing imbeciles!" He looked sideways at her. "Is it okay if I say 'effing'?"

"Say anything you like. What has Douglas been saying to you?"

"He won't believe me. Even after Tyrone has gone all the way back to London to fetch his data, PC Plod doesn't believe it and I don't blame him."

"What?" She was suddenly alarmed.

"Everything we have is at best circumstantial. We have circular arguments which rely on all the other arguments being true, and of course they are all logical deductions, but the law demands fact, not logic."

Tyrone squelched his way across the path churned to sludge by police boots. "No dice, boss?"

"Did you tell him about Temple-Brooke?" Vikki asked.

"What was the point? We have nothing on him, he's clean."

"He plays golf with Douglas, you know," Vikki informed them, "and Arnold, my editor, which is how I found out. One can't accuse one of the chaps, can one?"

Flint simply stood with his hands on his hips and let the freshly falling rain spatter on his face. He thumped the megalith. "Go on, Gaia, give me pneumonia too."

"Who's Gaia?"

"Mother goddess." Flint thumped the stone again.

The reporter looked at the the other two, willing something to happen to break the stalemate.

"If only I'd got the number of that Range Rover," Tyrone moaned.

"What Range Rover?" she asked idly.

He retold the encounter on the country lane with the Range Rover on Halloween.

"The great poet drives a Range Rover, I chased him back to it after the poetry reading."

"What colour was it?" Tyrone interrupted.

"Green, aren't they all green?"

"No. It didn't by any chance have a little picture of a dog . . ."

". . . in the window behind the driver?" she asked, with a warm sensation welling within her. "A Red Setter?"

"Yes, it's him, it's him!" Tyrone gave a little jig, Vikki almost burst with the chance discovery, her prayer had been answered, instantly. Perhaps there was a power hidden within the stone. She turned to Flint. "So, what do you think now?"

He clapped them both on the shoulders and pulled them into a close huddle. "Liking Red Setters is not an indictable offence."

"It should be," Tyrone said.

"But it's proof!" Vikki burst out. "Go back and tell Douglas."

Flint began to walk away from them.

"I'm coming." Vikki clutched at his sleeve. "I want to see his face."

"I'm not bothering with the flatfoots any more, I'm going to see Monica, to find out how we get to talk to Temple-Brooke."

Flint drove the Land-Rover back to Kingshaven and wasted time trying to find somewhere to park amongst the eager Christmas shoppers. He had changed into his driving shoes, but still wore his old donkey jacket and the digging jeans with clay caked up to the thighs. He tinkled the door chime in Monica's shop.

"Jeff, Jeff, my!" She stopped mid-sentence to look at his unwashed, unshaved state.

"Sorry, this is my business suit. I haven't much time, so I'll come straight to it."

Her face creased with concern.

"Did you hear the news?"

"You found your student?"

He nodded. "Now I need your help to get me to her killer."

"Jeff, I've done all I can."

"I must speak to Temple-Brooke, I know he was involved."

"No, he can't be."

"Yes he can, he fits the bill perfectly."

Monica shook her head furiously. "Jeff, you're mistaken, he's brilliant, he's gentle, he's not a murderer."

"Okay, so he knows who the murderer is, because any ordinary killer couldn't have covered his tracks without money and influence and organisation and your Mr Temple-Brooke has all three."

"Have you told the police?"

"No." He repeated his doubts about the evidence. "I'll give it some thought over the weekend."

Monica stood wringing her hands and making well-meaning but ultimately hopeless suggestions. He gazed around her shop for inspiration, taking in the sign saying "Closed for the Week-End" and its sister, "Wednesday is Half-Day Closing". Down on the floor were sacks labelled "Split-peas" and "Kidney-beans". Monica had a very neat writing hand and had mastered several styles. She had probably done calligraphy once.

"Just phone him, Monica, tell him he's my number one suspect and that I'm taking the story to the cops unless he talks to me and finds me a better suspect."

"Jeff, that's cruel. It's moral blackmail."

Flint felt his eyes watering. Monica had a store of sympathy for every troubled soul in the world.

"I have to go. When this is all over, we'll have to have dinner some time."

Monica laid on a bright veneer for a few moments. "Fine, that will be nice."

*   *   *

274

Jeffrey Flint left Kingshaven once more, collected Tyrone and asked him to drive back to London. It had been a cold, muddy, tiring week of conflicting moods. He would spend the weekend bathing, sleeping, eating, watching anything on the video, but not listening to a single news broadcast. He wouldn't hear Vikki repeating her story for the agencies, nor see anguished pictures of Barbara or Mrs Gray. He would not be reminded of his agonising telephone call with its clumsy words of regret. For a day he would put the trauma aside, then on Monday, he would start again.

His first Monday lecture was at two, and he habitually turned up late. Flint made no exception for the last week of the autumn term, arriving just after eleven in a sombre, determined mood. Sally stopped him at the top of the stairs with a comment along the lines of, "Oh Jeff, how totally ghastly."

He followed Sally into the office and went for his mail on reflex, finding thirty items, most of which were seasonally stamped and Christmas-card weight. All these were forgotten in a moment, when Sally opened the cake box which sat on the counter.

"You have a secret admirer," she said.

He let his eyes roam around the chocolate cake, its centre overflowing with butter icing, its top rippling with thick, real chocolate and the six flakes added to boost the calorie intake.

"This is a cake and a half, who left it?"

"One of your FE people, she said she hopes you soon feel better."

Guilt twangs hit him. More sickness excuses had all but killed his night school class. Lucy had drawn him away from all normal responsibilities. The neatly written card simply read, "Hope you are better after the Christmas-holiday Doctor Flint".

"Which one was it?"

"Forty-ish, grey, wears a head-scarf and glasses, dresses a bit dowdy. Susan? Sharon? Sheila?"

"Sheila?"

"Probably."

"The old darling, get me a knife and you can have a chunk. If you spot Tyrone, drag him in too, he needs building up."

Sally answered the external phone and handed it directly to Flint, who was within sniffing range of the cake.

"Doctor Flint?" It was him.

"Rupert Temple-Brooke, I presume."

"We must talk."

"Well, I've been wanting to talk to you for . . ."

"Now I'm ready."

Ready huh? What was that supposed to mean? "Okay, your place or mine?"

"Look, we need to meet, without that girl reporter present. I would just like you and me to have a quiet walk and a talk. I think we have a misunderstanding."

"Right." Pretty big misunderstanding, thought Flint.

Sally returned with a knife and half a dozen plates and cut generous slices, oblivious to the nature of the negotiation taking place.

"This affair must end. We must meet, alone, tomorrow." The Poet started to give instructions. A lonely road out in the marshland beyond Kingshaven, a telephone box, a footpath. Four o'clock, it would be almost dark by then.

Flint signalled that Sally was to tuck in, then accepted a plate with his chunk of cake, vowing to munch it in defiance of etiquette. The anti-snob rose to the fore, and just to insult this pompous voice, he would wipe the crumbs from his chin with his sleeve. "I'll be there . . ."

"Good," the caller concluded.

Sally had a mouthful of cake and was mumbling delight, so Flint bit into his piece. How many people knew about his chocolate fetish? Was it written on his face? Had he told Sheila? No, but he had told someone. Someone who had an expertly neat writing hand. Someone who was a rabid hyphenator, writing "Christmas-holiday", "Week-End" and "Kidney-beans". Someone who knew Temple-Brooke. Someone who was an expert in herblore.

"Monica," he murmured, then spat out the cake. "Sally, spit it out!"

"Mmm?"

He grabbed the plate from her hand. "Poisoned . . ."

"You crazy . . . mmb."

Flint threw his arms around her and forced her to bend double, then began to thump her back. Seconds later, Sally was dragged across the hall to the ladies'.

"Puke it up."

"Jeff . . ."

He kicked open the toilet door and reached the sink. "Puke."
She squirmed as he thrust her head down.

"They are trying to kill me, Sally, stick your fingers in now!"
"Can't!"

Flint grabbed Sally's chin and stuffed a finger past her tongue.
She gagged, she struggled, then she was sick on reflex.

Two students rushed to the door, imagining an assault. He
brushed them away in a barrage of slaps and misunderstandings.

"Look, cretin! She's ill, get her to a doctor!"

Sally was still struggling, and was released. "Flint, you bastard,"
she coughed.

"Sally, get down to the health centre, quick, you've been
poisoned! Understand, poisoned, like all those other people I
told you about."

At last she seemed to get the message and stood panting, hands
on her thighs. She allowed the students to take her quivering
arms.

"Take her to the medical centre. Get them to supply some
sort of purgative. She's ingested a natural poison. Hurry, for
God's sake."

Which god? he thought, amongst the confused hubbub outside
the departmental office. Ignoring the chaos, Flint elbowed his way
towards the remains of the cake and picked it up.

"Evidence," Flint said aloud, hands trembling.

"Flint, was is going on?" It was the Professor, speaking from
the doorway.

"Evidence!"

"Are you still playing detectives in my department?" he shouted
as the junior lecturer pushed past him. "You're in serious trouble,
I say, Doctor . . ."

He continued to shout, but Doctor Flint was running through
the building, down the stairs and into the forensic archaeology
laboratory. "Doc" Savage and her staff were in the middle of some
meeting. "Doc" ceased reading from a document, whilst Jules and
Sasha turned their heads in awe at Flint's frantic, panting state.

"Jeff?" "Doc" Savage asked.

"Hi, sorry to barge in, folks, but I need cast-iron evidence,
to use an old cliché. I need you people to do some quick i.d.s
on this."

"It's a cake," Jules offered.

"It's a poisoned cake. It may look yummy, but don't eat it. What I want is fingerprints from the goo," Flint panted, "traces of body hair, clothes fibres. Most of all, I want to know what poison she used. Check for natural chemicals, mushrooms, belladonna, things of that nature."

'Doc' Savage put aside her clipboard and held out a hand for the cake. Flint hurriedly explained the drama upstairs, whilst the three scientists regarded the cake with as much awe as if it were Piltdown Man's last supper. None of them was more than temporarily shaken by Flint's sudden demand.

"So we're looking for the same as last time?" Sandra said in her cold, clinical way.

"More than likely."

Flint stood regaining his breath whilst the trio of scientists passed the item from one to the other, not without scepticism.

"If you have herbal poison in there really, you may find seeds or plant residues," Sasha suggested slowly, "and pollen might have got in as a by-product."

"Could you match it to a sample of the original blend?"

"Just like a fingerprint. We do it all the time, but working on a different time-frame. We could compare a batch of pollen from two herb samples and determine whether they were gathered in a similar location."

An idea was forming that was so perfect, that Flint could not remain in the laboratory another minute. "Brilliant. Could you compare them to those foxglove samples from Forest Farm?"

"Sure."

"Today?"

"What?"

"This is crucial, believe me, guys. Gotta rush." Flint backed away from them. "Save at least half the cake, we will need it in court."

An idea had taken root, grown and blossomed in the few moments Flint had spent in the lab. He had enough proof to tip the balance, enough evidence to turn the suspect into the accused.

Tyrone was lingering outside the lab, alerted by the rumour sweeping the department that Flint had tried to rape Sally in the ladies' loo. His supervisor jabbed a finger towards him. "Okay, Biggles, get your car round the front in five minutes."

"What's going on?"

"You were right, I was wrong, dear sweet Monica Clewes has been stringing us along."

"Vikki said she was out on Halloween."

"Yes, and Monica made up some story about being threatened and mug, here, swallowed it. I didn't swallow the cake, though, and that's what counts. Right, I'm going to the janitor's office, then we're going to try Plan C."

"What's Plan C, Doc?"

"We'll make it up as we go."

In under five minutes they were moving into London traffic and had soon broken free of the city. Tyrone drove at manic speed and for once, Flint was urging him faster. The placid archaeologist was fired, at last, with anger, with confidence and with desperation. He had been tricked cruelly by Monica, he was certain. All along she had spied on him and diverted the course of the investigation, with the sole purpose of protecting the one Michelle had called The Protector. One more day, a few more pieces for the puzzle and then he would go to the police. No force, corrupt, idle, complacent or incompetent would be able to ignore the truth.

Kingshaven was quiet that Monday afternoon. Even the dismal ritual of frantic Christmas shopping had eased as a miserable grey sky encouraged an early darkness and a bitter chill stalked the streets. Dropped at the end of The Passage, he jogged as far as the door of Naturella Wholefood Market. A sign was pinned to the inside.

"Sorry – we're closed."

He felt the thrill of success. Monica Clewes was lurking somewhere, building herself an alibi. Flint walked a few yards further away from High Street to where The Passage opened out into a cul-de-sac. A pair of ill-fitting blue painted doors bore the name of the shop and an instruction not to park before them. He squinted through a crack into what could be a garage integral with the stone-built terrace. The white van was not inside. He returned to where Tyrone sat with the engine running and collected the bag of tools scrounged from the college janitor: a mallet, a hammer, a multi-drive screwdriver kit and a pair of chisels.

"I hope you know what you're doing, Doc," Tyrone said. "If you get caught, I wasn't here, okay?"

"Just keep an eye out and hoot that klaxon if she comes back."

"If I see her."

No one was in The Passage. Flint had learned from mistakes made in the museum and came well armed with a definite plan. The sturdy padlock was bypassed in a depressingly easy forty-five seconds as he forced the catch away from the blue garage door. Slipping inside, he pulled the door closed. The garage was lit only by slits of light working their way through the ill-fitting main door, so he snapped on a light switch to see a wooden floor with a trapdoor above his head. At the far end of the garage was a badly painted internal door and his gloved hands pulled at it twice to confirm this was locked.

The door was old, but the lock was a new Yale type. Flint took the hammer and with a dozen blows stove in the panel and released the lock from behind. The building was empty, he surmised, as no one had rushed to challenge the brutal entry. For a moment he considered what to do, armed with a crowbar and lump hammer if suddenly confronted by gentle Monica. He subconsciously adjusted his gloves, then advanced up the stairs.

A low-roofed loft surmounted the garage, lit by a pair of dusty windows front and back. Sacks of oatmeal, lentils, nuts and kidney beans were clustered around the trapdoor down into the garage. A block and tackle swinging from the overhead beam probably saved Monica much back-ache. Another door led towards the body of the shop and was unlocked.

He creaked the door open slowly to see a short landing, with a stair down to the shop, and familiar fragrances wafting upwards. Two doors led off the landing, both marked "Private".

The first room was the bathroom, with an old white enamel suite, knickers hanging to dry, environmentally friendly loo cleaner and recycled toilet paper. Sharp odours were masked by a dangling pot-pourri but his interest in the room reached its end.

The second door, at the head of the stair, was locked. Cursing the woman's paranoia, he checked carefully. Like the door in the garage, this had an original tumbler lock, but a new Yale had been fitted above. His old Kensington flat had the same mismatch of lock and door and the laminated college ID card had saved him much aggravation from his landlord. That day it saved Monica from losing another door. A minute of wriggling wrecked the card but the door eased open.

He could have guessed at the contents of Monica Clewes' home, which was a tidier, more mature version of Michelle's Dulwich flat. The walls were draped with badly executed oil paintings of trees, the floor covering was home-made rugs over polished wood and the air carried the scent of herbs. He moved quickly to identify four rooms: lounge, kitchen, bedroom, shrine.

Monica had never invited him upstairs for tea, and now he knew why. The shrine was a modified box-room, with a residual reek of incense. Its walls were blue-black, its ceiling was painted with a representation of the polar constellations and the floor was deep green, painted with a white pentagram. Ogham runes rambled about its periphery whilst a small stone altar bore a pair of pottery candlesticks. No horned goats or Satanic images dangled from hooks, so he knew that at least Monica had some rational system of beliefs.

He moved to the bedroom, checking under beds and rooting through drawers, making a token mess to appear to be a burglar. To enhance the effect, he picked up a few pieces of costume jewellery. He felt no guilt, only outrage at how he had been tricked and used.

On the bedside table was a photograph of Him and Her. A gleaming Monica Clewes in smart ladies' suit, beside a familiar tweed-jacketed figure who would not look out of place on the back cover of a poetry book. Flint picked up the silver frame and almost kissed it. R. Temple-Brooke, poet and puppetmaster, pictured next to the woman who did his dirty work. The bedroom had provided its plunder.

A desk stood in the corner of the lounge. One drawer was locked, but only briefly. He shook its contents on to the desk and dropped the diary and the address book into his bag.

Behind the desk were shelves of books, with a familiar range of occult tripe, plus many works which had to be rare finds. None of them appeared to be the accursed *De Nigris*. The whole bottom row of the bookshelf consisted of hardback exercise books crammed with handwritten script, so Flint took a dozen, his bag now bulging with loot. At the end were a number of thick photographic albums, of the type with sticky pages. Quickly, he pulled one out, expecting a nest of family photographs and instead found postcards. Monica travelled the country and collected postcards. He stood each album on the table and scurried through the pages, hoping for the empty spaces. He found one, then another. Two of the albums were grabbed, causing his bag to overflow. He sacrificed a pair of the handwritten books to make room.

Finally, he entered the kitchen, which had a back window looking out on to a fire escape and empty washing lines. The shelves at the near end were a veritable alchemist's workshop of dried herbs, and powders: atropa belladonna, Adonis vernalis, briony, foxglove, senna, hemp, everything bar newt's eyes and bats' wings. Monica Clewes would perhaps pick her herbs in a limited location. Overlooking the local marshland, perhaps. A clever laboratory might be able to match samples with those from his chocolate cake or Piers Plant's stew.

Witch? Poisoner? Corrupter of the innocent? The more he discovered about the innocuous Monica Clewes, the more she frightened him. Flint knew he had spent so many evenings and days sitting beside death, idly chatting about travel or art. And she had sat and smiled and played her duplicitous game.

Taking a spoon from her sideboard, he put one scoop of the four most lethal herbs into separate sample bags, his hands trembling with anger as much as fear. Then he froze, he was not alone. He sensed company, movement. From the living room came the slow swish of paper slipping from a chair. Without time to rush for the stairs or to figure out how the back door opened, Flint acted on reflex, picked up his hammer and stood defiant.

Every witch has a black cat, but this one was tabby. It stopped in the doorway, fixed him with yellow slit-eyes and hissed. Had Flint believed in the power of the familiar he would have fled. Instead, he lunged at the beast, which flashed off towards the landing and did not reappear.

His nerve had been broken, so quickly he followed the cat into the lounge. One last look round allowed him to spot the inevitable poetry volumes on her bookshelves, then with pulse rate increasing and bowels churning, he succumbed to the urge to leave.

Panting with excitement he moved rapidly, soon reaching the battered blue door again. A youth cycled by outside, then Flint slipped out of the door and carried his heavy bag into the open.

Three more witnesses walked past as he hurried to the rendezvous with Tyrone.

"Success?" Tyrone asked.

"Ok, Wheels, hit it."

Chapter 27

Vikki had been surprised to find the itinerant Doctor Flint on her doorstep that evening, more surprised to learn he was staying the night and stunned when he told her what was in the kitbag and how he had obtained it. Tyrone gave her no more than a wave from the seat of his car before he roared away towards London, shouting an obscure parting line that Flint would need lots of money to feed the animals.

After the barest of explanations, she knocked up fish fingers and chips for two, keeping one eye on what Flint was doing on the kitchen table. He was rooting through books stolen from Monica Clewes' flat and describing them aloud.

Two were diaries written in code, the remaining handwritten books contained recipes for home-made concoctions or were do-it-yourself spellbooks. Vikki flicked the fish fingers over in the grill, then returned to gaze at the homespun occult armoury with fascinated disbelief.

Once dinner was served, and Vikki apologised for its carbonised state, they started to flick through the postcard folders. One section encompassed a selection of Scottish views, mostly castles and monuments, but with one glaring void.

"Isle of Skye?" asked Flint.

"Didn't Mrs Gray get a card from Skye?" Vikki realised. "So Monica sent the cards?"

"It looks like it. She uses hyphens all the time, I looked at the Christmas card she sent me, with a message full of hyphens and strange little looping 'g's, just like on the cards."

Monica had visited the Burrell Collection in Glasgow and filled two pages with their postcards. One was missing, presumed posted to Barbara. In the other folder, a tour of Wiltshire left another vacant space on the Salisbury page.

"I suppose she could have posted these to a friend and asked them to repost them to you," Vikki said.

"Easily. She might even have been the person faking those phone calls."

Finishing the meal without complaint, Flint turned his skills towards the code, puzzling, jotting notes on his pad. Before the coffee had fully worked its way through the filter, he declared, "Child's play. She's using letter substitution."

One minute later, he had a key and took pride in explaining it to Vikki.

"She uses 's' instead of 'i', q instead of 'a', what an amateur!"

Vikki watched fascinated as he exploded the code, then helped him fill in a table to decode the diary. The evening was spent composing a complete picture of Monica Clewes, woman, environmental campaigner, herbalist, witch and high priestess.

Just after nine o'clock, Flint closed the diary and closed his eyes. Vikki watched the way his brain visibly seemed to be ticking over.

"You know, you surprised me," she said.

"Me?"

"Of course, you. Who else is there? You know when I first met you, we didn't get on, did we?"

"Not exactly." By the way he shuffled in his seat, he seemed to be apologising for his frostiness that first day. "Don't you think I'm just another perpetual student living off the taxpayer?"

"I did, but not any more."

"Ah, my new image. This isn't the real me."

"Yes it is. Except now, you're not hiding behind a tatty jacket and protest badges. Losing the beard was a first class move."

"Glad the sacrifice was worthwhile. This whole episode has really chopped me up, Vikki, don't you know?"

"I know, you liked Lucy, didn't you?"

"I would have liked her, if I'd made the effort to get to know her."

"You've had a bad year," she said. "You lost your girlfriend . . ."

". . . Chrissie? No, we were just good friends. Still are, officially."

"What about that Irish girl?"

"No comment, and before you mention Monica, that has been

the worst twist of the knife, to find she's the one been covering up for Lucy's killer, whilst stringing me along."

He looked around her at the kitchen clock. "Well, tomorrow is make or break day, which means that me and you should go and find a little hotel somewhere."

She frowned, not understanding his intent. "What are you suggesting?"

"No funny business, honest," he pleaded, without too much sincerity, "my thinking is this. Dear Monica Clewes gets back to her shop tonight and finds what I've done. She will know who did it and she will tell her friends, at least one of whom is a practised arsonist."

Vikki nodded in sympathy. "There's a Travelodge about five minutes from here." Something was trying to wriggle free from the depths of her soul, but she squashed it. "They've got single rooms."

Single rooms were vacated late in the morning, after Flint had spent some time on the telephone to Tyrone and called at his bank. Vikki drove him out of Kingshaven and into the flat marshland which ran parallel to the river as it turned into salty estuary.

From the outside, the Magpie was a promising country pub, huge, square and half-timbered, but inside it was a draughty and under-used place. In a desolate corner of a desolate corner of England, it solicited trade by a bold black signboard on the B road from Kingshaven to Eastport. Before noon, Vikki parked between the Spitfire TYR-1 and the Central College Archaeological Department Land-Rover.

Inside the pub, nine students were doubling the lunchtime beer sales, and Flint immediately passed Tyrone a bundle of notes to repay for damage already done. He ordered a Coke, which spoiled his image, but kept his head clear for the afternoon.

Anthony "Ape" Anderson regaled Vikki with his recent exploits. He had already enlightened the whole room by reciting the rules of the Australian Biscuit Game (which he had probably never played). Next he described how his Animals had raided Chelsea College in a vain attempt to steal their mascot.

"We had a ransom note all done up from newsprint, three hundred pounds to the Rag Fund."

He drained his beer. Ape had straggling black hair which

dangled over puffy eyes, caused by playing wing forward in the first fifteen with gusto and violence. All seventeen stones of Bunny Beresford shocked the bar stool by his side.

"Coke, Doc?" He passed the drink and regarded Flint as if he were an alien. "Sorry there's not much change."

He handed over the remnants of a twenty-pound note.

"I'm driving," Flint muttered.

From his monogrammed briefcase, Tyrone drew a wallet he had prepared, then summoned the others from the bar. Once the team were assembled around the table, Tyrone stood up and began his briefing by ceremoniously displaying a map and tapping it with a ruler.

"Gentlemen, this is todays's target."

Ape and his team murmured with interest as Tyrone let them know the final details of Plan C. He hammed up the role of mission co-ordinator and received applause when he had concluded the briefing. Tyrone bowed.

"Are these kids reliable?" Vikki whispered to Flint. "They're all pissed as newts."

"Synchronise watches," Tyrone said. "At my call it will be one forty-seven."

Ape fiddled with an enormous wristwatch, which presumably was shockproof. The others played the game, which was what they were good at. As Tyrone sat down, Flint stood up, passing him a handful of ten-pound notes. "Car keys, Tyrone, time Vikki and I got going."

Tyrone took the money and drew out the leather monogrammed fob.

"Good hunting, Squadron Leader. Treat her like a lady."

Flint and Vikki went out to the Spitfire. The day was cold but bright and Tyrone had travelled down with the hood folded back.

Vikki climbed in the car, looking unsure of herself, "Tell me you're sure what you're doing?"

"We've got to meet him. It's just that now we do it on our terms."

"You don't really think he was going to kill you this afternoon?"

"Why not? Why else choose an isolated chunk of marshland, two miles from the nearest house, with a convenient channel of murky water close by. This guy is evil and desperate, Vikki."

"And you never thought of asking the police along?"

"Can we trust them? Honestly? After all you found out about Temple-Brooke and his contacts?"

"Okay, but this seems just a little complicated. I hope you know what you're doing."

Flint started the engine at the third attempt, crashed reverse gear, then jerkily manoeuvred the Spitfire out of the car park and on to the deserted road. He almost knew what he was doing, though his judgement was blurred by anger at the blatant attempt to poison him.

He found a disgusting thrill in mastering the Spitfire, enjoying its crude immediacy lacking in more modern cars. Coursing the straight, quiet roads of the flatlands, he was flying into battle with a damsel at his side. He felt confident and bouncy, the real danger had been side-stepped and a solution was within his grasp.

The Poet lived on an island, reclaimed progressively from the sea, now little more exciting than a promontory in the estuary. It was a bitter, ice-blue afternoon as the Spitfire crossed the girder bridge over an empty creek which was all that divided island and shore at the point of closest approach. Flat and bleak, the enemy's kingdom beckoned.

Nerves, excitement and sheer trepidation prevented any serious conversation so Flint jabbed one finger at the play button on Tyrone's tape deck. Blaring loud, clear and ominous, Wagner heralded their arrival; *Götterdämmerung*, the Twilight of the Gods, Act III, the Death March. Flint groaned. Tyrone knew he would play that tape. The boy was sick.

Foxstones was the name of Temple-Brooke's manor, a cubic block of buff sandstone which stood like a tomb against the bright southern sky. Visible for over a mile behind a thin screen of leafless trees, its very isolation permitted any excess on the part of its lord. Roads of decreasing grade led towards the target, a trio of cottages lined the road and lonely farms dotted the horizon. Somewhere in the direction of the sun, lay an arm of the river estuary. The tide was low at noon, scuppering Tyrone's first suggestion of making an approach by water, landing at the jetty some quarter of a mile or so beyond the house. The O.S. map had a ferry or ford marked near the same point, which might have offered a surprise southern route by which to approach Foxstones, but Flint could see no advantage worth the trouble.

Standing sentry were a pair of tall, lichen-scarred gateposts, each surmounted by a fox baying at the moon. The gates stood open, intruders were not expected this far from civilisation. One rutted roadway veered towards the farm which lay beyond the hall, whilst a metalled drive led directly to the front door. The house had pretensions to be a castle, with battlements around the roof-line and tiny turrets on the front corners.

Perfect, thought Flint. He should have come at night, alone, with the moon high and a mist rising. Then he would have been really frightened.

Valhalla was about to erupt in flames when Brünnhilde was silenced in mid-cry. Flint parked so as to box in the green Range Rover that stood before the Doric porch, and killed the motor. As Flint was climbing out he noticed the white wing of another vehicle just visible around the corner of the house.

Vikki set her Dictaphone running and slipped it into the pocket of her jacket. There was no need to ring the chain-pull bell, the Spitfire did not have a quiet engine and its approach had clearly been heard. The man who pre-empted them by opening the door was no butler. White stubble sprang from his chin and eyes that had known the marshlands for sixty years burned back at the univited guests.

"I have an appointment to see Mr Temple-Brooke," Flint stated, "the name is Flint, Doctor Jeffrey Flint."

A muffled question came from within.

"Flint," the rustic drawled.

Another set of commands.

"No, he's with a young lady."

With reluctance, the man allowed them to tread the stone floor of the hall. A double staircase swept off to left and right, to meet again on an oak balcony at first-floor level. From an open door ahead and to the left, came the figure of a country squire. Tweed jacket, no cap.

"We agreed four o'clock," The Poet stated in a brusque, irritated tone.

"I keep rotten time."

"And alone."

Flint let his eyes wander to take in the grandeur of oak and brass, oil paintings and ancient weaponry. He was no materialist, but this was material he could love and cherish.

"Hancock, check what he's carrying."

The underling, dressed for the outdoors, approached Flint from behind and frisked him. Flint raised his arms to shoulder height and permitted the indignity. Vikki presented her Dictaphone to prevent any embarrassment.

"Good afternoon, Miss Corbett," The Poet said with mock charm, taking the Dictaphone and turning it off.

Vikki gave a mock smile in response.

The master of the house was square-set, but not tall. In his mid-forties the man's features spoke of class and privilege, handsome, blue-eyed. Flint thought a face like that belonged in the Paratroopers or the Guards, or the SS, not amongst cheerful witches and eccentric old ladies.

Temple-Brooke looked at his servant and motioned towards the outside. "Check there is no one else, then close the gate." He turned back with an expression of suppressed annoyance. "Could you come into the study?" He turned and walked away.

They followed him under the sweeping stair, then through the oak panelled door. The Poet showed them in, with an "Excuse me for two minutes." Then closed the door.

Flint was relieved when a key was not turned in the lock. The study was the size of Flint's flat and its every feature delighted the conservative eye: walls lined with leather-bound books, a delicious desk, a bright but bleak southern aspect through massive leaded bay windows, and a log fire.

"Ready to do your interview?"

Vikki gave a smile. "I mentioned our poet to my boss yesterday and was given a final warning not to harass our shareholders. So here I am, harassing our latest shareholder." She gave a dismissive flick of her head. "But I thought 'What the hell?'"

He loved that cheeky grin and her careless way with the savage side of life, but Flint had only moments to watch Vikki's firm jaw laugh away danger, before the door reopened.

"We were to meet at four," The Poet repeated as he came into his study.

Flint turned to him, adopting a nonchalant pose, with hands in pockets. "I didn't fancy a deserted piece of marshland in the dusk. One loyal gamekeeper could have brought me down at two hundred yards. Duck shooting accident, oops, oh dear . . ."

The Poet's eyes narrowed. "You have a melodramatic imagination. Can you suggest one reason I would want to have you
killed?"

"A hundred and one."

"You flatter yourself, Doctor Flint. You seem to think you
threaten me. You are wrong, you're simply an irritation."

"Then why choose such a perfect spot for a murder, and why
insist I come alone?"

"Because I didn't want her present." The Poet jabbed a finger
at Vikki. "You and I could have sorted this out like men."

"Let's not be sexist."

The Poet turned and grabbed at a gun satchel by the fire. "Do
you know what's in here?"

"Twelve bore?"

"Money." He displayed a bag full of creased and very obviously
used notes. "I'm not rich, I'm no millionaire, but I have my reasons
for not wanting publicity."

"You know I couldn't be bribed," Flint said. "I'm an archaeologist, I have taken a vow of poverty."

"This is no time for clever puns, Doctor Flint." The Poet seemed
to have no sense of humour.

"Does your wife approve of you being a warlock?" Vikki asked
flippantly. "Or does she even know?"

"I don't need your meddling!"

"So you sent me a poisoned cake?" Flint said with anger.

The Poet showed surprise and lack of comprehension. It registered in Flint's mind, and immediately confused him.

"I was sent a poisoned cake yesterday."

The Poet winced, clearly ruffled by the news. "Again, melo-
dramatics. I am sure you are mistaken."

"Let's try a firebombing . . ."

". . . or having me beaten up," Vikki chipped in.

"Add that to conspiracy, kidnap, arson, adultery, murder . . ."

"And where is your proof? You are an academic. You should
know about proof." The Poet shook his head in sheer amaze-
ment.

"I have enough evidence."

"You have nothing."

"Try telling that to the tabloids, they will love it."

"And I'll sue you for every miserable penny you have. And

291

your college, and any newspaper which repeats the libel. You, Victoria, should see sense, you know I have bought shares in your miserable newspaper. One word from me and you are on the streets."

Vikki stuck out her jaw in a defiant gesture. "You can shove that job right up your trap-door, mate. This story is too big for that crummy rag."

"There is no big story," The Poet said, hands forming two fists to punch out his derison. "Will you be reasonable?"

Flint walked over to the window. "Okay, try this. Attractive but impressionable female student is drawn into the occult by Piers Plant, the High Priest of a coven. A confused, introverted man who believes his own gobbledegook. He becomes besotted by her and in no time, she is The Maiden, standing in the stead of The Goddess. But she has no time for him, she seeks the attention of another, one she cannot name, one who appears masked, but who holds mystery and power. The Horned Man, The Protector, higher even than the High Priest. She gives her all in what she believes are sacred rites. She becomes pregnant."

The Poet's face had set in concrete. "Pregant?"

"Lucy Gray was pregnant," Flint said. "So, come May eve, Beltane, the May Games, she could exercise her sacred right to claim the father of her child as her husband. It's the ancient lore, but terribly inconvenient if the man is married according to a different custom. Worse, if he is important and has ambition, the Sunday papers would not understand. So, Lucy never made it to May Day. On February eve, Imbolc, there was a mistake in the mixing of the Kat, the sacred potion. Someone introduced some additional, and fatal, ingredients. The girl is taken away by Piers Plant in his car to a little cottage. Some time that night, she dies and is buried at Harriet's Stone, secretly."

"I read all that fantasy in the paper."

"In the paper you read that Piers Plant concocted the brew and it was he who murdered the girl through jealousy. But Plant had already been fighting back in his own way, trying to find a copy of a supposedly magical book, which he imagined would help him wrest control of the coven, and Lucy, back from The Protector. Once we start to investigate, he goes completely insane and hides. He is an embarrassment, a risk to the one who really murdered Lucy Gray. He too is served a lethal concoction and someone else is conveniently out of the way."

"You still haven't mentioned how I am connected with this."

"There is evidence every step of the way. You are The Protector, The Horned Man, you are the father of Lucy's dead infant."

"Preposterous!"

"Ever heard of DNA fingerprinting? Lucy and her foetus were still in a good state of preservation when they were found. The police forensic team will be interested to take a sample of your blood . . ."

He gave a snort to protect his own disbelief. "The police have closed the case."

"I'm sure they would reopen it. We're talking double murder, it's hardly a trivial offence. You might imagine you have influence but you are wrong. This isn't the Middle Ages."

"I know everything about you, Flint. You are not the only one who can employ researchers. I know all about your background, know all your papers, understand your views. You, of all people, should understand what we are doing in the Valley."

He gesticulated heavily, the pair were boxing around the room, exchanging intellectual blows, both in their element. Flint's strike.

"I can understand Michelle and her immature friends having secret moonlight parties. I can't understand intelligent and wealthy people stooping to such antics." He employed flattery as a form of abuse. "Pagan beliefs is one thing, but black magic is just . . ."

"Means to an end."

Flint was stopped momentarily as he absorbed the brutal reality behind the poet of gentle vision. "So the end is to get kicks out of making people do as you please? That's why Plant couldn't find *De Nigris*, it doesn't exist. You just circulated a rumour that you had found a powerful occult work in order to awe the feeble-minded."

"Well done, bravo." The Poet made three slow hand claps. "Piers Plant was a sad person, mentally ill, who believed his myths and folklore too much, and did not grasp the new reality. What we are talking of is a Pagan revival. A whole new mass movement linking ecology, politics and religion. Capitalist Christianity has failed the West as Godless Communism has failed the East. The old social order is dying in a mess of drugs and violence, and people like yourself with no respect for authority."

"You talk about morality? Free sex, drugs, debased rituals, intimidation?"

He was ignored, the Poet was in full flood. "This is what we have to save." He waved out at the fields from his window. "This is what the Green revolution is really about. It's not about whales and rainforests, it's about England. The real England, the England of Mallory and Blake, Elgar and Wren. This is what I am going to save."

He used the personal pronoun singular. His hands switched to a grasp, his face to an intense appeal to reason. "We need a new code of morals if England is to survive into the next millenium. We need to strip away short-term materialism, insert new beliefs, strong beliefs, or we will fall into the pit."

Flint was warming to the debate, still manoeuvring his quarry, physically and intellectually. "So, you've given yourself the role of the prophet of the new Millenium."

"But don't you see where the true path lies? Everyone will know their place. There will be peace and good order and personal contentment, no continual striving for a bigger car or a bigger mortgage. No more strikes, no more inflation, no more balance of payments deficit, and no hankering for the afterlife. This is what I believe, and this is what my followers believe."

"So that's why you're buying all these silly little magazines," Vikki chimed, "so you can spread your daft ideas. Why don't you come out in the open and say all this? Give me an interview right now and we'll let the world know the Messiah has returned."

"One day I will," The Poet snapped. "When the time is right."

Now he was being sincere and sincerity is disturbing. Flint looked out at the green and pleasant land, washed by clean, wholesome winter sunshine. The Poet's vision was alluring, if dangerously elusive. For a few moments Flint considered this Eco-Fascism, this worship of a mythical Arthurian resurrection. His own hatred of cars, junk culture, capitalist imperialism, and brainless consumerism rose to attack his senses. Paganism had merits, Green politics had merits, the two merged neatly. Then he thought of Lucy in her cold, lonely grave, the terror at the museum and Amelia Winter's slaughter-house. This was not the way.

"I don't care about your views," he stated, "asinine or not. I don't care if you have a kinky fling at midnight. You can be a Pagan, Green, Fascist, Freemason, UFO-worshipper, whatever you like, I don't care. What I will not have is people murdering my students."

"I did not murder Lucy." His denial was flat, certain.

"He called her Lucy," Flint said to Vikki, "it sounds as though they were close."

"It was her name, Goddammit! I did not kill this . . . this student, nor did I murder Plant or arrange to have your miserable boat burnt, nor commit half a dozen other crimes you have accused me of."

"Then who did?" Vikki now intervened. "You are the all-powerful one. You seem to know what's going on, so who's behind it all?"

Flint sliced in again. "You are The Protector, you are in charge, you forced Monica Clewes to send the phoney postcards, you organised the threats and attacks. It all points in your direction."

"You can prove nothing."

"We can nail Monica for the postcards and for the cake. After that, the police wake up and start asking questions seriously. Sooner or later it comes back to you."

"Cakes! We are back to cakes."

"Are you familiar with pollen analysis?" asked the archaeologist. "Or land snail study, for that matter?"

"Should I be? They sound tedious."

"Piers Plant was a herbalist, he learned his skills from his aunt. Piers usually mixed the Kat, correct? At Imbolc, someone stirred an extra ingredient into Lucy's portion and she died a horrible, slow, agonising death. Someone that weak could easily be convinced that he had made some dreadful error."

"He did it deliberately," The Poet sneered, "the police know that."

"Okay, let's switch to Forest Farm, where Piers Plant is supposed to have killed himself from remorse, using poison of his own concoction. Except that the foxgloves which poisoned Piers were not picked in the Forest of Axley, but down here, near to the marshland. I've got the lab report if you want to read it. It will be interesting if the pollen profile matches that from the jar in Monica

Clewes' shop, and also, incidently, a cake which is sitting uneaten on my desk. I don't believe there are two murderers around, so logic says that if we can prove who poisoned my cake, and who poisoned Piers Plant, it tells us who killed Lucy."

It was as if a black hole had suddenly opened within the Poet's soul. His eyes seemed to sink and lose their fire.

"Yes, I suppose it might."

Flint saw that Vikki was grinning broadly at the discomfiture of The Poet. He seemed to be weighing things up, labouring under a growing weight. He nodded involuntarily as he visualised a cracking world. This was the culmination of his plan, to shatter The Poet's morale and force him into attempting something rash.

"When Monica is arrested for complicity, can you trust her not to lay the finger on you?"

The oak panel door opened suddenly. The Poet snapped with irritation. "Rowan, I told you to stay upstairs!"

Chapter 28

Rowan had been there all the while, trying to convince herself that a route out of her predicament existed. She had heard the Spitfire arrive and counted two occupants. The student had been left behind, perhaps he had been the first to eat the cake and now Flint had let his impulsive heart over-rule his cautious head. He could not have told the police he had burgled her flat, so could not have told them he was coming to Foxstones. He had given her one final chance.

Out of sight, she had stood at the top of the stairs, listening to the first words spoken by Flint, then Hancock, then The Poet. The group had adjourned to the study and Rupert had whispered an instruction to her.

"Keep out of sight!"

It was for his own sake that she ignored him once he had returned to the study. Hancock had gone from the hall, the other guests were still in their rooms, so no one saw her moving carefully down the stairs. Quietly reaching the study door, she placed an ear against the oak and heard it all. First she was warmed by the robust stance of The Poet, then chilled by how close Flint was growing.

The house keys hung in a great bunch inches from where she crouched, in seconds she had grabbed them and was letting herself into the gun room – a romantic name for a windowless cupboard. As she loaded the shotgun she had recalled distant days as a gamekeeper's daughter, but the past and the present were slipping by and merging as the future dimmed. She left the room, and reason, behind.

Flint noticed the shotgun before he noticed that Monica was holding it. In an instant, his brain realised what had really happened and kicked himself for not guessing sooner. The mistake could prove very expensive.

Confident and oozing malice, the unassuming shopkeeper closed the study door with her heel. So Rowan equalled Monica, and Monica had fooled him more than he could have guessed.

"What are you doing?" The Poet made a movement towards her.

"Keep back, just keep back!"

Flint could have felt a warm, smug pride had not cold fear penetrated him. He had anticipated a climax, but not this.

"Doctor Flint," she said, "dear Jeffrey, or shall I call you Jeff?"

Vikki groaned. "It was her."

"Shut up, bitch." The shotgun, held at waist height, wavered towards a new target.

For a moment, Flint considered remaining silent, then glanced at the mantelpiece clock and decided to buy time.

"You know, Rupert," he said to The Poet, "since I started on this case, I've had some pretty offbeat ideas, I even thought Lucy had been sacrificed at one point, but I was wrong, wasn't I? All this has got nothing to do with the Green Revolution, Mother Goddesses or any of that black magic nonsense. Lucy was killed for the oldest and basest motive: sexual jealousy. Lucy was besotted by you, wasn't she?"

The Poet simply glanced from Flint to Monica, then back again.

"And she wasn't the only one." Flint was aware that the shotgun was again pointed at him, but resumed his offensive to win The Poet's confidence.

"You had a sort of love quadrangle: Piers loved Lucy, Lucy loved you, but Monica worshipped you. Lucy never told you about the baby, did she? But she told Monica, right Monica?"

Cruel determination had replaced the subtle innocence of her looks, and Monica gave away nothing. "Finish your story," she said.

"Okay." Flint looked into her green, flashing eyes, then back to The Poet. "New theory. I don't think you did kill Lucy, I think it was Monica, here – or is it Rowan? It's difficult to make my mind up. She couldn't bear the idea of young, vibrant Lucy having your child, so she poisoned her and convinced gullible Piers Plant that he was responsible. Dotty Piers insisted that Lucy was buried at Harriet's Stone, then went into hiding. If he had kept cool, who knows, the grave might never have been found, but Lucy's death drove him over the edge. Monica couldn't risk him talking to the police, so she visited him at Forest Farm and cooked him a stew, letting down the tyres of his car just in case he had the strength to try to reach a doctor."

The face of the poisoner broke into a twisted smile, as though she enjoyed the revelation of how cunning she had been.

"It was so neat, she even stopped sending fake postcards and threatening letters when Plant died, just to make it look like he was faking them."

"And you can prove this," she stated, without question. Her voice almost purred, she was turning so completely into the archetype of the wicked priestess, that Flint ceased to think of her as Monica. Rowan the witch was all that was left.

"Monica, leave me to sort this out!" The Poet suddenly burst in. "He knows nothing, he's just trying to trick you! We can talk this out!"

"No, it's too late." Her thumbs hovered over the hammers.

Flint glanced at the clock. Not quite late enough. He shifted to put his back to the window and his attention towards Monica. "Listen to me, my people know I've come here, they know everything I know. You'll never get away with it."

"Yes, Tyrone Drake, is he still alive? Pity, I'll deal with him next."

Flint began to sweat as macabre thoughts came to mind. "Think of the mess. One shot from that, you'll need a new window, there will be bits of me all over the garden. You'll never be able to clear it all."

She nodded. "Right, so we'll go somewhere else." The shotgun motioned towards the garden. "We'll go out of the window, and down to the boat house. No one will see us." Her eyes flashed. "Afterwards, I will drive that horrible car through the village, hooting at everyone. There will be dozens of witnesses, everyone will remember seeing you leave."

"You can't do this!" Vikki was trembling, she took Flint's arm. "You won't get away with it."

"Of course I will." The stature of the Priestess had risen visibly, now she gloated with the confidence bred of fanaticism. "You'll regret crossing the path of The Goddess. You have already seen her power. The Earth is greater than any of us. You will go the same way as that silly little tart."

The clatter of a bell sounded in the hall.

"This will be the police," Flint exhaled, unable to bear any more tension.

Her smile was broad as it was unreasoned. "We know you didn't tell the police."

Thirty or forty seconds passed without words. Only bursts of recrimination flickered between Flint and the woman with the gun. The steady thump-thump of his heart increased its beat as Hancock's footsteps echoed in the entrance hall. The stakes were set, the hands about to be declared. A muffled roar was heard through the solid oak. The Poet cast a look at Monica, then rushed to the study door and pulled it open.

"What the hell is going on?" he cried.

The war cry began. "Ali zumbah zumbah zumbah!" as all eight of the Animals burst into the house. Hancock attempted to block their ingress, but disappeared under Bunny's inelegant tackle.

"Search upstairs!" bawled Ape, slurring from drink, as the other seven piled over the bodies on the floor.

The Poet whirled around. "Who are these animals?"

"They call themselves the Animals," Flint managed to murmur.

Monica's shotgun wavered and for a moment, Flint considered lunging for it, but was halted by fear of carnage. The hall was the scene of a mêlée, joined by two male house guests rushing down the stairs.

"Stop them!" commanded The Poet, but two lightweight Pagans versus a pack of hyperactive Rugby players was no match. Pushes and shoves turned to punches. Three of the college team burst through and charged towards the study yelling, "Doc, here we come!"

The Poet stepped back to Monica's side. Ape ran into the room.

"Hold it!" Flint warned.

"Stand right there!" Monica's command stunned the onrush. Ape froze in his steps.

The Poet glanced at the suspended Rugby players, then at the shotgun barrels. Quietly, as if trying to control his own hysteria, he said, "Will everyone please just vacate my house."

300

Ape looked at Flint, then back at the shotgun. Flint shook his head.

"You planned this!" Monica spat.

"Of course I did. You might have a mole at the police station, but I'm not stupid. You can't shoot eleven of us."

"They're trespassing," Monica said to her master, "you have the right. Take the gun, assert your right."

"Don't be daft, Rupert!" Flint intervened. "You've just been defending your privacy, she's been covering up for murder. She's the one going to jail, not you."

Monica trembled. "Rupert, we stand or fall together. Remember your position! The newspapers will ruin you, you'll be ridiculed! Your wife will divorce you!"

The Poet was looking at Flint, not at the woman with the shotgun as he spoke. "My wife? When did you ever care about my wife? No, Rowan, this is not the way. My lawyer is very good, very expensive. I will enjoy hearing Flint's accusations in court. We'll see who runs out of money first."

"Rupert!" Monica urged, but the Poet was no longer her Protector.

He turned to her. "Tell me it isn't true. About Lucy?"

Enemies divided at last. If not petrified, Flint would have been proud as he saw the tension between the two finally snap.

"Rowan, tell me you didn't kill her!"

"You couldn't love that silly girl!"

"She was like a daughter to me." The Poet's misted eyes strayed towards the wide view of the garden. "I should have guessed. Your loyalty to Oak could never have been so deep as to make you do the things you did. What a dance you have led us, but the dance is ended. Give me the gun, Rowan. This is England. We have a certain way of doing things."

Blissful in his soliloquy, certain of being obeyed, The Poet reached for the barrel of the shotgun, gripping it with his right hand. "Come on, Rowan, don't be . . ."

He would have said "stupid".

Blood spattered on the wallpaper, plaster burst, a picture shattered, the roar rocked the eardrums. Blood blew back at Rowan, splashing her frock as she staggered back under the recoil. The Poet fell sideways, clutching at his crippled arm. Ape made to move, Vikki shrank into a corner and the gun switched round from target to target. Tears trickled down Monica's cheeks and she let out an anguished gasp. Ape threw himself behind a heavy oak chest, distracting Rowan's aim, and Flint dodged out of the door.

He scuttled down the corridor, suddenly remembering Vikki and his student had been abandoned. Flint slid to a halt under cover of the banister. The woman with the gun did not follow.

"Who's been shot?" hissed Bunny.

"What's going on?" hissed someone else.

What was she doing in there? Grieving for her fallen idol or plotting revenge on the unbelievers?

"Vikki, Vikki, leave her alone," he muttered, dreading to see Vikki next as a mangled corpse, or hostage with shotgun under her chin.

Vikki put her chin around the door. "She's legged it."

Relief came as a huge rush, spurring him forward to embrace Vikki. The hug was sincere, on both accounts.

"Jeff, we could have been killed!"

He held on to her, steadying his own nerves. Over her head he could see The Poet, moaning quietly, rocking to and fro on the floor. The technicolour effects on the wall behind were spectacular. Flint released Vikki and yelled into the hall.

"Which one of you is the medic?"

The long-nosed one known as "Anteater" picked himself off the floor and edged into the study.

"Shit!"

Immediately, the drunken thug turned to trainee surgeon, calling out requests for assistance and material. Tyrone rushed in through the front door.

"She's got a gun, Doc!" he called, somewhat superfluously.

"I'll call the police or something," Vikki mumbled. "Even Douglas had better believe this!"

Back in the hall, the Animals were as shocked as the two free-thinking artists whose faces they were crushing into the tiled floor. Bunny had Hancock in an arm-lock, whilst one youth had seized a battle-axe from the wall. Flint yelled instructions to his private army. "Keep sitting on them."

The leaded bay window was open, Rowan the priestess had decided to flee and punish the sinners another day. With Tyrone at his shoulder, Flint dropped out of the window and on to the crisp

302

winter lawn. Advancing cautiously to the corner of the building, he could see the white Naturella van standing on a patch of gravel, with its owner leaning on the bonnet, sobbing and cursing her luck. She was not the only one who could deflate tyres. Tyrone had made quick work whilst battle had raged in the hallway.

For a moment, Flint hoped for total surrender but on noticing him, the priestess again clenched her hands on the shotgun.

"Monica, please." He made his last attempt to parley.

"I never liked you," she said, "I was never interested in you at all. Just like you with Michelle, I acted it out, only I kept myself clean."

Clean? What was her concept of dirty? He pulled his head back into cover as she continued to spite him.

"I still have friends. You will never find me until the day I find you!"

When he again chanced a look, she was running diagonally across the rose garden, towards the south, towards the river. Allowing her another fifty yards' lead, he jogged off in pursuit with Tyrone at his side. A row of thin hawthorns masked the fleeing figure for a minute or so. Then she could be seen again, running for the riverbank.

"She knows something we don't," Flint panted.

"Boathouse," Tyrone panted back.

"We just have to keep her in sight, keep out of range."

Tyrone stopped running. "I'll get the car, there's a track runs beside the river."

He turned and ran back towards the house, Flint ran on. Just me and the priestess now, he thought, and only the crazy one is armed.

The woman soon began to tire, she staggered and slowed. Flint saw this and slackened his own pace. No use doing anything dangerous! The priestess reached the sea wall and allowed herself to rest by raising the shotgun towards her pursuer. Flint spotted a slimy culvert off to the left and rolled into it, his feet ending in cold, stagnant water. He waited whilst the priestess stood blowing heavy clouds of vapour, then when she began to run off towards the right, he crawled from cover and renewed the pursuit.

Overheating in his flapping greatcoat, he removed it and rolled it under one arm like a Rugby ball, without losing his pace. Not that he was worried, there was a good half-mile of visibility on the flat landscape so she could have a ten-minute lead and still be in sight. He had no intention of actually catching her.

As Tyrone had guessed, the fleeing figure seemed to be heading for the boathouse, but on reaching it, she ran straight past. Arriving at the sea wall, Flint saw why. A quarter of a mile of glistening mud separated the island from the marshy shoreline. Water had crept into the channel from two directions, leaving an hour-glass of mud between island and shore. Creeks cut the mudflats and one finger ran towards the boathouse, but anyone launching a boat would have to fight against the tide flooding down the channel.

The priestess had used her rest to recharge her strength and was now running with all the power that drives a madwoman. Behind her, acid burned at Flint's lungs as he passed the boathouse. Another building lay ahead, and he read the O.S. map memorised in his head. Beside the words "Stray Farm", a narrow double line of dots connected island and shore. The Stray.

She reached the farm and disappeared over the rise towards the shore. It took Flint half a minute to arrive at the same position and he halted for a few moments to draw breath. Behind, he could see Foxstones, distant now, and beside it, the glint of setting sun on windscreen which said that the Spitfire was on its way.

Stray Farm was a grey, silent place where not even a dog barked at the chase. The Stray was a single, narrow causeway that led to the shore, providing a back exit for the islanders and an escape route for Rowan. Without a plan, Flint tossed his bundled coat on to the sea wall and broke into a jog again. His quarry was a hundred yards ahead, tiring, walking for nine out of ten steps, only managing a fitful sprint. Either side of her, threatening pincers of water lapped at the margins of the causeway. She was almost at mid-point and unless Flint followed, he knew she would escape. Probably she knew someone over on the far bank, friends, relatives, fellow Pagans, clients of The Poet who would hide her. By the time the police reached the isolated spot, she would have vanished.

Beneath his feet, the track was rough, rutted and water-worn. Running the first hundred yards from the island was ankle-breaking work, but further on, a figure in flapping dress staggered to a halt, bending at the waist. Flint slowed his pace and hailed her, hopefully beyond the range of a wavering, exhausted shot.

"Monica, give it up!"

She looked back, then turned away and stumbled on. Glancing sideways, the water seemed level with Flint's eyeline and an unpleasant thought washed over him. The priestess could reach the shore, then turn and hold the ford. It would be the Battle of Maldon, 991, all over again. He would play the hairy Norseman, she the defiant Saxon, standing firm with her shotgun until the tide sluiced him away. He ceased to chase her as water rushed across the roadway from two directions, separating pursuer and pursued. The track suddenly vanished and within moments ten, thirty, fifty yards of water cut both off from the far shore.

Rowan started to run as she sensed the danger, but slowed to a halt as she splashed into the water. She looked over her shoulder, immobilised by fear and exhaustion, knowing that one wrong step took her off the causeway and into the mud, depth unspecified. She stood motionless, seemingly standing on water. Then she screamed, turned and raised the shotgun. Her target threw himself on to the rough cinder track, crawling for a water-filled pothole and her shot fell hopelessly wide, pellets peppering the water some way beyond where Flint grovelled.

Now she was unarmed! He had her! On impulse, Flint stood and tried to run forward. For fleeting moments, he planned to Rugby tackle the exhausted woman, then drag her back to where Tyrone must be waiting with the car. His own feet splashed into water and fear gripped him. It was suicidal. He stopped twenty yards away from where simple Monica Clewes stood mesmerised by her own plight.

Monica looked at him with fear in her eyes, no longer the confident, all-powerful priestess. She turned to run once more, but lost the track almost at once and stumbled. Waist-deep in swirling brown water, she struggled to her feet and floundered on, but the soft mud of the estuary grabbed at her ankles and her forward motion ceased. Soft and liquid it held her and pulled her down as she struggled to wrench herself free.

Sharp and freezing water lapped around Jeffrey Flint's ankles and he glanced round to see a shimmering bight already lay between him and the island, advancing almost as fast as he could run. He could sprint for safety, risk tripping in a pothole, twisting an ankle or losing the path. Or, he could save Monica. He hated

305

her, wanted her to burn in a hell of her own devising, but he could not watch her drown.

He took half a dozen more steps towards her, but felt the causeway edge with his toes and realised that it was madness. She was up to her armpits, flailing and shouting for her gods. Even if he reached her, what could be done? Would she be rescued or would she fight to drag them both down?

The silhouette of the Spitfire could be seen atop the sea wall. Flint waved frantically and yelled, but no response came. A jetty ran down from the boathouse, and he imagined two figures moving upon it, so waved and yelled again. Surely, the shotgun blast had been heard for miles? Indecision paralysed him into inaction.

"Don't leave me!" a voice screamed from behind.

He took a few heavy, cautious steps back towards the island, before the fear of stumbling brought a halt. The sea reached his knees, icy cold and he felt the first real tug of current.

Monica was still screaming and pleading, blanking out his own thoughts. He began to think of swimming, the water was almost deep enough, but he was still panting. Could he fight the freezing water and be certain not to be swept away? Horror and cold steadily numbed his system, making the world unreal and decisions impossible.

From behind came another scream, summoning him to watch.

"Jeff! Jeff!"

Perhaps five minutes of motionless terror passed. He witnessed the splashing and heard the cries, the cries of a little girl who never anticipated punishment. He felt tears for the victim, for all the victims, for his own helplessness to save any of them.

The cries were no longer coherent, the churning of the waters simply frantic. The Maiden had been buried in the earth, the Priest had been consumed by fire and at last the Priestess was embraced by the waters. Plain Monica Clewes writhed then choked. Her head and waving arms burst from the waters for the last time, then, exhausted she allowed herself to fall.

Jeffrey Flint stood hip-deep, no feeling below the knees, straining now to keep balance. Mesmerised, he continued to watch until the trail of silver-blonde hair faded from sight. A tiny dot just beyond the jetty seemed so very far away and ceased to seem relevant. The same current that bore it closer tugged at his knees. Soon he would lose his footing and that would be it.

The boat was a minute or two away, forcing forward as fast as Tyrone and Bunny could row. To Flint, their idle, sluggish pace assumed a dreamlike quality from where he wavered, numbed by fear and shock. He staggered once, twice in the current, felt himself lift in the ripples, then stumbled over the edge of the trackway and was floundering. In moments, forgotten muscles kicked him to the surface and turned him on his back, trying to control breathing, stay upright, fighting cramp in the left shin. He began to drift away from salvation, heavy clothes weighing him down and the cold biting at his body. An effort had to be made to fight the current, but as soon as he moved, that cramp bit deep. He went down, up again, spat muddy, salt-and-oil-rich water, then lost sight of the boat and panicked.

Tyrone passed his oar to Bunny, who turned the boat and approached Flint from stern-on. Hanging over the stern, Tyrone grabbed at the collar of the floundering figure and was met by shocked and staring eyes.

"In you come, Doc."

Chapter 29

Jeffrey Flint spent two nights in the general ward of Kingshaven District Hospital as "real doctors" checked him for shock and exposure. The students had found difficulty holding the boat against the current and an eon had passed whilst the lecturer sat shivering on the thwarts. An open-top car is not the best way to get an exposure victim to hospital, but Tyrone, being Tyrone, succeeded. In a private room within the same wing, R. Temple-Brooke lay shrouded in bandages and tubes, his conscious hours spent contemplating criminal conspiracy charges, a smashed right arm, a divorce writ and public humiliation.

After Flint had been discharged, he had to make one final journey into the valley. The week before Christmas was not the best time to go to a funeral, when normal life dissolved into parties, feasting and jovial irrelevance. By some ironic quirk, Lucy Gray was buried on the day of the winter solstice below a bowl of perfect blue. Mrs Gray had asked Flint to choose a hymn, putting the sometime atheist on the spot. He was tired of religion, but even more tired of alternative religion, so he offered to choose a Bible reading. In the warm sandstone church of St Michael, Jeffrey Flint stepped up to the pulpit in his jacket and tie and read aloud from Revelations, 21. The new heaven, the new earth and the new Jerusalem might just have appealed to Lucy. The end of death, and pain, and tears appealed to the congregation.

Only one house in Nether Durring did not have festoons, Christmas cards or a pagan tree, but Mrs Gray had lavished love into baking very fine vol-au-vents. In a quiet corner of the family home, Jeffrey Flint ate in near silence, wishing the English had a more cheerful way of sending the dead on their way. Munching in polite reverence, he longed for a New Orleans jazz procession or a boozy Irish wake. Instead, he was embarrassed with the rest, making small talk, thinking of Lucy not with joy for her life, but sorrow for her death.

Flint had been driven down by Tyrone, who was working his way through the salmon sandwiches as a way of hiding his own emotion. Vikki Corbett had been asked to stay away, but she came anyway, in neat grey check skirt and black jacket, with notepad slipped into and out of a half-moon handbag. Flint knew she had resigned from the *Advertiser* and wondered who she was working for.

Barbara came over, her white face contrasting with the new black dress. Flint was conscious of his outdated grey suit and blue college tie, but nothing else he owned was even remotely suitable.

"I'm so glad you came." A smile cracked the pain. Some relief at last was visible.

He said something polite and meaningless.

"I don't know how we can thank you." Barbara tried to kick-start the conversation again.

He shook his head. If Lucy had been found alive, he could have accepted praise.

"The newspaper made what you did sound very dangerous."

"Vikki exaggerates. As always."

"You could have been shot, or drowned."

"It wasn't planned that way."

"No." She looked pleased with him, proud almost. "I still can't understand it all, Jeff, all this awful business with those people!"

"Nor me. One day I must sit down with a pencil and work it all out."

"Well, you got those responsible." There was an assured air of satisfaction in her voice.

"They got themselves, poetic justice."

"Well, thank you anyway. For Lucy. I think she can rest now."

It was as if this was the last release for Barbara, the tension seemed to be slipping from her features by the moment. "Mother loved the passage you chose, and you read it so well." She gave a nervous grin. "I'm not much of a churchgoer myself, not even high days and holidays."

"Me neither, I'm a bit of an atheist really."

"Like Lucy." She smiled sadly.

"Lucy was no atheist, she had firm beliefs. Although most people will think badly of her, she did have faith of her own. Faith in the Earth, in the sky, in that." He gestured out of the window towards apple trees and to the rolling hills beyond. "Nature and beauty."

"Strange gods and demons," Barbara added.

"That too."

Barbara sighed, it was the sigh of someone who could not yet understand the loss. "Will she hate us for burying her in the churchyard?"

He gave a slight shrug of his shoulders.

"What else could we have done?"

Leave her at Harriet's Stone, was his first thought. Then he considered the girl, lost, confused, misled. Left to a lonely grave on a hillside, without even a hurried, made-up Pagan ritual. She may have forgiven her family for drawing her back into the conventional world.

"I think you did right."

This reply seemed to please Barbara, who turned to practical matters.

"How much do I owe you?"

"I'm not sure, Tyrone has it all written down somewhere."

"The insurance money comes to eleven thousand pounds. I want you to have it, repair your houseboat and pay your student for all the work he's done for you. If there is any left, buy something for the college, some books for the library, or an essay prize. Something they can remember Lucy by."

"The Lucy Gray Bequest?"

"Something like that." She offered her hand. It was a kind of farewell. The circle was squared, the Gray family was wishing for peace.

Tyrone was amongst the first to leave, he waved farewell to Vikki and Flint, then roared away towards his family Christmas. For the lecturer, there would be one more interview and one more ride in the red Metro.

"There are still things I don't understand," Vikki said as she drove towards Kingshaven. "Perhaps I'm thick, and you're the one to put me right." She smiled at him and the car wobbled around a bend.

"Don't ask me, I'm brain-dead for the rest of the year. There are loose ends lying all over the shop and we'll never be able to tie them all up, even if the police manage to trace all the circle."

"Like, for instance, who set fire to the museum?" Vikki asked.

"Piers Plant? Monica? Both of them together? I don't know, and I don't think it matters any more."

She suggested they have an evening out at a restaurant, but he pointed out that celebration was a little irreverent, so they had called at a corner shop for a pile of boxes to push into Vikki's microwave. Taking home a clinking carrier bag of Mexican beers would add a little seasonal cheer.

Changed and freshened, Vikki cooked a mean three-minute vegetarian chilli.

"I do eat meat," Flint said, striving for once not to be too offbeat.

The pair made an odd contrast. Still clean-shaven, but wearing his favoured red glasses, Jeffrey Flint in shirt and tie strained towards normality. Opposite him, Vikki had minimised her make-up, changing down into tight jeans and baggy purple jogging top, meeting him halfway and almost passing in the attempt.

"I feel I haven't eaten for a week, and there were all those canapes at Mrs Gray's," she said, clearing her plate by the scoopful. "I've had my busiest week ever. I just need to write up that funeral."

"Is that necessary?"

She winced at his sincerity. "It's my job."

"Don't you ever feel bad about it?"

"All the time. Don't you feel bad when you dig up someone's great-grandad and whip his gold ring?"

Those eyes of hers were so lovely and round, almost black in the dimmed light.

He gave in. "All right, I suppose we all have to trim our morality. Has your editor taken you back?"

"Stuff him, it's next stop Fleet Street; everyone loved my last piece."

"KILLER PRIESTESS IN DEATH HORROR?" He grimaced at the memory.

"Okay, so it's corny, but it's what people want."

"So you'll be moving to London?" Flint was tired of visiting the provincial town, and Vikki's move opened possibilities.

"Not actually Fleet Street, of course, but I'm on a daily from the New Year. Between now and then, do you know what my next deal is?"

He mumbled through the last tacos. "Shock me."

"'MY LIFE AS A WITCH.' Serialised in three parts."

"Sorry, I don't follow you."

"Michelle, you remember Michelle? The police tracked her down and I got talking to her. She's moving back to Ireland, but first she's giving me all the dirt on the coven, moonlight orgies, goat sacrifices, it's terrific copy. I found an agent who thinks it could even make a quick-selling paperback."

So Michelle had succumbed to disillusion too.

"I hope she's getting a good deal."

"My agent is auctioning the rights today. Michelle might walk out of this with a few thousand in her Christmas box."

He had to smile. "I suppose I have to be happy for her, she's not a bad girl, just sad and lonely and very mixed up."

"But crazy about you, at least she was crazy about Grant Selby."

He turned red.

Vikki had a broad grin on her face. "She's been telling me her life story, and she told me all about you."

"Including the mucky bits?"

Those pupils were as wide as they would go. "Especially the mucky bits. I know all about you now."

Another glass of beer was what Flint needed.

"Does that mean you're going to do a feature on me too? MY LIFE AS AN ARCHAEOLOGIST. You can have exclusive rights: ten grand, cheap at the price. Do you need any more detail, or do you have it all?"

"Well, I already know all about you and Michelle and I know something about you and Monica, but there is one thing I want you to tell me."

He would play her game, hoping she would play his. "Ask away."

"Do you treat all your women so badly?"

"No."

"Good."